W9-CJZ-792

REDEMPTION

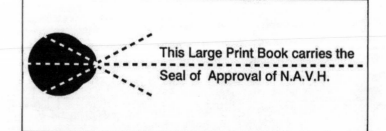

This Large Print Book carries the
Seal of Approval of N.A.V.H.

REDEMPTION

Gary Smalley &
Karen Kingsbury

Thorndike Press • Waterville, Maine

SOMERSET COUNTY LIBRARY
BRIDGEWATER, N. J. 08807

Copyright © 2002 by The Smalley Publishing Group, LLC, and Karen Kingsbury.

Redemption Series #1

Additional copyright information on page 558.

All rights reserved.

This novel is a work of fiction. Names, characters, places, and incidents are either the product of the authors' imaginations or are used fictitiously. Any resemblance to actual events, locales, organizations, or persons, living or dead, is entirely coincidental and beyond the intent of either the authors or publisher.

Published in 2005 by arrangement with Tyndale House Publishers, Inc.

Thorndike Press® Large Print Christian Fiction.

The tree indicium is a trademark of Thorndike Press.

The text of this Large Print edition is unabridged. Other aspects of the book may vary from the original edition.

Set in 16 pt. Plantin.

Printed in the United States on permanent paper.

Library of Congress Cataloging-in-Publication Data

Kingsbury, Karen.
    Redemption / by Karen Kingsbury with Gary Smalley.
        p. cm. — (Thorndike Press large print Christian fiction)
    ISBN 0-7862-7324-0 (lg. print : hc : alk. paper)
    1. Large type books. 2. Married people — Fiction.
    3. Adultery — Fiction. I. Smalley, Gary. II. Title.
    III. Thorndike Press large print Christian fiction series.
    PS3569.M33R43 2005
    813'.54—dc22   2004025474

To Our Families
who dream with us,
challenge us,
and daily remind us
of the reality of
Christ's redemption.
And to God Almighty
who has, for now,
blessed us with these.

National Association for Visually Handicapped
serving the partially seeing

As the Founder/CEO of NAVH, the only national health agency solely devoted to those who, although not totally blind, have an eye disease which could lead to serious visual impairment, I am pleased to recognize Thorndike Press* as one of the leading publishers in the large print field.

Founded in 1954 in San Francisco to prepare large print textbooks for partially seeing children, NAVH became the pioneer and standard setting agency in the preparation of large type.

Today, those publishers who meet our standards carry the prestigious "Seal of Approval" indicating high quality large print. We are delighted that Thorndike Press is one of the publishers whose titles meet these standards. We are also pleased to recognize the significant contribution Thorndike Press is making in this important and growing field.

Lorraine H. Marchi, L.H.D.
Founder/CEO
NAVH

* Thorndike Press encompasses the following imprints: Thorndike, Wheeler, Walker and Large Print Press.

AUTHORS' NOTE

The Redemption series is set in Bloomington, Indiana. Some of the landmarks — Indiana University, for example — are accurately placed in their true settings. Other buildings, parks, and establishments will be nothing more than figments of our imaginations. We hope those of you familiar with Bloomington and the surrounding area will have fun distinguishing between the two.

Chapter One

From the front seat of his beat-up Chevy truck, Dirk Bennett stared at his girl's third-story apartment. He watched the shadowy figures of two people come together and stay that way.

A minute passed, then two. Then the apartment lights went out.

Dirk's fingers trembled, and his heart ricocheted against the walls of his chest. He glanced at the revolver on the seat beside him and shuddered. What was wrong with him? He was a nice guy from a nice family. People like him didn't carry guns, didn't lose sleep at night hating a guy for stealing his girl.

Maybe I'm going crazy.

Or maybe it was the pills. They could do that to a person, couldn't they? Make you crazy in the head? No, that was paranoid. Dirk calmed himself down. The pills had nothing to do with the way he felt. They weren't even steroids — not exactly. And they *were* working. He'd packed on ten pounds in the past six weeks — ever since he doubled his regular dosage. Ten pounds of muscle.

Dirk gripped his forehead and tried to remember what his trainer had told him when he sold him the bottle. *Get the formula right. Too little and the lifting would be worthless. Too much and . . .*

Rage, depression, irrational behavior.

Was that what this was, this constant buzzing in his head? Too many pills? Dirk tapped his fist against his forehead. It was impossible. The pills were completely natural; that's what everyone said. Half the guys at school were on them, and no one else was having any kind of reaction.

He stared at the gun again.

It's what anyone would do. He wasn't going to hurt Professor Jacobs, after all — just scare him. Then Dirk and Angela Manning could be together the way they should have been all along.

He had known from the beginning that Angela was the one, the only woman he could ever love. She'd felt it, too, at first, before she met the professor. Dirk shifted his gaze to Angela's apartment. What could she possibly see in that guy? He was at least ten years older than she was, with thinning hair and gray in his beard and the beginnings of a paunch.

Besides, Professor Jacobs was married.

Dirk had seen the man's wife up in the journalism department a time or two, a beautiful, dark-haired woman who laughed and smiled and seemed to be in love with her husband. The whole thing didn't make sense — an old man like the professor with *two* gorgeous women. Dirk bit the inside of his lip. That part would change soon if he had anything to do with it.

In the glow of a streetlight he glanced at his watch and saw it was after ten o'clock. If he wanted to pass history, he'd better get home and write the paper on Civil War generals. It was due tomorrow. Dirk worked the muscles in his jaw as he grabbed the gun and tucked it underneath his seat.

He'd have to scare Professor Jacobs another time.

Then, just as he started his engine, he got an idea — an idea so sound and strong it caused a surge of hope to rise in his heart. Maybe he wouldn't have to use the gun. Maybe there was another way to scare the professor into backing off his girl.

He chuckled out loud as he pulled away from the curb.

Ten minutes later he sat on the floor of his Indiana University dormitory room,

11

staring at a single entry in the Bloomington white pages as his fingers began punching the numbers.

Not many blocks away, Professor Tim Jacobs lay awake in his girlfriend's off-campus apartment, wondering what was happening to him.

He was used to the guilt and insomnia. But the tears were something new.

Since he'd begun violating his wedding vows, there had been too many times when he was supposed to be at work reading student papers or at one conference or another but instead had been sharing a bed with Angela Manning, possibly the most promising student ever to grace Tim's advanced newswriting class. She was young and idealistic and achingly beautiful, and Tim knew their affair was more than a passing distraction.

Sometimes the realization caused the guilt to grow so loud that it almost took on a voice — a voice that kept Tim awake even when he was dead tired.

The voice was not audible, but many nights it woke him all the same. Tim would be nestled against Angela, intoxicated by the kind of sin he'd never even dreamed about, when from out of nowhere the voice would come.

Repent! Flee immorality. I stand at the door of your heart and knock! Flee...

Tim would roll over, hoping to find his way back to sleep, to the imaginary place where his wife, Kari, would not be waiting at home alone, trusting him to be faithful. But the voice of guilt would come again and again — persistent, relentless, tirelessly calling him home regardless of his lack of response.

His lack of worth.

Tim shifted onto his side, trying not to waken Angela. He stared at her plain white apartment wall, and a memory came to mind — the day Angela Manning first visited him at his office and made her intentions clear.

They had talked for fifteen minutes, teasing and laughing and sharing sentiments of mutual admiration while Tim twisted his wedding ring, hiding it behind the fingers of his right hand.

When Angela left the room, a scent of musky jasmine remained. And enough heat to warm the building. Tim spent the minutes before his next class savoring the way she made him feel. But as he left his office that day his eyes settled on a plaque Kari had given him for their first anniversary. It bore the engraved image of an eagle in flight and words he remembered even now: *The eyes of the Lord search the whole earth . . . to strengthen those whose hearts are fully committed to him.*

In that moment everything about serving the Lord had felt binding and restrictive. Without too much thought he swept up the plaque, dropped it in the nearest file drawer, and strode out of his office.

It remained hidden in the drawer to this day.

Tim blinked as the memory faded. The plaque no longer applied to his life; it was best left out of sight. His strength didn't come from having a heart committed to God. Not anymore.

Since the hot August night when he and Angela first slept together, Tim's strength had come from being with her. And from his professional accomplishments, of course. Tim had devoted his career to excellence in print, first as a working journalist, then as a teacher of the craft, training a yearly crop of reporters who would carry on America's devotion to preserving a free press. In relatively little time, he had become a respected professor who also wrote a regular column for the *Indianapolis Star.* In the most influential circles of the discipline, Tim's name was gaining recognition.

That was a kind of strength that made a difference in life.

Another reason for his power was his absolute commitment to journalistic integrity both in the field and in the classroom. Back when he was reporting, he had never revealed a source. And even though he was a churchgoer — well, he *used* to be a churchgoer — he had never let his religious faith stand in the way of his ability to practice objective journalism. Religious bias had no place either in the newsroom or in the educational process — not when a reporter could do his best work only with an open mind.

Kari had always struggled a bit with Tim's thoughts about faith and the press. But not Angela.

She treasured the fact that Tim was a "man of faith," as she put it. But she also admired him for his ability to put aside his personal beliefs when he wrote a column or lectured to a class. "We never knew exactly where you stood on issues," Angela had told him later, transfixing him with her electric blue eyes. "But we always knew you stood for good journalism. We knew you'd never cave, never give in. Do you know how rare that is these days?"

He was Angela's hero, no doubt. It was something he'd known from that first day when she had showed up at his desk after class the spring of her junior year and had asked him out.

"Professors can't date their students," he told her, stifling a smile.

She simply held his gaze, her directness both disconcerting and alluring. "Can they have lunch together?"

They had lunch. The office visit happened a week later.

After that, month after month after month, he fought the temptation. After all, it truly was policy that a professor couldn't date a student currently in his classes, though the university's Ethics and Harassment Department had long since agreed that there was nothing wrong with a mutually consenting relationship once the shared class had officially ended.

So Tim had held back, flirting with Angela, enjoying lunches and study times with her, but refusing to cross the line. When summer came and Angela returned to her hometown of Boston, Tim felt relieved, glad to be free from the guilt of their flirtation. He tried to put Angela behind him, to focus on his marriage. But

Kari was gone nearly every day, too busy to spend time with him, often too tired to respond lovingly to him at the end of the day.

When Angela returned to school, Tim finally had to admit the truth to himself, even if he wasn't ready to admit it to his wife.

He was in love with Angela Manning. Deeply, completely in love. It was wrong, no doubt. But he couldn't deny his feelings or the way she left him unable to choose anything but time with her.

And it was since that realization that the voice of guilt had been nothing short of relentless.

Repent. . . . The thief comes only to steal and kill and destroy.

The voice spouted Bible verses at him, passages he'd memorized as a boy but hadn't read in years.

I have come that you may have life, and have it to the full.

Tim liked that one least of all. *Life to the full.* As if reading a Bible or going to church every time he earned a day off could possibly compare with the way Angela made him feel.

Life to the full?

The Bible was obviously mistaken on

that point. In Angela's arms life had never been more full. So Tim had gradually let go of the beliefs that had once been the foundation of his life — a foundation that now seemed flawed and almost ridiculous.

He'd doubted some of the details for a long time, of course. A world made in six days? An ark with hundreds of animals, floating above a world of water? People cured of diseases by simply taking a bath or having their eyes covered with mud? Tim had long ago written off such events as either symbolic or simply irrelevant.

But recently he had started to ask even more fundamental questions. What if God didn't exist after all? What if the Bible had been made up by a group of religious leaders intent on dictating the moral fiber of a society gone bad? What if real life, real truth, lay in the finding of one's soul mate? Someone whose soul seemed like a missing piece to one's own?

Someone like Angela.

In the weeks since he and Angela had begun sleeping together, the questions had gradually become statements in his mind, until now he was ready to let go of the crutch of religious tradition entirely, ready to embrace the reality of new life with his new love.

What he wasn't ready to do was tell his wife, and therein lay the struggle. He knew that the only right thing was to confess the affair. But when Kari met him at the door each evening, he couldn't bring himself to look her in the eye and tell her the truth. That he wanted a divorce. That he was in love with another woman — a student, no less.

It did not take a psychiatrist to figure out the most likely source of the guilt that interrupted his days and kept him awake at night. And it wasn't hard for Tim to convince himself that the whispered flashes of Scripture were figments of his imagination, a consequence of confused brain signals or perhaps the manifestation of an overactive conscience.

So he chose not to dwell on the fact. The guilt would pass in time, once he acted on his decision to leave Kari, once the stress of a double life was behind him. The voices would eventually stop, though for the time being they made sleeping almost impossible.

And that's where things were different now. For weeks the guilt had awakened him with gently persistent preachy sentiments about truth and repentance.

But lately, that same guilt had been

waking him with something else.

Tears.

These thoughts, all of them, came in the time it took to realize it had happened again. In the midst of a perfectly good night's sleep next to a woman who had captured his heart and intoxicated his senses, Tim Jacobs, respected professor and ace columnist, was crying.

Weeping quietly as if someone had died.

Tim blinked to clear his vision, and suddenly he knew that someone had indeed ceased to exist. Himself.

Quietly, discreetly, he silenced the sobs and wiped his tears, but none of that erased the sadness in his soul, a sadness so deep and true he ached from the power of it. As if a veil had been lifted from his heart, he saw everything he'd once been — the idealistic boy, the energetic teenager, the God-centered college student, the hardworking journalist, the romantic groom. The loyal husband.

That man was dead.

His betrayal of Kari had fired a final, fatal bullet into what remained of the man he'd once been.

There in the darkness, with Angela curled up beside him, lost in sleep, the sadness within him grew. He cried for Kari, the sweet young woman to whom he'd promised a lifetime. He cried for the children they'd never have and for the growing old they'd never do together.

Tim swallowed back a lump in his throat and tried again to clear the tears from his eyes. Where were these feelings coming from? Why were they hitting him now? His love for Kari had cooled long before he met Angela. Still, Kari was his wife. As much as he longed to be with Angela, Kari deserved better.

Why have I let things get so bad? What's happened to me? What have I become?

The answers were ugly and came as quickly as the questions, forming a stranglehold on Tim's heart. As strong and capable as Tim thought himself to be, the depth of sorrow that surrounded him now was enough to destroy him. It was a moment that would normally be accompanied by the voice of guilt, assuring him that even now redemption was his for the asking.

But as Tim cried quietly into Angela's pillow, mourning for the first time the man he'd once been, the marriage he was about to lose, and the fact that he had no intention of changing his mind, he realized something that was more heartbreaking than the other losses combined.

The words on the plaque Kari had given him were right. Without God he wasn't as strong as he'd thought. Not at all. And that's why the tears flowed so easily these days. Because in its hardened state, his brittle heart had done something he'd never expected when he first took up with Angela Manning.

It had broken in two.

Chapter Two

The phone rang as Kari Baxter Jacobs was washing the makeup from her face that night. She dropped the washcloth in the bathroom sink and quickly patted a towel across her cheeks and forehead.

It was a gorgeous fall night in Bloomington, Indiana, the type of night that inspired artists to paint masterpieces of moonlit farms and rolling hills. As busy as Kari and Tim were these days, as tired and ill as she often felt lately, she welcomed the change of seasons. The shorter days and coloring leaves seemed to promise the coming of quieter times, long, dark evenings when she and Tim could catch up and talk about the idea that had been nearly bursting in Kari's heart for the past six months.

The idea of helping minister to other married couples.

It wouldn't be anything full-time or all-encompassing, she thought — maybe a midweek meeting for couples wanting a closer walk with God and each other. Couples like her and —

The phone rang a third time as she picked it up. *It's probably Tim, calling to check in.* Tim was attending a conference three hours away and wouldn't be home until Sunday afternoon.

"Hello." She sat on the edge of the bed and glanced at the clock. Ten-thirty. Just about the time Tim usually called when he was away. She waited for his voice, but there was only the faint sound of breathing on the other end. Kari lowered her eyebrows and wondered if they had a bad connection. "Tim?"

"Uh . . ." The voice was raspy and belonged to a younger man. Kari's smile faded. He didn't sound professional enough to be a salesman. And even across the phone lines Kari could hear something odd in his tone. Fear, maybe. She rolled her eyes. *Prank call.* She was leaning over to hang up when the man cleared his throat. "Look, I have something to tell you."

Kari's breath caught in her throat, and she chided herself. There was nothing to worry about. Tim would have been safely registered at his hotel the night before. Her parents and siblings were all well according to this morning's conversation with her mother. She exhaled, forcing herself to be calm, professional. "Is this a sales call?"

"No." The man's answer was quick. Too quick. "Like I said, I have something I got to tell you."

Kari sighed, and her mind raced. She barely noticed that her breathing had quickened. "Look, I'm busy." She uncrossed her arms and absently drummed her fingernails on the nightstand. "Just say it."

"I can't give you my name." The man drew a shaky breath. "But what I'm going to tell you is the absolute truth. You can check it out."

The struggle to make sense of the call was growing more intense. What was the man talking about? Who was he and why wouldn't he give her his name? And what exactly did he have to tell her? Anger rose inside her. "What's your point?"

The caller drew another deep breath. "Your husband's having an affair."

Her heart began a free fall that took her stomach with it. She blinked and uttered a single shallow laugh. "What're you talking about?" *What a terrible trick, calling me at home and making up a lie that couldn't possibly be* . . . "You don't know my husband."

"I guess you don't either, lady." He paused. "I thought you deserved the truth. I've got to go."

"Wait!" Adrenaline flooded Kari's veins, pounding its way through her arms and legs and heart, and again she felt herself falling, farther and farther down into a terrifying, dark abyss. She gave her head a fierce shake and tried to hold on to anything that might make sense. The man was lying; he had to be. Tim was in Gary, Indiana, at a conference on freedom of the press. He hadn't even wanted to go; he'd told her so yesterday before he left.

Kari closed her eyes, and her heart seemed to stop. Tim's voice came back to her again. *I hate these things, but I have to do them, honey.* She could still see his earnest eyes, hear the sincerity in his voice. *The administration expects me to be there.*

A thud pounded in the depths of Kari's chest, and she felt her heartbeat return, this time twice as fast as before. She opened her eyes and fumbled for the notepad and pen she kept in the drawer of her bedside table. Her hands shook so badly that she could barely hold them. *It's impossible . . . this isn't happening . . . it's a lie . . .*

"Why . . . ?" Her voice was low and empty, as if her entire existence had been snuffed out in the time it took the caller to deliver his message. She struggled to find the words. "Why should I believe you?"

The caller hesitated. "Let's just say I'm doing both of us a favor. He's off campus, at the Silverlake Apartments. He was there last night, and my guess is he'll be there tonight.

He's staying at Angela Manning's apartment. She's a journalism student at the university." He hesitated. "Now do you believe me?"

Kari shook her head, slowly at first and then fiercely. "No, no, I don't." Tears flooded her eyes, and the falling sensation intensified. "You . . . you have him mixed up with someone else."

"Look, lady —" The caller was getting impatient. "The man I'm talking about is Professor Tim Jacobs. He's your husband, right?"

Kari's eyes grew wide, and her stomach locked up. She dropped the receiver as if it were suddenly on fire. Then, without stopping to pick it up, she raced back into the bathroom. She dropped to her knees and barely got her face over the toilet bowl in time.

Again and again her stomach convulsed until there was nothing left. Not in her stomach or her heart. Weak and shaking from head to toe, Kari struggled to her feet and wiped her mouth on a piece of toilet

27

paper. *It couldn't be true, could it? There'd been no signs. . . .*

That thought struck an off note, and Kari remembered details from the past few months. Fall was often a busy conference time for Tim, but this year had been the worst ever. So many weekends away that Kari had to struggle to remember exactly how often he'd been gone. Four weekends? Five?

Another wave of nausea crashed in around her, but she stayed on her feet. She had no time to hover over toilets, fearing the worst, wondering if it was possible that life as she'd known it had just come to a crashing halt.

Kari looked at her reflection in the mirror and shook her head. "It's all a mistake," she whispered. "It has to be." Her hair had come free from the big clip and now hung in thick clumps around her face. She pulled them back with one hand and leaned closer, studying her eyes and the corners of her mouth. She saw no visible lines, even with her face scrubbed clean of the thick pancake foundation she had worn for her shoot that day. Kari modeled part-time for department-store catalogs, and today's shoot had been for evening wear. The heavy makeup was a must for sessions like that. But without it, she looked even younger than her twenty-eight years.

She examined her cheekbones and chin and grabbed at her loose-fitting T-shirt, tightening it behind her so she could see her figure. Well, maybe she had put on just a little weight in the past months, but not enough to cost her any jobs. Surely not enough to . . .

She closed her eyes, and Tim's face came to mind. *You're gorgeous, baby, gorgeous. I can't get enough of you.* He'd said it as long as she'd known him, since her senior year at Indiana University — the year she and Ryan Taylor had finally agreed to go their separate ways.

The image in her mind changed. *Ryan . . .*

Kari gave a slight shake of her head. Just that morning she'd gotten word that he was back in town, had taken a job coaching at Clear Creek High School.

No, Kari, don't go there, she ordered her heart. Memories of her old boyfriend were better left to yesterday. Especially now when her marriage, her entire life, hung on the validity of a single phone call.

Kari opened her eyes and gazed once more into the mirror, as if it could tell her what she needed to know. Was there really

29

someone else, someone he was seeing on the side? Her stomach clenched in response. It wasn't possible. Tim Jacobs? Leader of his high school's Young Life club? President of his university's Fellowship of Christian Athletes? Onetime campus Bible-study leader?

He would never cheat on her . . . would he? She remembered the caller's voice and knew there was only one way to find out. She closed her eyes again and prayed for strength.

Are you there, Lord?

Don't be afraid. I will supply all your needs.

The words were part of a radio message she'd heard driving home from her photo shoot hours earlier. At the time the words didn't seem particularly profound, at least not for her. Kari wasn't fearful or needy, after all. She loved the way her life was turning out — great family, great church, great job, great husband. . . .

But that was before the phone call.

Her chest pounded, and she tried to swallow the anxiety building within her. **Don't be afraid. . . .**

The thought hung itself on a hook in Kari's heart and swung there for a moment. *All I want is for the caller to be wrong,*

Lord. I love Tim, really. Help me understand what's going on.

***Don't be afraid.* . . .**

Peace, warm and certain, eased over her, and she felt the muscles in her neck relax. It was a mix-up of some kind, or a mean trick. It had to be.

The phone in the next room was beeping a protest at being left off the hook. She returned to the bedroom to hang it up. Her arms and legs were still trembling, and her stomach ached. A bagful of possible scenarios spilled across her soul, and as she examined them, fear crept back to taunt her. Did Tim really have a conference this weekend? What about the other conferences — had he really attended them? If not, where was he . . . ?

Then she remembered. He'd scribbled the details about the conference on a piece of paper somewhere. In the kitchen, where she'd kissed him good-bye? Kari ran downstairs and searched the kitchen desk, moving stacks of papers and mail, desperately looking for Tim's handwriting. She hadn't paid attention because she hadn't thought she'd need the information. He'd called her the night before, and she'd been certain he'd call her again sometime today.

"Come on," she muttered. In her haste

she knocked over a stack of magazines. Finally her eyes fell on a yellow sticky note with a hotel name and phone number written in Tim's handwriting.

Kari picked up the receiver and dialed the number before she had time to reconsider.

"Marriott Hotel, Gary, Indiana."

She gulped. "Yes. I, uh, I need to speak to Tim Jacobs. He's staying there."

"Hold, please."

God, please let him be there. . . .

The man's voice came back on the line. "I'm sorry. There's no one here by that name."

Kari couldn't have felt worse if someone had walked up and kicked her in the stomach. The falling began again, and she had to steady herself against the desk. "He's . . . part of the conference. Freedom of the Press."

"Hold on." There was the sound of rustling papers. "We have four conferences here this weekend, but nothing about the press. Midwestern Chefs, maybe?"

Kari shook her head, her eyes filling fast with tears. "No. I must have the wrong hotel."

The blood drained from Kari's face, and she hung up the phone. Her heart and mind jockeyed for the lead in a race that seemed destined to kill her. She struggled to catch her breath as she buried her face in her hands and searched for a reasonable explanation. He'd accidentally given her the information from the last conference. Or the next one. He'd gotten the wrong hotel from his secretary. There had to be an answer. Something, anything.

Kari opened her eyes and realized there was only one other way to find out. "Fine." She drew a quick breath and grabbed her car keys. She'd lived in the Bloomington area all of her life and had spent years visiting friends in the off-campus apartments.

Ten minutes later she turned down South Maple and headed toward the Silverlake Apartments. She searched the opposite side of the street for Tim's black Lexus but saw nothing. Her racing heart calmed ever so slightly. The caller had been playing a sick joke. There was an explanation for everything. Tim was in Gary, not here at the —

She gasped. Up ahead on the right side of the street, just under the streetlight, her eyes picked out a familiar dark shape. *No, Lord. No.* She inched her foot onto the gas pedal, and as the black car came into view she saw it was a Lexus. Just like Tim's.

Lots of people drive a car like that. Lots of

people. The license plate . . . she couldn't be sure without reading the plate.

Two years earlier, she'd had a particularly good run of modeling jobs and surprised Tim for his birthday with the car of his dreams — right down to the personalized plates. Now she pulled up behind the Lexus and had a clear view of the back in her headlights. The letters were the ones she'd picked out herself: WRITE2U.

Her cheeks grew hot, and she was unable to draw a deep breath. Tears spilled down her face, and she clenched her fists. So it was true after all.

Everything about the past hour seemed like something from a nightmare, and Kari prayed she might wake up. Never once since meeting Tim would she have thought him capable of doing this, of lying and cheating and . . .

A hundred options raced through Kari's mind. She could park and go from one apartment to another until she found him. Or she could go home and call an attorney. The tears were coming faster now, and panic welled up within her. Black spots danced before her eyes, and she wondered if she was hyperventilating.

Was there still some possible explanation? Could he be helping a friend or meeting with another professor? Maybe he'd driven to Gary with someone else, someone who lived here in the . . .

The excuses faded, and in their place an idea formed. She parked and got out of her car. Then she walked up to Tim's car and threw her body against it with all her pent-up anger and fear.

Immediately, her husband's car alarm sliced through the quiet night, echoing ear-splitting cries off the fronts of the apartments. Kari returned to her car, climbed inside, and waited.

Don't be here, Tim. Please . . . let there be a reason. . . .

She fixed her eyes on the apartment entrance as the alarm wailed an entire minute, then another. The door to the complex suddenly flew open, and there he was. Her husband, the man she'd trusted with her heart and soul.

He was dressed in sweats and a white T-shirt, and his hair looked disheveled. A lump formed in Kari's throat. How could he? How could he have lied to her?

She watched him jog toward the street, aim his key chain at the Lexus, and press a button. Silence filled the air, and Tim surveyed the area. Before he could turn around, she opened her car door and stood up.

Her sudden movement caught Tim's attention, and from fifty feet away their eyes locked. His mouth hung open for what felt like an hour, and Kari watched the color fade from his expression. "Kari . . ." He took two steps toward her and stopped.

She wanted to slap his face or kick him or beg him to come home with her and tell her it was all a mistake. But the evidence was too much to bear. She considered falling against her car and weeping, but she didn't have the strength for any of it. Instead, she sank back into the driver's seat and started the engine, her eyes blurred with tears.

It was unfathomable, as if it were happening to someone else. Kari could barely breathe as her hands robotically turned the wheel and found the way home. Along the way she thought about going to see her parents or one of her three sisters, who lived minutes away. But there would be time for that later. Now she needed to be alone, to absorb the blow and give herself time to grieve until finally she believed the facts for what they were.

Tim was having an affair. With a student.

She took short, shuffling steps through the garage and into the house, where she threw herself on the living-room sofa and cried. Not the way she had cried when she and Ryan broke up back in college, or even when she miscarried her first child not long after she and Tim were married.

This was a deep, guttural weeping that came from a place in her soul she hadn't known existed until now. A dark place empty of all words except a wrenching *why*.

Why had this happened? What had gone wrong? Tim was still attracted to her, she knew that much. So what was it? She racked her brain trying to imagine why she hadn't been enough for him.

Then it dawned on her. Tim's student must be smarter, more academic, better with words. That had to be it. Wasn't Tim always coming home talking about this student or that one? Sharing examples from students' papers as if the clever crafting of words were the greatest talent a person could have?

She remembered a time when she and Tim attended a party hosted by the university. It was one of her first university gatherings, and she was thrilled to be there with him. They were standing together in a circle of witty, accomplished people when the talk turned to books. The chairman of Tim's department held forth for a while on some Washington exposé, and a woman Kari had met only briefly mentioned a collection of South American poems she admired. Then the tall, stooped woman on Kari's left leaned over solicitously and inquired what Kari liked to read.

She had nodded confidently and told the truth. "Just about anything by John Grisham. But *The Firm* was my favorite."

The pause that followed felt like an hour. Tim's chairman raised his eyebrows. The tall woman's mouth twisted into an uncomfortable smile that barely missed being a sneer. The poetry woman's face froze; then she let out a laugh as if just realizing that Kari had told a joke. A vague-looking older man was scratching his head and looking confused. "Grisham . . . don't think I'm familiar. . . . Was he that character at Iowa, wrote that analysis of corporate literature?"

By then Kari wasn't listening. She had seen the look on Tim's face, a mixture of irritation and determination not to let it show. He slipped an arm around Kari's shoulders and drew her close with a defiant look as if to tell the world, "Hey, at least she's beautiful."

The conversation had continued, but the moment stayed with Kari over the years.

Clearly Tim had been embarrassed, wishing her to be witty and intelligent and well-read like the other wives. That had to be the reason he was seeing someone else. The student must be brilliant and able to converse on a level Kari had never reached.

So what if she was beautiful? In the end it hadn't been enough to keep Ryan Taylor.

And now it wasn't enough for Tim, either.

Other memories came to mind, times when Tim had made her feel simple and inferior. Wasn't that why she spent so much time working and volunteering at church? Wasn't that why she had joined the book club and signed up as a museum docent? So he'd see her as more than a decoration? So he would be proud of her?

It was all so unfair. She loved Tim with her whole heart, intended to stay married to him forever. Wasn't that enough?

Hours passed, and Tim didn't come home. Kari was not surprised. What could he say? What was left to say?

The tears finally subsided, and she sat up. Her throat was swollen, and she struggled to draw a deep breath. She blew her nose and gazed out the front window at the dark skies beyond. How was it that yesterday she'd thought her marriage to Tim was a shining beacon of what married love was supposed to look like? What had happened? Even if the student had something Kari couldn't offer, was it that easy for Tim to walk away from all they had shared, all they had promised?

Her fingers tightened into two fists. If that's how he felt, he could go ahead and leave.

"Jerk." She whispered the word through clenched teeth. "We had it all, and you threw it away."

No answers came, and Kari closed her eyes, angry and defeated.

Where were God's reassuring whispers now? Where was God, for that matter?

She blinked and sighed deeply, knowing the answer even as she asked the questions. God hadn't disappeared just because Tim was having an affair. Even now, with her world upside down and every breath an effort, Kari knew the Lord would never leave her. And somehow he would help her and Tim sort through this mess, even if right now the idea sickened her.

Yes, things would eventually work out. Tim would come home and apologize, and they would get counseling like a handful of her friends had done when their marriages had been threatened. They would make it work, wouldn't they? Wasn't that the foundation of what she believed? That with God all things were possible?

Still, the thought of being married to a man who could lie to her, cheat on her, betray her, felt as welcoming as a life sentence in the state penitentiary. God could bring restoration, but she knew she would never be the same again after today. Tears stung at her eyes once more, and an overwhelming sadness settled like a lead blanket over her heart.

Kari pulled her knees up beneath her chin and thought about the woman she'd been that morning. Happy, idealistic, confident about her relationship with Tim. Trusting him implicitly and ready to launch a marriage group from their home. There hadn't been a single warning sign. She'd been busy, sure, but who wasn't? That had never come between them before.

And as the midnight hours bled into the early dawn, Kari grieved for the woman she'd once been. The woman she'd never be again.

A woman who had drawn her last breath at ten-thirty the night before.

Freshly popped corn and vanilla candles warmed the Baxter home, a sprawling Victorian in the nearby township of Clear Creek. The Dallas Cowboys had just won a close contest, and John Baxter used the remote to turn off the television. He shifted his gaze to Elizabeth, his wife of more than thirty years. She was still beautiful, but his attraction to her was more than that. She bore a certain charm and elegance that couldn't be taught.

The screen faded to black, but John was in no hurry to get up. After raising five children, silence seemed almost sacred. He ran his thumb over his wife's soft hand and savored her presence.

God, you're so good to me . . . thank you for letting her live. Thank you.

A holy reassurance massaged the rough edges of John's soul, and he felt the corners of his mouth lifting. He was fifty-seven years old, married to his best friend, and certain that when the clock ran out on his days in this life, he'd have an eternity together with his loved ones in a place that would put all of earth's goodness to shame.

Life couldn't get much better than that.

He was about to say as much when Elizabeth released a troubled sigh, stood, and slowly crossed the room, her gaze fixed on the framed photographs lined along the mantel above the fireplace. There they were, all five of them — Brooke, Kari, Ashley, Erin, and Luke. Oldest to youngest.

After a few minutes, Elizabeth dabbed at two silent tears. John's heart sank, and he went to her side.

"Which one?" He slipped his arm around her shoulders.

Elizabeth dabbed at another tear and made a sound that was part laugh, part bottled-up sob. "Kari."

John shifted his gaze and stared at the face of his second-oldest daughter.

"I'm worried about her and Tim." Elizabeth nestled her head on John's shoulder.

There were goose bumps on her arm, and John ran his hand down the length of it. "Did you talk to her?"

"This morning. Before her shoot."

"What'd she say?" He studied his wife, wishing he could ease her anxiety.

"Everything's fine." Another tear trickled down her face. "Maybe I'm the only one who sees it, but something isn't right." She wiped the tear away. "The distant look in his eyes lately, the way he's always too busy for family dinners." She paused. "He's out of town again."

John was quiet. He looked at the face in the photo once more. Suddenly the picture in his mind changed, and Kari was no longer a confident young woman in her twenties, married and living not far away in Bloomington. She was an anxious teenager wondering why Ryan Taylor hadn't called.

Daddy, do you pray for me every night? John could hear her precious voice as clearly as he'd heard it that long-ago day. He closed his eyes and let himself drift back.

"Of course." John remembered taking his daughter's hands, trying to will peace into her troubled heart.

"Will you still pray for me when I'm grown-up and married?" Her eyes grew watery and her chin quivered. "I'll need your prayers forever, Daddy."

Was her heart troubled now? Were there problems between Kari and Tim that none of them knew about? Elizabeth had always been perceptive when it came to their children, sometimes knowing their needs even before they recognized them.

"Okay." He gently squeezed Elizabeth's shoulder. "Let's pray."

Elizabeth nodded as they joined hands, bowed their heads, and placed their second-oldest daughter in God's hands where she belonged.

Even if she had no troubles at all.

Chapter Three

Tim Jacobs wished more than anything else that his upcoming meeting with Kari were over.

It had been wrong for him to stay at Angela's after seeing his wife out on the street, but he had felt paralyzed to do anything else. He had no idea what he was going to say to Kari, and anyway it was virtually impossible for him to walk away from a weekend with Angela Manning.

She captivated him like no other woman ever had; his feelings were that intense.

On Sunday evening, by the time he pulled up outside the home he shared with his wife, he had convinced himself that her discovery was a good thing. Now he could admit the affair and ask for a divorce. Yes, it would be sad, and it was bound to be difficult for both of them. But the outcome was fairly predictable. Tim would need to move out while the divorce was pending, and that meant one very wonderful thing.

He and Angela would never have to be apart again.

He killed the engine and stared at his front door. If only the whole ordeal were already over and done with. After all, he wasn't the first husband in the world to come home and ask his wife for a divorce. This kind of thing happened every day in neighborhoods across the country, right?

Tim swallowed and remembered something he'd heard in a sermon once. *The more bad choices you make, the less bad your choices seem.*

He dismissed the thought. Ridiculous. It was just his overactive conscience, nothing more. Life was about to be better than it'd ever been. His guilty feelings did not surprise him. He *was* guilty. And in some ways he felt awful about it. But during these past few months with Angela he'd felt like a kid in a toy store, lured away from his ordinary life by a woman who'd captured him heart, mind, and soul.

A sigh slid through Tim's clenched teeth as he climbed out of the car and went inside. She wasn't in the front room. He dried the palms of his hands on his pants legs, his throat so tight he could barely speak. "Kari?"

What he was about to do would be the hardest part. She would cry and carry on, and in the process he might even shed a tear or two. The truth was, he still cared about Kari. And he'd miss her like crazy when he was gone.

Images of Angela came to mind, and his heart rate doubled. Okay, so he wouldn't miss the bondage of being married. But he'd miss seeing Kari at the breakfast table, miss the way she looked with her hair messed up in the mornings before she took a shower and the way she hummed to herself when she worked around the house. Of course, he wouldn't miss her busy schedules, the way she made room for everyone and everything but him. The way their intimate moments had dwindled to little more than simple routine.

The truth was, Kari's life was full. Modeling, teaching Sunday school, church choir, her volunteer work at the museum, the time she spent with her family. In the long run, when the shock wore off, she'd be fine.

This was the kindest thing he could do — no matter how much he would miss her companionship. It was something he should have done months back, when he thought a few afternoons and evenings with Angela would cure him of his attraction to her.

Had he ever been wrong about that.

"Kari?" He set his bag down. His palms were sweaty again. He shoved his hands deep into his back pockets and exhaled hard. With every new development of his relationship with Angela he'd found a way to justify his actions. After all, his heart wasn't involved at first. That hadn't happened until the end of the summer.

Tim thought about how slowly, how insidiously his relationship with Angela had developed. He'd been attracted to her from the first day — it was hard to ignore somebody built the way she was — but that didn't signal an alarm. Dozens of attractive coeds had dotted the course of his career. Then he'd read her writing samples.

If he was honest with himself, he'd have to admit that he'd fallen in love with Angela less because of her physical beauty than because of the way she could write. The combination of intelligence and emotion that poured from her text was striking, brilliantly so. And after spending a semester in his class, Angela had taken to crediting him with making her a better writer.

That had done unbelievable things to his ego. Even then, their relationship had been nothing more than admiration and desire until she returned from summer break in the middle of August.

On the first day of classes, they had shared lunch together — as they'd often done through the previous spring. But after a summer apart there was no denying that they both wanted more, needed more than a shared meal. After lunch they went to her apartment, and in the course of the next two hours Tim knew his marriage to Kari would never be the same again.

A week later his entire outlook on life had changed, and he was all but certain he wanted a divorce. Something about being with Angela made Tim feel better than anyone else ever had, even Kari. It was as if he was addicted to everything about his new love — the way she looked, the way she made him feel. Angela was aware of the effect her looks had on men. She was cool and self-possessed by day in her role as college student.

But by night . . .

Tim sucked in a slow breath. There were no words to describe the way she —

Footsteps sounded from down the hallway. *Okay. Get it over with quickly.*

Kari entered the living room through a side door, and Tim felt his words hit a logjam somewhere in his throat. There were streaks on either side of her face, and her eyes were red and swollen. Yet her beauty still caught him off guard. Pure, wholesome beauty, the kind that no longer excited him.

For a long moment they stayed that way, their eyes locked. No words were necessary. The expression on Kari's face told him everything he already knew — that his affair had caught her by surprise and slammed her heart into the ground.

Tim bit his lower lip and decided it was best to get to the point. "I'm sorry, Kari." His heart skipped a beat as he exhaled long and slow. "I don't want to be married anymore."

His words made a direct hit on Kari's heart and knocked the wind out of her. Not in her wildest nightmares had she thought he would start the discussion like that. This was the part where he was supposed to apologize and beg her forgiveness. She reminded herself to breathe. *Help me, God.*

She hadn't wanted to believe it, even after seeing him run from the apartment the day before. And after her initial breakdown, she had decided to withhold all judgments on the matter until he got home, until they could talk about what happened and why Tim wasn't at the conference as he had said he would be. In the meantime she'd had no choice but to act like nothing was wrong.

She'd gone to church that morning and taught second-grade Sunday school as always. For every question about her puffy eyes, she blamed allergies, saying nothing about the situation with Tim even when her mother asked twice if something was wrong.

After church she stopped to fill up the car. Every time thoughts of Tim came to mind her heart would race, her breathing suddenly fast and shallow. *There's a reason,* she told herself. *There's a reason . . . there's a reason. . . .*

And the anxiety would subside.

Three hours before Tim got home, she was putting away laundry, still insisting that somehow the situation couldn't be as bad as it seemed, when she walked by their wedding photo on the living-room bookshelf. She searched his intelligent eyes, his friendly face, soaked in the love that clearly existed between the two of them, and she remembered the caller's words from the day before.

Your husband's having an affair . . . having an affair . . . having an affair. . . .

In less time than it took her to inhale, the reassuring pretense disappeared. Choking sobs erupted from her angry soul and spewed hot tears down her face.

Immediately, the situation became clear. Yes, her husband had a reason why he had lied to her and spent the weekend at a student's apartment. It was the same reason the caller had given her, and no matter what lies she wanted to tell herself, the truth was blatantly obvious.

Tim was involved with another woman.

In that moment, the sorrow and anger in Kari's heart became fury. She grabbed the wedding photo, hurled it across the room, and watched the glass shatter into dozens of pieces. Then slowly, as if she were in a trance, Kari sank to her knees and began to pray.

"I hate him, God!" She shouted the words, weeping harder than before. "How could he do this to me?"

At the end of two hours, Kari's anger and sorrow, her sense of betrayal, were no less than before. But somehow a determination had come over her, and with it a clear and holy reminder of a truth — that same one her parents had lived by, the one she and Tim had agreed on before they married.

The truth was this: Love is a decision.

In the wake of Tim's unfaithfulness, her heart urged her to hate him, tell him he wasn't welcome back home, and then never see him again. God wanted something else. He wanted her to hear her husband's explanation and be willing to forgive, willing to find counseling and make things work. Not because she felt like it, but because it was something she'd decided to do nearly six years ago.

So, in the final hour before Tim's return, Kari pictured a hundred things he might say to her when he first walked through the door, when they first faced each other in light of what had happened. He'd apologize and tell her it was a mistake; he'd promise he'd never lie again. He'd insist the woman was nothing more than a distraction, a passing fancy. He'd blame stress at work and the fact that their marriage had fallen into a routine.

But the last thing she expected him to say, the thing she had never imagined he might tell her, was that he no longer wanted to be married.

Tim moved to sit on the sofa and anchored his elbows on his knees, his brows knit, his eyes searching hers. "Did you hear me?" His voice was quiet, laced with finality. "I don't want to be married anymore."

The rage within her was suffocating, but there were no sobs this time, no weeping. "That's it?" She crossed her arms, trying to ease the sick feeling in her stomach. "No explanations or promises? Nothing?"

Tim dropped his head in his hands,

groaned, and then looked back up at her. "I should have told you a month ago."

The sick feeling became a driving nausea, and it welled up in Kari's throat. She wondered if she should race for the bathroom or throw up on the carpet. *What's happening? What is this, God?*

Do not be afraid.

This time the silent assurance was too late. Amidst the feelings of pain and anger and even hatred, Kari felt a flash of sheer terror. Were divorce papers drawn up and waiting? Was he planning to move in with this woman? Could that actually happen? Could Tim leave her and marry someone else?

The questions pelted her like hail.

She couldn't live in Bloomington knowing she might run into Tim and his . . . his student.

The premonition of what her life might soon become was more than she could bear. She blinked, and the terror faded. In its place her fury was more controlled. "Who —" her voice was a whisper, her throat pinched — "who is she?"

Tim stared at his hands, and when he glanced up he looked ten years older than before. "It doesn't matter."

Again Kari was dumbfounded. "So

you're not denying it? You're seeing someone else?"

"I thought it was a phase." Tim's eyes remained fixed on hers. "That it would go away in time."

Kari tightened her grip on the back of a chair and tried desperately to make sense of what was happening. The nausea was still there, but it was being overtaken by a growing sense of panic. Her emotions swung wildly from fear to anger and back again, and she could think of nothing to say.

After a long pause his gaze fell to his feet again.

He's afraid to look at me. The thought settled like a rock in her empty gut.

"There's no other way to say this, Kari. I want a divorce." He looked briefly at her. "I still care for you, but I'm not . . . I'm not in love with you."

The panic became a tidal wave around her, consuming her. "You're in *love* with her?"

Tim made eye contact and gave the faintest shrug. "I am."

What was he saying? She could almost feel the hands of angels keeping her from collapsing on the floor. She straightened and paced across the living room and back, stopping directly in front of her husband. "She's a student, Tim. What is she — nineteen? twenty?"

For the first time since he'd gotten home, Tim's expression became defensive. "She's twenty-four, okay? And I met her almost a year ago."

Kari's head was spinning. "A year ago?" Her voice was barely a whisper. Who was this woman, and what did she look like? Was she one of the students he had raved about last year? The whole situation was impossible. "You've been seeing her for a *year?*"

Tim shook his head and massaged his fingertips against his temples. "I met her at the beginning of the spring semester. It didn't get serious until . . . until a few months ago."

He stood up and threw his hands in the air. "There's no point to this, Kari." His voice was loud, frustrated. "What I do with my life after you and I divorce is my business."

The tidal wave came crashing down, and Kari fell back into the chair again. Her heart raced dangerously fast, and she couldn't grab a full breath. Pain shot down her arms, and there was a heaviness on her chest that grew worse with each passing second.

Lord, help me. I'm falling. Father . . . help!

I am with you.

The gentle whispers in the depths of Kari's soul brought only a fraction of relief, but it was enough to ease the pain and allow her to inhale. "You owe me more than that, Tim." She steadied herself and stared up at him. "She's not your wife. I am."

Tim opened his fists, took hold of his wedding ring, and slid it off his finger. "Don't you get it, Kari?" He tossed the ring on the coffee table, shook his head, and sat down. "It's over. I want out. I don't want to be married anymore."

As the ring clattered onto the table, something in Kari shut down. It was almost as if a protective shield had gone up around her heart, a kind of armor that simply would not allow her any more pain. She felt dizzy and sicker than before, yet somehow detached and clear-eyed, as if she were observing the whole scene from a distance.

Her husband was nothing of the man she'd thought him to be. Instead, he had lied and cheated on her, and now he was saying their marriage was over. She looked at him sitting there, his long fingers clenched together, his head lowered, giving her a clear view of the bald spot just beginning to show on the top of his head.

She remembered a verse from their wedding: *And now these three remain: faith, hope and love. But the greatest of these is love.*

Acting with what she could explain only as supernatural power, and without so much as a single tear, she studied her husband and steadied her voice. The anger was still there, but her determination was greater. "We need counseling."

Tim's mouth hung open. "Counseling?" He rolled his eyes, his tone louder than before. "Kari, I'm sorry this is hard for you to accept, but you need to hear me. I want a divorce, not counseling. I'm in love with someone else."

"That doesn't matter." Kari leaned back and crossed her arms tightly in front of her. "God can forgive you."

Her husband swore under his breath and stared at her as if she'd just stepped off an alien spaceship. "I don't want God's forgiveness." His voice filled the room. "Not now, not ever. It's my life . . . however I choose to live it." She opened her mouth to say something, but he held out a hand to stop her. "I don't want *your* forgiveness either. I don't want to be married. It's not fair to either of us." He paused, and the dejected calm returned to his tone. "I want a divorce. Nothing less."

Again a strength she couldn't explain coursed through her. "You're my husband, Tim. We promised each other forever. Whatever you've done, God can help me forgive you. We can get counseling and work it out."

Tim glared at her, got up and crossed the room, and grabbed the overnight bag he had brought home with him. He stood that way for a moment; then he let it fall once more and slowly came to stand with his feet nearly touching hers. "I loved you, Kari." He shrugged, and his eyes were sadder than they'd been since he arrived. "I never meant to hurt you with this. But I'm not staying married to you. I can't live a lie." His voice grew softer. "I'm moving in with Angela tonight."

"No . . ." The comment was out before Kari could stop it. The veneer of calm was giving way, threatening to release an avalanche of rage and pain and heartache. She could feel her limbs shaking from her scattered emotions, and her mind raced as she considered her options.

Tim raked his fingers over the tops of his thighs as if he was trying to keep from shouting at her. Then his hands relaxed, and he spoke quietly, simply. "I'm sorry, Kari."

Without waiting another moment, he grabbed his bag again and headed toward their bedroom.

"Don't do this, Tim." Her words trailed after him, but he didn't look back. She closed her eyes and screamed, "Help me, God! I don't know what to do."

For the next thirty minutes she stayed anchored to the chair. She heard him searching through the closet and pictured him finding his suitcase. She listened to the sound of dresser drawers and closet doors opening and closing, and finally he appeared in the living room once more.

He had a suitcase in each hand, the overnight bag hanging from his shoulder.

She felt like a dazed accident victim. "Don't go."

Again the words seemed strangely out of place, as if they were coming from someone else. Tim was in love with another woman and wanted a divorce. He'd become the cruelest man he could ever be. He'd broken their wedding vows and done the one thing that would give her a scriptural excuse for ending their marriage.

But despite her anger and grief, despite the shock that still shook her body, she knew one thing for certain: She didn't want a way out. She didn't want to give up on her promise to stay no matter what, to love no matter the cost.

Her anger subsided. "Stay." Sorrow and fear smothered her voice. "Work it out with me. Please."

Tim hesitated, and she almost thought he might change his mind. She looked deeply into his eyes and willed him to hear her heart. *Come on . . . don't give up on us. . . .*

"Good-bye, Kari. I'll call you tomorrow; we need to talk about the legalities." He took one step toward the front door. "You can reach me at work."

Kari stood. She thought of a dozen things she wanted to say and do. She wanted to walk up and slap him across the face, spit at him, or kick him in the leg. She wanted to punch a hole in the wall or collapse in a heap and have a complete breakdown — the one only God was holding at bay, the one she was certain to have in the hours and days and weeks ahead.

Instead, she looked at Tim as he walked out the door and said just one thing.

"I won't give you a divorce."

Chapter Four

She slept on the couch, crying so hard she thought her ribs would break. Countless times Kari considered going back to the woman's apartment, finding Tim, asking him if it weren't all a bad dream. Begging him to tell her it wasn't true, that he wasn't in love with one of his students, determined never to come home.

But in the end she stayed on the couch.

The truth was so real it was suffocating. Sometime around three o'clock in the morning, her heart began skipping about in irregular patterns. Sweat broke out across her forehead and she felt flushed. Kari recognized the symptoms. She was having an anxiety attack.

Small wonder.

She turned on the table lamp and reached for the Bible she kept beneath it. *Show me something, Lord . . . give me peace. I can't make it through the night.*

Flipping through the pages, she settled into Psalms and began skimming verses, looking for promises of peace or vengeance or at the very least, deliverance. Her eyes scanned Psalms 48 and 49, and then from deep in the sea of pain her feet hit solid ground.

It came in the form of Psalm 50:15: *Call upon me in the day of trouble; I will deliver you, and you will honor me.*

Nothing about what Tim had done was honorable; in fact, she was deeply ashamed for him, for both of them. But here in God's Word, among all the other promises that would always be true, was one that seemed written just for her. To think that God would not only deliver her but also give her a chance to somehow honor him in the midst of this disaster. It was enough to make her heart rate return to normal and the flushed feeling fade.

Call upon me in the day of trouble; I will deliver you, and you will honor me.

"Help me, Lord," she whispered into the night. "I'm so lost."

She closed the Bible, flipped off the light, and lay there repeating the verse in the dark, believing the promise within. It was the only thing that got her through the rest of the night.

In the morning, when she remembered that Tim had left her for another woman, when the reality of that settled around her consciousness like a vise grip, she called her parents' house.

"Hello?"

It was her mother. *Help her understand without asking a lot of questions, God . . . please.* Kari knew she sounded awful; no doubt her mom would be worried. She closed her eyes and began to talk. "Hi, it's Kari." A fresh bunch of sobs collected at the base of her throat, and she could no longer speak.

"Kari — honey, what's wrong? Are you okay?" Kari felt strangely reassured by the alarm in her mother's voice, as if she'd finally stumbled onto someone who cared.

Kari coughed, trying to clear away the thick and heavy sadness blocking her airway. The anger and fear from yesterday were gone. In their place was a sadness she couldn't begin to describe. "I need to talk to you."

"Want me to come there?"

"No." Kari's sinuses were swollen shut from hours of weeping, and at the moment it was all she could do to carry on a conversation. "I'll be there in an hour."

Minutes later she stepped into the shower and considered what her life had become. She had no idea how long Tim would be gone or how serious he was about the divorce.

And there, while the hot water washed over her body, she allowed herself to drift back to the days when she first met Tim Jacobs.

She remembered so many good things about him — his friendly looks, his sense of humor, his intelligence. His stalwart faith. Who wouldn't have jumped at the chance to date him?

Kari mulled over these points and realized there was one thing about Tim that had stood out more than all the others combined. Ultimately it had been the thing that convinced her to marry him.

He made her forget about Ryan Taylor.

Kari Baxter's senior year in college had been a difficult time for her. Some days her heart had been in such a shambles that she wondered how she got dressed in the morning, let alone survived the day.

Back then Tim Jacobs had seemed like the answer to all her prayers. Especially after the way things had ended with Ryan.

Kari sighed. It would do her heart no good to dwell on Ryan. Not now. Better to skip the part where the boy who had been her best friend, her first love, made his sudden and lasting exit from her life.

It was spring when Tim made his entrance, and Kari was in her final semester at Indiana University. Though she was still reeling, she had started to think she might survive. She even made a plan to attend a campus Bible study at the Indiana Memorial Union.

Kari remembered feeling indifferent that day, as if she were merely going through the motions. She showed up ten minutes early, slipped into a booth in the lounge where the study would be held, and rested her head on her backpack.

Tim was one of a few people setting up that day, and for several minutes she watched him talk with a short, redheaded girl. He seemed older than the average student, and Kari wondered if he was a professor. Most campus clubs had a faculty advisor.

"I know it might not be spiritual, but the way to really lure people in is with trips." The girl spoke with her hands, her voice tinny and flirtatious. "Lots of trips. I think a camp-out at Lake Monroe would be perfect."

Kari peered at Tim and noticed he was good-looking in a simple way — about six feet tall, with dark hair that already showed some distinguished gray. Eyes full of good-humored confidence.

Tim smiled as he shook his head. "I don't think so, Ruth."

The redhead threw him a teasing look. "Why not?"

"A bunch of college kids on a camp-out?" He shook his head. "Then what? Next year we start a campus nursery for single mothers?"

"That's what I like about you, Tim." A blush fell across the redhead's face. "Always thinking."

The girl put her hands on her hips and stifled a smile. *She won't let it drop,* Kari thought absently. *I wonder if he knows she has a crush on him.* She shot a look at his left hand. No wedding ring. At least the redhead wasn't flirting with a married man.

Tim sorted through a stack of flyers on a nearby table. "Maybe a movie night, something like that."

Ruth ran her fingers through her hair and batted her eyes at Tim. "Come on, have a little imagination." She flashed him a grin. "We could have Bible studies in the morning and at night, well . . . we could organize a swimsuit competition one night, a wet T-shirt contest another, maybe organize a dance party with a muscle-beach theme or —"

Tim raised his eyebrows. "I like your creativity, Ruth. But it's the first meeting of the semester, and we've got five minutes to come up with some suggestions that might actually fly."

The redhead moved in closer. "Don't you ever lighten up?"

Tim cocked his head and grinned. "Not that way. Not around students."

"So?" the girl whined. "I'm not your student."

Ruth's message was unmistakable, but Tim merely shook his head and returned to sorting through flyers.

Undaunted, the redhead leaned her face near his. "You think you're too old for me, don't you?"

At that, Tim's head fell back and he laughed. "Just how old do you think I am?" But then he leveled his eyes at her and spoke gently. "Look, I just don't date students. Okay?"

Kari watched, mesmerized. Though she wasn't interested in the man, she couldn't help but admire both his ethics and the smooth way he deflected Ruth's advances without totally deflating her.

When Tim and Ruth were finished preparing for the meeting, Ruth handed out name tags and welcome flyers to the students who were trickling in. Tim looked like he was about to take a seat when he spotted Kari. Their eyes held for a moment; then he looked away.

Instead of sitting down, he headed in her direction, greeting several students along the way. When he finally wound up at her table, it seemed nothing more than a polite gesture that he held his hand out and introduced himself. "Hi, I'm Tim Jacobs. I'm sort of the token faculty guy for this bunch. I teach part-time over in the journalism school." He smiled as their eyes met once more. "Anyway, welcome."

Something about the feel of his hand in hers made Kari's cheeks grow hot. "Thanks." She drew her hand back and buried it beneath the table. "I wasn't going to come, but . . ."

Tim waited, his expression curious, but without the slightest show of interest in anything more than her answer. "But . . . ?"

Kari shrugged. "I needed a change."

An easy grin filled Tim's face, and she felt his guard fall a bit. "We all do, now and then." There was an awkward silence between them, and Tim glanced around the room. "Good turnout. Bigger than we expected." His attention was back on her. "Guess we better get started."

They didn't talk again until the meeting was over. As Kari was leaving, Tim smiled at her. "Was it a good change?"

"Definitely." The hour of conversation and Bible study had been just what she needed.

"Okay. See you next week."

Kari's path didn't cross with Tim's until the next meeting, but several times in the next few days she kept on wondering about him. When she passed the journalism building on the way to lunch each day, she found herself looking for him, guessing about his personal life. He had to be in his late twenties or early thirties. Probably engaged. Most men that age were tangled up in some kind of relationship.

Four weeks passed, and Kari continued to attend the Bible studies. And though Tim did nothing inappropriate, made no suggestive remarks or flirtatious gestures, Kari had the uncanny sense that he was interested in her. At the end of the fifth meeting, Tim left the building at the same time she did and saw that she had an armful of books. "Want help?"

Kari struggled to get a tighter grip on two of the heavier tomes. "You don't mind?"

"No." Tim took most of the stack and slipped the books easily beneath his arm. "Where are you headed?"

She pointed with her elbow. "Parking lot."

They talked about the meeting while they made their way to her car. Then for nearly an hour they stood talking about her classes and his work and the churches they attended and what they'd done before coming to Indiana University. Tim was finishing his Ph.D. from another school, teaching some writing courses, and doing editorial work on the local paper. He'd grown up as a missionary kid but had been away from home for quite a while, working as a journalist and pursuing his education. He had moved to Bloomington from Chicago.

"That's amazing." He smiled at her, and Kari had the sense that this was the real Tim Jacobs, the one who probably lived behind the confident, unflappable public veneer. "We've both been here on campus. I can't believe we never met before."

Kari could. She'd spent very little time getting involved at IU. Why bother, when she still lived at home and until November had spent all her free time with Ryan Taylor? "It's a big campus, I guess."

"I guess." Their conversation stalled, and Kari was about to say good-bye when he fixed his eyes on hers. "Hey, Kari, you seeing anyone special?"

Even now she remembered the way her heart had winced at the question. "Not anymore."

Tim's eyes sparkled, and she realized again that he was letting her see who he really was. "Well, if you're not doing anything, maybe we could have dinner sometime."

Kari remembered Tim's comment to Ruth, the way he held her advances at bay. "I thought you didn't date students."

He chuckled. "You mean Ruth?"

Kari nodded, biting her lip to keep from smiling. "You handled the whole wet T-shirt thing very well, I must admit."

"Ruth means well." His grin faded. "Actually, I don't usually date students. I'll be working here full-time soon, and —" he shrugged — "it isn't a good idea."

"But . . . ?"

"But the truth is I'm still a student myself."

She giggled. "How convenient."

They had dinner the following Friday after Bible study, and a month later they were getting together twice weekly at the library — she doing her homework while he worked on his dissertation. The more she got to know him, the better she liked him — and admired him. He was intelligent and focused, but beneath his intensity was a fun-loving guy whose quick wit made her laugh. She was convinced Tim Jacobs was going somewhere, and she was curious to see where that place would be.

They had had dinner together more often as time passed. Sometimes they had gone to church together or had taken in an occasional movie or concert. But Kari had been determined to keep things platonic. She hadn't been ready for a relationship. Not when she knew it would take a lifetime to get over Ryan Taylor.

Kari turned off the water, stepped out of the shower, and grabbed a towel. She remembered something her mother had told her later that spring.

"You aren't going to wait for him, are you, honey?" They'd been washing pans side by side while Kari's siblings filled the house with sounds of homework and conversation.

Kari's heart skipped a beat. "Wait for who?"

Her mother cast Kari a knowing look. "You know who."

"Ryan?" Kari's voice grew irritated. No one around the Baxter house had mentioned Ryan in months. Kari had absolutely forbidden it. "I told you, Ryan and I are finished. Over. End of discussion. He's moved on without me."

Elizabeth Baxter was silent for a minute. "He won't play pro football forever, Kari." She bit her lower lip and seemed to look straight into Kari's soul. "I hate to see you make a mistake."

"What's that supposed to mean?"

"I don't know. With Tim, I guess." She shrugged her shoulders. "Something about him feels, well, plastic. Like he works too hard to impress you. And I worry that he's too old for you."

Kari dropped the dishrag into the soapy water. "Tim and I are friends, nothing more." When she felt sure she'd conveyed her frustration, Kari reached for the rag and resumed scrubbing. "At least we pray together."

Her mother didn't say another negative word about Tim after that. Throughout the semester Kari and Tim remained good friends, casual companions, and Kari told herself that was all they would ever be. But one day three months into their friendship, Tim was particularly quiet over lunch.

They had finished eating, and Kari sipped a cup of steaming cinnamon tea as she eyed Tim. "All right." She could feel the way her eyes danced, hear the teasing in her voice. "What'd you do with Tim?"

"Hmmm?" Tim looked up from his plate as if her question had taken him by surprise.

Kari released a dramatic sigh. "Now I know you're an impostor. My Tim would've laughed a little, even if I'm not that funny."

Tim produced a fading smile. Something in his expression told Kari this wasn't a time to joke. She blinked and softened her voice. "What is it, Tim? What're you thinking about?"

"Truth?"

She nodded.

There was a hurt in Tim's eyes that she couldn't explain. Not once did he break eye contact with her. "Okay. I want to know about the special guy. Who was he?"

"The special guy?" Her heart lurched.

"That first day when we talked by your car, I asked you if there was anyone special, anyone you were seeing." His tone was gentle, and she knew he was being vulnerable with her.

Where is this headed, Lord? Don't let me hurt him. Kari let Tim finish.

"The way you said it sounded like what you had was over." Tim paused. "But that isn't true. You still care about him, Kari —

a lot. Maybe more than you're willing to admit."

She toyed with the handle of her mug. "How do you know?"

Tim shrugged, and it occurred to her that he was truly handsome, more so than she'd thought at first. Not like Ryan, who had a way of turning heads wherever he went, but very nice-looking in a friendly sort of way.

Tim sighed. "You absolutely never talk about him."

Kari leveled a gaze at Tim and grinned despite the sorrow that still filled her heart at the mention of Ryan. "Okay, I'll tell you. His name is Ryan Taylor, and he was a friend of the family."

When she mentioned Ryan's name, a strange look filled Tim's face. "Not Ryan Taylor the running back? Signed with the Cowboys out of Oklahoma University? Set a record for most passes by a tight end last year? Not that Ryan Taylor, right?"

Tim had been a sports reporter after college and still followed football. Kari should have known he'd recognize Ryan's name. She gazed down at her hands and nodded. "That's him."

A moment of silence passed between them, and then Tim brushed his fingers together and pushed back from the table, extending a single hand out to Kari. "Well . . . it's been nice. Now if you don't mind, I think I'll go find a woman I can really impress."

"Stop!" Kari laughed and grabbed his wrist. "Don't be stupid."

Tim eased back in his chair and stared at her, his eyes so wide she could nearly see the whites all the way around. "Ryan Taylor? He's the special guy? You're serious?"

Around the diner she saw other people looking at them, and she nodded quickly and put a finger to her lips. "Yes! Shhh . . . everyone's watching."

Shock played across Tim's face as he settled back in his chair. He looked as if someone had knocked the wind out of him. "Why would a woman who's dated the great Ryan Taylor share lunch with a guy like me?" He grinned and held up a single finger. "I know! Because you like my jokes! That's it, right?"

Kari held her hand to her face to hide her giggling. She leaned closer and took his hand in hers. "No, Tim. I don't like your jokes."

His jaw dropped in mock astonishment, and he silently mouthed the words, "You don't like my jokes?"

She laughed out loud this time, and when she'd regained her composure, she squeezed his hand and smiled at him. "What I mean is, it isn't your jokes that I like. I like . . . you."

Tim's expression changed then, almost as if he were determined to move past the truth about her onetime love. "Well, then, at least tell me what went on between you two."

And she did. For the rest of the hour she talked about her friendship with Ryan, the ups and downs and the fact that she had expected to marry him.

The conversation with Tim that day had been a turning point for them, deepening their friendship and hinting at something more serious ahead. But Kari still doubted that anything lasting would come from their time together because after graduation she planned to spend six months in New York with a few girlfriends — all of whom would be working for a modeling agency on the West Side.

Then, the night she graduated from college, everything about her relationship with Tim changed.

Her parents threw a huge open house to celebrate Kari's big day. That night the house overflowed with people, and Tim was among them. He spent nearly an hour talking to her father, and before the night was over, he helped her mother refill platters of snack foods and tidy up the kitchen.

Her mother pulled her aside before the party was over and whispered in her ear, "Maybe I was wrong about Tim."

"Yeah, maybe you were," Kari whispered back, her heart soaring at the success of the evening. "Not that it matters. I'm leaving in a few weeks, remember?"

A strange look came over her mother's face, and she hesitated, as if she was considering whether to say the next thing. Then she lowered her voice again. "Ryan called yesterday. He asked me not to tell you, but I didn't want you to be surprised."

Kari would never forget the way her heart dropped. Couldn't he leave her alone? Wasn't it enough to break her heart without haunting her? "Why?"

Elizabeth Baxter fiddled with a dish towel, and her features tensed up. "He wants to stop by tonight. Late. After everyone else is gone."

The panic Kari felt at that moment was almost enough to ruin the evening. She looked at the kitchen clock. "He wouldn't be coming this late, would he?"

A sheepish look crossed her mother's face. "He begged me not to tell you."

The number of guests was beginning to dwindle, and suddenly Kari thought of a plan. "Fine." She looked back at her mother as she took a step toward the living room where Tim and a dozen others were gathered. "Thanks for telling me."

Without waiting for a break in the conversation, she came up to Tim and took his arm. "Quick. I need to talk to you." If Ryan Taylor was going to show up unannounced, the last thing she wanted to do was appear interested. Or worse, as if she'd been pining away the months missing him.

When Kari and Tim were alone in the hallway, she told him what her mother had said about Ryan. As soon as she mentioned Ryan's name, Tim's expression fell. "You want me to leave?"

"No!" Kari's response was urgent, and she tugged on Tim's sleeve for emphasis. "I want you to pretend to be my boyfriend."

For a flicker of an instant, something dreamy and serious clouded Tim's eyes, but then almost immediately it was replaced by the teasing, twinkling look she was more familiar with. Moving like an actor in a movie, he took her face gently in his hands and lowered his lips to hers.

"Tim!" She pushed at his chest and stared at him, her heart beating hard from a mixture of mock indignation and some new, strange feeling she'd never had in his presence.

"What?" He gave her a lazy grin. "You said to pretend I was your —"

"Not like that! Come on now. Be serious." She pushed him again. "If Ryan shows up, I want you to hold my hand until he goes, okay?"

Again there was a flicker of something in Tim's eyes, something that made Kari's heart jump unexpectedly. Fifteen minutes later Ryan walked through the door, and Kari stayed in the living room, Tim at her side, the two of them holding hands just as they'd planned.

It took several minutes before Ryan worked his way into the room where Tim and Kari were sitting. Her breath caught in her throat at the sight of him, but she looked away, pretending not to notice. Still, she saw how his eyes took in the sight of her . . . and the fact that she was holding hands with Tim.

"Kari." He walked toward her, and she realized she'd almost forgotten how he commanded a room. "Congratulations!"

"Thanks." She stood up and Tim did the

same, keeping her hand in his.

There was an awkward silence as her mother and father followed Ryan into the room and both simultaneously stared at the spot where her hand joined Tim's. Kari's heart pounded so hard she thought everyone in the room could see it. She cast her parents a look that begged them not to give away her scheme.

Trying to shake off the memory, Kari wrapped the towel around her body and sat at the edge of the bed. Although it had been years since she'd seen Ryan, memories of him were as fresh as if everything had happened earlier that morning.

Kari remembered wanting to draw close to Ryan that evening, just one more time. To feel his arms envelop her against his chest, hear the way his heart beat against her face. Instead, she nodded politely and introduced Tim, whose hand still held hers. They talked about the Cowboys and spring training and summer camp, and Kari could see that Tim was impressed. There were a few more minutes of football talk, and then Ryan said his good-byes and left.

Though he still had a way of taking a piece of her heart with him, Kari watched him go without giving way to the desire that welled up inside her. The desire to run after him and forgive him for anything he'd ever done to hurt her. The desire to ask him if somehow he might still love her.

The moment he was gone, relief swept over her.

Ryan had made his choices long ago. There would never be anything between them again. Kari pulled Tim by the hand outside to a quiet place on the back porch. As soon as they were away from the others, she exhaled loudly and took a spot against the porch railing, staring up at the starry sky. "Thanks."

Tim was quiet, his gaze fixed upward as well. But after a few minutes he shifted positions so that he was facing her. "You're still in love with him."

There was no forgetting the way his statement made her stomach flip-flop. Had Tim read her mind? Had he known all along what she was feeling for Ryan? She squeezed her eyes shut for a moment and realized it didn't matter. She and Ryan had no future, no matter what indiscretions her errant thoughts committed.

Kari caught Tim's gaze as she adjusted her position so that they were facing each other. *Is he the one, Lord . . . ?* The thought came from nowhere and dangled in the subtle night breeze. She looked up at him. "It really is over between Ryan and me. It has been for a long time."

Tim studied her for a minute, his eyes tender and warm. "Are you sure?"

Kari nodded. "Why do you ask?"

Though the sticky hot days of July were just around the corner, this was June, and the night had turned cool. Tim moved gently, took her hands in his, and pulled her closer until their lips met in a kiss that left them both breathless. Kari drew back and searched Tim's eyes. Her voice was barely audible. "You're a convincing actor, friend."

Tim brought his hand to her face and tenderly ran his finger along her cheekbone. "It's not an act, Kari." He kissed her again, this time longer than before. "It never has been."

Kari's head began to spin. She closed her eyes and let her chin fall to her chest. "I . . . I don't know what to say."

He reached out, and with a touch so light she could barely feel it, he tilted her face up and made eye contact with her again. "I mean it, Kari. I've loved you since the day I met you."

Her mind raced, searching for a response, trying to sort through the feelings assaulting her heart. Fear, longing, doubt . . . and a strange sense of betrayal toward Ryan. "But I'm leaving for New York —"

Tim held a finger to her lips and then moved close again, silencing her with another kiss. When he stepped back, his voice was little more than a trembling whisper. "Think about me while you're gone. Think about what you want." His lips met hers once more, but only briefly this time. "When you get back, I'll be waiting."

I'll be waiting. . . .

Before walking her back inside, Tim took her hand once more and prayed out loud that God would show Kari the depth of his feelings and the sincerity of his intent.

After that, Kari's six months in New York passed in a blur of modeling and quiet time spent writing in her journal. When she came home, she was sure she'd finally put her feelings for Ryan behind her. Her feelings were for Tim and Tim alone. A week after her return to Bloomington, Tim Jacobs asked her to be his wife, and now she had no hesitation.

Five months later they were married. By then, Tim had finished his doctorate and landed a tenure-track position at the university. He left his job at the paper but retained his weekly column on the editorial page, hoping eventually for a syndicated spot. The phone rang almost daily with modeling jobs for Kari. They found a house they loved in an older subdivision just minutes from the university — and an easy drive to visit her parents or siblings. Back then, their whole life had been a promise.

Kari got dressed, brushed her hair, and flipped on the blow-dryer. The blast of hot air dried up the images from her past. Tears nipped at the corners of her eyes, and she wondered if she'd ever laugh again.

How did everything get so bad, Lord? Kari clenched her teeth. *How could he do this to me?*

She ran a brush through her hair once more and turned to leave. The air was chilly that morning, but she would be warm soon. She was minutes away from being back at the house where she had grown up, from falling into her mother's arms, and from trying to figure out how she was going to change Tim's mind about wanting a divorce.

And how she could ever love Tim again if he did want a divorce.

Chapter Five

John Baxter got news of his daughter's troubles during the break between his first and second patients that morning. Elizabeth's phone call had indicated no specifics, just that something bad had happened. Something between Kari and Tim.

"She's coming home to talk to me," Elizabeth told him. "I've never heard her like this, John. Please . . . please pray."

The news hit him like a Mack truck, and as soon as he finished with his last patient that morning, he retreated to his office, locked the door, and got on his knees. They creaked more than they had when he was younger, but that didn't matter.

John worked every Tuesday through Thursday in the office and spent Fridays teaching medical anatomy at the university. He made rounds at the hospital on Mondays. At every one of those places he was known for his medical expertise. But here, on his knees, he was just another sinner saved by grace, a man humbly awed that the God of the universe would care about his concerns. *I am nothing, Lord. You are everything. I come to you with a heavy heart.*

John's prayers moved from thoughts to words as he shared the fullness of his concerns with the only One who could do something about them. "Father, it's Kari. . . ."

He paused for a moment and wondered if Elizabeth was right, if indeed something had happened between Kari and Tim. What if the problem was serious? What if Tim was seeing someone else? A memory came to mind, something John had long since dismissed. He'd had lunch nearly a year ago with several professors, including an acquaintance in the journalism department. The man — a bitter scribe in his sixties — had asked about Tim.

"He's your son-in-law, right, Baxter?" the man barked across the table.

"Yes. He's married to my daughter Kari."

"Well," the man sneered, "tell him to remember his position. He's too friendly with the female students. Makes the rest of us look bad. Unprofessional."

John had dismissed the comment, assuming the man to be jealous or mistaken somehow.

But now . . .

John sighed and folded his hands in

front of him. If Tim had been unfaithful, he was perhaps the one person who should have seen it coming. He remembered that he was trying to pray. "Sorry, Lord, I'm distracted. It's just . . . you've put this fix-it thing in me that makes me want to understand a problem and work on it until it's better. It's why you had me be a doctor. . . ."

He hesitated and leaned forward, the weight of his concern for Kari more than he could straighten up under.

"But this, whatever has Kari so upset . . . I don't know how I'm going to fix it, God. I don't know how I'm even going to help."

John closed his eyes and waited on the Lord, deliberately loosening his clenched fists, listening intently for the familiar still, small voice.

Almost immediately a verse came to mind . . . his life verse, really. Psalm 73:26. The one that had always come to him whenever he reached the end of himself, when his need for a Savior was greatest of all: *My flesh and my heart may fail, but God is the strength of my heart and my portion forever.*

John repeated the words again and again, letting the meaning wash over him. "I understand." He whispered the words as a tear made its way down the day's growth of beard on his face. "I can't do anything this time. You will be the strength — not just of my heart, but of Kari's also."

Though John was prepared to spend more time in prayer, he felt a sudden urgency to go home. He stood and glanced at his schedule. It was his light day, and his patients were scheduled only until two o'clock that afternoon. He picked up the phone and within minutes had the appointments covered. Then he left the office and headed for his car, begging God that whatever had happened between Kari and Tim, they could overcome it as a couple.

Kari was sure she had gained her composure by the time she walked in the door of the Baxter home at nine-thirty that morning. But the moment she felt her mother's arms around her, the sobs that had gradually subsided rose again and spilled over. "Mom . . . you won't . . . believe it. . . ." Deep, gut-wrenching convulsions pummeled her body, doubling her over and causing her to gasp for breath. *Help me, God, I'm losing control.*

"Kari —" Her mother's voice was sharp, loud, as it had been when Kari was a small girl and had gotten in trouble for something. "It's okay. Whatever it is, we can get through it."

No, it's not okay. I won't get through it . . . not ever. The sobs continued, and between breaths she caught sight of her mother's pale face. "I'm . . . sorry. . . . I can't . . . help it."

Finally her mother led her gently by the arm into the front room, which was just off the foyer. As they sat on the old flowered sofa, Kari felt the slightest bit of calm come over her. *Help me, Lord. . . . I can't breathe.*

Don't be afraid. . . . I am with you.

Kari exhaled, and the sense of panic eased some. In its place was a nausea that she knew could be resolved only one way. "Wait . . ." She darted through the house and barely made it to the bathroom in time.

Her stomach convulsed again and again as she lost the small amount of food she'd eaten that morning. When she was finished, she felt worse, not better, and more tears coursed down her face. She was sick of crying, but she couldn't stop.

She rinsed out her mouth, clutched her sides, and made her way slowly back to the front room.

Both her parents were waiting for her.

91

Her father must have had someone take over his patients for the day. Typical. He had left work early other times, too, for one family crisis or another. It was his way of letting them know they always came first with him.

Her father stood to meet her. "Kari." She raised her eyes to his and saw that his face was lined with concern. He held his arms out toward her, and Kari went to him, needing his touch, yet racked with guilt for upsetting her parents. *I shouldn't be here. It's not their problem.*

Her father's silent reassurance was so strong that for the first time Kari had a sense she would survive. She allowed herself to be lost in her daddy's arms, sobbing as if she might never stop. This time, though, the hysteria was gone. In its place was a sadness deeper than a canyon.

"It's okay, honey." Her mother reached up and took Kari's hand. "You go ahead and cry. We're here . . . whenever you're ready to talk."

Kari cried for another few minutes and then eased herself down beside her mother as her father took the closest chair. Kari studied the floral pattern on the cushion near her knee and could think of no easy way to begin. It had been two days since she took the call that changed her life, and she hadn't told anyone yet, hadn't spoken of Tim's betrayal out loud. As if by keeping the truth inside, she could convince some part of her that it hadn't happened.

Her cheeks grew hot, and she felt deeply embarrassed by what she was about to say. No matter that the crisis was Tim's fault — she was the one who hadn't been able to keep him happy. And she was the one who had staked her entire life on the belief that her husband's faith was strong, his commitment to her deeply sincere.

She was a failure at the one thing she had prayed might never fail.

Kari lifted her head and saw her pain reflected in the eyes of her parents. The two of them waited, their faces expectant. "Tim and I talked last night." She could find no easy way to say it. "He doesn't want to be married anymore. He . . . he moved out."

Her head dropped, and sorrow choked off her words. Instantly her father moved over to join them on the sofa. She felt her parents' hands on her shoulders and savored the way they made her feel safe and protected. "It's okay, honey." Dad's voice was low, the way it had been whenever he had comforted her as a child. "We'll get through this."

Kari silently prayed for strength, and after a minute she looked up. "He's in love with another woman."

"Oh no, baby." Her mother's hand fell from Kari's shoulder, and she leaned in closer. "How long? I mean, what happened?"

A sigh slipped from between Kari's lips. "He's been seeing her about two months, I think." Her voice sounded dead, as if she'd reached her limit on feeling hurt and devastated and had let an unfeeling robot carry on in her place. "She's a student. It's been going on since the beginning of the semester. Or maybe longer — I don't know."

"Dear God . . ." For a few moments her mother covered her face with her hands.

In all her life, Kari had never seen her father look so helpless. Her every memory of him was marked by sure smiles and his confident way of handling whatever life threw at them. But those images stood in stark contrast to the man sitting near her now, his face pale, his shoulders slightly stooped as if he'd been blindsided and hadn't yet recovered.

"Kari, honey . . ." He made a slight shaking motion with his head, and she noticed that his eyes were glazed over. "I never would have thought . . ."

The nausea was back, but Kari held it at bay. *Get me through this, God, please.*

A verse came to mind, one that had comforted Kari before. It was the shortest verse in the Bible: *Jesus wept.* If he cried over Jerusalem, if he cried over the death of Lazarus, surely he was crying now over the death of her dreams, the death of her marriage.

Kari didn't know what to say. Her soul ached the way her fingers used to when she was a little girl and played in the snow without gloves.

"I'm so sorry, honey. I'm shocked." Her mother placed a hand on Kari's knee. "Has he filed for divorce?"

"I told him I won't give it to him."

"So . . . you *want* to work it out?" Her father sat a bit straighter and raised his chin. Kari felt suddenly scrutinized, like one of his patients.

"Don't look at me like that, Daddy. . . ."

"Sweetheart, I'm just trying to understand. It's a lot to take in at once."

Kari felt like a high school girl being questioned about a bad date. Her eyes grew wet again as she tried to explain. "I know it's a lot, Dad." She tossed her hands in the air. "I'm still trying to take it in myself."

Her mother searched Kari's eyes, and Kari could sense her astonishment as well. "You . . . you don't want a divorce?"

"Mother!" Was that the way it was, then? After all these years of teaching their children the strength of commitment, now her parents would so quickly advocate divorce? She folded her arms against her stomach, refusing the sick feeling. "I thought you two of all people would understand why I can't . . . why divorce isn't an option for me."

Her father cleared his throat, stood, and began pacing the small room. He stopped a few feet from Kari, and she could see conflict raging in his eyes. "Honey, you're absolutely right. And we'll do everything we can to support you in this." He slid his hands into his pants pockets, and Kari saw the muscles in his jaw tense. "It's just that I . . . I'd like to . . ."

His voice broke.

"I know." Kari rose and hugged him, and her mother joined them, placing her arms around them both. Kari whispered as loudly as she could, given the weariness of her soul. "Your little girl's been hurt, and you want to make it better, right?"

When her father didn't answer, Kari stepped back to see his face. What she saw tore at her almost as much as knowing what her husband had done. Her father, the man who had held the family together when her sister Ashley walked out five years ago, the man who had stayed upbeat and stood by her mother when her hair was falling out from chemotherapy — that same man was standing with tears running down his face.

Kari held on to her parents and prayed they would all somehow survive the coming weeks. She had no idea how her siblings or her friends at Clear Creek Community Church would react. Everyone had always known her as the good girl, the one destined to do right and stay married forever.

She hated the idea that now those same people were bound to feel sorry for her. The thought made her want to hide under her parents' bed like she used to do when she was little and a springtime thunderstorm would rock the house.

And there was something else, something she was afraid to admit even to herself. The truth was, the nausea and headaches and tired feeling she'd been fighting for the past few weeks might be more than a reaction to stress. It wasn't a thought she even wanted to entertain in light of Tim's admission. But that didn't make it less possible. If something didn't happen soon, she would have to take steps to find out.

Kari swallowed, and from the safety of the inner circle her parents' arms created, she calculated the dates once more in her mind. There was simply no denying the facts. She'd missed two periods in a row, something that had happened only one other time in her life.

That had been in February three years ago.

The first time she was pregnant.

Chapter Six

Dirk Bennett slipped into the storeroom of the largest cafeteria on campus, the place where he'd worked since the beginning of last year. He tipped three pills from a bottle marked "Natural Power" and downed them with a swig of water. Then he peered through a grate out at the seating area and saw Professor Jacobs having lunch with Angela. Again.

Anyone could see what was happening. The professor was having an affair with her. Dirk had been following them for the past few weeks, and now he was convinced they were living together.

Dirk clenched his teeth and wound his fingers into rock-hard fists. Anger burned within him, and he imagined opening the storeroom door, walking up to their table, and knocking out the professor with a single blow.

The thing that upset Dirk most was her lies. She'd been lying to him for the past eight months.

"I'm busy, Dirk. . . ."

"My classes are more demanding than I thought. . . ."

"I need space. . . ."

"You're too young to get so serious. . . ."

Her excuses felt like daggers through his heart. Dirk released a ragged sigh and thought back to the beginning. Back to the afternoon when he'd been pumping iron in the university weight room and Angela Manning first walked into his life. She wasn't pretty like the sweet girls he'd dreamed about in high school. Rather, she was striking, with an untouchable air and a taut, chiseled body.

That afternoon they had worked out for nearly an hour, sometimes only a few feet from each other. He caught her eye several times, and she met his gaze before returning to her work. When he finished his routine, he took a drink of water and paused as close to her as he dared.

He hesitated, knowing she'd probably laugh at him and send him on his way. Still he smiled at her and wiped his forehead with a towel. "New?"

"Mmmm." She ripped off a set of ten squats, straightened, and studied the length of him. For the first time that afternoon the haughty look in her eyes faded slightly, and she grinned. "You're a jock, right?"

Dirk remembered how his face grew hot as her question unwittingly hit a sore spot in his soul.

His brothers had played ball, but he'd stayed away. Who wanted to dribble a ball up and down a court for hours on end or spend long days with fifteen sweaty guys who thought life happened in a dugout? Guys whose greatest accomplishment was hitting a ball over a fence or kicking it over a goal line? Guys who were entertained by seeing how far they could spit a wad of tobacco?

Then there was the other problem, the one he never talked about.

Dirk was afraid of getting hurt.

Though his brothers reveled in the physical contact of sports, Dirk could see only the grim possibilities. The concussion in football, the broken nose in basketball, the pulled muscles in track. And in baseball . . . well, it didn't take a rocket scientist to figure out what would happen if a ninety-mile-per-hour fastball made contact with your face.

No, sports had never had a pull on him.

So Dirk had gone his own way and joined the marching band. Drum major. And like his friends, he had paid the price with hours of weekend practice. Sure, there were girls in the band who became his friends. But not the kind of pretty honeys who came calling for his brothers. In the high school social structure, girls who looked like Angela Manning recognized the fact that drum majors were beneath their rank. They rarely gave him more than a polite passing nod — and that only because his brothers were part of the golden circle.

Was he a jock?

Four years of high school memories swarmed in Dirk's head that afternoon in the weight room as Angela waited for an answer. He opened his mouth to lie to her, to tell her that yes, in fact, he was. But in that instant he caught a glance of his reflection in the mirror and realized something.

He wasn't in high school anymore.

His brothers were at separate universities a hundred miles away. He was tall and tan, and he'd put on twenty pounds of muscle since arriving at Indiana University. He smiled at Angela and said, "Drum major."

She arched an eyebrow, cocked her head, and let her eyes run lazily from his face to his feet. Her grin was just short of suggestive. "You don't look like a . . . drum major."

A new feeling coursed through Dirk's heart, and it took him a moment before he

recognized it: confidence. He allowed himself to be lost in Angela's bright blue eyes,
and he smiled again. "And you?"

She lowered her chin, eyeing him playfully. "Journalist."

"Journalist?" Dirk had never been on
this side of the game before, but he'd seen
his brothers play it a hundred times. He
imitated her, his eyes drifting over her
body and back to her face. "You don't look
like a . . . journalist."

She lifted the corner of her T-shirt and
wiped at the sweat on her brow, exposing
most of her stomach and causing Dirk to
inhale sharply. When the shirt was back in
place, she planted her hands on her hips.
"I'm free tonight. Want to show me
around?"

The evening had been like something
from a dream, and four days later they had
slept together. Dirk was only nineteen that
summer, four years younger than Angela,
but she didn't seem to care. They were together almost every night until school
started. She was bright and quick-witted,
and she admitted once that she wanted a
houseful of children.

Just like he did.

Dirk was sure he'd found the girl of his
dreams, the woman he was going to marry.

Things between him and Angela had cooled a little once school started last fall. He told himself that was to be expected because Angela was a senior and really dedicated to her studies. But they still had their moments, weekends when she spent the night and whispered words of love so sweet and true that Dirk had not a single doubt that one day they'd be married. He was so sure that a month before Christmas he had bought her an engagement ring. He told his parents about her, even told them he was going to propose.

"Are you sure? Isn't it a bit soon?" His mother sounded worried about the engagement, but Dirk had never felt more sure about anything in his entire life.

Then, one week before he planned to pop the question, he had seen Angela and the professor at one of the tables in the cafeteria. His stomach had slipped down to his knees as he watched Angela tip her head back and laugh when the professor spoke. The way her eyes danced from across the room, the way she seemed lost to everything but their conversation.

That same week she stopped answering his phone calls, refused to return his messages. By the time Christmas came around, they were barely speaking to each other. Still, Dirk remained undaunted. Angela was merely going through a phase — soul-searching, his father used to say.

She didn't love the professor. He was too old for her, too . . . too married.

No matter what Angela said or did, Dirk was sure that deep inside, her heart still belonged to him. Would always belong to him. He could wait for her to come around. She was worth it.

Time passed, and Angela went home to Boston for the summer. Dirk used the time to perfect his workout and hone his body. He was sure that come fall the professor would be out of the picture. But days into the new semester, he realized that Angela was spending more and more time with the man. And that was when Dirk started keeping closer tabs on the situation. Often Dirk was not far away when the two of them would leave the journalism building or the cafeteria or walk across campus together.

Dirk didn't think he was acting crazy, really. Just keeping an eye on a woman who would one day be his wife. But he had never expected to catch Angela and the professor together at her apartment. Alone. The way she and Dirk had been when they first fell in love.

Dirk imagined the gun, its smooth black handle, and pictured it in its box, safely tucked beneath his bed. He needed it, no question about it. He couldn't stand by and watch Angela be taken advantage of by a man who was supposed to be a trusted teacher, a mentor.

But even with all his determination, Dirk hadn't done anything to stop it. Sure, he'd called the professor's wife, but that had just made things worse.

He fingered the bottle of pills in his hand and watched the professor and Angela finish eating lunch, laughing, sharing quiet secrets. The whole thing made him furious, filled him with an unspeakable rage. That's why he needed the gun. In case Angela didn't come to her senses soon.

Dirk imagined himself cornering the professor, putting the gun to his head. Talking some sense into the guy with a little added persuasion.

He frowned, grabbed an industrial-size bottle of ketchup, and left the storeroom. He had work to do now, but the professor's day was coming. The gun would scare him away from Angela. It was just a matter of choosing the right time.

Chapter Seven

Tim Jacobs knew he was no saint. He had cheated on his wife. He had lied too many times to count. But even with all the questionable choices he'd made, the one that never even tempted him involved the liquid gold that came in a bottle.

Raised in a home of teetotalers, Tim had not been exposed to alcohol's seductive lure, and the stories he heard about its wily way of possessing a man left him determined to avoid it. In his high school and college days, he had no trouble saying no to the beer and hard liquor available at parties. Booze was a crutch, and back then Tim had prided himself on not ever needing one. Even in grad school and his newspaper days, when his friends relaxed with a beer after long days in the library or on the job, he had been perfectly comfortable enjoying the company but not the drinking that went with it.

Tim's parents had moved to Indonesia the summer before he entered college, and among the pieces of parting wisdom they left him with was this one: Don't join a fraternity; the hazing could kill you.

It was true. Tim had read about a case once where a 4.0 student who was his family's pride and joy entered college and a week later participated in a hazing ritual. The frat boys forced him to drink half a bottle of gin in an hour's time. Not wanting to be mocked or to fail the initiation, the student did as he was told and promptly passed out on the floor. Sometime before morning the gin worked its way through the boy's system, emptying the contents of his stomach. When his newfound frat buddies checked on him the next day he was dead, suffocated in his own vomit.

And death wasn't the only problem associated with drinking. There was also the chance that Tim might wind up like his uncle Frank, which, at least by his mother's standards, might actually be worse.

Uncle Frank was his mother's younger brother, and Tim had seen him only twice. The first time was when Tim was eight or ten and Uncle Frank came for Christmas. Even as a young schoolboy, Tim could tell there was something different about Uncle Frank. His hair was unruly, the soles of his shoes worn clear through. But the most obvious oddity about Uncle Frank that year was his breath.

Having no knowledge of such things, Tim wasn't sure what caused the smell until late that Christmas Eve. Everyone else was asleep when Tim sneaked downstairs to see if he could make out any surprises near the Christmas tree. Instead, he spied Uncle Frank near the coat closet, a bottle of amber liquid raised to his lips.

He remembered hearing his parents talk later that week about Uncle Frank and his alcohol addiction. When Tim asked his mother what that was, she told him some people could drink alcohol now and then and it wouldn't hurt them. Other people had a disease that, whenever they had even a little, would make them drink until they dropped.

Uncle Frank had the disease.

Every now and then — say in June, on Uncle Frank's birthday — Tim would catch his mother crying and know it was because of her brother.

The second time Uncle Frank came around, Tim was a junior in high school. That spring afternoon he showed up at their front door, staggering and reeking with a stench Tim had never imagined before. The man's clothes were tattered and stained, and he had a backpack of half-empty liquor bottles with him.

While Tim's father was in the next room getting a soapy washcloth, Tim stared at his uncle. "Why do you do this? Don't you know it hurts my mom and dad?"

Uncle Frank had leveled his gaze and given Tim an answer he never forgot: "It's one way to stop the pain."

Tim's father brought Uncle Frank in that day, cleaned him up, and gave him a sandwich. That night he drove Uncle Frank to a facility where he could "dry out." Drying out, Tim's parents explained, was a horrific process in which a person addicted to alcohol would sometimes undergo terrible hallucinations and bone-chilling pain, a mental place that would convince a man he'd died and gone to hell.

Tim's two encounters with Uncle Frank made such an impression on him that until he moved in with Angela, he had never considered taking a drink. After all, what if his parents were right? What if he had inherited the gene, the peculiarity in his system that would make him an alcoholic like Uncle Frank?

It simply wasn't worth it.

But after he moved in with Angela, Tim's attitude began to change. For one thing, she liked wine — found it fun to experiment with different types and vintages.

Often she enjoyed "loosening up" with a glass or two when she came home. She made it seem not only harmless but also pleasant, and Tim began to think he'd been a little too rigid all those years. After all, Angela was never drunk or out of control like Uncle Frank.

But something else was affecting him, too — a quiet, underlying pain in Tim's soul, a pain he hadn't known existed. It came as something of a surprise because, after all, it had been his decision to leave. And he still figured the best thing was for him and Kari to divorce quickly so they could get on with their lives.

Tim figured the pain came as a result of something he had no control over — a spiritual guilt that had been trained into him since childhood. It was a kind of guilt that chafed at him and made him wonder if Kari was praying for him. Not that her prayers would affect him, but either way he couldn't get around his feelings. The guilt was so strong at times it was paralyzing.

He was in love with Angela, true. In her arms he felt as if he'd been given another chance at life. But there were other times when he'd be lecturing to a class and catch himself in midsentence, not sure what he'd said or where his train of thought was going.

Then there was his office time. Sitting alone in the shadows of his own guilt, the pain of what he'd done to Kari was suffocating.

The problem was, these feelings had begun carrying over into his time with Angela. Though the holy whispers were gone, though the tears hadn't come for a while now, he couldn't shake the memory of Scripture verses he'd memorized as a boy.

And never had it been worse than that night. He'd had a long day and was about to use his new key on the apartment door when Angela opened it first.

He leaned against the doorframe and allowed a slow smile to creep up the sides of his face. "So," he drawled suggestively, "where were we?"

Some words from the book of Revelation kicked in before Angela had a chance to respond.

Remember the height from which you have fallen!

Angela must have said something because she lowered her brow. "Tim? Did you hear me? I was talking to you, and you had this . . . I don't know, this faraway look, like you weren't even listening."

Tim laughed, but it sounded nervous even to him. "Sorry . . . long day."

Her grin made his knees weak. "Well, then, welcome home." She moved her toned body to one side so Tim could see far enough into the apartment to notice lit candles and dimmed lights. Something freshly baked mingled with a smell that was sweet and intoxicating. Her hand found his. "I've been thinking about you all day."

He started to step inside when another Scripture verse flew through his mind.

The thief comes only to steal and kill and —

"Tim?" Angela angled her head and studied his face. "What's wrong with you?"

Flee from sexual immorality.

Tim sighed and tossed his hands in the air. "I'm sorry. I've got a lot on my mind."

"Yeah." Angela's smile faded. "Me too."

Tim felt his heart lurch. "Everything okay?"

"Sure." Her expression fell.

He lifted her chin, caressing her face as he did. "Tell me the truth, Angela. What's wrong?"

She shook her head. "Nothing."

He swallowed and forced a chuckle. "You're not having second thoughts, are you?"

Angela leaned her head against the wall.

"I wanted tonight to be perfect. But . . ."

The thud of his heartbeat sounded in his ears. He'd sacrificed his marriage for this woman. He had no idea what he'd do if she backed out now. "But, what?"

She looked at him. "I'm struggling, Tim. Really."

He searched his memory and tried to imagine why she'd be struggling. She had everything she had wanted. Including him. He brushed a finger along her brow. "Come on, Angela. Whatever it is, you can tell me."

She exhaled softly, and after a long while she began to speak. "My father left us when I was ten." Her eyes met his and held. "He ran off with another woman."

Silence hung between them for a moment, and Tim rested against the doorframe again. He wasn't sure where she was going with this, so he waited.

"I promised myself I would never date a married man." There was a catch in her voice. "And now here I am. No better than the woman who stole my daddy away."

Tim could barely breathe as he considered her words. "Should I go?"

"No. That's just it." She looked up, her eyes a mix of sorrow and desire. "I want you to stay. Forever, Tim. Really."

"Good." He felt himself relax. "I want that too."

She moved closer and ran her fingers along his hairline. The sadness eased from her expression. "You know what we need to do?"

Whatever it was, he would do it. How could he not, with her standing there, sweet and beautiful and vulnerable, mesmerizing him with her every movement? "What do we need to do?"

"Have a little wine." She smiled, holding up a hand to ward off his objections. "Now, look. I know you don't drink, but come on . . . just one glass?" She curled her lips into a pout that made Tim weak.

"Angela, I don't . . ." His argument fizzled, and another verse flashed in his head.

Be holy, because I am holy.

"Come on." She pulled at his hand again. "I'm tired of drinking alone." She led him into the apartment, but halfway across the entry she turned, rose on her tiptoes, and kissed him soundly on the mouth. The kiss lasted longer than either of them intended, and when Angela came up for breath she grinned at him. "Don't fight it, Tim. You can't tell me no, remember? Just one drink. For me."

And there it was, the offer he had never intended to accept, standing between them like a doorway. In that instant he knew instinctively that the Scripture verses would fade if he took the drink. What could it hurt, really? He wouldn't do anything crazy or over the edge, nothing life-threatening like the frat kid or Uncle Frank.

Just a glass of wine to please Angela, ease the pain, and help him think clearly.

The thief comes only to steal and kill and —

"You know, I think that'd be nice," he heard himself say.

Angela gazed back into her apartment and lifted her shoulders twice. "I just so happen to have a bottle of white zinfandel in the refrigerator." Her eyes danced, and Tim realized he didn't need a drink at all. He was intoxicated just being near her.

She led the way into the kitchen and nodded toward the table. It was set for two, and the lovely smell was bread baking in the oven. There were wineglasses at both their place settings. "Actually, you have a choice," she said. "The zinfandel or a nice little merlot."

He inhaled sharply and chuckled. "I'll trust your judgment."

She poured him a glass of pale pink liquid. It looked like the type of wine his friends used to drink years ago at more sophisticated college parties.

He gripped the stem of the glass just as yet another Scripture verse filtered through his mind.

I have come that you might have life and have it to the —

"To new beginnings . . ." Tim raised his glass to hers, and the two made a clinking sound.

He took a single sip and tried not to react as the liquid left a subtle burning sensation on his tongue, a feeling that worked itself down into his gut. *So this is it, huh? The great forbidden fruit.*

He took another sip, then another. A gentle floating sensation stole over him as he drank, gradually washing away the pain and anxiety Tim had felt in the past week. This wasn't so bad. He had no desperate desire to guzzle the liquid or finish off the bottle. When Angela offered, he accepted another glass, and as he drank it he felt his muscles warm and relax.

Before they made their way to the bedroom, he had finished off three glasses of wine and was still sober enough to recognize what seemed to be an important fact. He was not like his uncle Frank. The alcohol had helped him unwind, nothing more. The relief of knowing he didn't have a problem with alcohol felt almost as good as the gentle buzz that helped him sleep that night.

He considered Uncle Frank's statement about why he drank: *It's one way to stop the pain.* His uncle's words rang in his mind that night and again the next, when he and Angela finished off another bottle.

The next day he purchased a small bottle of vodka and hid it in his desk at the university. Lugging a wine bottle to work would look bad, but the little flask of clear liquid was easy to conceal. Besides, he guessed he would need only a single swig of vodka to give him the feeling he'd gotten from several glasses of wine.

It wasn't that he needed to drink. But if it helped him sleep, no doubt it would ease the emptiness and guilt he felt during office hours.

A week later — after sharing wine with Angela seven nights straight and nearly finishing off the vodka — Tim realized Uncle Frank had been wrong about something.

Drinking wasn't one way to stop the pain.

It was the only way.

Chapter Eight

Ashley Baxter was disgusted with her family's obsession with faith, but for the sake of her sister she was trying to keep her opinion to herself.

What sort of God would insist that Kari stay married to a creep like Tim Jacobs? That's what Ashley wanted to know. Kari had been living at their parents' house for two weeks, and Ashley still couldn't believe the conversation they'd shared the morning after her arrival.

"Let me get this straight." Ashley had sat perched on one of the kitchen stools while Kari leaned against the counter, sipping a cup of coffee. "Tim *told* you he's seeing another woman . . . but *you're* the one who doesn't want the divorce?"

"I don't expect you to understand." Kari had gray circles under her eyes again that morning. She held her mug with both hands and sighed. "He can tell me he's in love with her, but in his heart of hearts he doesn't believe that any more than I do."

"What?" An angry pit had formed in

Ashley's stomach. "He told you that? That he's in love with this . . . this student?"

"He's not in love with her, Ashley. He's mixed up." Kari straightened, leveling her gaze at Ashley. "I promised to love Tim Jacobs until the day I die, and that hasn't changed."

Ashley stood, her hands on her hips. "Don't you get it?" She and Kari were the same height, and as she approached her older sister, Ashley looked straight into her eyes. "Your marriage is over."

"Listen." Kari set down her coffee and studied Ashley with a quiet strength. "You can sit down, Ashley. And you don't have to raise your voice. I know my opinion is not popular."

"Not popular?" Ashley huffed out loud. "Listen, big sister, the guy should be hung from his —"

"Stop!" Kari's eyes welled up, and Ashley was seized with remorse. "Don't you understand? He's my husband, Ashley! I haven't had time to think it all through yet, but there's one thing I know for sure: If there's a way to get past this thing . . . to resolve it and put it behind us, that's what I want to do."

The memory faded and left a sour residue in Ashley's heart.

It was just after two o'clock, and Ashley's son, Cole, was sleeping. He was three years old, and naps were still a much-needed part of his schedule — not that Ashley was very good about schedules. That was her mom's area of expertise, and in some ways Ashley knew her son had two mothers. A young, single mother who liked feeding Cole his favorite ice cream, taking him to the park, and cuddling with him when he had bad dreams. And a more mature, responsible mother who made sure he ate bananas with his cereal and got a proper nap each afternoon. Sometimes the arrangement bothered Ashley, made her feel guilty and a little jealous. Other times she thought her son had the best of both worlds.

Right now, though, her mom was at a Bible study and Kari at the grocery store. With Cole asleep, Ashley had the house to herself. She opened her French impressionists art book and tried to tackle the third chapter. But every few sentences the image of Kari's husband, Tim, came to mind.

How dare he cheat on Kari? Ashley tapped her pencil on the open page and thought about where God fit into this mess. *You're still there, right, God?* She let the thought sit on the front porch of her mind for a moment before sweeping it away. Of course he was there. Ashley had no doubt about the existence of God. It was his caring about their everyday lives that Ashley tended to doubt.

A loving, involved God would have some sort of intelligent system whereby people like Tim would die suddenly in their sleep and people like Kari, people who taught Sunday school and read their Bible faithfully, would get some kind of break. If all Kari wanted from life was a marriage that would last forever, then that's what God should have given her.

But look at what Kari had instead.

Ashley exhaled loudly and turned a page in the textbook. What had God ever done for her big sister? A flash of remorse pierced her dark thoughts. Maybe she was being too hard on God. He'd helped all of them to some degree — by dying on the cross. Wasn't that the basic message of all those years of Sunday school?

Still, it wouldn't have hurt him to give Kari a better husband too.

Kari's unabated devotion to God in the face of Tim's affair was truly beyond Ashley. For that matter, it was beyond her how Kari could want such a simple life in the first place. Ashley gazed out the kitchen window of the Baxter home and took in the rolling hills and endless miles of red- and gold-decked trees.

The world was meant to be explored, conquered, tasted, sampled.

Wasn't that why she'd escaped to Paris the minute she finished her associate's degree? Wasn't it why she had done the things she'd done, why she'd decided to have Cole in the first place? Ashley closed her eyes, and she was arriving in Paris again, trying out her high school French on locals who pretended not to hear her, sampling new flavors and sounds and experiences wherever she found them, deliriously free of the expectations of living in a community where everyone knew her as the doctor's daughter.

The Christian doctor's daughter.

Of course, sometimes she wasn't proud of the lifestyle she'd lived in Paris, but those were the times when she thought like a Baxter, not like the expressive and free-spirited individual she knew herself to be. All in all, Paris had been worth it, regardless of the cost.

That's where she and Kari were so different.

Kari had spent six months in New York, but all she'd accomplished was some modeling and sightseeing. She hadn't immersed herself in the culture there, hadn't really *lived* in New York. Ashley sighed. It was one thing to be safe and conservative, to live a life based on your beliefs. Ashley could admire that, although it certainly wasn't her — not the safe and conservative part, anyway. But it was another thing entirely to pine away your days waiting for a faithless husband to come to his senses.

Especially with a hunk of a catch like Ryan Taylor back in town and wonderfully single.

Ashley thought about Ryan for a moment, the way he and Kari had been when they were younger. Kari had obviously opted for Tim because he seemed to be a safer bet, the type women wouldn't fawn over the way they fawned over Ryan.

Ashley had tried to support Kari's decision, but secretly she thought her sister had made the wrong choice. Ryan Taylor was fun and involved in their family. He loved all the same things Kari loved, and though they'd known each other since they were young teens, their relationship always had an air of electricity about it, something Ashley saw in few couples.

She smiled at the memory of Ryan. When she was a little kid, Ryan had always found a way to make Ashley feel important.

Maybe that's what she liked about him — he was the big brother she'd never had.

Most jocks had egos in direct proportion to their biceps, but not Ryan. Ashley had grown up hoping he would propose to Kari one day and be part of the Baxter family forever. When they broke up, Ashley had been nearly as upset as her sister.

That day had become something of a turning point in Ashley's life. After that, happy endings were no longer a guarantee. It was the same day Ashley determined she wouldn't allow herself to get involved with a man the way Kari had. The ending was simply too painful, too predictable. There were exceptions, of course. People like her parents. But by Ashley's assessment, exceptions like that were rare.

Anyway, regardless of Kari and Ryan's breakup, Ashley was sure of this: No one would ever love Kari the way Ryan Taylor had. The way he still did, as far as Ashley was concerned. Any doubts she'd had about that faded two months earlier, when she ran into him out by the high school football field.

Ashley had been jogging that afternoon, and as she rounded the track, she noticed one of the coaches watching her. He was tall and had the rough build of Ryan Taylor.

Then she remembered.

He was back in town. Something about his being finished with professional football and getting a job at the high school. Ashley slowed her pace, and on the next lap she watched the tall coach excuse himself from the others and jog purposefully in her direction. They met up at the end of the track nearest the football field.

"Ashley Baxter, I can't believe my eyes." They were both out of breath as they hugged and took a step back to study each other. "You were seventeen last time I saw you, and now you're all grown-up and gorgeous."

Ashley rarely blushed in the presence of complimentary men, and this was no exception. Still, she could feel the smile tugging on her cheekbones. "That's me. All grown-up." She met his gaze straight on. "So you came back to finish life in obscurity, huh?"

Ryan laughed. "I guess." He shoved his hands in the pockets of his nylon sweats and cocked his head. "What do you hear from Kari?"

Ashley shrugged. It was strange talking to Ryan now that she was a woman. Back when she was growing up, she had been Kari's kid sister. Now she was twenty-five and he was thirty. If he hadn't been in love with Kari . . .

She looked into his pale green eyes and saw not even a flicker of romantic interest. "She lives over at University Park. Her husband's a professor at the university. No kids."

Ryan inhaled slowly through his nose and seemed to weigh the words he was about to say. "If that ever changes . . ." There was a glimmer of raw pain in his eyes, but it passed, and Ryan smiled. "You be a good girl and give me a call, okay?" He flashed her a familiar grin, finished the conversation, and jogged back to his fellow coaches.

She and Ryan had spoken one other time at the track since then, but otherwise Ashley hadn't seen him. For all she knew, he'd met someone and was dating by now.

She looked down at her textbook and tried three times to read a single paragraph. Frustration worked its way through her veins, and without giving herself another chance, she shut the book and looked at the phone.

It couldn't hurt to call, right? He was probably listed. After all, he *had* asked her to call if anything changed.

Kari's words from the other morning filled Ashley's mind. *He's my husband, Ashley. . . . If there's a way to get past this thing, that's what I want to do.*

But what about Ryan?

Shouldn't he know that Kari's husband had abandoned her? Shouldn't someone at least tell him what was going on?

For the most part Ashley did not believe in prayer. But the childlike habit of conversing with God Almighty had stuck, and now and then — at times like this when she wasn't sure what to do — she uttered a silent bit of conversation to the Lord.

Nothing wrong with calling him, right, God?

Ashley even tried to be still and listen for a response, but she heard nothing. Not that she was really expecting one.

"Fine." She stood up and chuckled to herself. "I'll take that as a yes." She walked across the kitchen, flipped through the phone book, but found no Ryan Taylor listed. The listing was probably too new.

Feeling far more energized than she had moments earlier, Ashley tapped both sides of her head, and then it came to her. Clear Creek Community Church would have his number. Her mother and dad had seen him a few times at the Sunday night service.

Ashley looked up the church and dialed as quickly as she could. Kari would be home soon, and Ashley wasn't entirely sure if —

"Clear Creek Community Church. May I help you?"

Ashley resisted a smile. The church secretary always sounded so . . . well, so much like a church secretary. She was a seventyish woman who would have given a stranger the key to her house if it meant keeping him off the streets.

"Hi, Mrs. Mosby. Ashley Baxter here. I have a quick favor to ask you."

"Oh, hello, dear." Mrs. Mosby was one of the few people at Clear Creek Community who hadn't made Ashley feel like dirt for coming home from Paris pregnant and single. "What can I do for you?"

Ashley held her breath. "Remember Ryan Taylor?"

"Yes, dear, of course." She giggled politely as if the effect Ryan had on women was not limited by age. "He moved back to town and comes to the evening service every now and then."

Ashley swallowed. She hadn't been to church since Easter, but she hoped Mrs. Mosby wouldn't hold that against her. "If you don't mind, I need his phone number. I must have misplaced it somewhere."

"Oh . . ." There was a pause, and Ashley could hear Mrs. Mosby searching. "Why, yes, dear. Here it is." She rattled off the number and then clucked her tongue against the roof of her mouth. "I remember when your sister and Ryan were teenagers. She'd bring him to youth group, and all the other girls would get jealous."

"Yes." Ashley smiled at the memory.

"I feel guilty for saying this —" Mrs. Mosby lowered her voice — "but I always rather hoped Ryan would marry your sister."

A smile tugged at the corners of Ashley's mouth, and she stared at the number she'd written down. "Yes, Mrs. Mosby. Me too."

"You know —" the older woman's voice was wistful — "I think we all did." Then she hastened to add, "But I was happy she married a nice Christian man."

Ashley didn't answer that one. "Well, I'd better go." She was suddenly in a hurry to get off the phone. She wound up the conversation and punched in the numbers Mrs. Mosby had given her. Then she closed her eyes and waited.

Ryan Taylor lived in a well-appointed two-bedroom cabin on a ten-acre ranch. The place was minutes from the country club, less than a mile from the boat docks at Lake Monroe, and only three miles down the road from the house where Kari grew up, the house where the senior Baxters still lived. His career in professional football had paid off financially. He had a savings account he could never deplete and owed nothing on any of his material goods, including the ranch and his loaded silver Chevy truck. Someday he planned to build his dream house near the front of his land, but so far he'd had no reason to break ground.

The cabin suited him perfectly. He had never planned on having the privilege of playing professional football, but now that those days were behind him, he knew there was only one thing that could fill the decades ahead.

That thing was coaching.

When the assistant position at Clear Creek High School became available at the beginning of summer, he knew it was the opportunity he'd been looking for. The opportunity to come back home.

Things weren't exactly the same, of course. Back when he'd grown up in Clear Creek, he was just one of the gang, a favorite son who was welcomed everywhere he went. Now, after his eight years with the Cowboys, people treated him like a celebrity. They stared at him in supermarkets, asked for his autograph at the movie theater, and wouldn't let him have a public meal in peace.

Sometimes he even wondered whether he might have made a mistake in thinking he could settle down in Clear Creek. But then it was still his favorite place on earth, the place where he'd grown up, where his mother and his sister and her family still lived. All his life he'd imagined settling down here.

He just hadn't imagined doing it without Kari Baxter.

He'd had plenty of opportunities to date when he returned from his stint with Dallas. Everyone had a daughter, a friend, a sister who wanted to meet the area's newest eligible bachelor. A time or two Ryan had actually followed through and asked one of them out. But he always stopped after a few dates when he found himself comparing each woman to Kari.

It wasn't that the women he saw weren't wonderful in their own right. They were mostly beautiful and bright and would have made great wives, no doubt. But they hadn't sat cross-legged next to him on a summer's night the year he turned fourteen and told him the secrets of their hearts the way Kari had. They hadn't stayed beside him all day fishing on the shores of Lake Monroe the summer he was seventeen or run for cover with him the afternoon the tornado siren sounded across the county.

The other women he met hadn't shared with him a first kiss or a first dance or that first taste of love. And they hadn't shown him for the first time what it meant to love God. To really love God and want to please him.

Ryan understood very well that Kari was married; clearly she was not the woman for him. He simply wasn't in a hurry to find one who was.

"I don't know, Ryan, you're getting awfully old," his mother would say to him every other Sunday when they got together for dinner. "At this rate, I'll be toothless in a rocker before you get me some grandbabies."

Ryan would laugh and pat his mother on her shoulder. "You're stubborn enough to live a hundred years, Mom. At fifty-three you're young enough for anything. You'll probably outlive us all."

Practice had finished up early that day, and for some reason Ryan felt lonelier than usual, as if a piece of his heart weren't fitting quite right. He slipped on his work boots. A few hours outside in the yard would help clear his head.

He tackled the bushes in front of his cabin first and was inside getting water when the phone rang. Max, his white Lab puppy, cocked his head and stared at the receiver as Ryan picked it up. "It's okay, Max, boy." He whispered the words and stooped to scratch Max's ears before clicking the button and answering the call.

"Hello." Max whined and gave two high-pitched puppy barks.

"My goodness, Ryan, I didn't know you could sing."

The voice was Kari's, but the tone was Ashley's. Subtly sarcastic and mixed with a teasing they'd always shared.

He smiled and cleared his throat. "I'm working on that number. Takes me a while to warm up."

She giggled. "Bet you don't know who this is."

"The voice police? Calling to tell me I'm under arrest?"

Another peal of laughter erupted on the other end. "Ah, yes, same old Ryan. You never change, do you?"

"Nope, Ashley, not really." He hesitated, curious. Ashley had never called before. "Okay, what's up? No, wait, let me guess.

Kari's husband left her high and dry, and she's pining away for me but couldn't bring herself to call." He grinned at the audacity of his statement, certain Ashley would be doing the same.

Instead, her laughter died, and there was silence.

"Ashley?" Ryan's heart beat twice as fast as before. "Ashley, talk to me. What is it?"

Her voice lacked any teasing. "Kari's husband left her high and dry, and I don't know if she's pining away for you, but either way, I had to call."

Now it was Ryan who was silent. His mind reeled at what she was saying, trying to determine if she could possibly still be joking. "Be serious, Ashley."

"I am." She hesitated. "Tim's having an affair. He moved in with one of his students." She paused, and he felt the wood floor give way beneath him. "Kari's spending a lot of time at my parents' house. She's been here the past few days. I thought you should know."

Ryan found the nearest chair at his small dining-room table and sat down. His knees were trembling. "Is she . . . is she okay?" It was the first thing he could think to ask. His emotions were bubbling within him — pain and sorrow, rage and revenge. *How dare he do that to you, Kari girl? How dare he —*

"She's pretty messed up, Ryan. She says she doesn't want a divorce; she's praying for Tim to come around."

Ryan gritted his teeth and ran through a host of possible actions he might take, actions like driving to the university, finding the guy, and leveling him there in his office. Or driving to the Baxter home and holding Kari until the pain went away. The ideas fell flat.

Obviously he would see her again; he'd known that since he moved back three months ago. He'd expected to see her sooner than this. They couldn't live in such a small community and not run into each other somewhere — at church, if nowhere else. But it wasn't his place to do anything about what was happening to her. Not unless she asked for his help.

The realization suffocated him. Kari was hurt — the kind of hurt that some people never recover from. And though he was just three miles from her family's home — from her — he could do nothing to help.

"So." Ryan could hear the tightness in his voice as Kari's pain became his. "Why'd you call?"

Ashley was quiet a moment. "I'm not sure." She sighed and sounded as frustrated as he was. "I remember a time long ago when everything seemed good and right with Kari, when the five of us Baxter kids were close, and never in a million years would any of us have dreamed this might happen to our sister. You were always there for her back then, Ryan."

He squeezed his eyes shut and massaged the bridge of his nose. Those days were so real that he could reach back over his shoulder and touch them. "Yeah . . . I remember."

"I guess I always thought you'd be there. And now . . ."

"What can I do?" Ryan closed his eyes again. "She's in love with her husband. You said so yourself."

Ashley seemed to consider that for a moment. "You know what I think, Ryan?"

The ache in his heart was so great that he literally had to force himself to stay seated, stop himself from bolting out the door and driving to Kari before common sense got the better of him. "What?"

"No matter what she says . . . I think she's still in love with you."

Chapter Nine

A pregnancy test was the only real way to know.

Kari had been late before, but not this late. And besides, she could hardly deny the fact that she was almost constantly nauseous. At first it had been easy to blame the missed periods on her busy schedule. And feeling sick was certainly understandable in light of the changes in the past three weeks.

But very little could account for her being this late and this sick.

In the weeks following Tim's departure, she had gradually moved from total paralysis into a kind of functional routine that had very little to do with the terrible reality of his absence. Though she desperately wanted to save her marriage, she felt frozen, unable to take any action at all — especially when every thought about Tim and his affair threatened to dissolve her into tears.

Kari's photo shoot schedule was light for the next few months, nothing that couldn't be handled by the other models at the agency. She had called her agent and asked for time off. But that left her with nothing to fill her days, and she hated being at home by herself, so she'd set up temporary quarters in her parents' guest room — the very room that used to be hers when she was growing up. At least at her parents' house she had company and distractions. It was better than sitting in her own empty house listening to the deafening silence shout that her husband didn't live there anymore.

The best distraction at her parents' house was the cleaning. Elizabeth Baxter had always prided herself on keeping a neat, organized home, but that was before she started baby-sitting Cole three days a week. Now there were closets that needed cleaning, cupboards that hadn't been gone through in years. So Kari had spent most of her daytime hours doing housework, cleaning the garage, and, when the nausea grew too strong, taking naps.

As far as she could tell, there were enough projects around here to keep her busy for weeks — or at least until she knew what to do next. And by Saturday of the third week since Tim had moved out, Kari knew exactly what she had to do.

Even if the results terrified her.

Just before lunch she found her mother and little Cole in the kitchen. "I'm going out for a while." She grabbed her keys and smiled. *Please, God, don't let her be curious. Not today.*

Elizabeth looked up from the table where she and Cole were coloring pictures. "Can you pick up a gallon of milk?"

Kari felt a warm rush of relief. She was terrified enough about the possible results of the test without having to tell her mother. That could come later, if the test turned out to be . . . she couldn't bear the thought. "Sure. Anything else?"

Her mother thought for a moment. "Actually, yes. Two loaves of bread and some mustard. Thanks, honey." She held Kari's gaze a moment longer. "Any word?"

For a brief instant Kari thought her mother was talking about the pregnancy test. She could feel the color drain from her face. "About . . . ?"

Her mother knit her brows and lowered her voice, as if Cole might somehow understand what they were talking about. "From Tim. Has he called?"

"Mom . . ."

"I know, I know." Her hand came up in a gesture that told Kari she didn't need to belabor the point.

Kari had begged her parents that first day not to ask about Tim. "I'll keep you up on what's happening," she'd told them through her tears. "If he calls, if we make any progress at all, I'll tell you. But otherwise, don't ask. Please."

"I'm sorry." Her mother stood and drew her into a hug. "Your dad and I are praying. It's just . . . I don't know. What's he doing, Kari? He's a married man. I keep asking myself — what could be more important than loving my little girl?"

The obvious answer hung in the air between them like a newly sharpened sword. Her mother's eyes misted over, and she pulled Kari close once more. "Oh, honey, that was a dumb thing to say."

"It's okay." Any other day Kari might have broken down in her mother's arms and silently cried out yet again for God to change Tim's heart. But now that she'd made up her mind to find out whether she was pregnant, she wanted desperately to get to the store. "God's going to get us back together somehow. I really believe that. Just keep praying, Mom."

Her mother nodded, too choked up to speak. "Always."

With the precision of one who'd spent most of her life in the Bloomington area,

Kari navigated her way up the two-lane highway lined with rolling hills and autumn leaves and onto the busy streets of the city proper. At the store she grabbed the first pregnancy test she could find and hid it in her cart beneath the bread. She saw an older couple from church and made small talk for a few minutes but was relieved to see no one else she knew.

What would I say if I ran into Ryan Taylor? The thought took her by surprise, and Kari had no answer for herself except for one: She wasn't ready to see him again. And to see him while she was purchasing a pregnancy test, of all things, would be utterly unbearable.

Thirty minutes later she pulled up back at her parents' house and hid the test in her coat pocket. Cole would be asleep by now, so she opened the door quietly.

Once inside she set the groceries on the counter and looked at her mother. Immediately Kari knew something was wrong. "Mom?"

Her mother was sitting at the kitchen table, her Bible open, her face ashen. "Come sit down, Kari. I have to talk to you."

A tremor made its way through Kari's veins and into her heart. Whatever it was, she couldn't take it. That much was sure.

She crossed the kitchen and sat down across from her mother. "What?"

Her mother met her desperate gaze. "Tim called."

Kari could feel her eyes fly open, her jaw drop. They'd been talking about him less than an hour ago, and then he'd called? That had to be good, didn't it? Maybe he'd come to his senses. She felt the slightest surge of hope. "What did he say?"

"He . . ." Her mother shook her head, and her eyes fell.

"Mother, what? Tell me what he said." It couldn't be worse, could it? Nothing could be worse than what he'd already told her.

Finally her mother looked up, and Kari could see how much she didn't want to answer. "He was drunk, Kari. His speech was so slurred that I could barely understand him."

Kari clutched her forehead as her mind searched desperately for explanations. "Maybe . . . maybe he was tired." She stood and took a few steps to one side and then the other. "He's never had a drink in his life."

She'd heard the stories about Uncle Frank and how Tim never wanted to find out if deep inside him lived an alcoholic like his mother's brother. He would never have started drinking, would he? And if he had . . . tears stung at Kari's eyes.

"It can't be true." Her hands began to shake. When would the nightmare end?

Her mother took hold of Kari's fingers. "He was drunk." Her tone was calmer and completely convincing. "I'm sure of it."

Kari broke free of her mother's grip, rested her hands on the table, and hung her head. After a while she looked up, and for a long moment she stared at her mother, searching her face for answers. "What did he say?"

Her mother tenderly placed a hand over Kari's. "You won't like it."

Why, Lord? Kari blinked back fresh tears. "It's okay, Mom. Tell me."

"Oh, honey . . . he said he still wants a divorce. He told me to tell you he's getting a lawyer."

Kari threw her hands up and moved into the living room. Her mother came up behind her, gently taking hold of Kari's shoulders.

"My whole life's a mess."

Her mother leaned her cheek against the back of Kari's head. "He's serious, isn't he? About the divorce?"

Kari stared out the window at the tree-lined driveway and the grassy fields where she'd played as a child. Back when she'd known for sure she'd grow up to marry Ryan Taylor. Back when she —

"I won't give him one. He's crazy and . . . and he's in a bad place." She turned and stared at her mother, silently pleading for her to understand. "He'll come around one day." Kari gulped, feeling for the pregnancy test in her pocket. "Besides . . ."

Her mother's eyes softened, and she ran her fingers along Kari's cheek. As if she knew what her daughter was going to say, she locked eyes with Kari and spoke in a voice that was almost too quiet to hear. "Besides, what?"

There was no point in hiding it. If she was pregnant, it couldn't possibly come as a shock. After all, Tim was her husband, and ten weeks earlier Kari had known nothing of his unfaithfulness. She drew a steadying breath, her gaze still connected to her mother's. "I might be pregnant."

Her mother didn't move or cry out, but something in her eyes looked as if it had died. "I . . . I thought you might be."

Kari blew a wisp of bangs off her forehead and stared back out the window again. "I bought the test today." She made a noise that was part laugh. "If I am pregnant, I'll need you and Dad and . . . everyone else."

She blinked, willing the tears not to come again, but they were too close to the surface to be held back. "I need you, Mom," she whimpered as she felt her mother's arms surround her.

The landscape of Kari's mind was littered with questions she couldn't answer. What if the test was positive? What if Tim became an alcoholic like his uncle? What if he found a way to marry the student he was seeing? And most of all, where was God in all this?

Gradually a dim light dawned in Kari's heart, and she remembered the holy reassurance she'd felt the other day, the message from the radio.

Do not be afraid . . . I will be with you. I will defend you.

Kari sniffled and drew back, studying her mother, praying she would understand. "Mom . . . you get it, don't you? Why I want my marriage to work?"

Her mother smoothed her hand over Kari's hair. "Shhh, baby . . . it's okay." Her mother was crying now too. "Of course I get it. You want to do things God's way, and God will honor that. We'd love nothing more than to see your marriage work, Kari. You have our support, no matter what happens."

Kari managed the briefest smile because she knew it was true. No matter what others might say or feel about Kari's decisions, her parents would stand by her.

It was what the Baxter family was all about.

The directions on the pregnancy test kit suggested that an early-morning test would yield the best results. So she had set the kit aside until morning.

She was in the backseat of her parents' car and halfway to church before she realized she hadn't taken the test.

It wasn't merely a matter of forgetting, obviously. There was something final about taking the test, something Kari wasn't ready to face.

The view out of the car window provided a well-needed distraction for the fears jockeying for position in her soul. She stared at the familiar farms and billboards while her parents chatted in the front seat.

She had mixed feelings about going to church today. It would be her first time since Tim moved out. A few days after he left, Kari had called the church and explained that she wouldn't be able to teach Sunday school or sing in the choir for some time. When the church secretary asked if anything was wrong, Kari had said only that something had come up.

A part of her desperately wanted anonymity in this, her greatest season of grief and pain. But the desire to be surrounded by people who loved her and would pray for her was greater than her need for solitude. Besides, she'd sat around her parents' house acting paralyzed long enough. It was time to seek help, time to talk to Pastor Mark and arrange for counseling.

So she had decided to go this morning.

There was an expectant silence in the car, and Kari thought back to what she'd overheard her brother say in the kitchen earlier this morning. Kari had been coming down the stairs, anxious for crackers or something to stave off the constant nausea, when her brother's voice stopped her.

"What is it about my sisters?" The ring of indignation in Luke's voice surprised her. She and Luke had always shared easy laughter and mutual admiration, a bond that had never been threatened over the years. But this morning he sounded more fed up than fun loving. It was a side of her brother Kari hadn't seen before.

"Be quiet, Luke; she'll hear you." It was her mom, her hissing voice so low it was difficult to make out her words above the sounds of whatever she was cooking. "There was nothing Kari could have done about this, and you know it."

"I'm just saying," Luke's voice was only slightly quieter, "you'd think being raised in a family like ours, they might have made better choices."

They? Kari wrinkled her brows and dropped down two more steps so she wouldn't miss her mother's side of the conversation.

"Ashley and Kari are nothing alike. I think Kari would be hurt if she heard you say that."

"Okay, then at least get rid of the guy." Luke let loose an angry chuckle. "I mean, anyone who's doing what that jerk is doing shouldn't have the option of staying married to her."

Her mother stopped stirring, and there was silence for a moment. "You don't know the details, Luke. They're none of your business."

"Yes, Mother, I do know the details. I heard Kari and Ashley talking about it. The guy's living with his student girlfriend, he wants a divorce, he doesn't love my sister anymore." His voice fell flat. "But somehow Kari wants to give him a chance?" Luke uttered another laugh that was void of humor. "Even God wouldn't ask that of her."

There. That sounded more like Luke. He was upset and frustrated, but only because he cared. Kari slumped slightly against the wall and waited.

"She's doing what she thinks God wants her to do." Kari strained to listen. "She's asked only one thing from the rest of us."

Luke was eating something, and he spoke with his mouth full. "Mmm. What's that? Invite the guy over for Sunday dinner so we can all tell him how much we've missed him?"

Mother exhaled, and even from her hiding place Kari thought she sounded old and sad. Very sad. *Oh, Mom, I never wanted to bring this on you. . . . God, help me know what to do. Maybe I shouldn't even be here. Maybe I should go home and —*

"She wants our understanding." Her mother's tone became pointed. "Which is something you've never once given Ashley."

"Don't lay that on me. I wasn't the one who turned into some freak overnight. Ashley hasn't been the same since she got back from Paris, and that isn't my fault."

"Okay, fine. But this isn't about Ashley; it's about Kari. You and Kari have always loved each other, Luke. Always been there for each other. If you can't find it in your heart to support her now . . . I couldn't bear it any more than Kari could. That's all I'm saying."

Kari wasn't sure if she had been afraid of his response or eager to stop their conversation, but she took a few purposefully loud steps and turned the corner into the kitchen. "Hey, everyone." She ignored the nausea and forced a smile at her mother as she came up behind Luke and slipped an arm around his shoulder. "Good morning, little brother."

They ate their breakfast without further discussion of Kari's predicament or the degree of wisdom in her choices. Still, she sensed something different about Luke. Something missing from the easy relationship they'd always shared. As if his opinion of her had slipped.

Whatever it was, it made Kari want to crawl in a hole and cry for a hundred days.

Instead, she had finished breakfast, helped take care of the dishes, and gotten dressed for church. And had become so absorbed in getting ready that she forgot to take the pregnancy test.

Or hadn't really wanted to in the first place.

At any rate, now she was halfway to

church and wondering if she was crazy for going. Normally she and Tim attended on their own, and more often than not in the past year, Tim had begged off from going because he had papers to grade. Not until she learned of his affair did his absence at church finally make sense. Kari clenched her teeth and tried not to think about Tim. Not now.

She glanced behind her and saw Luke's truck. He had plans after the service and needed his own transportation. Their youngest sister, Erin, and her husband, Sam, would meet them at church. Brooke and Ashley attended only on holidays, and not always then.

Kari sighed quietly.

Of the five Baxter children, only Kari, Luke, and Erin had adopted their parents' faith. As the car neared the church her family had attended since she and her siblings were children, Kari's heart hurt at the realization. The families they'd grown up with at Clear Creek Community Church knew about Ashley's falling away and Brooke's independence. They had to know that John and Elizabeth Baxter grieved the way their close-knit family was no longer bound by their beliefs.

Kari smiled at little Cole, belted into his

car seat. Ashley had been out with her artist friends the night before, and Cole had slept at Grammy and Papa's, as he called them.

"You nervous?" John Baxter peered into the rearview mirror, and Kari could have cried at the compassion in his eyes. Her father had been her champion as far back as she could remember, and clearly this time in her life would be no different.

"A little."

Her mom turned slightly in her seat, her eyes noticeably softer than they had been moments earlier when she was hurrying them into the car. "There's not a person there who doesn't love you, Kari. You know that."

Kari nodded and felt a wave of tears straining to get free. She blinked them back. "It's not like I'm going to stand up and announce it to the congregation. But I need to tell Pastor Mark. And people are bound to find out. I feel like it's written all over my face."

Dad turned into the church parking lot, and a batch of butterflies took over Kari's gut. "Everyone has issues, sweetheart. Families don't get through life without a little sadness."

There it was. The kind of beauty-from-ashes thinking her father was famous for. As if he knew exactly how terrible she felt about the shame and pity her situation would bring on the Baxter name. His words washed over Kari's soul and somehow made her feel fresher, renewed.

Families don't get through life without a little sadness.

She reached forward and gently squeezed her father's shoulders. "Thanks, Dad."

Cole had been taking in the exchange, and he cocked his head at Kari. "Are you sad, Aunt Kari? Because I can share my ball with you if you're sad."

A peal of laughter escaped Kari's swollen throat, and it seemed to relieve the tension in the car. "No, sweetie, I'm not sad. You keep the ball, okay?"

Cole nodded, his eyes wide. "Okay. But if you ever get sad, just tell me. I'll give you my ball, and you won't be sad ever anymore."

Kari smiled. *If only it were that easy.* "Thanks, Cole. Now come on, let's get inside."

Something about the way Pastor Mark Atteberry preached always lifted Kari's spirits. It didn't matter if he was warning the congregation against stubborn sin or reminding them about the surprises of God's grace. What he said was seasoned with laughter and unforgettable stories that almost weekly moved the congregation to tears. Generally people who heard his messages sat spellbound, knowing that the words Pastor Mark delivered were the very ones they needed — regardless of where they had been or where they were headed the coming week.

Kari was certain today would be no different, and she silently chided herself for not coming sooner. So what if she broke down and cried? Wasn't that what church family was about? Pastor Mark had married her and Tim, after all. He'd known the Baxter family since he and his wife, Marilyn, had come as a young energetic couple and started the church twenty years earlier. He'd seen them through her parents' struggles back in the mid-eighties and then with her mom's cancer. The family at Clear Creek Community Church had watched the Baxter kids grow up.

Where else could she possibly want to be? Besides, being here was better than sitting at home convincing herself she was too heartsick to go.

Kari walked with her mother and tried to remember the last time Tim had accompanied her to church. Three months back, at least — early summer, maybe. Hadn't she sensed something was wrong back then? Hadn't she wondered if Tim was listening to the sermon or if he even wanted to be there?

"I'll check Cole in." Kari took the child's hand and smiled at her mother. "Save me a seat."

The church was sprawled out in a series of buildings. The sanctuary and fellowship hall made up the largest structure. Sunday school classes for primary children met in a separate building, teens in another, and adults in still another. As Kari and Cole entered the primary building and headed toward the open door of Cole's classroom, Noreen Winning stuck her head out and squealed. "Kari Baxter! I can't believe it! How long's it been?"

Noreen and Kari had been in the same grade growing up and had always shared a Sunday school class. A few weeks back Elizabeth Baxter had mentioned that Noreen, her husband, and their daughter had moved back to Bloomington. Kari hugged her and smiled. "Two years at least. And it's Kari *Jacobs*."

"That's right. You married a professor, didn't you? Your mother told me. Tim, is it?"

"Yes. Tim teaches at the university."

"I'm this little guy's Sunday school teacher. Filling in for the day." Noreen bent down and tousled Cole's curly blond hair. She leaned close to Kari and lowered her voice. "Ashley's little boy, right? He looks more like his mother every day."

Kari studied Cole's fine features and delicate cheekbones and nodded. Though they'd all been blessed with nice looks, Ashley was easily the most striking of the Baxter girls. Her son was a male mirror image of her. Kari bit her lip. "I wish Ashley would come."

Noreen shook her head as if she'd just been given tragic news that could have been avoided. "I hear she hasn't been the same since —"

"Since coming home from Paris . . . I know." For some reason, Kari was bothered by Noreen's tone. *Leave her alone, Noreen. She's my sister.*

Noreen looked both directions and then pointedly at Kari. "Well, do I get to meet this Tim?"

Here we go. Kari drew a deep breath. Her eyes dropped and then lifted again as she spoke. "He didn't come."

Noreen cocked her head slightly, searching Kari's eyes. "Everything's okay, right?"

157

"Not really." Kari could hear the weariness in her voice. "Not really. I'm staying with my folks for a while." She studied the toe of her shoe and blinked back tears as she absently twisted her wedding ring. "Tim and I are having some trouble."

Noreen stopped short of gasping, but her wide eyes expressed her shock. "What happened?"

Noreen had always probed beyond what was kind, and this was no exception.

Get me out of here, God.

My grace is sufficient for you, daughter.

Kari blinked twice. Since the beginning of this ordeal, this time of pain, God seemed to be promising her deliverance and peace. But this . . . *grace is sufficient? What do you want from me, Lord?*

Much.

Much?

"Uh —" Kari cleared her throat and tried to focus on Noreen's question. "It's a long story. He's not . . . walking with the Lord."

Noreen's eyes grew even wider, if that were possible. "Oh, Kari. How did it happen?"

Kari wanted to walk away, let nosy Noreen figure out an answer for herself. But something in the Lord's persistent silent

158

voice stopped her. *Much, Lord? You want much from me? Now, when I have nothing left to give?*

My grace is sufficient for you.

An image came to mind of a small group meeting in the living room of a house. Couples filled the circle — hurting couples, hoping couples. And Kari and Tim were in the middle of the circle, teaching the couples how to love.

Is that it, Lord? You'll bring beauty from the ashes of our love? Restore the crumbling foundations?

My grace is sufficient.

Her heart filled with a deep gratitude and peace, the kind she hadn't felt since before Tim's announcement.

Cole's class was filling up, and Noreen tapped her foot. "If you can't answer me I understand." The tapping stopped. "I'm here for you, Kari. Call me, okay? I'm listed."

Kari gave a quick shake of her head as if she'd suddenly realized she hadn't answered Noreen's question. "I'm sorry. It's a long story."

Noreen leaned close one last time. "So . . . are you . . . you know, does he want a divorce?"

Kari forced a smile. "He doesn't know

what he wants." She remembered the Lord's persistent whisperings from a moment ago. "But God's in control of our marriage. I really believe everything will be fine."

There seemed to be nothing left for Noreen to ask, and she shrugged. "I'll pray for you." She paused and looked more serious than before. "I don't know your situation, but I can tell you this. Whatever your trouble, you're doing the right thing. God can clean up even the worst problems, you know? Your marriage could be better than you ever dreamed, better than before this happened." She squeezed Kari's hand. "Don't give up, Kari. Please."

Kari wasn't sure what to say. Ever since Tim left she'd been longing to hear those exact words. *You're doing the right thing. God can clean up even the worst problems . . . don't give up.* Funny that now they would come from this annoying woman, this long-ago friend who didn't have a clue about Kari or Tim or their marriage.

Kari's heart softened in gratitude. "Thanks."

Kari glanced at her watch as she headed for the sanctuary. The last thing she wanted was to walk in late after missing so many weeks.

She spotted her father and headed toward him, trying to ward off the sadness welling within her. She had planned on feeling hopeful at this point, surrounded by church family, about to hear Pastor Mark's message — especially after Noreen's encouragement.

But as she took her seat beside her father, she could think of only one thing.

Somewhere across town in an off-campus apartment bedroom, her husband would be waking up in the arms of another woman.

Chapter Ten

Ryan Taylor slipped into the back row of the sanctuary five minutes before the service began and wondered if this would be the day. There was no denying he'd attended this service in hopes of seeing Kari. He'd done little more than think of her since talking with Ashley.

He searched the congregation, knowing he'd recognize the back of her head even in a sea of people. Poor Kari. She must be devastated. Maybe too devastated to make a public appearance at church. He scanned the pews. *Lord . . . where is she?*

His father's favorite verse flashed across his mind: *The fear of the Lord is the beginning of wisdom.*

Ryan blinked.

The fear of the Lord?

How long had it been since that verse had come to mind? Ryan's gut tightened, and he absently rubbed the back of his neck, the place where football had nearly cost him his life. He knew exactly how long it had been. In November it would be eight years. Eight years since he lay motionless strapped to a hospital bed, fearing he'd never find a way out. Fearing God in a way he'd never done before.

Back then he barely breathed without praying, begging God for mercy and healing. But over the years, after the scars from his injury faded, life found a way of gaining ground on his best intentions, taking up more and more time and leaving fewer hours for spending time with God.

It was simple, really. The urgency was gone.

Ryan let his gaze fall to his hands, and he felt a mantle of conviction settle across his shoulders. Why was the realization hitting him so hard here and now? Had God chosen this moment to call him on the months and years of gradual decline, the complacency that resulted in . . . well, in the type of spotty church attendance and communication with God he'd been guilty of since he'd returned to football a year after his injury? Sure, he attended a night service now and then, but his faith-driven passion was limping badly.

He felt a sting in his soul, as if the Lord himself were poking needles at his conscience. He winced as he realized the truth. Even today he was there only because of Kari. Thoughts of her, memories of her had consumed him since the moment Ashley had spoken her name.

Kari . . . his precious Kari girl. His mind began to drift again, lazily taking him down dusty lakeside paths to a time when a brown-eyed beauty with laughter like wind chimes was his best friend and constant companion, down the trail of years to a place where . . .

The fear of the Lord is the beginning of wisdom.

Ryan sat up straighter in his seat, jolted from the memories that distracted him. *I'm sorry, Lord . . . I'm trying.*

Huge, holy eyes seemed focused directly on him, penetrating his mind and soul, seeing his thoughts and motives and intentions. His very heart.

He opened his bulletin and looked at the sermon title on the top left page. As he read the words, he could feel the blood leaving his face, the slight trembling in his fingers. Whatever was happening, God had him here for a reason — and somehow Ryan doubted it had anything to do with Kari.

The sermon title was "The Fear of the Lord Is the Beginning."

Ryan closed his eyes and began to pray.

As soon as Kari took her seat, her father leaned over and put his hand gently on her knee.

"You made it."

She smiled. "Barely." A weariness settled over her. It had been harder than she thought, telling Noreen why she was alone, admitting out loud that she and Tim were having problems. She slid down in her seat and leaned on her father, trying to soak in some of his strength and stability.

The worship music began, but Kari couldn't bring herself to sing along. Instead, she stared at the song sheet and let her mind wander. When exactly was the first time Tim had cheated on her? Was he such a good pretender that she hadn't even noticed? Or had she suspected even last spring that things weren't what they'd once been? that something was wrong?

I didn't want to see it. . . .

Kari blinked, and two tears fell to the paper in her hands. The music stopped, and she looked up as two dozen children filed across the steps of the stage. They wriggled and giggled and squirmed about until an older woman got their attention.

Noreen's daughter was probably up there, and as Kari scanned the group, she saw the children of several old friends. Her hand moved firmly over her lower abdomen. *What about me, Lord? Am I really pregnant? Will I have to raise a child alone?*

The music started, and the children began to sing a song that had been Kari's favorite ever since they'd sung it at a retreat when she was sixteen years old: "Jesus loves me, this I know. . . ."

Ryan Taylor had been on the retreat too. They'd sat side by side as the speaker explained the options Christ might have if he were to get one of them face-to-face in a room alone. Kari closed her eyes as the children continued to sing, and she could still hear the retreat speaker's voice.

"He could yell at you and tell you how badly you've messed up, order you to get things right, and then hand out some sort of punishment." The speaker had been passionate, walking back and forth across the stage as the teens sat spellbound.

"Or he could shake his head and tell you what a disappointment you've been."

Then the speaker's voice had grown quiet as he stood still, only his eyes moving deliberately about the room, making contact with as many teens as he could. He pointed at a teen in the front row and asked him to come onto the stage. Surprised and a little unsure, the boy hopped up and at the speaker's direction stood facing the man.

"You know what Jesus would do instead?" The speaker's voice was softer than it had been all night. Slowly, lovingly, he put his arms around the boy's shoulders and pulled him into a long embrace. When the speaker drew back, he kept one arm around the boy as he led the group in what became the theme song for the retreat.

"Jesus loves me, this I know. . . ."

Every teen in the room had been crying that night, and Kari had glanced over to see tears trickling down Ryan's cheeks as well.

The visual effect of that scene, combined with the simple message of the song, had stayed with Kari every day since. Even now, with her world upside down and her heart hanging heavy within her, Kari didn't for a minute doubt Christ's love. She sniffed softly, and her mother reached over and handed her a tissue. Kari lifted her eyes just long enough to thank her. Pastor Mark began his sermon. Kari knew she should be listening, but she still couldn't get beyond the thoughts that vied for her attention. What would she do if Tim was really serious about a divorce? Could he do it without her consent? Would a baby change things? And even if it did, could she raise a child with a man who seemed to have abandoned his faith along with his marriage?

What's going to happen to me, Lord? Where do I go from here?

Once again she was overwhelmed by a strong sense of comfort, as if the Lord had slipped into the pew beside her and put his arms around her. Just like the picture the retreat speaker had painted so many years earlier.

The sermon was winding up — something about the fear of God and not running away — and before she could force herself to think clearly, Pastor Mark was praying. "Lord, I know there are people with us today who are hurting and in trouble. I believe you've brought them here for a reason." In the background, the pianist began playing a slow, haunting arrangement of "Jesus Loves Me."

Pastor Mark continued his prayer over the music. "Father, help us hear you more clearly. Help us have a healthy fear of your power, that whatever you call us to do, we can do it in your strength."

Kari kept her eyes closed, her face downward, trying to hear what the Lord might be saying to her.

"We have the prayer room open now." He paused, and Kari felt as if he were speaking directly to her. "This is one of those times when you have a choice. You can hear God and ignore him, or hear him and do what he's asking. We're all in this together, people. Come and let someone pray with you."

From the back of the church, Ryan felt like a man who'd just had his sight adjusted. The sermon was strong, pointing out the truth that God is not only Savior and Friend and Prince of Peace but also the Almighty One. He is powerful and just — a God to be feared, respected, held in awe. So gripping were Pastor Mark's words that thoughts of Kari had been pushed from Ryan's mind. If she was in the service, he hadn't seen her. And now, with his heart broken wide open by the message, he knew that was a good thing.

He still had no idea why God had chosen this morning to get his attention after his years of mediocre faith. But Ryan knew without a doubt he was here for a reason, as if he'd shown up for a divine appointment. And when the pastor called for people to come up for prayer, for the first time since Ryan had given his life to Jesus, he was on his feet and headed down the aisle before he had time to change his mind.

Though her eyes were closed, Kari could feel tears trickling down her face and onto her hands. If only she could get past her shame and go forward. But even from where she was sitting, near the front of the church, the walk seemed a mile long. Too far to go by herself, crying and alone, without the help of a husband who no longer loved her. A husband living a life of adultery.

Go, daughter . . . where two or more are gathered, there I am.

Kari adjusted her position and hunched over her legs, her face in her hands. *I won't know what to say, Lord.*

Her dad seemed to understand that God was working on her heart, and he gently elbowed her ribs, nudging her, encouraging her to heed the only voice that mattered.

The pianist continued.

"They are weak, but he is strong. . . . Yes, Jesus loves me, yes —"

Kari squeezed her eyes shut and wiped her cheeks as well as she could. Then she stood up and made her way into the prayer room with the strongest sense that she was no longer alone.

She saw him the moment she walked in

170

— Ryan Taylor sitting in a prayer circle holding hands with the Millers, an elderly couple who'd been at the church as far back as Kari could remember. The three of them were the only ones in the room, and Ryan was explaining something to them in hushed tones when he spotted her.

"Kari . . ." Their eyes locked, and he was on his feet, moving out of the circle and then stopping short of her, his hand stretched in her direction.

Something in Ryan's eyes, a depth that she couldn't quite define, told her he knew about Tim. She reminded herself to exhale and politely nodded in his direction. *What am I supposed to do now, God? I can't talk about Tim in front of —*

My grace is sufficient.

"Why . . . Kari. It's so good to see you, dear." Mrs. Miller stood up and pulled Kari into a hug. When she drew back, she studied Kari's face. "Honey, you look like you need some good praying."

She led Kari by the hand back to the circle and directed her to an empty chair next to Ryan's. Mr. Miller smiled sympathetically. "You two kids haven't been in the same prayer circle since high school, I reckon."

Kari's heart slammed at the inside of her

chest, and she had no idea what to say. The nearness of Ryan Taylor made her mouth dry, her thoughts jumbled. *Help me, God. Why'd you bring me here if he was going to be —*

Mr. Miller cleared his throat. "Ryan's asked us to pray for his focus." The older man smiled at Ryan. "That he'll have a healthier fear of God and get his priorities straight."

Priorities straight? Kari wondered what would send Ryan to the prayer room to seek prayer about his priorities. She forced herself to concentrate as Mr. Miller looked from Ryan's face to hers. "Kari?"

This couldn't be happening. She couldn't be asking for prayer for her failing marriage seated next to Ryan Taylor. "Umm . . ." Her eyes stayed fixed on a spot near the door. She couldn't say it, couldn't spell out the fact that her husband was cheating on her. Fresh tears burned their way down her cheeks, and she could feel her heart pounding in her temples.

Help me, Lord . . . please.

She exhaled slowly and found a supernatural strength within. What did it matter if Ryan knew about her and Tim? She'd gotten her answer about Ryan's feelings for her a long time ago.

Ryan Taylor did not love her; he never had. Not the way she'd dreamed of back when she was sixteen and he was heading off to college.

And Ryan was beside the point anyway. Tim was her husband, the man God wanted her to stay with. She lifted her eyes and looked first at Mr. Miller, then at his wife. "Please . . . pray for my marriage." Her gaze drifted down again. "I love my husband very much and . . . well, he doesn't want to be married anymore."

A soft gasp escaped from Mrs. Miller as she reached out and took hold of both Kari's hands. "Child . . . I'm so sorry."

Kari could feel Ryan looking at her, but she refused to meet his gaze. This moment wasn't about her and Ryan. It was about hearing the voice of God and knowing that this place, this circle of prayer was where she needed to be. Sitting among church family, lifting up the shreds of her tattered marriage to the only One who had power enough to fix it.

If Ryan Taylor was part of that prayer circle, so be it. She could use all the prayer she could get.

Silence hung in the room for a moment, and then Mr. Miller bowed his head and reached out his hands — one to his wife and one to Ryan. Mrs. Miller let go of Kari's left hand and took hold of her husband's.

The circle was intact except for the place where Kari and Ryan sat. From the corner of her eye she saw Ryan raise his hand in her direction, and she took it without hesitating. As she felt the warmth of his stronger, larger hand in hers, a piece of her heart began to melt.

Noreen and Ashley and Brooke had peppered her with questions, but not Ryan. Even if they had been the only two in the room, he would have let her talk and then simply taken her hand. It was what he'd always done even back when they were kids. As if he didn't need her to fill in the missing places of a conversation because he already knew what they were.

They had been that close.

Long before she loved him and imagined that he loved her, Ryan had been her friend — maybe the best friend she ever had. Now, with her hand in his and his strong presence beside her, she remembered why.

Mr. Miller led the prayer, pleading with God to help Ryan remain clearheaded and focused and aware that the fear of the Lord was the beginning of wisdom. For Kari he prayed that God would change Tim's heart, that he would remind Tim of the height from which he'd fallen, and that the Lord himself would quickly and miraculously restore their marriage.

The prayer lasted several minutes. When it was over, as they were releasing the hold they had on each other's hands, Kari thought she felt Ryan squeeze ever so slightly. Almost as if he was seconding the motion, agreeing with Mr. Miller in his desire to see Kari's prayer answered.

Mrs. Miller looked from Kari to Ryan and smiled. "I'm so glad you came for prayer."

She has no idea how awkward this is. Kari urged the corners of her mouth upward. "Thanks."

Another hug, and Mrs. Miller took her husband's hand. The two left with promises to continue praying. Then the door shut behind them, and Kari and Ryan were alone.

She looked up, and her eyes met his. She could see no spark or attraction, only a kindness that surrounded her with comfort. They were two old friends whose grown-up lives had taken them in different directions. But they were friends who still cared deeply. As their eyes held, she was frustrated to feel tears welling up again.

Without saying a word, he came to her and wrapped his arms tenderly around her, pulling her into a hug that erased the years in a single instant. A combination of feelings consumed Kari's heart. She realized she was at once grateful for his friendship and brokenhearted at the distance time had placed between them. Here in his presence she suddenly felt the loss of him more deeply, and that grief, piled onto all the rest, made her erupt into fresh sobs.

He lowered his head so that it hovered next to hers, and his hand worked soothing circles into the small of her back. "Shhh . . . it's okay, Kari girl."

Kari girl . . .

His words acted like a balm to her soul, and she ached at having gone so long without hearing her name on his lips. His very presence felt like a gift from yesterday.

She stayed that way, her hands at her side, sheltered in the warmth of his arms, until finally he pulled away. His eyes met hers, and he searched the secret places of her soul for a long while, reading her heart as easily as he'd always been able to do. "Want to talk about it?"

No questions or guesses or inquisition. Just the same offer he might have made if they were teenagers again.

A shaky sigh escaped from her heart's darkest closet, and slowly she allowed the door to open. It was strange, in a way, because they hadn't seen each other for years. She really didn't know the man Ryan Taylor had become. Yet somehow she knew she could still trust him, this friend whom she'd grown up adoring. With her life crashing in around her, she was simply grateful beyond words for his concern.

"He wants a divorce." The pain of the confession was so intense that she was unable to maintain eye contact. Her gaze fell to the tiled floor, and Ryan reached down and took her hands in his.

If he had questions, he still wasn't asking, but suddenly she wanted him to know. She kept her gaze downward and spoke in quiet whispers. "He's been cheating on me for . . . for a while now. I'm staying with my parents for a few weeks so I can think about things."

Ryan crooked his finger and gently caught her chin, lifting it so that their eyes met. Every word, every inflection of his voice was kind and deliberate. "You still love him, don't you?"

With that, something between them changed, and the distant sounds of music and people talking faded entirely. They stood there, eyes locked, while Kari considered his question. Who was she fooling? She could never see Ryan Taylor as merely a friend. *God, I've missed this man. What am I doing here?*

She felt as if her heart had fallen from her chest, the same way she had felt on the roller coaster at the county fair last spring. The way she felt the first time she kissed Ry—

Her eyes closed, and she stepped backward, steadying herself in the process. *I do love him . . . Tim, I mean . . . don't I, Lord? Give me the strength to be Ryan's friend without these other feelings.*

Ryan was waiting, and Kari opened her eyes. "Yes . . . I love him." The words were bitter on her tongue. "God wants me to love him until . . . until he changes."

She'd be going home in a few minutes, taking a pregnancy test in the morning. She was probably already a few months pregnant with a child who would be raised without a father. She wondered what Tim was doing . . . Tim and his girlfriend.

Suddenly Kari was overwhelmed with the need to be away from Ryan Taylor. He was her friend, yes. But he was also her first love, and clearly her heart had not forgotten. She took another step backward and smiled sadly. "Ryan, I've got to go."

Ryan caught her hand once more, and she saw no ulterior motives in his eyes. "Listen, Kari, I'm here . . . if you need a friend."

If he was a magnet, then she was solid steel. The air between them grew more charged than before, and she knew better than to linger in a dark and quiet prayer room in the presence of Ryan Taylor.

God had allowed her heart to be comforted by the understanding of an old friend.

Now it was time to go.

She nodded and locked eyes with Ryan one last time. Then she turned and made her way quickly out the back door toward her family's sedan before he could see the fresh tears in her eyes. Or the way his presence had stirred a memory within her of a boy she'd once dreamed was her knight in shining armor. A boy she thought for sure she would marry.

Thoughts she'd long since assumed were dead.

Until now.

Chapter Eleven

The car door was unlocked. Kari slipped inside and leaned her head back, trying to figure out in which direction her heart was traveling and what she could do to regain control of her emotions.

A strong breeze had kicked up, and she left the car door partially open, allowing the autumn air to wash over her. Had she just spent the past half hour with Ryan Taylor? Praying with him about her marriage to Tim? It didn't seem possible.

Ten minutes passed, and her parents returned with Cole. They said nothing to her then or on the ride home, though her eyes were swollen from crying. Before they got out of the car, her father turned and winked at her. "I know it was hard, honey. But I'm glad you went."

He and her mom knew nothing of Ryan Taylor, obviously, and Kari nodded, too confused to say anything about their encounter just yet. "Yeah. Me too."

She managed to avoid questions from Ashley, who was curled on the sofa sipping from a mug. There was no way Kari could talk now. She desperately needed to be alone.

Once upstairs she went to her room and stared out the window. The leaves were half gone from the trees, scattered across the yard and driveway. The image of her parents' front yard blurred, and she remembered one fall a few years before she and Ryan broke up when he was home from college for the weekend. The two of them had raked the Baxters' yard until they had a leaf pile four feet high.

"Let's jump," Ryan teased her.

She threw her hands in the air and did a back flop on the pile. From beneath a layer of leaves, she yelled at him, "Your turn."

"Okay." Ryan laughed. "Look out." He fell in alongside her. There under the cover of a foot of leaves they kissed until they both broke free of the pile, laughing and gasping for air.

She closed her eyes. The last thing she needed to think about was Ryan. But how could she not after spending time with him again, feeling his arms around her? She blinked and turned away from the window, plopping down on her old bed.

Long ago when she had first fallen for Ryan, she'd learned a technique to control her randomly impure thoughts. The Clear

Creek Community Church youth pastor had taught it to the youth group, and somehow it had stayed with her to this day.

"Put arms and legs on whatever thought you don't want, and then picture yourself handcuffing the little guy," the youth pastor had said. "Once he's all bound up, toss him out of your head."

Thoughts come, he'd told them. There's nothing anyone can do about that. "But when they come we can sit them down, give them a Coke, and entertain them . . . hope they stay for a while. Or —" the kids had snickered at the imagery — "we can handcuff the little so-and-sos and be done with them."

If ever there was a time when she should be handcuffing her thoughts, it was now. Kari stared at the ceiling, but all she could see was Ryan's face. She drew a steadying breath. *Lord, you know my heart. You know I'm mad at Tim. This is all his fault. But sometimes I think Ryan knows me better than I even know myself.*

Silence.

Her fingers tapped out a rhythm on her knees. This was no time to be remembering Ryan. Her future with Tim would never happen if she didn't start thinking about it soon.

A plan. That's what she needed. The shock of Tim's affair had left her emotionally frozen, but now it was time to act. She was angry, yes, and betrayed. But she was willing to fight for her marriage, willing to do whatever was necessary to get him back.

She put together a mental to-do list. She'd forgotten to find Pastor Mark and make an appointment; first thing tomorrow she'd call and do that. Then she'd call Tim. There was no point waiting for him to make a move toward reconciliation. No, she needed to talk to him, and soon. In fact, she needed to see him. Maybe she'd drive to his office tomorrow and reiterate that she wanted to work things out.

The plan began to take shape in her mind, and she felt herself relax. Tim still loved her; he had to. He wouldn't tell her no, especially if . . .

She crossed over to her suitcase and pulled out the pregnancy test she had bought the day before. Resettling on the bed, she reread the directions; maybe she *could* go ahead and do the test now instead of waiting for morning. She needed to know, needed to move out of her denial. If she *was* pregnant, she would be into her second month, and that meant she'd be showing soon.

Kari ran over the dates in her mind as

she'd done many times since Tim left. She saw no way around it. If it did turn out she was pregnant, she would have conceived sometime in August, and that meant . . .

That meant Tim had slept with her when he was already in love with another woman. The timing made her feel dirty and used. Most of the time she tried to convince herself it wasn't possible. That she had certainly not gotten pregnant in a moment that was nothing more than physical release for Tim. At a time when he no longer loved her.

She crooked her arm so that it covered her eyes. And as she lay there, the image of her and Ryan in the prayer room returned. What a welcome distraction it had been to see him again, to hug him. To remember again the way he'd graced her teenage years.

Years of thoughts and memories drifted in, and though she knew she should, Kari couldn't summon the energy to handcuff them. Instead, she let them gather around the table of her mind, sipping Cokes and enjoying themselves.

The years had definitely dulled the pain of that harsh November day, the day of Ryan's injury. The day she knew for certain that she and Ryan had no future together.

Was the medicine of time always that effective? Did it so easily soften the blows of yesterday, so strongly magnify the joys? Her thoughts of Ryan were growing in number, throwing a full-blown party at the table now, but Kari didn't mind. She wanted them to be there, wanted to walk back through the years with them, swept up in the currents of yesterday's river, back to a barbecue the summer she was twelve years old.

The first time she had ever laid eyes on Ryan Taylor.

Warren B. Taylor had served on the administration staff at Bloomington's St. Anne's Hospital the year Kari's father began an internship there. The men were both in their mid-twenties and quickly became friends.

Kari knew from her father's stories that busy schedules caused the two to drift apart for a while. But the summer Kari turned twelve, the Baxters moved into a five-bedroom colonial in Clear Creek, just three doors down from the Taylors. And that evening, Mr. Taylor invited their family over for a barbecue.

Kari was unpacking boxes in her new bedroom when her father poked his head in and grinned. "Take a break. We're going down the street for dinner."

She knew better than to complain, but at

twelve years old she was more interested in getting her bedroom together than stopping progress for a social event. "Can I stay? I'm almost done."

"Mr. Taylor's a friend of mine." The look her father gave her conveyed his answer more clearly than any words. "I want us all there."

Dressed in white jean cutoffs and a dusty blue T-shirt and determined to get home as soon as possible, Kari led the way as her parents and four siblings headed down the street. A half hour later they were sipping iced tea on the Taylors' back porch when a dark-haired, shirtless boy breezed into the yard. Kari set down her glass and studied him discreetly. He was tall and lean, with a V-shaped back and a football under his arm.

"Hey, Dad, I'm home. I'll be out front."

Mr. Taylor was flipping burgers. He shut the lid of the grill and looked pointedly at the family of seven seated around the picnic table, then back at his son. "We have guests."

"Oh, sorry." The boy raised a hand in the direction of the seven of them and did a double take as he caught sight of Kari. Their eyes met for a moment, and Kari remembered the way her stomach fluttered under his gaze. "Hi." His tone was friendly and curious, his greeting directed at her alone.

Mr. Taylor cleared his throat, and Ryan blinked, the spell broken as he looked back at his father.

"We're eating in five minutes. Go wash up."

"Yes, sir." Ryan nodded, but before he darted back in the house, he cast one last look at Kari. The moment he was inside, Kari noticed something she hadn't before.

Her heart was gone.

Ryan sat across from her during dinner that night. Since Kari's family had moved from Bloomington, she'd be attending a new middle school. Ryan tried to fill her in on everything she should expect.

"I can't believe you're only in seventh." Ryan's short, dark bangs hung in damp clumps off to the side of his face, and he was deeply tanned.

Kari could feel her face grow hot. "I look older."

"How old are you, anyway?"

"Twelve." Kari set her burger down and tilted her head. "You?"

"Fourteen. High school in the fall."

Kari nodded her chin toward the football. "You play?"

"More than I breathe." He grinned and pushed his plate back. "Want to go out front?"

She nodded and left most of her dinner untouched. They played outside, laughing and teasing and tossing the ball until the summer sun set and lightning bugs began flashing at the base of the trees.

It was then that Kari realized she could not possibly be the only girl in Clear Creek, Indiana, dazzled by Ryan Taylor. He was two years older, about to start high school, and she was just starting middle school. But she lived three doors down, and that had to count for something.

Fall came that year, and Kari saw far less of Ryan than she'd originally planned. She was involved with Clear Creek Community Church's youth group and taking tennis lessons at the country club; Ryan was busy playing whatever sport was in season. But come June they seemed to drift together naturally, playing kickball with the neighbor kids, fishing at Lake Monroe, counting stars and talking out in the yard on summer nights. Fall came again too quickly, and later that year Ryan's parents bought him a shiny dark-blue Chevy truck for his sixteenth birthday. After that he was almost never home, and though she thought of him often, Kari saw him only in passing.

But all that changed Kari's first day of high school. She was a freshman at Clear Creek High School that year and had made the cheerleading squad. Practice was under way outside the gym that afternoon when Ryan and a handful of his teammates walked past and headed for the drinking fountain. He was well over six feet tall and by far the best-looking boy at school.

Ryan caught her eye and held it as he made his way across the quad. "You're finally here."

She smiled in a way that wasn't overly eager. "Yep." No matter what she thought of Ryan Taylor, she wasn't going to become one of his groupies, following him around school, giggling and hoping he'd notice her. Not with Ryan's varsity football player friends standing there.

The football players had finished their drinks and headed back to the field when Kari saw one of the guys whisper something to Ryan. She turned around and began one of the warm-up stretches, reaching an arm over her head. Mandy Morken, Kari's best friend from middle school, had made the squad too, and as the boys filed by, she elbowed Kari and leaned close. "He likes you."

"What?" Kari switched her stretch and leaned in the other direction. "Who likes me?"

Mandy released an exaggerated huff. "Ryan Taylor's friend. The blond guy."

Kari could remember the way her heart sank. Mandy turned out to be right, and that weekend after the football game, Ryan introduced his friend to her. His name was Josh, and he was nice-looking in a plain sort of way. The three of them made small talk for a few minutes, and then Josh joined the rest of the team. Ryan hung back and anchored himself a few feet from Kari, a lazy grin making its way across his face.

"All the guys are talking about you."

Kari was grateful the stadium lights had been dimmed. The last thing she wanted was for Ryan Taylor to see her blush. "Yeah?" She jutted her chin out and tossed her dark ponytail.

His expression changed, and he suddenly looked more like the boy he'd been two years earlier. "You still know how to toss a football?"

She giggled and felt her facade melt. "Maybe."

He picked up her bag, and they walked

to the team bus together. Cheerleaders rode back to school with the players after away games, and this was the first of the season. Ryan kicked at her tennis shoe as they walked. "So, you like him?"

Kari let her gaze fall and she shrugged. *I like you,* she wanted to scream at him. Instead, her voice grew soft. They were almost at the bus, and she wanted to end the conversation before they boarded. "I don't know."

"He's seen you before. At my house. I told him you can't date until you're sixteen."

The surprise in her voice was genuine. "How'd you know that?"

"You told me once." He grinned at her again. "I remember those things."

It turned out that Josh was one of Ryan's best friends, and the dynamic that had been established that first week of school remained for the next two years. She and Mandy often went out for pizza with a group of their friends after football games, and somehow she always wound up sitting near Josh, with Ryan across the table or at the other end. At times she could have sworn he was watching her, staring at her. But when she met his eyes, he would only wink and look away.

But the flirtatious game playing that

seemed to take up most of the school year fell away when summer arrived. This time they did more than play games and count stars together. They shared their hearts. Kari's best memories were of the times they spent in a quiet, sunny cove on Lake Monroe.

"We're so different in the summer," Ryan told her as they fished together one Saturday afternoon.

"I know." They were sitting side by side on a fallen tree at the lake's edge, their bare feet hanging in the water.

"I wish we were like this all the time." Ryan was quiet. "I can tell you anything."

Their fathers were fishing a hundred yards away, but that didn't matter. They were so caught up in talking with each other, confiding in each other, that Kari figured they might as well be on a deserted island.

That lazy, hot summer they shared their feelings on everything from life at home to their dreams for the future. Ryan was the first person Kari ever told about her academic insecurities.

"Brooke's so smart." Kari played with her reel and let out an extra foot of line. "Sometimes I wonder if I'll ever measure up."

"That's crazy." Ryan spent the next ten

minutes detailing her strong points, how kind she was and how genuine. How fun she was to be with.

There was only one topic they stayed away from, and that was their feelings for each other.

"Are you guys going out or what?" Mandy would ask when they'd talk on the phone every few days.

"No. It's not like that." Kari would laugh at her friend's perplexed tone. "Don't worry. If anything changes I'll let you know."

Nothing changed. But they fished at Lake Monroe almost every day and spent so much time together that her parents grew a little concerned. But they trusted Kari, and she had a strict ten-o'clock curfew. Besides, the lake was so crowded they were never really alone together — except that one afternoon when they ran for cover as a tornado siren rang through the still air.

Storm clouds had kept most of the lakegoers away that day. When the siren sounded, Ryan took her hand, and they ran to a clearing. Crossing the lake half a mile away was the whirling sliver of a waterspout.

For a moment they stared at it, mesmerized. Ryan was the first to react. "Come on, let's get out of here." He pulled her from the spot and led her to a ditch not far from the beach. They lay there side by side, their hearts pounding as the small tornado made landfall, tore limbs off several nearby trees, and then dissipated before their eyes.

Next to Ryan that day, Kari had felt safe and protected — the same way she'd felt in the prayer room earlier this morning.

The only other times they were alone that summer were the evenings when they met in front of her house and sat on her parents' porch swing — or at his house, where they'd sit in the bed of his pickup, staring at the stars and dreaming about their future lives.

One particular night stood out among a bouquet of memories from that summer.

She and Ryan were tanned and tired, worn-out from a day of record-breaking temperatures, and they sat side by side in the back of his truck with their legs stretched out and their heads against the cab. For two hours they shared whatever thoughts crossed their hearts.

"I'm going pro, Kari . . . you watch." Ryan's eyes shone with the reflection of the moon.

"I will." She smiled at him and gazed up at the Big Dipper. "Every game."

They were quiet a moment, staring at the sky. Suddenly a star shot across the dark canopy above. Kari uttered a soft gasp. "Did you see it?"

"Yep." Ryan grinned at her. "A shooting star. You know what that means."

"We get to make a wish."

"No." His eyes danced. "It means you have to answer one question, any question I pick."

She clucked her tongue. "If you get to, I get to."

"Okay, deal." He glanced at her, and she noticed he was sitting closer than usual. "The guys were over yesterday, and one of them wanted to know whether you really liked Josh last year." His eyes held hers. "Did you? Don't worry; I won't tell him."

The streetlight shone in the distance, leaving them relegated to the shadows of the night, and Kari knew something was different. Something in Ryan's tone. She decided to be bold. "No, I didn't like him — not like a boyfriend, I mean." She lowered her chin, suddenly more daring than ever before. "Now it's my turn."

"Shoot."

"Which of the guys wanted to know?"

He turned to her, and their eyes locked — as they would do so whenever they met up in the years that followed. "Someone."

Kari refused to look away. "Someone, who?"

Then in the slowest, dreamiest motion, he leaned over and kissed her tenderly, lightly on the cheek. In an instant he was on his feet, jumping from the back of the truck and heading inside. "I've got to run. See you."

She watched him until he disappeared behind his family's front door, too stunned to move. Had that actually happened? Had Ryan Taylor leaned over and kissed her in the light of the summer moon?

Kari nearly danced home from Ryan's house that night, thinking where things might go in the future now that he'd made his feelings known. His kiss confirmed everything she'd wondered about since summer started. They were best friends, but the attraction was there for both of them.

That night when her mother came into her room and sat on the edge of her bed, Kari told her what had happened. "I think I've loved him since that day we went to dinner at his house."

Her mother looked so beautiful; Kari hoped she could be half as beautiful when she was a grown woman. "I know how that feels, sweetheart." She angled her head as if there were many things she'd like to say. After a pause she ventured, "You know how we've always prayed about the man you'll marry?"

Kari nodded. "Ever since I was a little girl."

Her mother's lips parted, and she hesitated a moment. "Honey, you know we like Ryan a lot. But he doesn't share the same beliefs as you."

A rush of peace came over Kari. If that's all it was, then she had nothing to worry about. "He hasn't missed youth group all summer."

Her mother raised her eyebrows. "I think we both know why Ryan goes to youth group. It's not because he believes, Kari."

She sighed, frustrated. "It's not like he *doesn't* believe. Anyway, he will one day, Mom, I know it."

"Okay." Her mother smiled doubtfully and took Kari's hand. "But until then, be careful with your heart, honey."

For the next ten minutes her mother tried to explain the reasons God wanted a couple to share common beliefs. But for a fifteen-year-old girl living every moment through the filter of a three-year-old crush that was finally coming to fruition, it was difficult to grasp.

Not that it really mattered. She still couldn't date until she turned sixteen. When school started that fall, she had no choice but to go the entire year without anything even remotely resembling a date. She complained about the rule, but she was secretly glad for it. She knew Josh still liked her, but he was too shy, too quiet for her. And her heart already belonged to the boy three doors down.

Ryan's senior year was a busy one for all of them, but it was especially so for Ryan. He had sprouted to six feet three inches and weighed just over two hundred pounds. He was good in the classroom and brilliant on the football field. Major universities contacted him daily until he made his decision: He would go to the University of Oklahoma in Norman on a full football scholarship.

A month after his graduation, Kari turned sixteen. It was a day she would remember as long as she lived.

That Thursday morning Kari's father was already at the office seeing patients when she heard the doorbell ring. Glancing in the mirror and tousling her hair, she ran downstairs. Probably one of her sisters' friends, she figured. But as she opened the door, her mouth dropped.

Ryan stood on the porch holding sixteen long-stemmed red roses. Kari covered her mouth with one hand, her eyes wide. All she could think was, *He remembered. He actually remembered.*

Ryan's eyes twinkled, and he grinned at her. "Happy birthday."

She took the roses from him and stood there, too shocked to speak.

"So that's what I have to do to get you to be quiet. Bring you roses on your birthday." He touched her cheek with his fingertips. "Come on, Kari girl, do you like them or not?"

Kari looked from the flowers to Ryan and back again. "They're . . . they're beautiful." She knew that red roses meant something different from, say, yellow roses. But she had no idea if Ryan understood the meaning. She looked up and searched his eyes. "Why did you . . . ?"

Her question trailed off, and Ryan took a step closer. "Will you go out with me tomorrow night, Kari? Please?"

And with that question all Kari's hopes and dreams seemed instantly fulfilled. Of course he'd go to church with her one day. He went to youth group, after all; he'd kept going even through his busy senior year. He was bound to become a believer eventually. Why wouldn't he? What was there not to believe?

Her parents agreed to the date, but not without warning her. "I trust Ryan," her mother said. "I like him a lot. Just remember, he's two years older than you."

The date was unforgettable. Ryan held her hand and bought her popcorn, and after the movies they went to Lake Monroe and walked out on the pier, skipping rocks and watching the way the ripples grew in the light of the stars. It was wonderful, all the comfort of being with a best buddy along with the excitement of finally knowing for sure that he didn't see her as "just a friend."

All night she wondered if he was going to kiss her. She wondered how it would take place and when it would happen and how she would respond. Her head was so filled with images of what it would be like — her first kiss, with the boy she really loved — that she almost didn't notice how quiet he had grown as the night progressed.

But when they pulled up in front of her house, Ryan cleared his throat and removed his baseball cap. "I'm not going to kiss you, Kari. I can't."

In that instant everything good about the night came to a sudden, grinding halt.

"What?"

"You've been my friend through the best years of my life." She noticed he was trembling, and she couldn't understand why. Why was he telling her this now?

He must have read the bewildered look in her eyes because the muscles in his jaw flexed, and he gripped the steering wheel, his arms locked into position, his gaze straight ahead. "Look, I'm leaving for college soon. Training starts early." He looked at her over his shoulder. "And you're . . . you're too young. Where could it possibly go?"

The lump in Kari's throat kept her from speaking. After that, their good night was hurried, and Kari said little to her parents before turning in and crying herself to sleep. Why the roses? Why the date, after all . . . ? Kari couldn't come up with any answers for herself. And she couldn't ask Ryan — couldn't even bring herself to face him.

He called a few times, but she wouldn't talk to him, and she dropped her eyes to avoid her mother's questioning gaze. She stayed inside when she thought he was likely to be in the yard, and she made a point of spending her time where she thought he wouldn't be. Her efforts just made everything worse because she desperately missed his company, missed their times at the lake, missed talking with him in the evenings under the stars. That was the worst part — not only did he not want to be her boyfriend, but she also felt uncomfortable around him. And that meant he couldn't be her friend either.

Three weeks later, Ryan knocked on the door. This time her mother insisted she talk to him. He was standing in the front room as Kari came down the stairs, his hands shoved deep in his pockets.

Kari looked at him, and it was as if she were seeing him for the first time. He had the kind of looks that were bound to stop college girls in their tracks. No wonder he didn't want to kiss her. He was right. What was the point, if he was busy dating college women?

"My folks have the truck packed." He looked at her the way he'd always done, holding her eyes and seeming to see straight into her soul. When she didn't say anything, he kicked at her foot. "Kari, look, I'm sorry. I didn't mean . . ."

Kari nodded but couldn't find her voice. Again, the lump in her throat was too big. She wanted to shout at him, tell him he shouldn't have asked her out in the first place, shouldn't have made her think he cared for her that way and then crushed her when the night was over. This good-bye was something they'd known was coming, even a year earlier. It was supposed to be a time when they wrote letters and kept in touch, but now everything felt different.

She swallowed back her tears and lifted her chin. "Good luck. You'll do great at Oklahoma."

Ryan sighed and shifted his position. For a moment she thought he might lean forward and kiss her on the cheek again — the way he'd done that summer when she was fifteen. Instead, he lifted his shoulders once and cocked his head. "See you around, Kari."

The pain of that summer morning felt almost as raw today as it had all those years ago. Ryan had been right, of course — she had been too young. Nothing good or lasting could ever have come from a relationship they might have started that summer.

Still, it had been weeks before she went a day without thinking of Ryan Taylor. Months even. Kari felt the memory fading now and knew there was much more to the story — the best part, really. But either way, she knew that a piece of her — the young-girl part that a woman carries with her — would always think of him that way. Would always remember him standing in her front room and telling her good-bye for what felt like the last time ever.

Kari blinked back the memory and sat up on the bed. Why was she lying here reliving her past with Ryan when she needed to be thinking about her future with Tim? When she moved to get up, her hands fell on the directions for the pregnancy test. She stared at them and steeled her resolve. She couldn't wait another minute. She had to know, had to take it and find out for herself. If there was any doubt, she could always do another one later. But right now she had to do something.

She hurried to the bathroom, locked the door, and performed the necessary steps. It was easier than she remembered from the last time she'd been this late, and when she was done she set the test stick on the bathroom counter.

One minute for early results, three minutes for a conclusive answer. She waited a full three minutes, then reached for the stick and brought it close, purposefully avoiding the test result window. If she was pregnant, then there was no doubt that somehow, someway, she and Tim would one day work things out. God wouldn't have let it happen otherwise.

If not . . .

Thoughts of Ryan crowded about in her mind again, and she ordered them silent. *I'm sorry, Lord. . . . Help me not to think that way. Help me know what your perfect will is for me because that's all I want. I love Tim, really, Father. Keep my mind from wandering where it shouldn't.*

Without waiting another moment, she focused her eyes, and there it was, clear as day. Two plus signs, side by side.

She was pregnant, carrying Tim's child.

Surely that was a sign. Surely, somehow, she and Tim would get back together. They would get counseling and whatever help they needed, and they'd fall in love again.

Her only hope was that it would happen fast.

First, because she had a limited time to make things work with Tim before the baby came.

And second, because now that she and Ryan Taylor had connected, it would take another miracle to keep them apart again.

Chapter Twelve

Tim Jacobs was lying in Angela's bed, switching channels on her television set, when he came to a talking-head shot. A conservative-looking man in his early fifties appeared to be holding a book, and Tim squinted in the darkness to make it out. He'd gone through most of a bottle of wine in the past two hours, and he had to work to make sense of the imagery on the screen.

Angela was down on her exercise mat beside the bed doing stretches. She looked up, annoyed. "Hey, c'mon, change the channel. I can't stand those TV preachers."

But for some reason, Tim couldn't bring himself to turn it. The preacher man — if he was a preacher — wasn't one of those big-hair types. His eyes had a look of compassion and . . . something else. Urgency, maybe.

Tim let the remote fall to his side. "I was gonna be a preacher once." His words slurred together, and his eyes struggled to focus. "Gonna tell the worl' about Jesus."

Angela sat up and stared at him, her eyes mocking him as a single burst of laughter broke through her pursed lips. "You? A preacher?"

Something in her tone irritated Tim, set his teeth on edge and brought his pain close to the surface. He reached for the wine bottle and poured himself another glass. Some of the liquid sloshed onto the bed, and Angela grimaced. "Hey, babe, you've really got to back off on the wine. A little bit's good for you — not this much."

Her words were measured and in control. Though she drank with him now and then, she did not share his urgency for alcohol, an urgency that seemed to grow with each passing day. She had even tried to limit his drinking in ways he found profoundly annoying. Who did she think she was, anyway? His drinking wasn't a dependency or an illness like Uncle Frank's problem. It was a life preserver. Every drink did a bit more to keep thoughts of Kari from suffocating him.

Tim looked around the room. The walls seemed to be closing in on them. Angela's bedroom had always been small, especially with her exercise equipment in the corner. Now it was getting claustrophobic. He downed half the glass in a single, practiced gulp and shook his head, trying to clear his vision.

He hated the way his words ran together when he drank, hated the nausea and headaches and the way his body demanded more whenever the effects of the drink wore off. As a way of proving to himself that he was in control, he'd kept his drinking down to three or four nights a week and an occasional swig from the flask in his desk drawer at work.

Nothing more than what his coworkers might do.

The preacher was saying something, and Tim squinted again, trying to follow the man's words. "The message of Christ's love is found in Isaiah, chapter sixty-one," the man was saying. "God himself will restore the crumbling foundations of your life. He will give you beauty for ashes. He'll provide redemption, no matter who you are, where you are. . . ."

Angela huffed, and Tim turned in time to see her roll her eyes. She chuckled in a condescending way.

"Wha'so funny?"

She grinned at him, and through his blurred eyes she swayed like a person caught out at sea. "Don't you get what he's doing?"

The room started to spin, and Tim felt a growing frustration deep inside. He set his wineglass down and scowled at her. "Get what?"

She pointed at the television screen. "Exactly what we talked about in class. It's just manipulation — just another ad campaign." She lifted herself from the floor in a single fluid movement and climbed up beside him on the bed. She snuggled close to him, kissing him on the shoulder and neck and finally on his lips before finishing her thought. "First he tells you how awful things are, makes you feel really bad about it; then he tells you what you ought to do." She smiled. "Selling God is like selling diet pills. 'Oh, you're so fat. Here, I've got what you need.' "

"What are you talking about?" He wasn't quite sure what diet pills had to do with evangelists or God, and his growing dizziness wasn't helping him understand her any better.

"I mean —" she kissed him again — "that we don't need what he's selling because what we've got here is beautiful just the way it is."

She looked at him and seemed to be waiting for him to say something. Then she sighed hard and leaned back on her elbows, stretching long, pale legs in front of her. She rotated her ankles a few times, then turned back to him, propping herself on one forearm, her blue eyes focused. "Listen, Tim, I know you're having some bad feelings about . . . the divorce. But you've got to stop letting it get to you. You need to take care of yourself. You could start going to the gym with me . . . get some exercise. That would help, don't you think?"

Tim stared at her, bristling a little at her solicitous tone, and realized for the first time that the passion he felt for her was fading. What had seemed brilliant and intoxicating less than a week ago now seemed cynical and self-serving.

"Don't get me wrong," she was saying. "I still think you're gorgeous." She smiled and moved toward him again, kissing him, obviously intent on more of what they'd spent the past weeks doing.

But suddenly he knew he was going to be sick. He gently pushed her off and stumbled into the bathroom.

The first wave of vomit dropped him to his knees.

"Are you okay?" She sounded worried, but there was no way he could answer.

By the time the convulsions stopped, his head was so far inside the toilet that his chin was nearly touching the water. He gasped for air and slowly eased himself back to a kneeling position. Angela's words and the preacher's wove together in his head, tormenting him. *He'll give you beauty for ashes. . . . It's just manipulation, just another ad campaign. . . . God himself will restore the crumbling foundations. . . . What we have is beautiful just like it is.*

He stayed there a long time, sitting on the floor beside the toilet. Angela knocked at the bathroom door a few times, her voice first concerned, then annoyed. He replied with single syllables. After a while she stopped knocking, and finally he felt the apartment grow silent.

Fear settled over him then, thick and ropelike. It wrapped itself around his throat and made it difficult to breathe. He stood up, wiped his mouth with the back of his hand, and used the walls to help him navigate his way back to the bedroom.

The room was dark. Angela lay with her back to him, her hands tucked under her head like a child, her lean body stiff and still. He couldn't tell if she was asleep or pretending, but something about her was different. This was the woman who had sent his body into a fever pitch of desire, but now she made him feel sad and old and somehow . . . disgusted. The choking feeling intensified, and he absently brought his hands up to his neck as if there might be some way to relieve the pressure.

I'm choking to death. Help me, God.

In response he felt the faintest nudging, something else the television preacher had said. Tim dropped to the floor, his eyes closed, as he tried to recall the words.

Repent . . . flee the bonds of the enemy.

Tim held his breath. Had his memory finally kicked in, or was that the Lord talking to him? Now, after all these days of silence? After all Tim had done to walk away from him?

Tim circled his hands around his throat and tried to swallow. Yes, that was it. Bonds of the enemy. That's what was choking him.

He struggled to his feet, found his clothes and shoes, and managed to get dressed. It was after three o'clock in the morning, and he needed to be at school by nine. He trudged into Angela's living room and spent the next few hours dozing in a chair. Before Angela was awake, he crept out, and for the first time since leaving Kari, he drove home.

His key still fit in the front door — something he'd wondered about. He glanced around. "Kari?"

There was no answer. He tried again, this time making his way slowly toward their bedroom. The bed was made, and Tim realized Kari was probably still at her parents' house. He felt a pang of irritation, then a wave of remorse. How could he blame her for not wanting to be home?

As he looked around the room they had shared, an image came to mind, then another and another. He and Kari saying their vows before Pastor Mark at Clear Creek Community Church. He and Kari walking hand in hand through the park. He and Kari laughing and talking and . . .

The choking fear was back, and Tim sank down on the clean bedspread. His eyes fell on the nightstand and a book that still lay there, calling him, reminding him of his other life, the one he'd lived before meeting Angela. He stood up and stared at the book. It was leatherbound and had his name engraved on it.

His Bible, the one Pastor Mark had given him when he joined the church after becoming engaged to Kari.

Like a man clinging to a life rope, Tim sat down gingerly on his bed and clutched the book to his chest. *Help me, God . . . I'm not going to make it.*

How long had it been? Tim thought

back and remembered months and years when he'd pretended to read . . . told Kari he was reading. But really? Truly? He couldn't remember the last time he had read his Bible.

His hands shook from the hangover. He clutched the Bible more tightly and then steadied his hands enough to open the front cover. There were words scrawled inside, words from Pastor Mark.

Tim shook his head, forcing his mind to clear at least enough to make out the writing. He looked again, lowering his face to the open page, scrutinizing the wording. It began with a quote from Isaiah: "But now, this is what the Lord says . . . 'Fear not, for I have redeemed you; I have summoned you by name; you are mine.' "

Underneath the quote the pastor had added these words: "Remember, Tim, God's offer of redemption is forever. Pastor Mark."

Redemption? God's offer of redemption? Tim closed his eyes, and drums began beating somewhere close to his temples. He had the strongest sense that if he so much as took one hand off the Bible, a cloud of demons might descend on him then and there and take him straight to hell.

Redemption?

Tim looked again and saw that Pastor Mark had scribbled the church phone number under his inscription. He closed his eyes again. The room was spinning. Not fast like before, but just enough to build within him another wave of nausea, worse than the last.

Redemption. The television pastor had talked about that, hadn't he? Or maybe the whole thing was nothing more than a bad dream, a crazy nightmare meant to scare him into giving up the things he loved, the lifestyle he'd chosen.

A memory flashed across his mind. Someone talking, saying something serious. The words grew sharper.

God will always honor your choice.

Tim shook his head once more and tried to make sense of the familiar words. God would honor his choice — where had he heard that before? Seconds passed and then minutes, and suddenly he remembered. They were Pastor Mark's words, spoken at his and Kari's wedding. What had the man said? Something about making a choice to love one another . . . or love God. Making a choice about something.

It was coming back to him now, and he squeezed his eyes shut, willing himself to remember everything. It was a warning.

The pastor had told them that if ever they decided not to put God first . . .

Now the pastor's voice was so clear in Tim's mind, it was as if he were speaking directly to him. *"God will always honor your choice."*

Was that what this was?

Tim had chosen a lifestyle of freedom, independence from God, and now God was honoring his choice?

The alcohol was fading quickly from his system, and in its place was a pounding headache. Three times his stomach convulsed with the nausea that welled up inside him. He wanted a drink so badly he could taste it, could feel the liquid burning its way down his throat.

What have I done, Lord . . . ?

He pictured Kari, wondered how her family had handled the news. Another emotion clawed at his gut, and he realized it was hatred. Hatred for himself. How could he let her handle the news of his affair without even calling her? Other than the time he'd talked to her mother and —

Tim felt liquid building in his eyes, and he squeezed them shut. What kind of man was he, anyway? Nothing about him was worth redeeming — nothing at all. He tentatively took hold of the cordless phone and cradled it as he considered his options. He opened the cover of his Bible again. There it was, written clearly under Pastor Mark's name. The number for Clear Creek Community Church.

The phone was still in his hand. Tim gulped twice, clicked a button, and began punching in the numbers. He was one number away from Pastor Mark, one number away from confessing it all and begging him or anyone who might listen for a second chance. A single number away from the redemption the preacher had talked about last night.

His hand hovered over the final number, and suddenly his fear dissipated. In its place was an anger so strong and real that he could taste its acid residue in the back of his throat. He clicked the Off button, stood, and slammed the phone back on the base unit.

What was he, crazy? Calling a preacher because of something the man had scribbled in a Bible years ago? Then what? Would he tell the man that he was in love with someone other than his wife? or that he'd taken to drinking occasionally to ease the guilt? or that he wasn't sure what God had to do with any of it — if anything?

He clenched his teeth and calculated his

next move. It was morning, time to eat and brush his teeth and get to work. There would be no alcohol today, not until tonight. An image of Kari, hauntingly beautiful and all alone, drifted into his mind until he banished it. His marriage was over; everything about his old life was dead and buried.

Pastor Mark had been right. Tim had made his choice and left God no option but to honor it. So it was up to him to live with the results as best he could. With Angela, of course. He popped three Advil tablets from the bathroom cabinet and downed a glass of water before heading into the kitchen.

Redemption? He blinked back the idea and started rummaging in the pantry for something to eat.

Redemption? He'd lost that chance months ago, the first time he cheated on the woman who once had been his whole world.

Dirk Bennett sat in his truck and kept his eyes on the professor's house. His breathing was fast and shallow, and his heart was racing. Of course, that was nothing new. His trainer said it was one of the side effects of getting stronger. A small price to pay.

With a shaky hand, Dirk jotted the professor's address on a notepad. He wasn't sure whether he'd need the information later or not, but it was worth getting anyway.

Dirk glanced at the dashboard clock and saw that it was 6:32 in the morning. He'd been here since sometime around five, when he'd followed the professor from Angela's apartment. He'd thought maybe the professor would stop in for a minute or two and head back to Angela's — in which case, the plan was simple.

Dirk would follow at a distance. Then before Professor Jacobs had a chance to walk up to Angela's apartment door, Dirk would sneak through the shadows and put the gun to the man's head. Dirk would explain to the professor as calmly as possible that the affair was wrong. That he needed to go back to his pretty wife and leave Angela alone.

But now the night had gotten away. Dirk sighed in frustration. He needed to be at the gym by seven o'clock for his weight-training class. He started his engine. This wasn't the time to confront the professor. In fact, it was possible he'd never need to scare the man at all. His long stay at home could mean he'd decided to go back to his wife. But even if he hadn't, Dirk had a new plan, one he'd formed in the past hour.

He couldn't spend every free moment following Angela and her lover around Bloomington. What would that prove? That he was some sort of deranged stalker?

No, nothing good could come from that.

But what if Dirk simply trained harder, got in the best shape of his life, and then looked for his chance to catch Angela alone and propose to her? As he should have done last year. That made sense. Surely that would cause Angela to walk away from the professor on her own.

He opened the glove box and saw the gun next to another bottle of Power pills. He was going through them three times as fast as before. Nothing dangerous, the trainer told him. Nothing illegal. Just a little something extra to enhance his strength and pack on another twenty pounds of muscle by Christmas.

He drove away, and by the time he pulled into the university parking lot he had a smile on his face. It was a good plan. But he liked knowing where Professor Jacobs lived, all the same. It expanded his options.

And as far as Dirk was concerned, options were always a good thing.

★ ★ ★

Angela woke up an hour before class, and for the first time since Tim had moved in, his side of the bed was empty.

She stretched and moaned. Her muscles were stiff, tense, especially around her neck. She remembered the night before, and a ripple of worry coursed through her.

What if Tim had changed his mind? Maybe he'd gone back home to work things out with Kari and make another go at his marriage.

Angela cringed at the thought. As awful as it was to be having an affair with a married man and as worrisome as his new drinking habit was to her, it was worse to imagine him leaving, going back to his wife. She lay back in bed and wondered how her life had gotten so complicated.

The choices she'd made were the very ones she'd been determined to avoid since the day her father had walked out on them. She could see herself as she'd been that year, just a child, listening to her parents fight downstairs. The dialogue rang clear in her mind even now.

"I don't love you anymore; it's over. I'm in love with someone else." It was the same voice her father used when she'd stall bedtime as a little girl. The voice that meant he was serious, his mind was made up — no more discussion.

"Don't leave, please." Her mother was crying, and her tone told Angela this was more serious than the other fights they had. "I'll do whatever you want; just don't leave. We need you."

Her father hadn't said another word. He merely walked upstairs to Angela's bed, bent down, and kissed her as he ran his fingers over her hair. "Good-bye, sweetie. I'm sorry."

Her mother was never the same after her daddy left. She kept working and going through the motions. But the spark in her eyes was gone forever, and Angela grieved the fact to this day. That night in her room was the last she had heard of her father until she'd gotten word about him her junior year in high school. He'd been killed in a car accident in California.

Angela remembered how she'd felt when she heard the news, the mix of emotions that assaulted her heart, the resolutions that steadied her soul.

First, she would never do to another woman what the nameless woman had done to her mother. She would avoid married men at all costs.

Second, if love could destroy a person

the way it had destroyed her mother, then she'd stay single all her days. She would never be like her mother, saddled down with a child and begging some man to stay. Absolutely not. Single and independent, responsible all by herself to keep the spark of joy alive within her.

Sure, she'd dated before. Guys like Dirk Bennett, who were good for nothing more than passing the time. Still, she had kept her heart too far buried to worry about losing it to any man.

But all that changed when she met Tim.

Don't fall for him, she'd warned herself. The professor was a married man, a man already given over, heart and soul, to his wife.

But ever since she'd come back to school that fall, Angela had known for certain Tim's heart was no longer given over to the woman he'd married.

It was given to her.

She drew in a slow, cleansing breath. She had nothing to worry about. Tim would be back. Because no matter how he'd annoyed her last night, no matter where he was this morning, no matter how far she'd fallen from the person she'd intended to be, she wasn't letting go of what she'd found. She felt safe in his arms, safer than she'd felt since she was a child. He was witty and charming, a brilliant writer and teacher with a charisma that had drawn her from the first day.

Other than her father, Tim was the only man she'd ever really loved. The only man granted permission to see completely into her soul.

Angela closed her eyes and imagined the heartbreak his wife must be suffering. For just an instant she felt the pierce of guilt and regret, and she thought about the television preacher's words from the night before. Redemption. As if people like Tim and her might have a chance to make things right with a holy God.

She rolled over on her side and stared out the window of her apartment. She wasn't worried about God or redemption or anything but being with the man she loved.

Besides, she'd already found heaven. It wasn't some faraway place in the clouds where she might go when she died.

It was right here in the arms of Professor Tim Jacobs.

Chapter Thirteen

Kari let herself into Brooke's house and called out to her sister. "I'm here."

"Good." Brooke darted out of her upstairs bedroom and smiled over the railing. "Thanks. You're a lifesaver. Our sitter's never canceled on us like this."

"No problem. Where're the girls?"

"Hailey's already asleep. Maddie's got a fever. She's resting in bed, but not quite out yet. I'm almost ready. Be down in a minute."

"Okay."

Kari looked around. New carpet, new furniture. She yawned and headed for the living room. Something about Brooke's pristine house made Kari feel strangely out of place in her jeans and sweater. She cozied up in a leather recliner and wondered about her older sister. She was not glamorous or even particularly beautiful, but something about her exuded confidence and energy. She stood out in a room.

Kari leaned back and stared at an elegantly tasteful art piece on the opposite wall. It had always been that way with Brooke, even back when she was in high school and still attended church with the rest of them. She'd always insisted on the best. Back then she was one of the best swimmers in the state and played captain on the school's state championship volleyball team.

Kari remembered asking her once whether she prayed before competition. A strangely foreign look had filled Brooke's expression. "Not really. I just imagine myself winning, and then I go out and win."

That was how Brooke lived to this day. Married to Peter West, one of the top internists at St. Anne's Hospital, and months away from having her medical license to practice pediatrics, Brooke had always played out her life as smoothly as one of her sporting events.

For Brooke, everything from her job and her gorgeous estate home to her adorable little blonde daughters had been a simple matter of imagining herself winning and then going out and doing it. Being the best. Having the best. All without even a remnant of the faith she'd been brought up in.

Kari thought about her own life and inhaled slowly. It didn't seem fair.

Brooke came lightly down the stairs dressed in a conservative black evening gown. She smiled at Kari and sat in the big chair beside her. "You look seventeen."

Kari's eyebrows lifted. "Me?"

Brooke nodded. "Maybe it's the jeans."

"Maybe." They studied each other for a minute, a comfortable silence between them.

"Ashley told me you saw Ryan."

Kari bit her lower lip and gazed out the window into the dark night. "At church the other day."

"Well?" Brooke raised a single eyebrow, and the corners of her mouth lifted. "How did it go?"

Kari adjusted her position so that she could see Brooke better. "Meaning?"

Brooke hesitated. "Meaning the guy's been in love with you since the beginning of time. He's single, gorgeous . . . you know what I mean. How'd it go?"

Anger grabbed Kari's heart, and she crossed her arms, pinning them against her body. "I think you're forgetting something."

"What?" Her sister's expression was blank.

"I'm married, Brooke. Remember?

Doesn't that count for anything?"

Brooke uttered a short laugh. "Is that what you call it?" She leaned over her knees and locked eyes with Kari. "Listen, little sister. By the time a guy moves in with his girlfriend and asks for a divorce, marriage is just a technicality."

Kari's anger doubled. "It's more than a technicality to me. I made a promise before God and everyone."

Brooke rolled her eyes and smiled sadly. "So that's what this is about. Some commitment to an all-powerful God who wouldn't have the sense to release you from a marriage like yours?"

Kari's jaw dropped, and her eyes opened wide. "Brooke, listen to you! How can you say that?"

"It's true."

Kari had no idea Brooke had fallen this far in her faith. "Don't you believe even a little?"

There was a hesitation. "Of course I believe. It's how we were raised."

"I'm not talking about how we were raised." Kari splayed her fingers over her chest. "I'm talking about a relationship with God." She paused, searching Brooke's face. "That's what keeps me going. Even when I don't think I'll last another minute."

Brooke studied her and nodded slowly. "So you're not going to divorce him?"

"No. I told you that."

"But I thought the Bible gives you a way out if your husband's sleeping around? Isn't that right?"

"Never mind." Kari held her hand up. "You don't get it."

"I get it. Your husband is a two-timing jerk who can't keep his pants zipped up. No matter what else happens, you'll never be able to trust him again." Brooke lowered her voice. "I'm sorry. All I'm saying is that I think the Bible gives you a way out in this case."

"I'm not looking for a way out." Kari struggled to keep from screaming. "I want my marriage to work. Is there something wrong with that?"

A single cry came from upstairs, and Brooke looked toward Maddie's room. When the child fell silent again, Brooke turned to Kari. "Her fever's down a bit, but she's still feeling sick."

"Are you worried?" Kari's tone softened. "She seems to be sick a lot lately."

Brooke shrugged. "It's just a bug. Nothing a little pain reliever won't help." Compassion eased the lines on her forehead. "Hey, I didn't mean to make you mad with the Ryan comment. Obviously it's too soon to talk about you and him."

Kari took a breath to explain that no matter how ridiculous her determination to remain married might seem, it was not a passing phase. And Ryan Taylor had nothing to do with the situation, especially now that —

She let the air leak out in an exasperated sigh. This was obviously not the time to go into all that, not while her sister was getting ready to leave. Besides, what was the point of explaining when she knew Brooke would disagree? "You didn't mean anything by it." Kari's tone was terse. "It's okay."

Resting her hands on her knees, Brooke frowned. "No, I don't think it is. What were you going to say?"

Kari sighed again. What did it matter anyway? "I have to tell you something."

"Tim's already filed?" It was less of a question than a statement.

Kari shook her head, and her eyes narrowed. "I'm pregnant, okay?" She met Brooke's eyes once more. "I took the test Sunday."

Her sister's mouth hung open for a moment, and her face grew a shade paler. "Does Tim know?"

"No." Tears clouded Kari's vision. "He hasn't called since I left — well, once when I was gone, but he just told Mom he wanted a divorce."

Brooke sat very still as if she were weighing her words. "Are you . . . you know . . . are you going to keep it?"

"Brooke!" What was her sister thinking? Brooke couldn't possibly think she'd have an abortion. And did that mean Brooke thought abortions were okay?

"I'm sorry." Brooke let out a heavy sigh. "What I mean is, if Tim's been promiscuous, there could be disease involved. And with everything else you're going through, the last thing you need is an unwanted pregnancy."

A strangled laugh escaped Kari's throat. "I can't believe I'm hearing this." She stared out the window for a moment and then back at her older sister. "Let's get one thing clear, Brooke. I'm not one of your patients. And you should know better than to say such a thing to me." Her hand slipped to her abdomen as she continued. "The timing may not be ideal, but I want this baby more than you or Ashley or anyone else knows."

"All right, all right." Brooke held up a hand. "I won't bring it up again." She paused. "How far along are you?"

Kari sank deeper into the chair. Didn't her family know her at all? "Almost three months."

Brooke seemed to let that sink in for a moment. Then she crossed the room and knelt down, slipping her arm around Kari's shoulders. "I'm sorry."

The muscles in Kari's back relaxed, and tears filled her eyes again.

"You must be scared to death."

A tear fell on Kari's jeans, and she sniffed. "I just want things to be right with Tim and me." More tears trickled down Kari's cheeks. She offered Brooke a pitiful smile.

"Hey." Brooke squeezed Kari's hand. "I love you, even if I think you're crazy."

"I know." Kari wiped her cheeks with her fingertips. "I love you too."

Peter came bounding down the stairs and stopped short when he saw the two of them, Kari crying and Brooke huddled close by her.

Brooke was the first to speak. "Ready?" She gave Kari a final squeeze, stood, and flashed her husband a look that seemed to stop him from asking questions.

"Ready."

"We'll be back before eleven." Brooke

gazed upstairs once more. "Don't worry about Maddie. The medicine should hold her over until after we get back. But if you get worried, you can page me."

Kari listened as Brooke and Peter pulled away. When they were gone, she drew the shades and plopped on the sofa. Now everyone in her family knew the truth.

"You'll be fine, Kari Baxter," Ashley had told her, giving her a heartfelt hug. "Being a single mom's not so bad."

Kari winced now at the memory of how those words had stung her heart. She was *not* a single mom. And she wasn't Kari Baxter; she was Kari Jacobs. For better or worse, until death took one of them from the other. Why was everyone having such a hard time understanding that?

Tim would come around . . . he had to.

Or maybe they were struggling with it because deep in the center of her heart, she was struggling too.

She thought about how often she'd called his university office today. Several times during his office hours and at least once between each class. Times when the old Tim would have been at his desk.

Each time, the phone rang once, then kicked into the main office of the journalism department. Kari's first call had been at eight this morning.

"Journalism." The terse voice belonged to Eleanore, the blunt secretary who had served in the position for three decades.

Kari did not try to disguise her voice. "Hi, it's Kari Jacobs." She wondered if everyone in the department knew about Tim's affair. "Is my husband around? He should be in his office, but he's not picking up."

"I haven't seen him, Mrs. Jacobs." Eleanore paused. "I'll tell him you called. Or I could give you his voice mail."

Kari was dying to ask more questions, find out if Tim was openly carrying on with his girlfriend or whether he was keeping his private life a secret from others in the department. But she stopped herself. What good could come from asking such a question? Besides, there was no guarantee she'd get the truth. Eleanore had always had a soft spot for Tim; her allegiance was bound to be with him and not Kari.

She had opted for leaving Tim a voice mail. Over the course of the day, she left a series of them, with no response.

When she was unable to reach her husband, she called Pastor Mark and made an appointment to see him the following day.

"Is everything okay?" The pastor sounded concerned.

"Well —" Kari's voice broke, and it took a moment before she could continue — "not really."

"I'm sorry, Kari." Pastor Mark waited.

"Tim . . ." She swallowed back the sobs that seemed always ready to burst to the surface. "He moved out a few weeks ago."

Kari could hear the pastor exhale, as if the news made a physical impact on him. "Will he come with you tomorrow?"

A sob slipped from her throat, and she struggled to regain control. "He moved in with another woman. I haven't talked to him since he left."

Before the phone call ended, Pastor Mark prayed for her and assured her that God still loved her and was looking out for her, that he would redeem even this seemingly impossible circumstance. They set the appointment for Tuesday at noon. "I'd like it if Tim would come," he told Kari. "Keep trying to reach him."

Kari got up and checked on Brooke's daughters. Now, with the girls asleep and a lonely night ahead of her, Kari's anger was back. The emotions that had washed over her since Tim moved out seemed to change as often as the tide. One hour she'd miss her husband so badly her chest would ache. Then she'd imagine him with the other woman, and suddenly she'd be angry enough to do something crazy — like send a letter about the situation to the university's ethics board or find him and pound her fists against his chest.

On top of that she was pregnant, her body steeped in rising hormones. There seemed to be no balance, no even-keeled moments; she'd even been getting heart palpitations lately.

Kari exhaled slowly. No matter what he'd done by having the affair, Kari missed Tim so badly it hurt to breathe. She needed him to walk through the door, take her in his arms, and tell her it was all a nightmare, that he wasn't in love with someone else and that, in fact, he would love her until the day he died.

"Where is he, Lord?" She whispered the question out loud. "Why didn't he answer my calls?"

She thought about Pastor Mark's final comment. *I'd like it if Tim would come.*

Slowly an idea began to form. Why not call him at Angela's apartment? So what if it was awkward? If she was going to fight for her marriage, she would have to endure some awkwardness. Who knew? Maybe the phone call would help bring him to his senses.

Kari braced herself against the kitchen counter and stared at the telephone. She remembered the woman's name; it had been hovering in her mind since she'd received the anonymous call the day before Tim left.

Angela Manning.

How many Mannings could possibly be listed in the city of Bloomington? Kari's heart beat faster in response. She reached for the phone, dialed information, and was connected with an operator.

"For what city?"

"In Bloomington, the number for Angela Manning, on South Maple."

"Hold for your number." In three seconds Kari had the number for an A. Manning at an address that had to be the Silverlake Apartments. She scribbled it on a notepad near the phone and stared at it for nearly a minute. Her breathing was shallow and fast, and she felt faint. But there was no other way to find him.

She punched the numbers quickly before she could change her mind. A woman answered on the second ring.

"Hello?" She sounded older than twenty-four.

"Yes." Kari cleared her throat. *Help me, Lord . . . give me the words.* "I'm looking for Tim Jacobs."

The woman said nothing.

Kari felt her courage building. What did she have to fear? She wasn't the one having an affair, after all. She could call her husband if she wanted to. "I said I'm looking for Tim Jacobs. Is he there?"

"Who is this?"

The anger was returning. "This is his wife. Who's *this?*"

Again the woman was silent, but Kari heard her set the phone down, and after nearly a minute Tim picked it up with a huff. "Kari?"

She wasn't prepared for the warring emotions that came over her at the sound of his voice. Should she cry and beg him to come home or curse him for leaving? Kari closed her eyes and prayed for strength. "Hello, Tim." Her voice shook, and she felt nauseous. "We need to talk."

Tim's voice was furious. "What are you thinking, calling me here? Did Eleanore give you the number? I can't believe she'd do that to me."

That answered one question; the journalism department definitely knew about his affair. Kari held back the tears and clenched her fists. "No . . . the operator gave it to me. I know who she is, Tim. There's no other A. Manning listed."

He lowered his voice. "Listen, there's a time and place to talk about things, Kari, and this is neither."

Kari could barely catch her breath from the shock of Tim's attitude. *He isn't even a little sorry, God. What am I supposed to say?*

"I tried calling you at work all day, and you weren't in your office." Kari blinked her eyes and felt the first tears spill onto her cheeks. "I left you eight messages."

A frustrated sigh sounded in Kari's ear. "I was going to call you in a few days. You're right. We need to talk."

Kari noticed that her husband's words were not slurred, and she felt the slightest bit of relief. "I'm meeting with Pastor Mark tomorrow." Kari shielded her eyes with her free hand and gripped her forehead with her thumb and forefinger. "He asked if you'd come."

"What?" For the first time since he'd gotten on the phone, Tim's voice held traces of weary sadness. "Kari, give it up. Please. I want a divorce, not a counseling appointment. For God's sake, I'm living with Angela."

The tears came harder, and she sobbed

softly, searching for her voice. "It's for God's sake that I want you to come with me tomorrow. I'm still your wife, Tim. We can work through this."

Tim sounded exasperated. "We should've gotten counseling a year ago when I was so lonely that I didn't even feel married." He exhaled hard. "Look, I wanted to end things on good terms with you, Kari. But nothing you or anyone else might say could convince me to stay married. I've already moved on; it's too late to turn back."

"All I want is for you to give us a try." Kari was weeping openly now. "Is that too much to ask, Tim? After all we've shared?"

"And all I want is a divorce." He sucked in a breath, and Kari thought he sounded tired. "Quickly, quietly, and without fanfare. The same way other couples get divorced." Tim's tone had turned cold as winter wind. "Is *that* too much to ask? After all we've shared?"

Kari's pain turned to raging fury. "I don't know what kind of monster you've become or what you've done with the man I still love, but I know this much —" She shook with fury, her fists so tight the fingernails dug into the palms of her hands. She opened them then, spreading her fingers out against her still flat abdomen. "I will never give you a divorce. Our baby deserves more than that."

Without saying another word, Kari slammed the receiver back on the base. There. Let him chew on that while he slept in Angela Manning's arms tonight. She relaxed her hands and went back to the living-room sofa, where she lay on her side and felt the anger drain from her body. In its place was an odd sense of detachment, as if her body and emotions had gone numb.

She sat up, replaying her conversation with Tim. She would have given anything to see him try to explain the phone call to Angela, all the while hiding the panic he had to be feeling now that he knew he was to be a father. He'd have to be frantic with concern, desperate to talk to her. She'd probably get back to her parents' house that night and find a dozen messages from him.

But then she gave a single, bitter laugh, remembering the hurtful things he'd said and the chill in his voice.

Who was she kidding?

Tim didn't want counseling or conversation. He had no interest in making things work between them. He was never going to

241

come around — he probably didn't even want the baby. She wrapped her arms protectively around her midsection. Ashley was right. They'd be single mothers together, and Kari's dream of helping other married couples would always be just that.

A dream.

Still feeling strangely empty, she glanced idly around the room. On a low shelf across from her she spotted what looked like a scrapbook. Funny. She hadn't remembered that Brooke liked to work on scrapbooks. Kari wiped her fingertips under her eyes and wearily made her way over to the bookcase. The scrapbook was bound in leather and weighed a ton. Kari carried it back to the sofa and opened it to the first page.

There in fancy lettering were the words *The Five of Us.*

Kari knit her brows and flipped through the book, stunned at what it held. Somehow amidst studying for medical exams and raising a family, Brooke had found time to put together a scrapbook of the Baxter kids and their lives growing up. Brooke, who in recent years had become little more than a nonbeliever? The Baxter daughter who seemed absorbed in her medical training and elitist lifestyle? That same Brooke kept a scrapbook of their childhood?

Kari and the other siblings never would have guessed that Brooke gave them more than a passing thought. But if she kept this book, she must have cared more than any of them knew.

Kari turned the pages back to the beginning and savored the memories as they came. She and Brooke on tricycles some long-ago Sunday morning before church. Kari felt the corners of her mouth lift as she remembered how close the two of them had been back then. But not because they were similar — though when they were little their mother tended to dress them alike, and people sometimes did mistake them for twins. Actually, from the beginning their likes and dislikes had been totally different. For that reason there was no leader, no follower in their relationship. They almost never argued and were always a help to each other. They shared the same values and saw most things eye to eye.

Way back then, anyway.

She flipped another page and saw a photo of the four girls together when Erin was only a baby. The family was picnicking at the lake — something they did often. Dad had made it clear that, though he often was on call and sometimes away for conventions and medical seminars, he would always find time for his family. There had been family softball games at Monroe County Park, boating at the lake, trips into Indianapolis to see plays and concerts.

Theirs had been the kind of family Kari imagined she would have one day.

She shook her head and turned the page, only to burst out laughing. There stood Kari and Brooke and Ashley at nine, ten, and six, their arms wrapped around each other, standing in front of their family tent in just their underwear. The family had been swimming when Daniel, their shaggy dog, had dragged the duffel bag into the lake, submerging their clothes.

"I know," Kari had said as everyone stood about the campsite, slack-jawed. "Our underwear's in Mom and Dad's bag!"

Brooke's eyes danced as she caught on. "Right."

Ashley giggled and followed Kari and Brooke into the tent, and three minutes later the girls piled out in only their underwear — ready to tackle the day.

We were so silly back then . . . not a care in the world.

A few more pages, and she saw Ashley pulling Luke in an old red wagon. Kari smiled and ran her finger lightly over their young faces. *Where'd you go to, Ash? A part of you got lost in Paris. What happened there, anyway?*

No answers came as Kari stared at the photo and thought about the changes in her sister. Obviously something bad had happened to her there, something she hadn't been able to share even with Kari.

Whatever it was, Ashley wasn't talking.

It hadn't come between the two of them, but a strain definitely existed between Ashley and the others. Especially between Ashley and Luke. Kari stared at the picture again and remembered something she'd forgotten before. Ashley used to call their brother her "little Lukey." Even though he was closer in age to Erin, he and Ashley had practically been joined at the hip as kids. Ashley, the big sister who could do no wrong, and Luke, the little brother her friends oohed and aahed over.

Luke.

The blond prince whose presence filled their home with laughter and lighthearted memories. It tore at Kari's heart to see how he and Ashley were now — the way they avoided each other, the snide remarks they threw out under their breaths. If Kari were a stranger just passing through, she would have thought the two had been at odds forever.

She stared at the scrapbook again. The pictures told a different story.

Kari lingered on one photo after another until she came to a classic — her mom and dad on their twentieth anniversary. Next to it, Brooke had fixed a copy of their parents' wedding photo. Kari could almost feel their love emanating off the page.

Wasn't that the type of love Kari had always dreamed of? Wasn't that what she and Tim were supposed to have? She thought about her parents' love story, the way her silly dad still sat them down every Valentine's Day and shared it with whoever would listen.

Kari closed her eyes and could hear the story come to life — how her father's parents had wanted a big family but her dad's father, John Sr., had been killed in action in World War II when her dad was just a baby. Because of that, he'd grown up an only child.

"Whenever you kids get tired of sharing your things and your place at the dinner table, take a minute and remember how lucky you are that you have each other,"

her father would tell them at that point in the story. "Every day I wished for brothers and sisters, but it never happened."

His mother had offers but chose not to remarry, never really getting over the death of her husband. When her dad was in college, his mother died of what seemed to be a broken heart.

"I was very lonely back then, but I always knew one day I'd have a huge family." Their father would grin and cut his eyes over toward his wife. "Of course, when I met your mom, I knew it had to be up to her. Because whether she wanted one child or ten, she was the one for me. I loved her so much that it didn't matter."

Kari's mom had been a home economics major at the University of Michigan and her dad a med student when they met at a campus Bible study. He liked to say Elizabeth was easily the most beautiful girl at the university that year, and Kari didn't doubt it. There was something stately and elegant, fragile and unforgettable about that old picture of Elizabeth Baxter, with her dark hair and huge eyes and porcelain complexion.

The same way Ashley looked now.

To hear her dad tell the story, he and her mom were pretty much married from the moment they said hello. And when he asked her how many kids she wanted, she was sure there'd be no more than three.

Ashley liked to tease Erin and Luke, telling them they were lucky she was a good baby. Otherwise their mother would never have given in and had more kids.

The story always ended with John Baxter's casting a loving look at his wife and saying something like, "You, my dear Elizabeth, are gold. I could never live long enough to grow tired of your company." Or, "I treasure your every breath, Elizabeth. The day I met you I became a man blessed beyond any other."

Kari would always see her parents as they were in moments like that, literally glowing in each other's presence. The Baxter children never needed to wonder what love was — their parents defined it every day of their lives.

She shut the scrapbook and leaned back against the sofa. She stayed there, motionless, as the feeling of numbness opened up into a hollow sadness. All her life she had dreamed of having a love like her parents had, sharing those same glances and smiles, memories and magic. Taking a lifetime to celebrate oneness with the man she married.

In the light of those dreams, Kari's loss felt greater than at any time since Tim had left home. Even if they did get back together and managed to work things out, what memories would the two of them have now? Their good times would forever be tarnished by Tim's affair. The reality of that grieved Kari beyond words.

Kari closed her eyes and prayed for sleep. She simply could not imagine being old and gray and reminiscing about the past with Tim Jacobs.

Not when she would have to work every day for the rest of her life to forget it.

Chapter Fourteen

Pastor Mark was working on his sermon Tuesday afternoon when Kari knocked on his office door.

"Am I early?"

He pushed away from his desk and stood to greet her. "Not a bit. Come in."

She struggled to make eye contact with him, embarrassed about how she looked. She knew there were dark circles under her eyes, and despite her pregnancy, her clothes hung on her. Pastor Mark kept his office door open, returned to his chair, and pointed to a vinyl sofa that had been in his office for years.

Kari sat down and crossed her legs. Her hands were shaking.

"You couldn't get Tim to come?" The pastor's voice was gentle, and Kari relaxed some, her heart still heavy.

She shook her head and tried to speak, but her emotions got the better of her.

"That's okay, take your time." He smiled sadly. "I'm not in a hurry. You can tell me what happened whenever you're ready."

Kari released a sigh and eased back into the sofa. "He moved out almost a month ago. He's having an affair with a student — moved in with her the same day he told me about it." She pulled a tissue from her purse and ran it beneath her eyes. "I called him at her apartment last night. He wants a divorce."

"And you?"

"I want to make it work." She exhaled and covered her face. When her hands fell back to her lap, the dreaded tears were back. "Everyone else thinks I'm crazy."

"No." Pastor Mark angled his head thoughtfully. "You're not crazy, Kari. I officiated at your wedding, remember? As long as I live, I'll remember the way Tim looked at you that day."

Kari nodded, and the image of Tim's face on the day of their wedding came to her mind as well. Never could she have imagined he'd ever love anyone but her. A tear slid down her cheek, and she dabbed at it with her fingertips. "My family's having a hard time remembering."

Mark's eyebrows lifted. "Even your parents?"

Kari shrugged. "They're trying. They think I'm doing the right thing, but they hate seeing me hurt." She gave him a half-hearted smile. "My sisters think I should wrap him in baling twine and toss him over a cliff."

He winced. "I guess that's understandable."

"Yeah," she sniffed, "I guess."

"You already know this, but I'll say it anyway." He paused. "You can't base your decisions on anyone's opinion but yours and God's."

Kari nodded. "That's why I'm here." Her voice broke, and she struggled to find the words. "I'm sorry. I . . ."

Pastor Mark handed her a tissue and waited until she could speak.

"I'm here because I want my husband back and I have absolutely no idea how to make that happen."

The pastor let his gaze fall to the floor for a moment. When he looked back at Kari, she could see in his eyes a depth that wasn't there before, and she was struck by how much he cared. "You can't *make* it happen, Kari. Tim has to be willing."

"Do you think he ever will?"

Pastor Mark folded his hands and hesitated. "Do you?"

Memories of the initial days of her marriage flashed in Kari's mind. Finding a jellyfish on a Mexican beach the week of their honeymoon. Buying furniture for their first home — a tiny apartment — and falling down laughing when they got home and found out the sofa was bigger than their living room. Crying together in the emergency room after they lost their first baby.

Those and dozens of other shared moments came to mind, and Kari smiled through her tears. "I don't know." She wanted to be honest. "I know he used to love me, and I think a part of him still does. Most of all, I think God wants me to keep trying to love him, not just give up."

The pastor smiled. "Then hold on to that, Kari. Don't let it go for anyone or anything. No matter how long it takes."

She stared at him, searching his eyes for wisdom she neither had nor knew how to find. "There's something else." Pastor Mark waited. "I'm pregnant. I found out a few days ago."

If he was shocked, he didn't show it. Instead, he drew a slow breath and nodded.

"I told him last night, but then I hung up on him. I haven't talked to him since."

"You hung up on him?" There was no judgment in the pastor's voice, just curiosity.

"Yes. He told me all he wanted from me was a divorce, and I got mad." She pursed her lips. "I'm mad at him a lot lately. Kind of crazy, I guess. Here I'm doing every-thing I can to get him back, but I'm also so mad at him that sometimes I actually hate him."

"That's not crazy, Kari. You wouldn't be human if you weren't mad." He paused. "So Tim knows you're pregnant and . . . you hear the ticking clock."

"Yes." Kari swallowed back the sorrow in her chest. "I need him home with me. I'm already almost three months along." She let out an exasperated huff. "Then there's Ryan Taylor."

"Ryan Taylor?" Pastor Mark's right eye-brow lifted ever so slightly. "I remember. You two were quite an item once."

"I guess you could call it that." She was telling him more than she'd planned, but it felt good. If she told her sisters about her unwanted feelings for Ryan they'd have a wedding date set before the end of the con-versation. "I was young, but he was very special to me. And now —"

"He's back in town."

Kari was amazed. The man ran a church and counseled many people every day, yet she felt as if he'd had private access to her deepest thoughts. "Right." Kari let her gaze fall to her ring finger. "I'm scared and alone and . . . part of me wants his friendship." She searched for the words. "But after being in love with him for so many years . . . I don't know if I could be his friend."

Pastor Mark's eyes narrowed, and he bit the corner of his lip. "Ryan's a good man, but I think you are making a wise choice. It would be easy to get confused if you spend too much time together. You're in a lot of pain right now, and pain can cloud your judgment."

Kari felt her cheeks grow hot and knew the pastor was right. It didn't matter that she loved Tim and wanted to win him back. She still had a heart, after all, and her heart would always be vulnerable where Ryan Taylor was concerned.

The topic changed, and Pastor Mark suggested she keep a journal, maybe write letters to Tim as if he actually were open to reconciling. This would help Kari work through her feelings and possibly, one day down the road, give them a tool they could use to make their relationship stronger.

"If you really want to save your marriage, Kari, God will show you how. He'll give you something you can do, the right words to say." Pastor Mark reached into his cabinet and pulled a piece of paper from a small file. He slid the sheet across his desk. "Take this. When Tim's ready for counseling, this program is something I strongly suggest."

Kari scanned the paper. The heading read "Marriage Intensive Seminar." "Marriage intensive? What is it?"

"It's a day's drive from here, in the Ozarks. It involves two days of intensive counseling between a couple and two counselors — a male and a female." Mark shrugged. "The results are amazing, from everything I hear."

Two days of counseling? Kari couldn't imagine Tim's agreeing to that type of therapy. But she took the paper. "Thanks." There was more doubt than faith in her voice.

Mark's expression softened. "I know you're not optimistic, but God has a plan, Kari. I'll be praying. You too, okay?"

"Okay." Kari folded the sheet of paper and slipped it into her purse.

"Beyond that, I really believe God will show you what to do."

Kari nodded. "He's already shown me one thing. I can't keep staying at my parents' house. I'm going back home tonight, at least for the weekdays. That way, if Tim comes around, I'll be there."

"Good idea."

Their time was over, and Kari wanted to have a fresh outlook. She'd expected to feel as if a ten-story building had been lifted from her shoulders. But all she felt was nauseous and tired. The idea of working to win back a man who'd walked out on her without a warning was suddenly more than she could fathom.

As she thanked Pastor Mark and walked to her car, she kept hearing his voice reassuring her that God would make it clear what she should do, how she should go about actively fighting for her marriage. She believed he was right. But the more the pastor's words played in her mind, the more she was certain of one thing. In that instant — even though it was wrong — there was only one person she really felt like being with, and it wasn't her husband.

It was a tanned, green-eyed football player who'd stolen her heart the summer she turned twelve.

After Kari left, Pastor Mark was unable to get back into the sermon he was writing. What had happened to the Baxter family? Weren't they the shining example among the congregation? He thought about Elizabeth and John, their early years, the way they'd seemed to have such a strong relationship with their children.

So why did everything seem to be coming apart now?

He and John Baxter had been meeting once a week for most of the past decade, encouraging each other in their faith, sharing each other's burdens. John was on the church board, and it had been a relief for Mark to know he could unload some of his own trials to someone as trustworthy as John Baxter.

As a result, Mark knew more about the Baxters' tragedies and triumphs than anyone else.

There was Brooke, who with her husband had clearly chosen the pathways of medical science and professional achievement over the truths of the faith.

Ashley's situation was possibly worse. Not only had she walked away from God, but she also harbored a secret, something she refused to discuss though it isolated her from everyone who might have mattered in her life — everyone including Landon Blake, the young fireman who had pursued her since they were both teenagers.

And lately he'd noticed trouble brewing with Luke. Something in his critical comments and sharp tones, tones that had been kind and gentle the year before. John hadn't mentioned it, but Mark was concerned all the same.

Worries about Elizabeth's health were ongoing, of course. And now, on top of it all, came Kari's difficulties. Pastor Mark's heart broke for her — both for her pain and for her temptation.

Pastor Mark thought about the Baxters' struggles for a moment and knew there was only one possible reason for them. It was spiritual warfare, pure and simple. Something great and amazing must be standing on the other side of these dark times; otherwise, the enemy wouldn't work so hard to discourage this family.

Yes, that must be it.

Surely good times were right around the corner.

Pastor Mark allowed himself to imagine Brooke and Peter remembering that true knowledge and success come from God alone. Ashley confiding in her family, telling the truth about her past, finding healing and maybe even love. Tim Jacobs changing his ways, falling to his knees, and begging Kari's forgiveness. Elizabeth living to a joyful old age.

It was possible that none of this would turn out the way he hoped — the way he prayed. But even then, Pastor Mark was certain God would faithfully see the Baxter family through their difficulties.

He thanked the Lord for that even as he wondered how much worse life could get for the Baxters before they arrived on the other side.

Mark leaned back in his chair and gazed out his office window. He thought about Kari and Brooke and Ashley and John and Elizabeth.

A lot worse, he guessed. A whole lot worse.

He would pray for them daily, as he'd been doing for some time now, ever since he and John had begun meeting together. But there had to be something else, something tangible he could do to help.

His fingers found their way to the computer mouse, and he clicked open a file of church member profiles. He hesitated a long time before making the next move. If Kari had been any other member, he wouldn't have considered breaking a confidence and making the call.

But this time . . . maybe it was what was needed.

Mark scanned the alphabetical list until he found the work number for Tim Jacobs.

Okay, Lord, use this phone call. Please . . .

And with that he began to dial.

Chapter Fifteen

Kari was dusting her parents' piano when Luke walked in, tossed his gym bag on the bench in the foyer, and flopped onto a chair a few feet away, his basketball still under his arm. He was playing on an intramural team at Indiana University that semester, and his games were on Saturday mornings.

"Hi." She kept dusting, but she could see him staring at her. He looked frustrated, as if he wanted to say something but couldn't quite find the words.

Finally he cleared his throat. "I owe you an apology."

The dust rag froze in Kari's hand, and she looked over her shoulder at her brother. "What for?"

"Because —" he pinched his lips together — "because I'm sorry you married the jerk." Luke's eyes twinkled, and he tossed his ball at her.

In a single fluid motion she dropped the dust rag and caught the ball. Kari could feel the patience draining from her expression. "Am I supposed to laugh?"

Luke turned and gazed out the front window, his eyes narrowed. "I just hate what he's doing to you."

She was still holding the ball where she'd caught it, inches from the piano, as she studied her brother. She clutched the ball to her midsection. Everyone had handled news of her pregnancy fairly well — except Luke. He had seemed even more distant than before, and Kari had not known how to bridge the gap between them.

But now, here was her baby brother, all grown up with a mop of blond hair and a lanky frame larger than their dad's, trying to find the words to connect with her again. It was the first effort he'd made since she'd been home.

A tear slid down her cheek, and she wiped it with her free hand, waiting for Luke to finish saying what was on his heart.

After a while, he shook his head and turned his gaze back to hers. "I haven't been —" He dug his fingers into his hair and released a frustrated burst of air. "I'm sorry, Kari. The last thing you need is two jerks."

Kari tossed the ball back to Luke, and he caught it deftly in one hand, drawing it securely against his body. She leaned against the piano and gave him a crooked smile. "Two jerks . . . hmmm, let's see. My husband, Tim, and . . ." She was teasing him, speaking the language he knew best.

He grinned, and the lines on his face eased. "Me, goofy. Ever since Tim left, I've treated you like —" he waved his hand in the air — "like you have some kind of disease."

She angled her head, seeing him as the towheaded little kid he'd been when she was in high school. Her heart swelled with understanding. "Thanks."

A sigh slipped through Luke's clenched teeth, and he looked like he was about to cry. "He makes me so mad, Kari. I respect what you're doing and all, but part of me wishes you'd dump him and get on with your life. You deserve better."

Kari crossed the room and sat in the chair next to him, their knees nearly touching. "I know. I feel like that some-times too." She willed him to see her point of view. "But I really believe he's going through a stage, a bad time or a midlife crisis or something, and somehow we can get through it."

Luke studied her, and Kari saw that the hard edge was gone, even if he still struggled with her decision. "*You* believe it . . . or you believe that's what God wants you to say?"

The air leaked from Kari's lungs as she sat back in the chair, her eyes still fixed on his. "I can't separate the two. What God wants is what I want. Without him in our marriage we have nothing, anyway."

He nodded. "That's what I thought you'd say."

"You understand, right?"

"Not really." His eyes searched hers. "But these past few days, God's been on me every minute."

Kari smiled. "He has a way of doing that."

"He wasn't letting me off the hook until we talked."

Kari looked out the window. Though it was fall, temperatures hovered near the eighty-degree mark that afternoon, and after a week of cool weather Kari was glad for the change. She'd spent the past four nights at her own house and actually appreciated the solitude; it gave her time to follow Pastor Mark's suggestions. Since Tuesday she'd read a book about restoring broken relationships and written four letters to Tim, each of which she put in an envelope and placed on their dining-room table.

If Tim came home and she was gone, there was no way he could miss them.

She'd made some phone calls too. But since that first one, there'd been no answer at Angela Manning's apartment. Kari figured the woman had caller ID. She doubted they'd answer again unless she called from a pay phone or a friend's house — some number Angela and Tim wouldn't recognize.

Kari shifted her gaze back to Luke. Their parents were gone for the day, and Kari had decided to stay in the guest room for the weekend. Solitude was one thing, but after four days the loneliness, mingled with her fading morning sickness, had left her practically desperate for the comfort and welcome of the old Baxter house — especially in light of Tim's silence toward her.

Her throat was thick as she tried to explain herself to her brother: "When I take my marriage to God, the answer is always the same." Kari glanced out the window again at the red and yellow leaves sifting down from the trees in their yard. "Somewhere around the corner, I believe God has something very good planned for me. But I also believe he wants me to honor the commitment I made to Tim, at least for now. Even if Tim isn't doing the same. Does that make any sense?"

"I guess." Luke's eyes still held a layer of bewilderment, as if the concept of standing by someone like Tim was as foreign as living on the moon. But he was listening, and that much made her feel better.

"Anyway . . . I'm glad we talked." She leaned forward and jabbed her finger at his side, the place where he'd been the most ticklish since he was a boy. "At least I know my little brother still loves me."

A blush spread across Luke's cheeks, and he tossed the ball to her once more. "Want to play? Out front . . . like old times?"

Kari laughed. "Maybe that's what I need."

"Get changed." He was out the door apparently without another thought to the depth of the conversation they had just had.

She watched him go and remembered months when the two of them played basketball out front nearly every day, times when Brooke was away at college and Ashley was learning to play guitar and Erin was giggling with her friends. Back when Ryan was off at Oklahoma University and Kari was looking for ways to pass the time until his next visit.

She ran upstairs and put on a pair of shorts and a T-shirt. She was losing a heated game of H-O-R-S-E when Luke hit a long-range shot, turned, and faced her straight on. "So what's the deal with Ryan Taylor?"

Kari grabbed the ball and dribbled between her legs. "That's the nice thing about big families." She was out of breath but invigorated by the fresh air and exercise. "No secrets."

Luke used the toe of his shoe to point to the spot where he'd made the bucket, and Kari tried but tossed up an air ball. "H-O-R-S." Luke grinned at her. "Erin told me." The ball settled a few feet away from the basket. Luke jogged over, scooped it up, and did an underhand layup.

"The deal is nothing. Nothing at all." Kari took a bounce pass from her brother and made a similar shot. "Take that!"

Luke grabbed the ball and held it, turning his attention completely on Kari. "Are you sure?"

At that moment a truck pulled into their driveway and parked fifteen feet from the basketball court. Kari knew the driver's profile as well as she knew her own. Her heart flip-flopped inside her.

It was Ryan Taylor.

She watched Luke's eyes narrow as he studied the man behind the wheel. He passed the ball to Kari. "Nothing, huh?"

Ryan climbed out of the truck and caught her eye as he came toward them. *Lord, what's he doing here . . . and why does he still move me after all these years?*

She heard no holy response, just the thump of her heart beating twice as fast as before.

Ryan had nearly reached them when he pointed down the road. "Sign back there says there's a H-O-R-S-E tournament today." He held out both hands, and Kari passed him the ball, feeling herself relax in his presence, as if no time had passed since those companionable summers long ago. "This must be the place."

Luke grinned, and Kari saw on his face how much her brother admired Ryan. "Kari's got H-O-R-S. I'm still clean. Pick your shot."

Ryan winked at Kari and eyed the basket. "Let's see if we can't dirty up your record a little." He dribbled across the court, searching out the perfect spot.

Kari stood back some and studied him, keenly aware of the impact he had on her emotions, her memories. Whatever his real reason for coming by this afternoon, he was keeping things light and at a surface level. If she hadn't known him so well, she would have thought there was nothing more to his visit than the chance to shoot a few baskets with some old friends.

A particular memory flitted across her mind, something her friend Mandy had said the year they graduated from high school. Mandy had been over at Kari's house that day, and Ryan had stopped by on his way back to college after a long weekend at home. The two had spent a half hour outside talking while Mandy stayed in chatting with Brooke. When Kari came back inside, Mandy clucked her tongue against the roof of her mouth and leveled a knowing look at Kari. "You and Ryan need each other the way most people need air."

Brooke had nodded her agreement. "I'll say this for you, Kari. What you and Ryan have isn't something that goes away with time. If you don't marry him, you'll spend a lifetime wishing you had."

The memory faded as Ryan launched a long-distance shot that slid down the center of the hoop without even slightly disturbing the net. He pointed at Luke, his eyes dancing. "Can't touch the rim."

The contest went on for half an hour before Luke finally emerged the winner. "You guys take round two." He tossed the ball to Ryan. "I've got a poli-sci test to cram for."

Ryan bounced it back to Luke. "That's okay. Your sister would probably beat me, anyway." Luke laughed and took the ball inside, leaving them there alone. Ryan shoved his hands deep into his jeans pockets and gazed at Kari. "Want to take a walk?"

Be careful.

There it was. This time Kari was sure the silent voice was God's. *He's just an old friend.* But even as she tried to convince herself, she was riddled with guilt. Ryan had never been *just* a friend. Not when they were teenagers and not now. Brooke was right. What she and Ryan shared wasn't something that went away with time.

She clenched her teeth. Still, why couldn't she spend an afternoon with him? *I've been too lonely. I deserve this much.* The uneasy feeling faded. Kari smiled shyly at Ryan. "That'd be nice."

There was a dirt road that ran parallel to the main highway behind her family's property. It separated the privately owned acreage on one side from a meandering creek and state park property on the other. Since the highway was so busy, kids had always used the road for bike riding and as access to the neighbors' houses. Kari and Ryan had walked its three miles dozens of times before.

They set out south through the Baxters' backyard and didn't speak until they were headed east along the dirt road. In every direction the landscape was dressed in vibrant hues, set off by a brilliant blue sky. The smell of distant burning leaves hung on the gentle breeze.

"You left the prayer room in a hurry the other day." Ryan kept his eyes straight ahead as if he were taking in the serenity of the dirt road, the pristine beauty of the swiftly flowing creek to their right.

For just a moment Kari wanted to pretend she was single again, that she and Ryan still had a million options and a lifetime ahead of them, that she hadn't given up on him that day at the hospital, hadn't turned her love over to Tim Jacobs.

Hadn't married a man destined to do unspeakable things to her heart.

But there was no going back now, no way of undoing the past. Kari stretched her hands over her head, inhaled a full breath of clean Indiana air, and shrugged. "I had a lot on my mind."

They walked a ways farther, and their pace slowed. Ryan nodded toward a place just ahead where an oversized fallen log lay along the creek bank, half hidden by overgrown brush. It was a familiar place, one where Kari and Ryan had often wound up when they needed privacy.

"Let's sit." He led the way toward the spot.

The sun was low in the sky, the temperature falling fast, but Kari nodded and followed him. When they were both seated he searched for a rock and skipped it expertly across the water. "I already knew about Tim. Before the prayer room."

Kari frowned. "Who told you?"

"Ashley." He looked at her, and whatever casual pretense he'd demonstrated for her brother back at the house was gone.

Looking at him now was like looking straight into his soul — and what she saw there made her wonder if she'd been wrong about him, if maybe he hadn't stopped loving her all those years ago. Whatever his feelings, his eyes told her this much: His concern for her had not dimmed with time. She tried to focus on what he'd said. "Ashley told you?"

"She called me a couple of weeks ago and filled me in. The short version, anyway."

Ashley had called Ryan? Kari's mind raced, trying to make sense of the idea. "What made her do that?"

Ryan picked up another smooth stone. "It was my fault." He skipped the rock and looked back at her. "I ran into her a few weeks ago at football practice. We were joking around, and I told her to give me a call if your husband ever left you high and dry."

Kari nodded and pursed her lips as her eyes followed a pair of squirrels playing on the grassy shore across the creek. "I see."

"So in a way she kind of owed me the call."

Her eyes met his again. "You didn't act like you knew."

"Yeah, well —" his gaze stayed locked on hers — "I had a lot on my mind."

"That's what you said." They were sitting several feet apart, but still Kari felt trapped in his gravitational pull, the same way she'd always felt around him.

He uttered a sad laugh. "The other day I didn't say half of what I wanted to." He found her eyes again and waited a long while. "Don't you get it, Kari?" He sifted through the rocks near his feet until he found the right-sized stone and sent it skittering over the water. "The reason I needed to focus was because ever since I heard about you and Tim —" he shifted his gaze to hers — "ever since I heard what your husband had done to you, I couldn't think about anything else."

"Other than . . . ?" Her heart was pounding again, and if the holy warnings coursing through her mind had been audible, neither of them would have been able to hear above the noise.

"Ah, Kari girl." His voice grew soft, and Kari saw an overwhelming sorrow in his face. "Other than you."

The world began spinning out of control. It was one thing to guess at Ryan's feelings, but now, here in the seclusion of their special place, a place where they'd kissed and talked and made plans of forever, it was almost more than she could bear. She tore her eyes from him and stared at her feet. "I . . . I don't know what to say."

Ryan slid over and took her hand tenderly in his own. "Don't say anything." He moved still closer, so that the sides of their arms were touching.

Lord, get me out of this.

My grace is sufficient for you.

Why was that verse playing across her heart so often? *Grace? I need more than that, Father. I can't think with him so close, my hand in his.*

There was nothing in response, and she closed her eyes, trying to get a grip on her emotions.

Ryan exhaled hard. "I know how you feel, what you want. I'm not trying to come between you and Tim." He ran his thumb over the top of her hand. "I just want you to know how I feel. How I've always felt about you."

Anger made its way up through the sea of desire within her. How dare he say he'd always had feelings for her? What about Dallas? What about that night at the hospital? Everything in her wanted to challenge him on his comment, make him go back with her to his accident and all the awful details of that terrible day.

She opened her mouth to speak, but then she closed it again. Going over the past now would prove nothing. It would do nothing but bring more pain. Still, she was grateful for the anger, which helped her back off and remember what was important. She wriggled her hand free from his and crossed her arms. "How are you these days anyway, Ryan?" She forced a smile and saw that he read her eyes perfectly. There would be no more talking about how he felt about her, how they felt about each other, or anything that might remotely be linked to what they'd once shared.

She needed to win her husband back, not start an affair.

He cocked his head. "Okay . . . I'm sorry for bringing it up. I've never kept anything from you, and I thought —"

Kari held up her hand and shook her head. "Don't, Ryan." Tears filled her eyes. It wasn't her fault things hadn't worked between them. "I have to get back."

It was dusk now, and she was starting to shiver. Her entire body ached for Ryan to slip his arm around her, pull her close, and ward off the cold of the impending darkness, of her impending future. Instead, she stood and wrapped her arms more tightly around herself. Two tears made their way down her cheeks as she stared down at Ryan. "I can't explain it, but I want my marriage to work."

Ryan clenched his jaw, opened his mouth, and said nothing. He stood and gently pulled Kari into a hug, one that could have been taken only as an embrace between two old friends who'd found each other again. "I'm sorry. The last thing I wanted was to upset you."

The longer Kari stayed in his arms, the less platonic the hug felt. Finally she knew she had to pull away or face doing something she would regret for a lifetime. "We need to go."

Ryan didn't argue, and she knew it was because he was feeling the same way. They walked back to Kari's house while he entertained her with stories of his last season with Dallas. "So there he was, wrong-way Leonard, carrying the ball for all he was worth, headed straight for the opponent's end zone, and I'm seeing that no one, not a man on our team, is going to catch him and turn him around the right way."

He ran ahead of her a few steps to illustrate the story. "I took off as fast as I could, and finally at about the ten-yard line he saw me and froze, dead in his tracks. They replayed the thing a dozen times on ESPN." Ryan waited for her to catch up and then fell in step beside her again. "At that point the team gang-tackled him."

Kari laughed at the image of Ryan's poor teammate, and Ryan elbowed her in the ribs. "I can't believe it." He walked backward a few steps, studying her face. "I actually made you smile."

She thought about what her life had become — Tim's affair, the pregnancy, the way Tim hadn't called except to say he wanted a divorce, the way she could not even consider letting herself have feelings for Ryan Taylor again, no matter how she felt.

It *had* been a while since she'd laughed.

Now she felt her cheeks grow hot under his gaze, and she pushed him teasingly in the chest. "Stop staring at me."

He fell beside her once more and spent the last ten minutes of the walk recalling stories and funny incidents from their past. By the time they were back at the Baxter front drive, Kari felt like she'd been given a new lease on life. She tilted her head as they walked up onto the porch, and she smiled at him. "It was good to see you again."

The silliness in his expression faded, and his eyes seemed to bore into hers. "For me too." He hesitated. "Kari, I —"

She held up her hand. "Don't." They'd found their friendship again on the walk back, found a tenuous way to laugh and tease and enjoy each other's company without treading on the dangerous ground of attraction. She couldn't bear to hear him say again that he had feelings for her, especially now, when except for her faith and convictions, she would gladly have run off with him and never looked back at Tim Jacobs and the life he'd left her with. "I'm married, Ryan. I'm planning on staying that way. Please . . . be my friend. Nothing more."

His eyes grew wet, and she thought how rarely she'd seen him this emotional. It triggered something deep inside her, and her eyes, too, felt the familiar sting. "I respect your feelings, Kari. I may not understand them, but I respect them." He held out his arms and hugged her quickly this time. "I'm here for you. Whenever you need me."

She thought about telling him she was pregnant, but something told her to hold back, as if sharing something so intimate might cross a line she didn't want to cross. Instead, she blinked back her tears and smiled at him. "Thanks."

Then before he could say anything else, before she might toss her convictions to the wind and kiss him the way she was dying to do, she turned and disappeared into the house. She listened as he trudged down the porch steps, across the driveway, and into his truck. As he pulled away, she stole up to the guest room and shut the door, questioning whether she was losing her mind.

Time was when she would have given anything to have Ryan Taylor standing on her doorstep declaring his feelings for her. But now, when she desperately needed him and just as desperately needed to avoid him, she had turned him away.

The tears came in earnest, and she knew there was only one way out of the despair that gripped her soul. She slid off the side of the bed and landed on her knees. With head bowed, body convulsing in sobs, she buried her face in the bedspread and cried out to the only One who could make sense of her life.

I need a miracle, Lord. . . . I'm at the end of my rope.

My grace is sufficient for you.

The Scripture passage came to mind again, and this time she remembered the rest of the verse.

For my power is made perfect in weakness.

Her weeping subsided. God was here; he saw how weak she was. And he knew what she needed — not just one miracle, but a couple of them.

First, that Tim would stop his wayward lifestyle and return to her. And second, if he did return, that she could somehow learn to enjoy loving him once more.

Even after knowing how good it felt to be in Ryan Taylor's arms again.

Chapter Sixteen

Angela was busy with a study group for her modern history class that Saturday night, and Tim decided to go back and get a few things from his house. He'd called, but Kari didn't answer, and he figured she was either working or at her parents' house.

Actually, he rather hoped she'd show up while he was there. That way he could look her in the face and find out what she'd meant by the baby comment. He'd gone over the dates a hundred times since then and couldn't imagine how she might just have found out she was pregnant. The last time they'd been together was back in August, back when he was doing everything he could to get Angela out of his mind and make things work with Kari.

If she'd gotten pregnant then, she'd already be three months along. Wouldn't she have found out sooner? Tim was almost positive she would have. They had those tests, didn't they?

He thought about the possibility as he drove the few blocks to University Park, the upscale area of older, restored homes where they'd planned on spending forever. What if she really was pregnant? How many times in their early years had he longed for a child, imagining the wonderful life Kari and he would have once their home was filled with little ones?

The thought of Kari's raising their child alone made him feel sick to his stomach. There would be no pleasure sharing an apartment with Angela if Kari was forced to live the single-mother life ten minutes away.

He pulled into the driveway and entered through the kitchen door. The answering machine held only one message.

Tim hit the Play button.

"Hi, Tim. It's me, Pastor Mark, over at Clear Creek Community Church. I talked to Kari today and left a message for you at work. Not sure if you'll get this, but if you do, I'd appreciate a call when you get in. If it's too late, I'll be at the office first thing in the morning." The pastor rattled off a few phone numbers and hung up.

Tim felt his face grow hot. Why had Kari gone to see *him?* And what was he doing calling Tim at home? Tim cursed under his breath. Preachers were all alike — a bunch of do-gooders trying to save the world. Well, he for one did not want saving. He had tried that route and failed miserably. There was nothing left now but for him to build a life with Angela and try to make his own happiness.

As long as Kari wasn't pregnant, that is.

He moved into the dining room and came to an abrupt stop. There on the table were four envelopes. Each one had his name scrawled across the front with a date from the previous week.

What was this?

Tim could hear his heart beating. He picked up the envelope with the earliest date and opened it. *I could use a drink.* The thought filtered through his mind, and he silently chastised himself. After overdoing it that night at Angela's, the night that preacher was on television, Tim had decided not to drink during the day. As long as he could keep to that promise, he was pretty sure he'd never have a problem. At least not one like Uncle Frank's.

Tim found a letter inside the envelope. He took it out, unfolded it, and saw that it was a handwritten letter from Kari. He sighed, and his eyes found their way to a portrait that hung on their dining-room wall, a portrait of Kari in her wedding dress.

His breath caught in his throat as he studied her face, her smile. Her trusting eyes. No matter what plans he had for the future, there was no denying her beauty. He studied the picture, and he could hear her laughter, feel her touch on his skin.

He tore his eyes from the portrait and made his way across the living room to an oversized chair. Then he held up the letter and began to read, a lump lodging in his throat.

Dear Tim,

The one thing I would tell you if you were here right now is this: I love you.

Even after all that's happened, even though you've moved in with her, I still love you. Isn't that crazy? Because the thing is, I know the real Tim Jacobs. The man I married loves God and wouldn't in a million years think of doing this to me, to us. So whatever's happening now is something we need to get past.

The letter went on to recall in detail some of Kari's favorite moments since they were married. As he read, he was swept away, drawn back to the days when he would never have considered having an affair, let alone moving in with another woman.

He kept reading, but when he reached the last few paragraphs, his heart skipped a beat.

By the way, I meant what I said the other night. I'm three months pregnant, Tim. And when I'm so mad at you I could break something, when I'm all alone crying myself to sleep, when I hate you for what you've done, I have only to remember the precious life growing within me to know the truth.

I will wait a lifetime for you to return, believing that someday you'll remember who you are and what we shared and find your way back to me. To us.

Loving you still,
Kari

The moisture flooding Tim's eyes made it impossible for him to see. He blinked and felt a trail of tears burn a path down his cheeks. Over and over again he read the last part of the letter, unable to fathom the emotions that coursed through him. A part of him ached for what he'd already missed — being with Kari when she found out about the baby, helping her through the morning sickness. Just like last time.

Only now, if she was already three months along, the danger of miscarriage was largely past. And that meant . . .

He let his head fall back and uttered an audible groan. He really was going to be a father. At a time when he'd fallen in love with another woman, he was finally going to father his wife's child. The thought was more than he could bear and made him desperate for a glass of wine or a shot of whiskey. Anything to dull the pain.

He stifled a sob. Suddenly he missed Kari more than he would have thought possible a few days before. He wanted nothing more than to take her in his arms and beg her forgiveness. If only there were some way to go back in time, back to the days before he'd met Angela.

As if scales were falling from his eyes, he began to see himself as he really was. What kind of a creep had he become? No matter how busy or inattentive Kari had been, that didn't justify his taking up with Angela.

He closed his eyes and wondered what to do next. He could call Pastor Mark. Or he could call Kari, drive to her parents' house, and tell her he was sorry.

But there was one problem.

The feelings he had for Angela Manning were as strong as ever. She was young and vulnerable, despite the veneer of cool toughness she displayed around campus. Over the course of the past year she had bared her heart to him, and his love for her was not a passing fancy. It was real — as real as his feelings for Kari had ever been.

He closed his eyes and saw himself dancing with Kari at their wedding reception. She was beautiful beyond words. A wave of desire washed over him, and he was disgusted with himself.

He wasn't a player, not like some men. But somehow he had managed to end up in love with two women. One in a familiar way that tugged at his heart, the other in a new and exciting way that made him feel needed and important.

The image of Kari at their wedding remained. Her hair had been up in some kind of amazing design that day, and just a few pieces hung in soft wisps near her face. Her expression was fresh, hopeful, impossibly tender.

And what about him? He'd been happy and full of life that day, ready to take on the future. How had everything gotten so bad? How had they gone from the couple in his memory to the people they were today?

Even now, he was sure he'd never loved anyone like he'd loved Kari Baxter back then. Hadn't he meant it when he promised her forever? For that matter, hadn't he also promised God forever? He massaged his temples. What in the world had happened to him since then? Had he betrayed his faith as surely as he had betrayed his wife?

He hadn't always been serious about God — not as a child or a teenager. When he was growing up as a missionary kid, believing had been little more than a well-practiced routine. But all that changed not long after he entered college.

He remembered a long-distance conversation he had had with his father midway through his freshman year. Tim had told him he was on the leadership team of Christians in Action, and his father had nearly wept at the news.

"I'm so proud of you, son." The overseas connection wasn't clear, and his father's voice broke up every few words. "Your mother and I have been praying for you, believing you'd come to really know Jesus one of these days. And now it's happened."

The change, Tim knew, could be traced back to a retreat they'd had at a lakeside Christian camp. The speaker had been talking about the end of the world as if it might happen tomorrow, and suddenly Tim's heart had begun beating erratically, pounding out a strange rhythm inside his chest, threatening to break free from his body.

In those days, prayer was not something Tim typically took part in, unless it was praying out loud for a group. He did not normally carry on silent conversations with the Lord — not until that day at the retreat. But then, with his heart beating wildly, threatening to take his life then and there in the assembly hall, he gulped and uttered the most sincere silent prayer he'd ever said.

Lord, what is it? What's happening to me?

And he heard an answer deep in his heart:

Hear my Word, and obey it.

It was as if God were speaking the words to him directly. So clear was the message that it might have been relayed over the loudspeaker for everyone at camp to hear.

Tim remembered paying close attention to the speaker after that. When the man mentioned Christ's return and how his followers would be taken to heaven, Tim no longer found himself rolling his eyes and wishing for the dinner break. Instead, he listened like a man whose minutes were numbered.

"You think you're young and invincible and that life lies stretched out for decades in front of you? Let me tell you what the Bible says about that: 'What is your life?' " The speaker's voice boomed, quoting from the book of James. " 'You are a mist that appears for a little while and then vanishes.' "

Tim remembered the impact those words had on him as he sat on the floor shoulder to shoulder with hundreds of other college kids. For the first time in his life, Tim felt like the words applied directly to him.

He listened as the speaker continued. "You can play around with God today, but one day . . . one day that kind of hypocrisy will catch up to you. The truth is clearly spelled out in Scripture. . . ." His voice was softer now, more compassionate. As he spoke, he made eye contact with a number of the students until finally his eyes rested on Tim. "One day every knee will bow, every tongue will confess that Jesus Christ is Lord." He paused, his eyes still linked with Tim's. "And on that day, if you've been playing with God, if your name isn't written in the Lamb's Book of Life, there remains only one eternal place for you. A place of torment and fire and everlasting desolation."

Tim's chest pounded even harder, and right there, surrounded by the crowd of guys who looked up to him and girls who found him funny and attractive, Tim Jacobs bowed his head and talked to the Lord again.

I'm sorry, Father. I know he's talking about me. I've only played with you and not believed your truth until now. Forgive me, Lord. I believe you now. I want my name in the Lamb's Book of Life from this minute on.

With that, his heart skidded into a normal rhythm, and he felt washed with the freshness of supernatural peace. In the weeks and months and years that followed, Tim tried hard to do exactly what the Lord asked of him. He took God at his word and studied the Bible. He went up the aisle at a church he'd attended sporadically and publicly rededicated his life to Christ. Every day he learned something new and life-changing about God and his truth.

He had even toyed briefly with going into the ministry, but he had quickly found his passion was for journalism. He finished his degree, then moved from one newspaper job to another while he took graduate courses. And somehow in the process he had managed to hold on to his convictions — not an easy thing to do as a journalist.

Those days were wonderful, filled with new experiences and a love for reporting that seemed to grow from deep within him. It led him to his ultimate goal — teaching journalism at the university level.

And eventually it led him to Kari.

But all that seemed so distant now. How had his love affair with God and the things of heaven cooled into an obligation, then an embarrassment? Tim knew the answer. It had happened gradually, as he pushed for professional success and struggled to fit in with his colleagues.

And when had his devotion to Kari become routine, boring even?

The answer to that one was more specific. It had happened the day Angela Manning walked into his classroom.

Whereas Kari expressed little interest in the columns he wrote or the manner in which he taught, Angela had been practically starstruck. She had made him feel worthwhile and wonderful, and it had been only a matter of time before he found himself tempted by her attentions.

Now, back in the home that he and Kari had shared and thinking about the baby on the way, he found his heart racing much as it had that day at the college retreat, back when he'd really heard God for the first time. Suddenly everything he was about to lose lay out in his mind like a smorgasbord of goodness.

His baby's first smile, first steps, first birthday. The satisfaction of seeing his family grow together, and the inner joy of knowing he was with the woman to whom he'd promised a lifetime of love. The peace of a life free of guilt and condemnation.

A renewed faith in God.

All of it hung in the balance. If he didn't stop now, if he didn't heed the feeling deep in his soul to turn and walk away from the life he'd chosen, he wouldn't have another chance. He knew this as surely as he knew how hard it would be to tell Angela good-bye.

Tim's arms and legs trembled as he pulled himself out of the chair. There was no question about what he had to do, and he was certain it would be as difficult as walking on the ceiling.

He had to find a way to break it off with Angela. And he had to do it soon, before he became so entangled with her that he no longer cared about the good things set before him or the future he might share with Kari and the baby.

He could do only one thing. He knew only one way out of the hell he'd created.

On unsteady feet he plodded toward the kitchen, played the message one more time, and wrote down the phone numbers.

Then he did what he should have done weeks ago. A year ago.

He dialed as fast as his fingers could move, and then he waited for Pastor Mark to answer.

Chapter Seventeen

Fishing with Ryan Taylor might not have been the wisest choice she could make, but Kari was going anyway. Tim wasn't taking her calls, and she was weary of waiting and wondering and trying to be faithful without the least indication that anything would change. She was tired of defending Tim to others, tired of defending her own decisions to friends and family.

So when she saw Ryan this morning in church and he suggested an afternoon on the lake, she had thought, *Why not?* He seemed to respect the boundaries she'd set the last time they were together.

Besides, she could use some fresh air and good company.

Kari was peering out the window looking for Ryan's truck when she heard the phone. Her parents were upstairs in her dad's home office, and when they didn't answer, Kari rushed and picked it up on the third ring. She smiled. Her nausea was almost completely gone. In fact, she felt better than she had in weeks.

"Hello?"

"Kari? It's Pastor Mark. How are you?"

Kari's stomach slipped to her ankles, and her mind raced. "Fine, thanks." Had the pastor known she was about to go out with Ryan? She leaned against the kitchen counter and kept her focus on the driveway. He would be here any minute. "Sorry I didn't meet up with you at church."

"Yes, I saw you with Ryan Taylor." The pastor hesitated. "How's he doing?"

Pastor Mark didn't have to ask whether Kari was sticking to her promise, keeping her distance from Ryan as much as possible. His tone said it all.

"Fine." Kari cleared her throat. "He knows where I stand."

"I'm glad. Listen, I have some news for you." There was another pause. "Tim called last night. He found your letters and read them. If he didn't take you seriously about the baby when you told him, he's taking you seriously now."

"What?" Kari's heart skipped a beat. "Why didn't he call *me?*"

"He knew you were at your parents' house. He wasn't sure it would be appropriate."

She drew in a sharp breath. "What does he want?"

"He wants to meet with us next week. It

sounds like the answer we've been praying for."

Kari tried to feel something. This was the moment she was waiting for, wasn't it? She should be thrilled. Happy tears should be streaming down her face, and she should be thanking God for even this slightest sign that Tim was sorry, that he wanted to work things out.

Instead, she felt flat, as if the wind had been sucked from her. "Did he say anything else?"

"Yes." The pastor's tone was kind, warm, as if he understood her confusion, her mixed feelings. "He said he'd made a mess of things and he was sorry."

Anger tore at the frayed edges of Kari's heart. "What does he want me to do, run home and pretend everything's okay?" There was silence at the other end. She exhaled slowly. "I'm sorry. That was uncalled for."

"You have a right to be upset, Kari. In fact, you *have* to have those feelings. But the bottom line is this: You want your marriage to work, right?"

Kari blinked back thoughts of her anticipated afternoon with Ryan and held her breath, struggling to get her feelings back in line. "Right."

"Okay. Last night your husband said he's willing to try."

A glint of silver flashed at the edge of the driveway, and Ryan's truck appeared. Kari's face grew hot. "Okay, thanks. Look, I need to go." She didn't want to hear about Tim now. Not with Ryan waiting outside.

A pang of guilt poked at her. The pastor would never approve of her fishing with her old boyfriend, not after Tim's phone call. But she was feeling defiant, not contrite. After all Tim had put her through, she had a right to a little fun. "I'm sorry. I'll call you soon."

Pastor Mark barely had a chance to say good-bye before Kari hung up the phone. She opened her eyes wider, turned around, and found herself face-to-face with her father.

"Who was that?" He wasn't angry or accusatory, but his voice told her that he knew something wasn't right.

"Pastor Mark." She sidestepped her father and swung her bag over her shoulder. "Tim called. He wants to meet this week."

Her father smiled broadly. "Hey, that's great. You've been praying he'd come around. Maybe this is the answer."

Kari shrugged, suddenly nervous.

"Maybe." She glanced outside, then back at her father. "Ryan's here."

Her father kept his eyes fixed on hers and raised a single eyebrow so subtly that Kari was certain no one else would have caught it.

"What?" She shrugged and let her bag fall to the floor. "What's the look for?"

"You're a big girl, Kari. You can do what you want." Her father's expression softened. "But do you really think going out with Ryan Taylor is a good idea?"

Kari dug her fists into her waist. "Yes, as a matter of fact, I do. I've been sick and alone and desperate to understand why I wasn't enough for my husband, why he wouldn't even take my calls. I've had my heart broken, and truthfully, I don't know how I'm ever going to love him again." She let her arms fall to her sides as the fight left her. "So right now, yes, I think it's a good idea to go out with Ryan Taylor. In fact, I can't think of anything I'd rather do."

A knock sounded at the door, and her father gave her a smile that said he thought she was wrong but he would let her find out for herself. Kari knew he meant it as a reassurance of his love. But it made her feel sixteen again and anxious to leave.

"Okay." Her father took hold of her

shoulders. He looked at her for a long moment, then pulled her close. "I love you, Kari. No matter what you do. I'm proud of you for staying strong and trying so hard to do what God wants." He smiled. "You'll do the right thing. I know it."

Kari sighed. "Thanks. I'll see you later."

And with that she grabbed her bag and lightly ran out the door to where Ryan was waiting for her. Just as he'd waited for her all those years ago.

Elizabeth Baxter sat on the edge of her bed, her back ramrod straight, and looked out the window as Kari and Ryan climbed into his truck.

John slipped on a sweatshirt and eased himself beside her, following her gaze. "Worried?"

"Of course." She turned and studied her husband's face, amazed at the serenity she saw there. "Everything's falling apart, John. How can you be so calm?"

He gave her a practiced smile, the one that always had a way of working a degree of peace and warmth into her heart. "Because Kari and Ryan are spending a day together? Everything's falling apart?"

She sighed and turned her attention back toward the window and the pickup truck that was pulling away. "Kari's three months pregnant, and I heard your conversation. Tim wants to talk to her." She felt the sting of tears. "She says she wants her marriage healed. So why is she spending a day at the lake with Ryan Taylor? You know very well she's fooling herself when she insists they're just friends."

John squeezed her knee gently and gave her a half-smile.

Elizabeth crossed her arms and gripped her elbows. "It's not just Kari, you know. What about Ashley . . . even Brooke? She and Peter drift further away from the Lord every day. And why's Maddie always sick?" Elizabeth wiped at an errant tear. "Makes me wonder what's going to happen to Erin and Luke."

John was quiet a moment; then he wove his fingers between hers. "Once, a long time ago, there was a boatload of disciples trying to cross the Sea of Galilee." She relaxed some and felt the hint of a smile tug at the corners of her mouth. The story was John's favorite, and she loved hearing him tell it.

"They had followed their Teacher for months and months, and they trusted him implicitly. In fact, he was in the boat with them one night when a terrible storm came

301

up. The wind and waves were wild, tossing the boat like a child's toy until the disciples cried out for their Teacher's help."

John paused, and Elizabeth could see the men, hear their cries. Almost feel the water on her face.

"Where was Jesus? Sleeping at the back of the boat. But at their desperate request, he rose and stretched his hand out toward the sea. 'Be still!' he said. And suddenly the wind and waves grew calm again."

Elizabeth leaned on her husband's shoulder. This was one of the reasons why she loved him so, why she'd easily promised him forever and cared for him more with each passing year. He was her lover and friend, and so often when her own ship was sinking, it was John who righted it. Even now, in this season of uncertainty and terrifying possibilities, his trust in God was absolute. That gave her an anchor, a rock to stand on no matter how difficult the situation seemed.

"That same Teacher knows about the storm we're in," he reminded her. "He hasn't abandoned ship, and we can't either."

She smiled through her tears. "I know . . . you're right. It's just . . . sometimes I can't help worrying."

With that, John took both of Elizabeth's

hands in his and bowed his head. He prayed out loud that God would direct the hearts and decisions of their adult children and protect them from making choices they'd regret.

Even choices they might make that very day.

Kari and Ryan arrived at the lake just after one in the afternoon, and Ryan parked in a private lot near the boat dock.

"Is it still true?" Kari grinned at him as they gathered their gear from the back of the truck and made their way toward the boats.

"What?"

"That only snobs moor their boats at the country club?"

It was something their classmates used to say back when they were in high school together. Kari and Ryan were both members back then, enjoying their fathers' privileges and taking part in everything the club offered, from boating to tennis. But though their families had boats at the club, the two of them preferred puttering around the lake in Ryan's beat-up boat, which they could pull behind his pickup truck. The rowboat was more fun — not because they feared being thought of as snobs, but because the rowboat felt simpler, more adventurous.

Now, though, the old boat was gone. Ryan not only moored his boat at the club but also was a full-fledged member, with golf privileges.

They arrived at Ryan's cruiser, and whistled low under her breath. "This is nice, Ryan . . . really."

It could hold eight people easily and had a canopy that could enclose the entire front. "Let's put it up." Ryan worked his way around the other side of the boat and began latching the canopy in place. "Until it gets warmer."

She glanced at the sky. "I doubt it'll get warmer than this."

There was a bite in the air, and the water temperature couldn't have been much above fifty degrees. Most late-fall weekends would never have been warm enough to consider boating. "Do the fish bite in water this cold?"

"What?" He shot her a teasing grin. "Has my former fishing partner forgotten about our secret spots?" He shook his head dramatically. "I'll have to get you reacquainted with the terrain."

She smiled, and her earlier feelings of guilt faded. "You do that, Ryan."

"Okay." He started the engine and

pushed off from the dock. "Hold on."

They set out over slightly choppy water, and for a while they didn't speak. The roar of the motor filled the empty spaces, the unanswered questions between them, and Kari allowed herself the chance to soak in the sight of him. Tall and filled out in all the right places, Ryan was even more handsome now than he'd been the last time they'd shared a day on the lake.

Ryan was taking her to their favorite spot, a quiet cove on the other side of the lake and down several miles. It would be twenty minutes before they got there, so Kari leaned back, enjoying the slap of the waves against the bow, letting her mind simply drift. She could have predicted where her unrestricted thoughts would take her, but she was tired of fighting them. She'd be back at it next week, fighting for her marriage, attending the appointment with Tim and Pastor Mark.

In the meantime, she wanted to relax. So she let her memories carry her where they willed, back to the days when she and Ryan had been in love. Back to a time when they believed they always would be.

The summer Ryan left for college, Kari had been about to enter her junior year in high school. He had been her adolescent crush, her first love, the boy of her dreams. But their one date convinced her he didn't share her feelings, and when he drove away that day she figured their time together had come to an end.

Instead, Ryan had surprised her by staying in touch. In the eighteen months that followed, he wrote letters now and then and made a point of stopping in and saying hello whenever he was home. But he never asked her out, and she was afraid to ask him for details about his life at Oklahoma University — afraid of what she'd find out.

Then, on a bitter cold day in early December of her senior year, her dad phoned from his office. "Kari, I'm so sorry to tell you this."

"Tell me what?" Her breath caught in her throat as she waited for him to continue. Her father rushed on to explain that he'd gotten word from a friend at the hospital. Ryan Taylor's father had suffered a brain embolism that day and had died just after noon.

Kari was crying before she hung up the phone. She spent the rest of the day in her room, remembering the first picnic the two families had shared and so many other outings the families had taken together. Ryan was very close to his dad, and Kari knew he'd be devastated by the news. She waited until the next morning before heading over to his house and knocking on the door.

When it opened, Ryan stood there, cheeks tearstained, eyes bloodshot. "Hi."

She moved into his arms, wrapped her hands up around his back, and held him, telling him over and over how sorry she was. They took a walk around the block and into the next neighborhood, holding hands while Kari let him talk about his father.

Her attention should have been focused on Ryan's grief, but all she could think about was the way her hand felt in his.

The next week was full of heartbreaking moments for Ryan — viewing the body, the funeral service, the gathering of relatives all wanting to wish him their condolences.

Through it all, Kari was at his side.

She remembered one afternoon that week when her mother pulled her aside. "I see what's happening." She kissed Kari on her forehead. "Be careful."

Kari feigned innocence and gave her mother a questioning look. "If you're talking about Ryan and me, you don't have to worry. He just needs someone to talk to, someone who isn't his mother or his family." She shrugged. "I'm only trying to help."

"Really." It wasn't a question, but a statement of doubt, and it frustrated Kari. Was it that obvious that she was falling for him again? And what about Ryan? Did he really want her company only because he was grieving the loss of his father?

Ryan's father had died shortly before the beginning of Ryan's four-week Christmas break. He had arranged to test out of his courses by mail and stay to help his mother and sister until classes started up in January.

But the truth was, he spent less time with them than with Kari. They took long walks and spent hours on his front porch, talking about Ryan's memories of his father, his feelings now that the man was gone. With each passing day, each passing conversation, they grew closer.

Finally on a Friday two weeks after the funeral, they drove to Indianapolis and spent a late afternoon Christmas shopping at one of the city's oversized indoor malls. Kari had wondered if it would be hard for him, but he seemed relieved to escape for a little while the sadness at home. They walked hand in hand — something they had never done in public — through the elegantly decorated stores. Kari noticed every time he slid his fingers along hers. Her heart beat faster with each subtle squeeze or brush of his thumb against her palm.

A barrage of questions hit her as they walked that way. Why was he holding her hand if he didn't want to date her? Had something changed since he'd been home? And what would it matter anyway, since he was going back to school at the end of break? To keep her mind from wandering, she caught Ryan up on the news at the high school. She was telling him how one of the cheerleaders had come to a football game with three hot rollers stuck in the back of her head when Ryan laughed out loud.

It was the first time he'd done so since his father died, and Kari basked in the sound. As the evening wore on, there was no question that something had changed between them. She wondered if either of them would be bold enough to talk about it.

They teased and shared stories and searched for treasures and checked items off their lists. After eating in the food court, they made their way back to his truck in the underground lot. The structure was only dimly lit, and once they climbed into his truck the darkness lay thick around them. Kari waited for Ryan to start the engine, but instead he turned to face her.

"Do you feel it?" The space between them was so dark she could make out only the sparkle in his eyes.

She reminded herself to exhale as she nodded. "For a long time."

He inched closer and took her face gently in his hands. "I love you, Kari. I've always loved you."

Her heart thudded inside her chest. "But . . . what about our date . . . on my six-teenth birthday? I thought . . ."

He held a single finger to her lips. "What good would it have done? You were too young to be dating a college guy. I had no choice but to wait."

No choice but to wait? Kari thought she might explode from the way her heart swelled within her. All this time . . . all this time Ryan had cared about her as more than a friend? He really *had* wanted to date her? It was more than she dared dream, even in the secret places of her heart. Before she could give his feelings further thought, he brought his lips to hers and kissed her in a way that made time stand still.

The moment lasted forever as he kissed her again and again, soothing away any doubts. Certainly whatever issues they hadn't resolved between them would all work out in the long run.

Or at least it seemed that way back then.

Ryan killed the engine, and the memories fled. Kari watched him drop anchor and gather up the fishing equipment, appreciating again how much he'd grown and matured since those days when they'd been inseparable.

If only we'd stayed that way . . .

Kari blinked back the thought. She could let her memories go only so far. Thinking about him like that now, in the present, couldn't possibly help her — not when Tim was finally ready to talk. Or so he said . . .

She shook off the niggling doubts and pointed to the fishing poles. "Which one's mine?"

He handed her a slim fiberglass rod, and they moved out from under the canopy to the back of the boat. "Okay." He opened the box of lures. "Let's see if the fish in Lake Monroe bite when the water's cold."

The air between them was easy, and Kari wasn't surprised. They sat side by side fixing their lines, then casting them out behind the boat.

Minutes passed while they sat in silence, working their reels. Then, without saying a word, Ryan reached out his free hand and quietly worked his fingers between hers. The touch of his skin was electrifying, and she couldn't speak, could barely think. Everything in her knew she should break free, find some excuse to change seats or distract him from making contact again.

But in that moment she was carried back to another place and time, back to the days when sitting together this way was as easy as breathing.

What am I doing, Lord?

The wind chimes of uncertainty played softly in her mind. She closed her eyes, and nothing else mattered — not her convictions or her confusion or her questions. Because then and there, alone on a lake they both loved, hand in hand with Ryan the way they hadn't been for years, Kari was sure that nothing could have made her pull away.

Not even God.

Chapter Eighteen

They tried to pretend the attraction wasn't back, but despite their talk of fish and lake water and proper lures, they couldn't deny the feelings between them. Kari laughed when Ryan reeled in an old sock early in the day, and later she helped him land a king-size bass that nearly broke his line.

The cold temperatures and icy water didn't matter. In Ryan Taylor's presence, Kari felt warmer than she had in weeks.

When they fell silent, the space between them was quietly inviting, as it had always been.

Kari gazed out at the lake and remembered the golden weeks they'd spent together after that first kiss in the underground parking lot. After they finally admitted their feelings for each other there had been no turning back. The two of them were together every moment, and three weeks later Kari's parents made their doubts known. She was seventeen by then, Ryan nineteen. Her parents thought she was too young to be so serious.

"We love each other." Kari shrugged, making eye contact with her parents, pleading with them to understand. "Maybe we always have."

Her mother leaned forward, her voice kind and firm. "We believe you, dear, but that doesn't change the fact that you're just seventeen. You both have so much ahead of you. We don't want you to get hurt."

Kari had crossed the room and hugged them both. Her parents' concern made her feel loved and protected, but it did nothing to change her feelings for Ryan. "I'll be careful. I promise."

With every passing day the connection between them grew. They took walks along the icy lakeshore and went ice-skating at the park. They cuddled in his truck at the drive-in movies and tried to pretend time wasn't running out. The night before Ryan went back to college they made plans to see a movie, but the moment Kari climbed into the truck, they began kissing.

"Lake Monroe?"

Kari pulled away, breathless, and nodded. She needed no words.

They parked in a remote spot overlooking the lake and talked about what would happen next.

"I don't want to go back. Not now, not

ever." Ryan took her hands in his and looked deep into her eyes. "Football used to mean the world to me, Kari, and now it's just a silly game. All I want is you."

The air was cold and dark outside, and a delicious, dangerous electricity filled the spaces between them. "I wish I could go with you." Kari slid across the bench seat and laid her head on his shoulder. He was breathing hard, and the sensation of his nearness caused feelings in her she hadn't felt before.

Her parents didn't expect her home for two hours, and before either of them knew what was happening they were kissing again, taking in all they could about each other, pushing the limits in a way they hadn't before. Finally Ryan eased himself away from her. He looked straight ahead and gripped the steering wheel. "We can't . . ."

Kari ached with feelings she knew were forbidden. She tried to steady her heartbeat. "I know."

"I can't believe I'm leaving tomorrow." He gazed at her by the light of the moon, his eyes filled with passion. "I need you, Kari."

They'd never run out of things to talk about before. But that night, sitting in his truck, they agreed that no amount of conversation could ease the temptation they both felt. And nothing they might talk about could take away the pain of good-bye.

They went home early, and Ryan parked in front of Kari's house. "Have you ever wanted to run away? Just forget about the things people expect of you?"

She studied him, unwilling to let go now that their hearts were bound so completely. "I wish you didn't have to leave."

He kissed her one last time and whispered into her hair words she remembered to this day. "Wait for me, Kari girl. Please."

She couldn't speak, couldn't answer him. Instead, she nodded and quickly climbed out of the truck. When she waved good-bye they were both crying.

For the next five months they spoke on the phone several times a week, biding their time until summer vacation. From the moment he attended her graduation that May, they were inseparable — boating on the lake, day camping on the shore, playing Frisbee and Ping-Pong and H-O-R-S-E, and living each hour as if it might be their last.

Intensely aware of the electricity between them, they came up with the idea of a Passion Patrol and took turns being on duty. One weekend she'd be in charge of making sure they got home without incident; another weekend it was his turn. Though their feelings for each other grew with each date, so did their determination to wait. For her, it had been a matter of her faith. For him, it was more a respect for her and a determination to help her honor her convictions.

But Ryan often attended church with her as well, and halfway through that summer she was surprised when he answered an altar call and accepted Christ as his Savior.

"Guess all those years of youth group paid off." He grinned at Kari after the service. "I don't know why I waited so long."

She was thrilled, believing nothing could separate them now that he was a believer. For a brief instant she wondered if his decision wasn't a bit too convenient, more about pleasing her than God. Even so, she couldn't wait to share the news with her parents. "See," she told them that night, "I knew he'd get there one day."

After they parted in August, they spent each day wondering how they'd survive being apart until Christmas.

Kari started college at Indiana University and buried herself in schoolwork and her first modeling jobs, while Ryan took his emptiness out on the football field. That fall he averaged more yards per catch than any of his teammates, and by midseason he was on course to break several school records. More often than not, the weekly write-up on the team included his name.

It was about that time that Kari first began to sense a change in him. His letters and phone calls were briefer. He talked more about what *he* was doing and less about what they would do together.

Then, toward the end of the season, Kari and Brooke flew out to Oklahoma to watch Ryan play and meet some of his teammates. He was obviously glad to see her, but he was just as obviously caught up in how many yards he'd gotten and how many he'd get the next game. He spoke about little but opposing defenses and passing routes and offensive strategies. He took her to parties where he and his friends were so caught up in football talk that he had almost no time alone with her.

It was on that trip that Kari realized what was happening.

First place in Ryan's life no longer belonged to her. It belonged to football.

"You're really serious about this, aren't you?" Her question came late that Saturday night as he said good night outside the hotel room she was sharing with Brooke.

Ryan shrugged, and she saw the answer in his eyes. "When I'm out there, running plays, catching passes —" His eyes drifted heavenward, and he shook his head. "I don't know . . . it's like I'm the wind, and nothing can stop me."

The next year was more or less the same. Fewer phone calls, shorter visits home. When he did make it to Indiana, they still attended church together, still promised their love to each other. Still talked about sharing a future together. But the talk grew more and more vague.

By the spring of his senior year, Ryan's letters had all but stopped, though he still called occasionally and his mother kept her posted in the meantime. By that time, the ache of missing him had softened to a kind of wistful loneliness. Kari studied hard, kept herself busy, even went on occasional dates with friends — but she always made it clear she was waiting for Ryan.

Whenever he was ready to be serious about their relationship.

In May of his senior year, he told her he wouldn't be coming home for the summer. He was scheduled to try out at several NFL camps, and he had decided he could stay more focused between tryouts by staying in Norman.

"You watch," he told her on the phone, "I'm gonna get drafted. Coach is sure of it."

Then, in late July, she was chopping vegetables for soup when the phone rang.

"Kari, you won't believe it!" Ryan was breathless on the other end. There was static in the background, and she guessed he was at a pay phone. "They offered me a contract!"

Her pulse quickened. "Who? What do you mean?" It had been a month since he'd last called, and she wasn't sure what city he was in, let alone what he was excited about.

"The Cowboys." He let out a hoot that echoed in her ears. "Can you believe it?"

"That's great." Kari wasn't sure how to respond. "What happens now?"

"I join them for summer training. Then in fall I move to Dallas. Preseason starts in late August."

A dozen questions banged about in her head. *What about us, Ryan? Where do I fit in? Haven't I been patient? Haven't we waited long enough?* She swallowed all of them. "Congratulations." Her voice was as upbeat as she could make it. "Are you coming home first?"

"There's no time." He was silent a moment. "Training camp begins first thing tomorrow."

A chilly breeze pulled her from the memory, and she tightened her jacket more closely around herself. Ryan glanced at her. "What're you thinking?"

She smiled. "About yesterday."

"Yesterday?" He was still holding her hand, and he slid closer to her on the bench. The warmth of his body worked its way through her, and she knew she couldn't pull away if she wanted to. "You look cold."

"Mmm. Yeah, I guess."

He gazed out at his fishing line. "How many yesterdays ago?"

"A few."

"Yes." His eyes narrowed. "I've done that a lot myself lately."

Kari dug her elbows into her knees and propped her chin on her hands. "We had our chances."

Ryan reeled in his line and cast it again at another angle. "Why was I so stupid? Lots of guys were married and doing great for the Cowboys." He stared at her, his eyes a deeper green than the lake water. "What was I thinking?"

"I don't know."

She hadn't really wanted to venture into

this conversation, but clearly it was at the front of both their minds. An eagle soared above the treetops across the lake, and Kari closed her eyes. Something her father told her before Ryan's graduation echoed in her mind. *A dozen guys at the university would give their right arm to take you out. If Ryan wanted a serious relationship, you'd know it by now.*

Kari opened her eyes and took a drink from her water bottle. Despite her best intentions that this day be nothing more than a diversion on the path to reuniting with Tim, she leaned closer into Ryan's shoulder. Her father had been right. What had happened during Ryan's time with the Cowboys was better left in the past. The accident, the girl — obviously, God had never intended Kari and Ryan to be together.

Ryan released her hand and reeled in another catch.

"I haven't even caught a sock," she complained. They both laughed, and she helped him secure the flopping fish. "It must be your day."

His hand came over hers as they steadied the line. He caught her eye. "It is."

Her heart swelled, and she looked away, suddenly shy. They said little for another hour, and when Ryan had his limit, they boated back to the dock. Kari helped him cut and clean the fish at an outdoor sink near the beach, and together they built a fire in a pit on the shore. "You didn't know we were catching dinner, did you?"

She smiled. "I guessed."

He grabbed his backpack and two beach chairs from the back of his truck and set the chairs up near the firepit. From inside his pack he pulled out utensils and plates, everything they needed for a fish fry. Once the fire was started in the pit, he snagged a Frisbee from his backpack. They played for half an hour and then sat side by side while he cooked the fish. When they were finished eating, Ryan stood and held a hand out to her. "Walk with me?"

The temperatures were falling fast and it was dark, but Kari knew she had no choice. She was seventeen again, crazy in love with Ryan Taylor and wondering how she'd ever found the strength on that fall day to walk away from him.

He kept hold of her hand as they made their way to the shore. Long minutes passed before he stopped and took her shoulders, searching her eyes by the light of a crescent moon. "May I tell you something?"

She couldn't find her voice, so she nodded, her gaze locked on his.

"It wasn't fair what you did to me after the accident."

Kari was thankful for the cover of night. Otherwise he would have seen the way the blood left her face. "What *I* did?" *How could he* —

"Just leaving like that. You never even came in to see me."

She moved back a step, and her hands fell to her sides. "You asked me to wait for you, but you promised me nothing, Ryan. You didn't owe me an explanation. I only wished you would have told me about her before —"

"About who?" Ryan took a step forward and once more placed his hands on her shoulders. "I loved *you*, Kari." He shook his head, and tears glistened in his eyes. "I know it's too late. No matter what your marriage looks like, you . . . you love him. But I wanted you to know how I felt."

Her eyes flooded, and she swallowed a lump in her throat. The determination she'd felt days ago to resist temptation, to remember she was a married woman, was fading like a springtime tulip. Her father was right — she shouldn't have come. "You . . . you had a girlfriend in the hospital room, Ryan. What was I supposed to think?"

He opened his mouth to say something, but then stopped. Peace filled his features, and he took her hand once more. "It's cold. Let's go sit by the fire." They walked a few steps, his fingers fitting between hers in a way that was so familiar it scared her. "I think we have some talking to do."

Why was he looking at her that way? "Talking?"

"About what happened that day." He reached out and wiped at a tear making its way down her cheek. "Even if we can't go back, I want you to know what really happened."

Kari nodded, terrified that somehow Ryan might have an explanation for what took place that far-off day. And if he did . . . if the only reason the two of them weren't together today was some mistake . . .

She couldn't bear to think about it.

He led her back to their seats. Then without waiting another moment, with a firm hold on her hand and an even firmer one on her heart, Ryan Taylor began to tell her a story she'd never heard before.

One that, had she heard it sooner, would have changed the course of her life.

Chapter Nineteen

Elizabeth sat on the living-room floor across from little Cole, helping him work a jigsaw puzzle. "Look for the edge pieces, honey." She held up a straight-edged piece. "Like this. We have to find these first."

John entered the room with two steaming cups of mint tea. Apple pie was baking in the oven, and the aromas mixed in a way that filled their home with warmth and peace. In the background, Kathy Troccoli sang about beauty for ashes. And as Elizabeth worked on the puzzle with her grandson, she realized her earlier fears were gone. In their place was a holy assurance that somehow everything would work out.

The troubles with Brooke and Peter. The trials with Ashley. Her own health. And even the alarming fact that Kari and Ryan had been together all day. None of it seemed overwhelming now.

John's story had done it, of course — the way he wove Scripture into their conversation. That explained the peaceful feeling she'd had ever since. God had calmed the sea before, and he would do it again — whether it raged inside her heart or all around her.

"Did Ashley say when she'd be back?" John sat in the closest chair and rested the hot mug on his knee.

"Cole's spending the night." She gave John a knowing look, then smiled at the little boy. "Five more minutes, and it's bedtime, okay, pumpkin?"

Cole nodded. "I get to sleep over, right, Grammy? That's what my mommy said."

"Yep, in your special bed. Billy Bear's already up there waiting for you."

"Know what I dreamed about, Grammy?"

"What, honey?"

"I was making the hugest sand castle in the whole, wide world, and all the sudden a big shark came right up on the beach. Only know what, Grammy?"

"What?" Elizabeth made her eyes big.

"He was a nice shark, and he sat down beside me and helped me make the sand castle, and it was the bestest one I ever made."

The story went on to involve a variety of sea creatures and sudden storms and magic treasure. Elizabeth remembered that they had watched a nature special together a few days earlier. She marveled at how everything the little boy saw or heard became part of his reality.

"And know what happened then, Grammy?" Cole gathered himself to a standing position. He raised his hands high over his head. "A big, tall daddy came out of the water and walked up to me. He told me he'd been gone a really lot of time, but now he wasn't going away anymore. And he said he loved me more than even the bestest little boys all over the whole wide world."

Elizabeth blinked back tears and worked to find her voice. "That's wonderful, sweetheart."

They finished their puzzle, and Elizabeth and John walked the child upstairs. "Can you carry me, Papa?" Cole reached his little-boy hands up to John, and Elizabeth's heart melted. At times like these it nearly strangled her to imagine Ashley's boy growing up without a father.

John scooped him up. "You're my boy, Cole. Always and forever."

Cole responded by laying his head on John's shoulder and wrapping his chubby arms around his neck. "I wish I could sleep over every night."

Elizabeth trailed behind, blinking back tears as she watched her husband kiss the child's cheek.

John's voice was choked when he answered, "Me, too, son. Me too."

They prayed together, tucked Billy Bear in beside Cole, and left with promises of pancakes in the morning. When they were downstairs, Elizabeth walked to the front room and stared out the window.

John was at her side instantly. "They'll be back soon."

She smiled. "How do you know which one it is tonight?"

"It's Kari. She's had the number-one worry spot for a while now."

Her head tilted back against his chest. "But it could be Ashley."

"True."

"Or both of them."

"Absolutely."

"Actually, I was thinking about Cole." Elizabeth felt her smile fade. She turned as John wrapped his arms around her. "It breaks my heart to see him growing up without a dad."

John kissed the top of her head. "He's such a great little guy."

"You know why, don't you?" She leaned up and wondered again at the depth of love she felt for John Baxter, a love that grew with each passing year as if there were no limits to how she could feel about him.

"Why?"

"Because he has you, of course." She smiled but knew he could read the seriousness in her voice. "I thank God he has you, John."

"Ashley tries."

Elizabeth smiled in a tired sort of way. "She has so much to learn about being a mother."

He nodded. "I watch Cole on the floor making puzzles and telling you his pretend stories about sharks and treasures and big, tall daddies, and I want to shake her and ask her, 'Ashley, what are you doing tonight that could possibly be more important than being here with him?' "

Melody Blues was nearing the end of its first set at The Coffee House. Ashley Baxter and two of her friends sat at a back table, sipping mochas and comparing notes.

Her friends were nothing like her family, but they were loyal. And they didn't expect from Ashley anything that she wasn't willing to give. There was Anika, the

Alaskan transplant who talked constantly about getting to New York and playing violin for a Broadway orchestra, and Billie, the art student who'd been saving for years to buy herself a summer in Europe. Since Ashley played the guitar and painted, the three of them fit well together. But beyond their shared artistic interests, they had something bigger in common.

Their discontentment with life.

Anika was twenty-three and divorced. Billie was living with a man twenty years her senior. And Ashley was pursued by a dozen guys every day but wanted nothing to do with any of them.

"Paris cured me of that," she'd told her friends. And though they didn't know the details, they were two of the only people on earth who had any idea at all of what she meant.

As far as Ashley was concerned, it was none of anyone's business what had happened in Paris the year she was twenty-one. Well, it was fairly obvious that Cole had happened that year, but she wasn't telling anything more. Her parents and siblings could ask all they wanted; she had no intention of dredging up the details. Not for them or anyone else.

"Hey, what's Cole doing tonight?" Anika

caught Ashley's eye and stirred the whipped cream into her drink.

"The usual. Spoiled by Grandma from seven to eight. Spoiled by Grandpa from eight to nine." She smiled, but her eyes felt soaked in a sadness she didn't quite understand. "His favorite kind of night."

Anika nodded and stared at the band. "I should be home practicing. I'll never be famous if I spend every night listening to someone else make music."

She launched into a comparison of off-Broadway musicals versus Broadway ones, and though Billie was immediately caught up in the interchange, trading ambiguous terms and meaningless opinions, Ashley wasn't in the mood.

Melody Blues was one of her favorite local bands, and The Coffee House was a place that always seemed to expand her creativity. Normally, a night like this would leave her feeling she could paint the Sistine Chapel in an hour.

But tonight was different.

In fact, the last four times they'd gone out — whether here or dancing at Kaverns — she had left feeling empty and sad. As if something was missing from life, something she couldn't put into words. It wasn't Cole — although the fact that he had more fun spending a night with her parents than staying with her didn't help her feelings any.

It was deeper, far down inside her heart, as if she had a hole nothing could fill.

"You okay?" There was a break in the conversation, and Billie touched her elbow, her forehead wrinkled in concern. "You don't seem like yourself tonight."

Ashley shrugged. "I just don't feel right."

Anika leaned back in her chair, her head angled curiously. "There's a flu going around."

"No, it's not that."

Understanding dawned on Anika's face. "Paris?"

Ashley stirred her coffee and felt the sting of tears. Because of Paris, she was sometimes seized by moments when she wanted to crawl into a hole in the basement of her heart where no one could find her — not even these, her closest friends. But Paris wasn't the problem tonight. "I don't know what it is."

Melody Blues took a break, and Billie motioned to the other side of the coffee house. "Want to browse?"

Half the building was a bookstore, an eclectic mix of new and used tomes —

mostly offbeat fiction, artsy how-to books, and various New Age titles. Customers drifted from one side to the other, finding books, taking them to the café, poring over them while sipping coffee and listening to music late into the night. Book purchases could be made until the two o'clock closing time.

Ashley shook her head. "You go ahead." Her friends finished their drinks and pushed back from the table. Ashley knew they might spend an hour or more looking at books, but that was okay. She welcomed the time alone.

A couple decked out in a kind of nouveau-hippie look — tie-dyed shirts, flowing glass beads, and leather-fringed pants — walked past and flashed her the peace symbol. She returned the same and smiled. Her parents would be deeply concerned to know she spent as much time as she did here, and they would be aghast to know she brought Cole sometimes. They were so straight, so — she searched for a word and thought of a hippie-era one her friends liked to use.

Establishment.

That was it. Everything about her family was establishment. Especially their brand of religion — the kind of white-bread, narrow-minded, Bible-bound faith that

Ashley had come to despise. She couldn't understand why Kari still bought into it.

Maybe that's what bothered her the most. The fact that her parents' faith seemed to have turned Kari into a robot.

When she and Kari were younger, Kari had been bigger than life to Ashley. Her older sister, beautiful and confident, dating easily the best-looking guy in all of Bloomington — at least that was how Ashley had seen Ryan Taylor back then.

When they were kids it all seemed so easy. They went to church and believed, and in return God took care of them and made sure everything worked out the way it was supposed to.

Paris had changed her thinking on that one — that and watching her sister give up any semblance of pride just to stick to some archaic rule about staying married no matter what.

Ashley stared at the melting whipped cream in her drink and swirled it slowly. Could God really expect that kind of devotion? Even when Kari's husband was an unfaithful jerk?

Bells on the front door jangled, and Ashley looked up. As she did, her heart skipped a beat, and she had to set her cup down to keep from spilling its contents.

Landon Blake?

What in the world was he doing at an artsy cave like The Coffee House on a Saturday night? And dressed in his firefighter's uniform, no less.

He didn't see her as he made his way between several tables to the take-out counter and ordered a drink.

Landon Blake . . . Ashley's heart grew instantly softer. If Ryan Taylor was the best-looking guy in Bloomington, second place — without a doubt — belonged to the boy who had chased her since the first day of middle school. The boy who'd gone off to Texas to become a veterinarian — until he spent a semester of his junior year volunteering for the fire department.

Something must have happened that year, because he came home from college right afterward. He abandoned his dream of working with animals and instead joined the City of Bloomington Fire Department.

Other than that, little had changed about Landon.

He was still as gorgeous as ever, still a little too religious for her taste, still attending the big church across town and, according to everyone who knew him, still carrying a quiet torch for Ashley Baxter.

They'd been in the same Sunday school class when they were kids, back when his family attended Clear Creek Community Church. Every summer they had gone to the same camp on the same church bus and shared the same friends. All her life, in fact, everyone had expected her to marry Landon one day.

And all her life she'd been determined to prove them wrong.

There had to be more to life than the predictability of spending a lifetime with someone like Landon. Someone with whom she'd rarely have a surprising moment. The wildest thing he ever did was switch career goals halfway through college. Since then he'd been as predictable as winter. She could never be interested in Landon.

At least that's what she told her parents.

The truth was something she rarely admitted even to herself.

The summer after his first year of college, Landon Blake had come home for two months, and Ashley had caught herself doing the very thing she'd promised never to do.

She was falling in love with him.

Just as her mother and father and everyone who knew them always thought she would, that summer she fell hard for the boy who'd always been there for her.

Ashley studied him now. Wasn't that the reason she'd gone to Paris in the first place, running scared from everything predictable and ordinary to a country where she could be someone no one knew? Wasn't that why she'd traded her safety and security for a chance to paint a masterpiece by starlight or stay up all night listening to the lap of a lake against foreign soil?

Still, the question remained.

If she'd been willing to work that hard to keep herself from falling for Landon, why now — years from those church-camp days — was her heart still moved by the sight of him?

She watched him order, watched the way the girl behind the counter blushed in his presence, and took in the fact that he had to be every bit of six feet four inches now. She saw it all as she waited for the inevitable.

He would see her. He always did.

Ever since their early teenage years, it hadn't mattered if they were in church or a crowded cafeteria or at opposite sides of a local supermarket. If Landon Blake entered a place where Ashley Baxter was, he would find her.

Landon leaned against the counter and waited for the girl to fill his order. He slipped one hand casually into his pocket, and Ashley wondered if he bought coffee here often and whether he knew she was a regular. He turned and leaned against the counter, and almost immediately his eyes found hers.

Ashley hated the way her palms grew sweaty under his slow, easy smile. He made his way toward her, unrushed, moving with the grace of an athlete. His eyes held hers. When he reached her table, he sat down and looked at her for a long while before talking.

"Hi." He still had the same dimples that had set him apart as a schoolboy.

"Landon." She returned his smile. "What brings you here?"

"Coffee." He cocked his head and, though his tone was light, he looked further into her eyes than she was comfortable with. "Of course, if I'd known you were here, I would've come sooner."

"Somehow I believe you." She leaned her forearms on the table and looked into the bookstore, wondering whether Anika and Billie had spotted him. Though she and Landon lived in the same town, they ran in completely different circles. He was straightforward and good, the type who divided his time equally between church, the gym, and the fire station.

Ashley didn't spend time in any of those places, so though he'd been back home for more than two years, she could count on one hand the number of times they'd actually run into each other.

"Where's Cole?"

A part of her heart was touched that he remembered her son's name. He'd seen the boy only once — when she'd had him dedicated at an evening church service just after his first birthday. Landon had heard about it from her parents and showed up with a present, an engraved picture frame that still sat on Cole's nightstand.

"With my parents. He likes it there."

He leaned back in his chair. "How long's it been, Ash?"

She thought about that for a moment. "A year at least."

He nodded, and the faraway look in his eyes told her he remembered their last meeting as if it were yesterday. "So . . . what's new?"

Ashley doubted that was the question he wanted to ask. The real question, the unspoken one, hung around them like a cloak, and she decided not to make him guess. "I'm not seeing anyone, if that's what you're wondering."

He nodded thoughtfully. "I'm not either."

The girl from behind the counter placed a steaming drink on the take-out shelf and searched the room. Ashley gestured toward the cash register, leaned close, and whispered, "Your admirer has your drink ready."

"My admir—"

He turned, and the girl gave him a cutesy-type wave. Ashley whispered again. "That one."

Landon turned to her again and settled into his chair, making no effort to retrieve his coffee. After a while he crossed his arms, his eyes never leaving hers. "May I call you sometime?"

Her heart rate sped up, and she worked to look indifferent. "Why?"

"Relax, Ashley." He chuckled and shook his head. "I'm not asking you to marry me. Just talk a little, catch up on the years."

Her better sense screamed at her to say no, to tell him to leave her alone and let his feelings for her die. But being in his presence now was more enjoyable than she liked to admit, and she let her gaze fall to her hands. What harm could there be in talking to him now and then? She lifted her eyes and met his. "I live on my own now."

He raised his eyebrows, and a slow grin worked its way across his face. "Call me crazy, but the way you said that almost makes me think you're saying yes."

A giggle slipped from between her lips, and she silently scolded herself. Why was she doing this — leading him to believe there was any hope? "Okay." She reached into her oversized crocheted handbag, grabbed a pen, and scribbled her phone number on a napkin. She dropped her chin, gazed up at him, and slid the napkin across the table. "You can call."

He took the paper, folded it, and slipped it into his wallet. Then he studied her for another moment and tapped his finger on the table two quick times. "Good seeing you, Ash."

She leaned close and whispered once more. "Your coffee's getting cold."

He left then, moving back to the counter as easily as he'd come, taking his drink and looking at her over his shoulder once more before leaving.

The moment he was gone, she silently cursed herself for giving in. *What's wrong with me?* Were his looks that hard to resist? She dried her palms on her jeans and knew the answer. Forget the fact that they were as different as night from day. Something about him was flat-out irresistible.

That's why she had felt compelled to go as far as Paris to get away from him.

But where could it possibly lead? Landon was everything she was not. Stable and steady, the type of guy who deserved a — what did her mother call it? — a Proverbs 31 woman, someone who would honor him and make him proud and sit by his side at church.

Quite simply, Landon was the marrying type, and she was not.

Something occurred to her then, a thought that had irritated the delicate places in her soul a handful of times since she'd been back in the States. It wouldn't be that hard to lose Landon if she wanted to. He didn't know about what happened in Paris.

If he did, he would toss her phone number in the nearest trash bin.

In fact, he wouldn't have asked for it in the first place.

Chapter Twenty

Kari's legs shook as Ryan led her back to the beach chairs by the fire. He slid his chair closer to hers so that when they sat, their legs and arms touched. Heat from the fire warmed Kari's freezing legs, but it was nothing compared to the way Ryan's nearness warmed her body.

"Cold?"

She shook her head. "I'm okay." It was partly true. She could survive the falling temperatures. It was the story he wanted to share that concerned her.

"I've looked for a way to talk about this ever since I got hurt." Ryan gazed out at the silvery reflection of moonlight on the water. "We should have done it a long time ago, but . . . I don't know. I'm not sure exactly what happened." He looked at her. "Obviously you walked away believing something that wasn't true."

Her mind swirled with possibilities, trying to understand what he was saying. The events of that day were perfectly clear, weren't they? The nurses at the hospital had confirmed it. "I . . . I guess I don't know what you mean."

"Let's do this." There was a softening in his features, and she saw that whatever the misunderstanding, he didn't hold it against her. "You tell me what you think happened, how you remember the day I got hurt and . . . everything that followed it."

Kari nodded and stared out at the lake, her thoughts drifting back to a time she'd never been able to delete from her memory. "It was November. I was a junior in college."

"Right."

She closed her eyes and pictured her family going about its business that Sunday afternoon. Brooke was already away at medical school in Indianapolis, but the others were home. Mom was in the kitchen. Ashley, Erin, Luke, and Dad were watching the football game on television.

Kari bit the inside of her lip. "By then I'd been hearing things from your friends, you know . . . here and there."

Ryan's eyebrows raised a bit. "About me?"

"About how you were spending your time." Kari had a group of friends she hung out with back then, several of whom had known Ryan in high school and still followed his career. Two of them had even flown out and caught a game a month before Ryan was hurt.

"What'd they tell you?"

Tears stung at her eyes as she struggled to find her voice. "A bunch of us went bowling after they got back. They were full of stories."

"Like what?" The surprise on Ryan's face was genuine, and Kari felt increasing tremors of doubt ripple across the foundation of everything she'd believed.

"Like how well you were doing, how much money you earned . . . and the girls."

Ryan laughed and ran his hand over the top of his head. "I took them to a players' party."

"That's what they said. All they could talk about were the women around you."

"Sure, there were women. There always were at those parties. I introduced the guys, and that was it. After that, I stayed with the team. I wasn't interested in those girls, Kari. I told you that."

A dozen conversations played in her mind. Ryan was right. He'd always claimed that his feelings were for her alone, that when football was over their life together could begin.

An ache settled in her heart, and she traced small circles in the sand with the toe of her shoe. "Yes. You always said that."

"You didn't believe me?"

"I tried." She stared at him, her mouth open. "Look at it from my point of view."

"I want to, Kari." He was calm. "Why don't you tell me what happened after I got hurt? Maybe I'll understand better."

Kari took a deep breath and continued.

She had watched the game on and off that afternoon, doing laundry, catching key plays every now and then, when suddenly she heard her father's voice.

"Kari! Ryan's hurt."

They were words Kari would never forget, words she had always feared. As she hurried into the television room, she told herself it couldn't be serious. An ankle or knee or bruised rib, maybe. But the screen showed Ryan lying motionless on the field while the announcers talked in hushed tones.

Kari eased herself, trancelike, into a spot on the sofa beside her father and watched as the network replayed the injury. Ryan had caught a pass in the air and then instantly been sandwiched between two defenders. One pulled him from behind, causing him to lose his balance. The other met him with a direct blow from the front. By that point, Ryan was parallel to the ground, and his head took the full brunt of the impact.

His head and his neck.

The camera cut back to the scene on the field, and Kari could barely breathe as she watched a team of people working on Ryan. Seconds earlier he had been doing what he loved best — running like the wind, his body strong and responding to every signal his brain sent it. But in a single moment, a single hit . . . Kari stared at his image on the screen, unable to believe her eyes.

His legs lay at an unnatural angle, utterly still.

The announcers' voices cut in. "He hasn't shown any signs of movement."

"No, it doesn't look good."

A somber silence filled the air.

"Our thoughts and prayers are certainly with Ryan Taylor and his family right now."

The fear of that moment came back in all its fullness now, and Kari was silent for a while. "I was so scared for you."

Ryan took hold of her hand and stared at the water. "It still feels like yesterday."

Looking back, it seemed odd that she

and Ryan had never had this conversation, never gone back and talked about what it was like for him, lying on the field unable to move. "How much do you remember?"

Ryan's features darkened. "My face was planted in the grass. They had to carefully move me so I could breathe." He clenched his teeth. "My mind was screaming at my feet and legs and arms to do something, move, get my body up and running again."

He leaned back in his chair, and his grip on her hand tightened. "Look at my legs."

Kari shifted her gaze to Ryan's knees. "Okay . . ."

"Try to make them move."

Kari stared for a few moments, understanding. She looked up at him and winced. "That's how it felt?"

"It was like my arms and legs belonged to someone else. No matter how hard I tried, I couldn't move." Tears glistened in his eyes. "I might have already made a decision to love God, but I guarantee you, that day I was praying like never before. I promised God if only he'd give me a second chance, I'd get serious about him."

It was a detail she'd never heard before, and Kari was terrified at what other truths he might share. What if she'd been wrong about what happened?

It would be more than she could bear.

She swallowed back a lump in her throat and nodded. "Dad called us together in the room, and we prayed. Then we watched along with everyone else in the country. Waiting and wishing you would move. Even a little."

Instead, paramedics had arrived, strapped him to a backboard, and carried him off the field. The announcers had promised to keep the viewers updated, and the game had resumed.

"I was so scared I could barely breathe." She ran her thumb over his hand. "That's when Dad made the plan."

The Cowboys had been playing at Soldier Field in Chicago that afternoon, and the hospital was only a five-hour drive away. Within thirty minutes, he'd phoned someone at the university and gotten the okay for a few days off from teaching. "Dad and I threw our things in a suitcase and set out to find you."

Ryan's mother had been at the game that weekend, so Kari and her father knew they'd find her at the hospital.

"I think my dad was as worried for your mom as he was for you." Kari inhaled sharply, her insides tense at the memory of the next twenty-four hours.

The drive up was one of the quietest Kari could remember. Her fears were so all-consuming she could barely think straight. What if Ryan died en route to the hospital? What if he never walked or ran or moved again? The possibilities were too awful to consider.

When they got to the hospital, they found Ryan's mother right where they'd expected. Sitting in the lobby in intensive care.

"She told us they were operating on your spine. That there was a chance — a small chance — you might walk again." Kari ignored the tears now streaming quietly down her cheeks. "Sometime that night my dad and I fell asleep on a couple of padded benches in the waiting room."

Ryan released her hand and turned to face her. "Here's where things get a little weird." His jaw muscles flexed. "My mom has tried to explain it to me, but I want to hear it from you. What happened when you woke up?"

Kari's stomach dropped. She could hardly believe she was here, at Lake Monroe alone in the dark with Ryan, discussing the events of that time. She exhaled slowly and found a way to continue. "Your mom was gone, and my dad was still sleeping." She angled her head, her eyes burning with tears. "I went to the nurses' station and asked how you were."

Ryan waited, his eyes locked on hers, hanging on every word.

"A nurse told me you'd come through the surgery beautifully." A sob escaped from a place in Kari's heart that had not forgotten. "They . . . they couldn't know if you might walk again, but there was a good chance." Kari caught two quick breaths and fought to maintain her composure. "I asked if I could go in, and they said maybe later because . . ."

His face came closer to hers, his features frozen in anticipation of what she was about to say. "Because . . . ?"

"Because right then your girlfriend was with you."

Ryan stood and let out a moan that echoed across the lake. He dropped his head back and stared straight up, then paced in a circle around the fire. "I knew it. I knew that's what happened." He stopped and stared at Kari, and for the first time his eyes blazed with a kind of anguish she'd never seen there before. "Why didn't you ask my mom about her?"

Kari's head was spinning. What was he saying? Certainly none of this was a surprise to him. She pictured the other girl at Ryan's side, comforting him, holding his hand, wanting a private moment for just the two of them. If that's what the nurse saw, then it was too late for Ryan to explain it away.

Her voice rose a notch, and she leaned forward, tossing her hands in the air. "I asked the nurse if she was sure it was your girlfriend in the room. I thought maybe she'd made a mistake, that maybe your mom was in there." Kari shook her head hard. "But she told me she was sure it was your girlfriend. Your mother had said so herself, told the nurses all about how your girlfriend had rushed to be there and how the two of you might need some time alone together."

Ryan stared at her for what felt like an entire minute. When he spoke, his words were slow and full of pain. "Yes, my mother said that." He uttered one very loud laugh that was anything but funny. "You know who she meant?"

Kari felt dizzy, and she closed her eyes, trying to regain her bearings. When she opened them, she forced herself to be calm. She had nothing to be nervous about; the answer was obvious. "She meant the girl in the room with you."

"No." Ryan came to where she was sitting. He dropped to his knees at her feet, resting his hands on her legs. "She was talking about *you*, Kari. You were the girlfriend. The girl in the room with me was one of the team trainers."

"What?" Kari's breath left her body. Her voice was barely a whisper, and she wrapped her arms around her waist, bracing herself against the explosion of pain that welled up within her. It wasn't possible. "Why . . . why did the nurse tell me it was your girlfriend?"

Ryan dropped his head against her knees and stayed there, even when he finally spoke. "I've talked to Mom about this a dozen times." His hands trembled against her legs. "She swore up and down there couldn't have been a misunderstanding about the trainer. She figured the accident just made you realize it was time to move on."

Kari's sorrow was so deep that she felt she was drowning in it. "I told my dad what the nurse said, and he went to find out more information. Before he could ask, he heard the nurses talking about you, how everyone hoped for a miracle and how devoted your girlfriend was, sitting by your side until you woke up."

Ryan lifted his head, and his eyes looked tired, as if he'd aged ten years in the past few minutes. "My mom couldn't stop talking about you. She told them how you'd waited for me while I focused on football, how you came the minute you knew I was hurt." He spoke straight to her soul, his voice barely louder than the breeze. "She was talking about *you*, Kari. Can't you see it?"

Fresh sobs lodged in her throat, and she shook her head. "It's impossible. I waited in the lobby and . . . when your mom came back, she told me you were doing better. She'd been in to see you. And the doctors were able to get you to move your toes . . . your fingers. She didn't say anything about the girl, and I figured she didn't want me to know. Otherwise, why was she telling the nurses and not me?"

The pieces were coming together, and neither of them liked the picture they formed — a picture of pain and hurt feelings and misunderstanding that had gone on to define their entire future. "You never came in to see me. I was drugged and half conscious, Kari. I didn't know the trainer was there. She was doing her job."

The sobs made their way up from Kari's gut like so many volcanic eruptions. "I stayed the whole next day . . . and when I left, I told your mother I didn't want to . . . to bother you." Kari hunched over, her head near his, and struggled to keep from falling out of her chair. "I thought she knew what I meant . . . that I didn't want to interrupt you and . . . and your girl-friend."

Ryan's hands were still on her knees, and Kari laid her fingers over them, grieving the loss, calculating what the misunder-standing that day had cost them.

For the first three months after surgery he had lived at a rehabilitation center in Dallas, his care supervised by the Cowboys. And when he was well enough to be re-leased, it had been to a condo in the team's training center where he was tended to three times daily by trainers and therapists.

"I called you, but everything seemed dif-ferent." Ryan's eyes glistened once more. "I was so busy trying to get better. I guess I figured we'd work it out later."

A soft rustling sifted through the branches above them, and Kari sniffed. "I wanted to ask you about the girl, whoever she was . . . but I figured you'd tell me if you wanted me to know." She tightened her grip on his fingers. "Besides, by then I was trying to forget about you."

Ryan sat back on his heels, his eyes caressing her face. "Did it work?"

She thought about Tim and the good times they'd shared, about her strong desire to salvage their marriage. Then she thought about Ryan and how she felt here, now, and she knew her answer as surely as she knew her name. "No . . . I never forgot."

He worked his fingers between hers and gazed at the sky. "I never understood why you changed, what happened. My mother's answer about your being tired of waiting made sense. I figured you'd finally decided to go on with your life." He looked back at her, his voice tired, as if the reality of their loss had drained him of something vital and life-sustaining.

"I kept thinking you'd tell me about the girl. Whoever she was, I knew she must be special or your mother wouldn't have talked about her to the nurses. And she wouldn't have been in the room with you hours after your surgery." Kari shrugged, her throat thick. "You and I talked only a few times over the next five months."

His eyes narrowed, and she could read the pain in them. It was no different from her own. He sighed. "Then you met Tim."

"The following year."

"You two were pretty serious at your graduation party." He was quiet a moment, his words slow and sad. "When I saw you that night, something told me you really had moved on, that I'd lost my chance."

Kari decided to tell him the truth. Her eyes fell, and when she looked up, she prayed he could see how sorry she was. "It was an act." Her voice faded. "Tim and I were just friends back then."

As the impact of what she said hit him, he fell farther back on his heels, pulling his hands from hers and bracing himself on his own knees. "Why would you do that?"

Anger welled up within her. "I thought you'd gotten serious with some girl and never even told me, never even given me the courtesy of knowing you'd left me behind." Her chin quivered. "When I heard you were coming, I begged Tim to pretend we were together so you wouldn't think I was stupid enough to be still waiting for you."

His voice was quietly resigned. "You know what I was thinking?"

She was afraid to ask. "What?"

The hurt in Ryan's eyes was so deep that just looking at him made her feel physically ill. "Now that I was finally well enough to come home . . . now that I had survived something most people never walk away from, I thought it was time to tell you how badly I'd missed you." His voice fell to a broken whisper. "I wanted to marry you, Kari. I never thought you might have found someone else."

The craziness of it all was more than she could bear. She stood, pushed back her chair, and took four steps closer to the water, wrapping her hands tightly around her waist again as the sobs had their way with her. Why hadn't she asked him these questions back then? She should have asked about the girl; then she would have known the truth.

My life's such a mess, Lord. . . . And you . . . you could have prevented all of it.

There were no silent reassuring words, only the echo of doubts as they rattled in her empty heart.

From behind her she felt the warmth of Ryan's body as he came up and circled his arms around her shoulders, pulling her close against him. She knew she shouldn't turn around, shouldn't allow him to comfort her here on the dark, secluded shores of Lake Monroe.

But even as she knew it, images flashed on the screen of her mind, images she'd worked night and day to shut out since her husband left: Tim kissing his new love, embracing her, caressing her. . . .

After what Tim had done, what loyalty did she owe him?

She cast her concerns to the harvest wind, turned, and melted into Ryan's arms, sliding her hands around his waist and up along his back in an embrace that felt achingly familiar. "I'm sorry, Ryan." She wept into his wool jacket, burying her face against him and repeating the same words over and over. "I'm sorry . . . I'm so sorry."

"Shhh." He rocked her gently, his body making her feel warm and safe, soothing her pain.

When her sobbing subsided, he pulled back enough to see her face. "It wasn't your fault." He leaned closer and kissed her forehead. Kari knew from the shadows of concern in his eyes that the kiss was a gesture of friendship. But the touch of his lips against her skin left her feeling nothing of the sort.

"Of course it was my fault." She shook her head and lowered her eyes. "I assumed something that wasn't true and . . . and that's why we . . ." Her voice trailed off.

Tenderly he lifted her chin with his finger until their eyes met once more. "I never should have waited so long to talk to you." His gaze was unwavering. "I thought there wasn't room in my life for football and you, but I was wrong, Kari. After I got better, after I started playing again, I found all sorts of time. But you were —"

"In New York. And then with Tim." Her mouth hung open a moment, and then it dawned on her. "Is that when you got serious about God?"

"I think I was in shock." Ryan blinked and winced a little. "Especially after I heard you were getting married." He tightened his grip on her, and for the first time since finding him again she saw deep, unrestrained desire flash briefly in his eyes. "I figured God had saved my life, pulled me through and let me walk and run and play again. Even though I'd lost you, I wanted nothing more than to live for him."

Kari could see the pieces fitting together, and the irony was almost more than she could bear. His initial conversion had really been nothing of the sort. But years later, in her absence, Ryan had given his heart and soul to the Lord, just as she'd always prayed he would. "When you were in the prayer room the other day . . . what was that about?"

He thought for a while. "I guess I was

missing those days when all I needed was Jesus. Ashley had told me about you and Tim, and —" his gaze dropped for a moment and then returned to hers — "I couldn't stop thinking about you. I missed you so much after I lost you, Kari. Your eyes, your laugh, your patient way with me. Your family. All of it. I knew I should have been praying things would work out for you and Tim, but all I wanted was . . ."

The moment changed, and the electricity that had always been between them was stronger than it had ever been. Their faces were inches from each other, and in a desperate move to stop herself from doing something she'd regret, she tried to conjure up the good times she'd shared with Tim.

But not a single memory would take shape.

"I know it's wrong, Kari." Ryan's voice was the gentlest whisper, soft as silk against her face. "But I . . . I still love you." His grip on her waist gradually tightened, and his face nuzzled against hers. The breeze all but disappeared in the warmth of his embrace, and Kari was caught in a tidal wave she could not fight and did not want to.

She closed her eyes and tried to remember all that was important and right and true about her faith, her belief in God and in marriage and forever. But all she could feel was Ryan Taylor in her arms.

"I love you, Kari girl." Ryan's words felt as if they were whispered into her soul.

"Ryan . . ." As she spoke his name, he brought his lips to hers and in a way they seemed helpless to stop, they kissed long and slow, savoring each other the way they had the first time.

The wind in the trees, the smell of the lake, the feel of sand underfoot — everything faded. She could no longer remember the reasons she should turn and run, the reasons she wanted to stay married to Tim, the reasons she hadn't stayed with Ryan all those years ago. All of it was gone, and in its place was only the sweetest feeling, the most incredible sensation she could ever remember having.

What did it matter if she kissed him, if she stole this one moment to imagine what life might have been like if they'd stayed together? Surely God wouldn't hold this against her after all Tim had done. All that Tim was doing.

Besides, it was just one kiss. One kiss between two people who would have been together had it not been for a series of horrible misunderstandings.

One kiss alone in the cold night on the shores of a lake they'd visited a hundred times before. It was so wonderfully real, so painfully forbidden. It was almost as if time had stopped.

He ran his fingertips up along the sides of her neck, her face, and she did the same, feeling the outline of his jaw, the day's growth on his face, breathing in the scents of fish and woodsmoke and cologne as their kiss grew more urgent. His hands trembled, and their breathing grew shaky and synchronized in a way that betrayed the urgency she knew they were both feeling.

One kiss?

Fresh tears stung at her eyes. Who was she kidding? Being with Ryan this way — feeling his lips against hers, his touch on her skin — she felt like a woman dying of thirst. These few sips would only leave her desperate for more.

Suddenly she knew she had no choice but to stop. "Ryan . . ." She broke away, tears spilling onto her cheeks as his lips found hers once more. But even as they kissed, she shook her head. She wanted nothing more than to follow Ryan back to his house and never give Tim Jacobs another thought.

But there was one problem: She couldn't live with herself if she did.

Not because of Tim or their shattered marriage but because of the sweet relationship she shared with the Lord. If she let herself give in to these feelings now, she and Ryan would both lose.

Because there was no way God could honor this. Not even for a moment, one that Kari wanted desperately to hold on to.

"You're crying." Ryan was breathing hard, and by the dim light of the crescent moon she saw her desire mirrored in his eyes. His breath was warm on her lips as he brushed his fingers across her cheek and erased her trail of tears.

No matter how badly she wanted to follow her feelings, to kiss him again and again, an urgency was building in her. One that insisted she run as fast as she could before everything she believed in, everything they both stood for, disappeared in a single instant.

God, give me the strength. She put her hands on his shoulders and pushed firmly enough to create a space between them, forcing herself to say the two most difficult words she could ever remember saying. "I . . . I can't. . . ."

She slid her hands into her pockets,

casting her eyes at the sand around their feet and letting her forehead come to rest against his chest. "I can't." Tears flooded her eyes again, but this time the words came easier, with enough conviction that she could almost feel Ryan pulling away, grabbing hold of his heart and burying it deep within him.

"I understand." He kissed her forehead once more.

They stood there that way for a while, catching their breath, trying to make sense of their feelings. He broke the silence first. "Come on. I'll get you home."

Her eyes lifted to meet his. "I want to. It's just that —"

"Shhh." His eyes welled up as he raised a finger to her lips. "You don't have to say it."

He released the hold he had on her and collected their things while Kari watched helplessly. "I hate this." Her voice hung in the autumn air a moment before he turned and caught her gaze.

"Me too." He waited for her near the firepit. "But if we don't go home now, you'll hate *me*." A sad smile worked its way across his face. "I can't have that."

"No, Ryan." Kari shook her head, blinking so she could see through her tears.

"I could never hate you."

He hesitated a moment, holding her gaze, but he said nothing. Moving completely against her will, Kari grabbed her bag, trudged up the beach, and followed Ryan to his truck.

Their arms brushed against each other as they loaded the chairs in the back, and for a moment Kari froze, reluctant beyond words to let go of what they'd rediscovered.

Kari had no idea how they managed to make their way into the truck, but fifteen silent minutes later they pulled into her parents' driveway. The house was dark, and Kari guessed everyone was asleep or out for the night. Ryan turned off the engine, but neither of them moved.

She turned to Ryan and found him watching her. His eyes conveyed a love that pierced her heart. A long, weary sigh crossed her lips, and she stared at her shoes. In all her life she couldn't remember anything as hard as this.

"Kari." He gently lifted her chin so that their eyes met once more. He didn't have to say it. Kari knew this was the last time they could be like this. Ever.

A lump formed in her throat as she searched Ryan's eyes, allowing herself to drown once more in the depth of emotion she saw there. She opened her mouth to speak, but every word was an effort. "I'm . . . I'm so sorry."

She wondered if he was going to kiss her again. But instead he searched her face and, despite the tears in his eyes, began to speak in a voice that was calm and controlled. "Don't ever apologize for doing what's right."

He smoothed a finger over her forehead, the connection between them unbroken. "May I tell you something?"

It was torture being so close to him, and she realized she was holding her breath. "Yes."

"No matter what happens next, I'll never forget tonight as long as I live."

Could he still read her that well? Did he know that this good-bye was more final than any they'd ever said? Tears coursed down her cheeks, and she was torn about how to respond. "Ryan, I —"

"No." His voice was choked but filled with compassion and authority at the same time. "Go, Kari. I'll see you later."

She nodded, swallowing hard. "Okay." Without hesitating, she leaned forward and hugged him, clung to him. And when she couldn't take the suffocating pain of his nearness, the impossibility of their situation, another moment, she pulled away, climbed out, and shut the door behind her.

Without turning around she took determined steps up the drive, onto the porch, and into the house. When she closed the door behind her, she heard him back out of the driveway, and she listened as the sounds of his truck faded into the night. Her heart plummeted, and the reality of her situation became painfully clear.

Help me, Lord.

She glanced at the wall in the entryway and saw the framed piece of needlepoint her grandmother had done decades earlier. The words stitched in a delicate faded lilac thread were a paraphrase of Philippians 3:13: "Forget what is behind. Press on to what is ahead."

The Scripture passage propelled her, prevented her from collapsing and dying from the pain of losing Ryan a second time.

Forget what is behind . . . press on to what is ahead.

The words ran over and over in her heart, and Kari knew they held within them her only hope for surviving.

She crept up to her bedroom, where she wept into her pillow. She was wrong to have spent time with Ryan. He was not her husband, not the man she planned to spend her future with. That man was Tim, and at this point God wanted her to press on toward her life with Tim and all that lay ahead for them.

But it wasn't the pressing on that concerned her; it was the other part of the passage.

The forgetting part.

After spending the evening with Ryan, after learning the truth about his feelings for her and knowing again the warmth of his arms and his kiss, after walking alongside him through the hallways of yesterday, the truth was clear.

Only a miracle could make her forget about Ryan Taylor now.

Chapter Twenty-One

Fog had settled over the water, and Kari strained to see across the deck. She heard a voice and realized there was someone else on the boat, someone besides her and Tim. It was a woman, and she was laughing.

"He loves me, not you . . . face the facts." Her cold, cackling voice sent a shiver down Kari's spine.

"Ashley?" Kari peered through the cloud cover once more, but couldn't make out the woman's face.

Whoever she was, Tim sat beside her, his arms crossed. And at the mention of Ashley's name he released a loud huff. "Ashley's not here. Don't you know who it is, Kari?"

Anxiety squeezed her ability to breathe. She stared at Tim and saw not even the slightest trace of love. "I guess I thought —"

"Kari . . . Kari, it's me!" Before she could finish her sentence, a voice she knew and loved called at her from the distant shore.

Ryan. It was Ryan Taylor — she was sure of it.

She spun in the direction of the beach, but through the thick cloud covering all she could make out was a far-off, shadowy image. "Ryan?"

Tim jumped up and grabbed her wrist, squeezing it until she winced in pain. "So that's it. You're still seeing Ryan Taylor? I knew it!" His voice rose. "It was always Ryan, wasn't it? You always loved him more."

Kari shook her head, her throat thick with fear. "That isn't true. I love you, Tim. I want our marriage to work. I want things to —"

"Aren't you finished with her yet?" A slinky blonde walked up and circled her arms seductively around Tim's neck. She leaned down and covered his throat with small kisses, working her way toward his lips.

Kari felt her eyes grow wide. "Get away from him!" She stood and glared at the woman, her heart pounding out a rhythm she didn't recognize. "He's *my* husband!"

There was a thud, and the boat made a sudden stop. Water rushed across the deck and came up around their ankles. Tim released his hold on Kari and glared at her as he leaned into the blonde. "I don't want you, Kari. I never have."

He laughed at her as his words faded into the damp air. The fog was lifting now, and Kari's heart rate doubled. There was a hole in the boat. They had two minutes — three at the most — before they sank. Even now the water was almost to their knees. Kari stared at Tim and the other woman and struggled to understand what was happening. "You have to try. You can't just give up on everything we promised each —"

"Kari, can you hear me?" Ryan's voice stopped her short, and she turned once more toward the shore. This time she could see him, tall and handsome, his eyes filled with a love that shone across the murky lake.

"I can't, Ryan." She began to cry even before she finished saying his name. "I'm . . . I'm married."

He shook his head. "You're going to drown, Kari. Jump! Get out of the boat before it's too late."

Kari's entire body shook with fear. Ryan was right. She looked back at Tim, but the woman was sitting on his knee now, running her fingers through his hair. Kari shouted the warning: "We're going to sink!" But neither of them made any response whatsoever.

Ryan's voice came again, more urgent

this time. "Jump, Kari . . . please. I'm here . . . I'll help you!"

The water was up to her waist, but before she could speak, before she could make up her mind about whether to stay in the sinking boat or swim for shore, she felt a sudden lurching followed by a crackling sound as the boat fell apart beneath her. Tim and the other woman disappeared beneath the water, their arms around each other as if unaware that they were sinking.

"Ryan, help me!" Water ran into her mouth. Just as she was about to swim away from the wreckage, her ankle twisted between two pieces of wood, trapping her foot and sucking her underwater.

"Ryan!" Her muffled voice sounded beneath the surface, but there was no way he could hear her. Foot by foot, she felt herself being pulled to the bottom of the lake, and no matter how hard she tried, she couldn't break free.

Her lungs burned, desperate for air. *Help me, God, I'm dying. . . . Get me out of this. . . . Get me —*

And then a desperate, primitive scream reached her ears, vibrating through the water closing around her. The scream came again and again and finally a fourth time.

"Kari?" Her mother was in the doorway, hurrying to her bedside. "Dear God, Kari, what is it? You scared me to death."

Kari shut her eyes tight and opened them again. There was no sinking boat, no far-off shoreline. The scream she heard had been her own. "Mom . . ." Kari was breathless as she looked at her mother and tried to remember what day it was, why she was at her parents' house and not at her own. "What's — what's happening to me?"

Her mother pulled her close, stroking her hair, causing her to release what was left of her tears. Her head sagged on her mother's shoulder as memories from the previous day all began to come back to her. The time on the lake, the memories, the realization that she and Ryan had misunderstood each other so many years before.

The kiss.

"Honey?" Her mother's voice was kind and gentle, as it had been when she was a little girl. At least she had this place, this family to come back to, this love that knew no limits.

She drew back, rubbing her eyes. "I was dreaming."

"I'm sorry."

Kari nodded and reached to the bedside table for a tissue. "I need to call Tim."

At the mention of his name, a shadow passed over her mother's eyes. "He called last night. I told him I'd tell you."

A quick breath caught in Kari's throat. "Last night?"

"Yes." Concern lined her mother's forehead. "Just after nine."

Just after nine. Kari thought back and knew exactly where she'd been at that time. Face-to-face with Ryan Taylor, her arms around him, holding him close and . . . "What did you tell him?"

"I said you were out with a friend."

Kari's shoulders dropped and she exhaled. "Thanks. He wouldn't understand about . . ." Her voice faded.

"About you and Ryan?" Her mother peered deep into her eyes, and Kari felt her cheeks grow hot.

"Yes."

There was silence for a moment, and her mother leaned over her knees. "You got home late."

"I won't lie to you, Mom." Kari sniffed and dried her cheeks once more. "I still love him. But that's the last time I'll see him." The lump in her throat was back, and a single sob escaped from her throat.

"Ah, honey." Her mother's arms were around her again.

Normally the tiny pink-and-yellow rose border that framed the bedroom walls and the picture window overlooking the dirt road out back were enough to help Kari feel grounded, but not today. This morning there was only one way she could find peace.

Her mother stroked her hair and studied Kari's face. "I'm going out to the mall shortly. Why don't you take a shower and come with me?"

Kari choked out a single laugh and shook her head. Go to the mall? When her life was in full-blown crisis mode? There was only one place for her to go now. "I can't." Kari blinked back the thoughts. "I'm going home. For good."

"Well —" her mother reached over and took her hand — "you know you're always welcome here."

Kari eased her legs from beneath the comforter and sat on the edge of her bed. "I know, Mom." Kari leaned over and laid her head against her mother's shoulder. "But my marriage will never get better as long as I keep running back here."

When her mother left the room, Kari stared into the mirror and realized something she hadn't before. For all her determination to save her marriage, for all her faith and ideals, this morning the facts were painfully clear.

She was no better than Tim. They were both unfaithful now, weren't they?

After being with Ryan, after picturing his face even this morning while she was making plans to reunite with Tim, the simple fact was this: The tears she'd shed the night before were not for her husband's faithlessness.

They were for a man she'd loved since she was a young girl, and for all she'd left behind on a familiar lakeshore near Bloomington, Indiana.

Tim Jacobs woke up on the floor of the bathroom close to the toilet. He had no idea how long he'd been there and only dim memories of the night before.

Everything about his life was a nightmare. And all of it — the whole messy situation — seemed to culminate in the emptying of his stomach hours earlier.

Why he had allowed it to come to this, he had no idea. But he knew one thing for sure. He was finished. Finished with the lies, finished with the cheating. And if he had any luck at all, finished with the bottle.

Maybe that's why he'd had so much to drink the night before. He'd told himself the only way to get the alcohol out of his system at this point was to consume as much as possible and get an honest taste for what it was doing to him.

It had done that, all right.

Look at you, Tim Jacobs. You're a loser. Pathetic. Kari wouldn't take you back now. Who are you kidding? You're the worst example of a —

"I know!" Tim shouted at himself.

He sank back against the bathroom wall and tried to clear his head. What time was it anyway? What day was it? He looked over and saw Kari's wedding portrait leaning against the tub; he must have carried it there last night. "Where are you, sweetheart?" he whispered. "What're you doing without me?"

Tim thought about his plan. He would get up, shower, get dressed, and call Kari at her parents' house. Then he'd tell her he wanted to move back home, once and for all. By evening they'd be together, and he would explain how sorry he was, how crazy he'd been to ever leave.

It wouldn't be easy to tell Angela goodbye. He still had feelings for her, and he didn't want to hurt her. But the whole affair had been a bad choice to begin with, and he was desperately sorry about it.

Kari and the baby and a normal life — that's all he wanted now. A life like the two of them had shared before he left.

He could still have it, he thought; it wasn't too late. He'd tell Kari that his cheating days were over and that he wanted to meet with Pastor Mark, get involved with church again. He could do it.

Because the truth — the truth he now saw so clearly — was that he still loved his wife. He had no doubts.

When he looked at his life and thought hard about when he'd been the happiest, Kari's face came to mind time and time and time again. She was beautiful and trusting and kind and compassionate and . . . there was no one like Kari. There never would be. More than anything else, Tim wanted them to be together again.

But where was she last evening?

A disturbing thought had come to him last night after talking with Kari's mother. The woman had been so vague about Kari's whereabouts, mumbling something about her being "out with friends."

Fear mingled with the leftover nausea, and Tim wondered again why he couldn't get the suspicion out of his mind. It was insane, really. Paranoid.

But there was this bit of reality: Ryan Taylor was back in town. According to the sports pages, he was coaching at Clear Creek High School — not far from where Kari's parents lived. Kari had once been in love with Ryan, after all. Maybe she still had feelings for him.

He blinked. What if they had run into each other and — ?

Jealousy clawed at Tim's gut even as he realized his own hypocrisy. Did he really believe Kari would cheat on him with Ryan Taylor? And could he really blame her if she did? He closed his eyes and pictured Kari in the living room the last time he'd seen her, the afternoon when he moved out. She had cried, but even then she'd been willing to work on their relationship. She believed in marriage, in God's plan for marriage, and despite the way he'd failed her, she believed in him.

And because of that, she could not possibly have been with Ryan last night. If he knew Kari at all, he knew that much.

Daylight streamed through the bathroom window, and he inched himself up until he was on his feet. His eyes cleared some as he stared into the mirror. There was a red mark on the right side of his face from the toilet seat. He leaned back, scrutinizing his appearance.

Very attractive. Very scholarly.

Cold water. That's what he needed. He flipped on the faucet and splashed his face, rinsing the rancid taste out of his mouth left over from the night before. *God, I'm sorry. . . . I don't know what to say. I've stayed away so long.*

It was the first time in months he'd prayed, but once the words penetrated his heart, a floodgate opened, and tears filled Tim's eyes. Then and there in the bathroom, he knew the worst days of his life were behind him. Kari would forgive him, and together they would move forward, make a home for their baby, and grow from the darkness of these days.

This time it would be up to him. He stared himself straight in the eyes and nodded with more determination than he'd ever felt in his lifetime. What Kari needed was a stronger Tim Jacobs. A man who knew what he wanted in his marriage and had a way to make it happen. A man willing to humbly come back to God, the way he should have done long ago.

"This is your day, Tim Jacobs. Everything's different from now on."

And with that he dried his face and

walked gingerly downstairs to the kitchen and filled the coffeemaker. While the coffee was brewing, he opened the refrigerator and poured himself a glass of orange juice. He was crossing the kitchen toward the telephone when he saw the half bottle of Jack Daniels he'd brought there the night before.

He picked it up and headed for the sink. He had no need for a bottle in the house now, not since he'd be starting life over as a new man. But then it seemed a waste to dump the contents down the drain, especially when his head was pounding so hard that it seemed it might split in two right there on the kitchen floor.

In as much time as it took him to cross to the sink, he revised his plan. He'd have a few shots of Jack Daniels in his orange juice and then call Kari. That way he'd be more relaxed and ready to talk. A little "hair of the dog" couldn't hurt; he didn't have classes on Monday.

Once that bottle was gone, he'd never drink again. Not ever.

He tipped the bottle to pour the whiskey into his glass of orange juice, then changed his mind and brought the bottle to his lips and took a long swig. "Aaah." He shook his head. "Good morning, Tim. It's a brand-new day! Yes, sir."

He raised the bottle and took another drink. And another and another and another.

An hour passed before he remembered the phone call he was supposed to make to Kari. By then he was having trouble understanding why they'd installed three telephones on the kitchen wall when one would have done quite nicely.

Chapter Twenty-Two

Four times that morning Kari tried to reach Tim at the office, but when he didn't answer, she decided to pack her things, go home, and face her future. In the deepest places of her heart she had no choice but to leave memories of Ryan Taylor — even recent memories — in the past.

Where they belonged.

It was time to make things right with Tim, especially now that he had contacted Pastor Mark. That call and the one he'd made last night to her parents' house were the signs she'd been praying for, proof that Tim wanted another chance.

As Kari showered and dressed, two things weighed on her: guilt and a dawning realization.

It had been wrong to kiss Ryan, wrong to act as if time had not moved on since their last time together. The fact that she could justify her actions did not make them less wrong. No, the guilt did not surprise her. It was the growing realization of her own responsibility that made everything seem so different this morning.

Before last night, she had been convinced that Tim was the cause of their troubled marriage. But since waking from the nightmare, she had been overcome with memories that suggested a slightly more balanced picture.

She remembered the time early in the summer when Tim had come home from work with a dozen roses and tickets to a show. She had thanked him for the flowers but begged off on the night out. "I have a photo shoot at eight tomorrow morning; I thought I'd get to bed early." The way Tim's expression had fallen was something that never hit her until this morning. He had wanted to surprise her with something nice, but she'd been too busy to notice.

There had been other moments too. Times when he would hand her one of his columns, anxious for her approval, and she would lay it aside to read later. Most of the time she never got around to reading his work. Looking back now, she was sure her lack of interest must have hurt him.

And then there were the conferences and university functions he wanted her to attend with him. Once it was merely a picnic with a few couples he knew from the university. She had imagined them mocking her for her lack of intellect and shaken her head.

"You go, honey." The memory of her response made her wince. "I've got a hundred things to do around here."

She'd made time to go to the lake with Ryan, but she couldn't remember the last time she'd gone anywhere with Tim — not just for fun and companionship. *When did I start treating him more like a fixture than a friend?* There were no answers, and she imagined her witty, charming husband growing silently disenchanted and lonely while she busied herself with a hundred more important tasks.

No wonder he'd been vulnerable to Angela Manning. The woman had probably jumped at the chance to do things with him, even something as simple as meeting him for lunch.

No doubt she was the companion Kari had once been.

Kari tried to remember what was so important that she'd so often declined his invitations, and she knew it was because she didn't feel like she measured up. Tim's columns were often about issues she didn't follow, and he sometimes made points she disagreed with but didn't really know how to argue. And Tim's colleagues and their spouses — well, she'd had enough of them after that awful dinner conversation about books. They were always talking about foreign affairs and compelling literature and "films" — never movies — when they weren't gossiping about university politics. Being with them always seemed like a competition to see who was the cleverest in the group and who could drop the most names.

She had neither the desire nor the courage to venture much into university society. So she had begged off from all but the most crucial functions. Now she could picture Tim at those same affairs, talking with other couples, being clever, dropping names. But always alone.

No, Tim was clearly not the only one contributing to the problems in their marriage. Kari still felt sick at the thought of his affair. It would take months, years of healing before their marriage might be again what it once was. But this morning — in the wake of her guilt and responsibility — she was ready to try, anxious to get home and start picking up the pieces.

She turned sideways in front of the mirror and checked her figure, noting that her abdomen showed just a hint of roundness. Their baby was growing within her, their child . . . part her, part Tim.

Suddenly she realized she was not only anxious to get home, she was also looking forward to it.

Those were still her feelings when she pulled into their driveway an hour later. The blinds were shut tight, the way she had left them, and the house looked utterly quiet. But the garage door opened to reveal Tim's Lexus. Had he come home?

"Tim?" she called out hopefully as she let herself in through the utility room. No answer.

Then she walked into the kitchen and saw the empty liquor bottle on the counter. What was this? Her breath caught in her throat. But after a moment she forced herself to continue through the house. Through the dining room, where unopened letters lay in a stack on the table and her wedding portrait had been removed from the wall. Through the living room, up the stairs, and down the hall toward their bedroom. *Get me through this, God. Please.*

She took the few remaining steps down the hallway and quietly opened the bedroom door. Tim lay sprawled across the bed, dressed in sweats and a T-shirt, his ragged snoring filling the air. The whole room smelled of alcohol and vomit and body odor. As her eyes adjusted to the darkness, a sudden storm of revulsion rained down on her.

It took everything God had given her to not turn around and drive back to her parents' house. *Help me, Lord.*

She tiptoed into the room, sure he would wake up from the sound of her heartbeat alone. Who had he been drinking with? Had Angela been here?

Kari gritted her teeth and settled her eyes on Tim.

Was this the man she'd married? The one who had once made her think it was actually possible to forget Ryan Taylor? The one who had sworn that no matter what, he wouldn't touch an alcoholic beverage?

The man who had promised to be faithful until death parted them?

She crossed the room in a trance and settled into a chair near their bed. Her stomach churned, and she was choked by a growing nausea. Three times she nearly made a dash for the bathroom, but she managed to swallow back the bile. She hadn't eaten since breakfast, and she knew her pregnancy was partially responsible for the sick feeling.

But clearly it was more than that. Tim rolled over in his stupor, and another putrid wave of alcohol and underarm sweat assaulted her senses. Dirty laundry littered the floor, along with scattered books and papers.

Kari stood to leave and then caught herself as a Scripture passage from their wedding flitted through her mind: *Love endures all things.*

She locked her jaw, sat down again, and gripped the arms of the chair. Gone were her feelings of guilt and responsibility — gone right along with her desire to work things out. In the depth of her being was a rock-bottom certainty that God wanted her to love her husband. But if this was what their love would be like, Kari had no idea how she'd endure a lifetime of it.

For two hours — until sleep mercifully took over — Kari watched Tim the way she might watch a horror film. Only this time the monster was her husband, and the terror was as real as her last name.

Tim Jacobs was certain the vision of Kari in the chair beside the bed was part of some alcohol-induced daydream, some stage of intensive hangover he hadn't hit before. He lifted his head and squinted at her before dropping back to the pillow. One thing was sure: Even in the midst of a dream Kari was still the most beautiful woman he'd ever seen.

Why are you here? He still wasn't thinking clearly from the alcohol he had downed earlier this morning, and he was hating himself with a passion for not dumping the liquor down the drain. He studied Kari's sleeping form as slowly, insidiously, guilt slithered into bed beside him and made its way around his midsection like a boa constrictor. *Did you come to torture me?*

It wasn't until Kari opened her eyes that he fully realized he wasn't dreaming. And suddenly he could see and smell and sense everything through Kari's perspective — his own drunken haze, the clothing and books littering the room, the whiskey bottle in the kitchen.

The realization sent him stumbling to the toilet, where for ten minutes straight his body tried to rid itself of every drink he'd consumed for the past month. But no matter how many times his stomach convulsed, it couldn't get rid of the fear inside him, the guilt and anguish at having Kari see him this way.

When he was finished, he wiped his

mouth with the back of his hand and shuffled toward the bed. He sat down and shifted so he could see Kari's face. There could be only one reason she was here now, and the thought made him blink back tears. She was the only good thing that had ever happened to him, and now he'd lost her.

No, he hadn't lost her; he'd destroyed her.

"You have divorce papers for me?" he asked.

Kari stared at him, and he cringed inwardly at the pain in her expression. "No."

No papers? Tim's mind raced, trying to imagine why she might come unannounced. As he searched for a reason, he saw a few tears meander down her cheeks.

She wiped the sleeve of her shirt across her face, and he sensed she was holding herself back. His breathing was shallow, and his heart raced near the surface of his chest. What could have happened to make her cry this way? Was it her parents? Was someone sick? He reached his hand toward her but stopped short of moving to her side. The last thing she would want now was his nearness.

"Why'd you come, Kari?"

"I'm your wife, and I'm pregnant." Kari

stood and sat on the bed across from him, tears now flowing freely down her face. "I need to be home. I need you."

She moved closer. His breath caught in his throat as he felt her hand on his shoulder, and he was instantly alert. "I'm here because I still believe in what we have. What we could have. We've got problems, but I believe God can heal us."

Each word, each syllable painted hope and life and possibility into areas of his heart that had been dead and buried. She was willing to forgive him after all. He deserved nothing but her wrath, but here she was, telling him they still had a chance. That she was willing to stay with him and have his child.

In his mind, one by one, he began to count off the reasons she should leave him. Angela, the lying, the drinking — all of it. Every bad decision he'd made shifted like a ton of dirt onto his back, and he knew he couldn't draw another breath until he got out from beneath it.

He met her eyes and silently begged her to believe the thing he was about to say. "I'm really sorry, Kari. So sorry." He moved his fingertips to the side of her face to convince himself she was really there, sitting beside him after all he'd done to her.

She opened her mouth, but no words would come. She simply nodded, her face red and tearstained. Then, as if she couldn't hold herself up any longer, she fell slowly against him. Tentatively and with fear in his heart, he brought his hand to the small of her back and held her while she sobbed.

Tim had no idea how much time passed, but finally he heard her draw a shaky breath. "I want . . . I want us to be together again. But I don't know." She sniffed. "We . . . we need counseling."

If she expected an argument, he had none to give. Tim nodded quickly as some of the weight eased from his shoulders. "I'll call Pastor Mark."

She was still leaning against him, and he felt the tears return. "I'm sorry. I didn't plan to fall ap—"

"Kari, don't." The idea of her apologizing now, in light of all he'd done, was too much for him to bear. He knew better than to breathe, knew that even the slightest movement of air in or out of his body would release a torrent of emotion he was not equipped to handle.

When his lungs were about to burst, he grabbed three quick breaths and gritted his teeth, squeezing his eyes shut as a torrent of sorrow released within him. Then he wept as he'd never wept in his life.

Eventually his other hand came around Kari's back, and he held her close, the kind of embrace he'd seen once on a news program when a man had wrongly received word of his wife's death in a plane crash. When the two were reunited at the airport, cameras had been on hand to capture the moment. The depth of feeling in the hug between those people was something Tim remembered to this day.

Now he knew what the man had felt.

Because until Tim woke and found Kari sitting across from him, everything in his life had been doomed. He had no right to what she was offering, no reason to feel worthy. Yet here she was offering him a new chance at life and everything that went along with it.

When he was able to catch his breath, he whispered words that he meant with every fiber of his being.

"Kari, I promise . . . I'll spend the rest of my life making it up to you."

Chapter Twenty-Three

A week had passed since Kari returned to her house, and still Ryan could think of nothing else. It was Monday night, and the coaching staff was meeting after school to discuss playoffs. The Clear Creek Golden Bears had their first chance at a state title in ten years, and the coaches wanted to be unified in their approach.

"You with us, Taylor?" Head coach John Sicora shouted at him from the opposite end of the table. "Which game are you thinking about, anyway — ours or the one on TV tonight?"

The others in the room laughed, and Ryan forced a chuckle. "Sorry. Got a lot on my mind."

"Well, disengage it, will you?" It was Tommy Schroeder, another assistant. "You're too quiet. Any playoff plan we make won't be worth the dirt we play on if you're not part of it."

Ryan sat up straighter in his seat and diverted his gaze for a moment, embarrassed by the compliment. Yes, he had a talent for coaching, but he was nothing without the rest of the staff. He smiled at the group of men seated around him at the table. He had no idea what they'd been talking about, but he trusted their decisions completely.

"What about the corner blitz?" Sicora leaned back in his chair. "Do we use it against these quicker teams or not?"

The meeting lasted an hour longer than necessary, with talk of getting together afterward for pizza and Monday Night Football. Ryan quietly left during the conversation and slipped out of the building before anyone could razz him about being antisocial.

The night air hit him like a slap in the face, and he gazed up at the sky. The ceiling of snow clouds was so low he could almost touch it. Normally Ryan loved the first snow of the season. Any other time, the gathering of coaches would have been at his house, anchored near his big-screen TV, warmed by a roaring blaze in the fireplace.

But since he and Kari had parted, nothing felt right. Worse, the hurt that racked his heart showed no signs of lessening as time passed. Just the opposite.

Now, as he made his way to the car, he remembered a conversation he'd had with his mother two weeks after his football injury, the one that had nearly paralyzed him.

He'd been lying on the hospital bed, staring out the window, trying to imagine why he hadn't heard from Kari, when his mother entered the room.

There was silence between them for a long time before his mother finally spoke. "I think it might be broken, son."

Ryan remembered the confusion he'd felt at her statement. He turned slowly so he could see her. His neck was healing well by then, but it was still difficult to turn. "What?"

"Your heart." She leveled her gaze at him. "There's a big hole there where a girl named Kari used to be."

He had sighed and let his focus settle on the ceiling. "Where is she? Why hasn't she called?"

His mother waited before answering him. "I don't have the answers, but I know this: You'll recover from your back injury." Her voice grew soft. "But if you let Kari Baxter get away, you might never be the same again."

Ryan climbed into his truck as the memory faded. All these years later he was still right where he'd been that afternoon in the hospital bed. Not sure how he was going to survive without her.

Especially after finding her again.

There was one difference this time. He hadn't let Kari get away; he'd consciously helped her go. She wanted to make her marriage work, and Ryan believed deep in his soul she was making the right decision. A God-centered decision.

He remembered some of what Kari told him about Tim Jacobs, the man she'd married. The man who didn't love her enough to be faithful. Ryan was simply amazed by her desire to stand by the man even after his affair. If she had been timid and dependent on Tim, the type of woman who never spoke up for herself, Ryan might have understood.

But Kari Baxter?

He chuckled out loud as he started the truck and pulled out of the school parking lot.

The high school stories about Kari were legendary. Although everyone wanted to be her friend or prom date, no one at school had to wonder about her thoughts on the typical teenage vices — drinking, drugs, sex, and even breaking curfew. Not that she was perfect. She got in trouble for talking during class or passing notes. But the really bad temptations were never a problem for Kari.

The moment she'd walk into a party, beer cans would begin to disappear. She'd look around, eyes sparkling with a joy that couldn't be bought in a bottle or bag. "I hope you guys aren't drinking, because that is *so* not cool."

In her presence her peers wanted to be clean. If it was good enough for Kari Baxter, it was good enough for them.

In fact, the more Ryan thought about it, the more he admired what Kari had done in going back to Tim. It hadn't been because she was weak-willed or lacking a backbone. No, she could have gone back only by God's grace, by asking him to honor her decision to love and help her stay strong in it.

Ryan remembered something she had told him about her motivation, and now he replayed it in his mind. *"I really believe that love is a decision. I decided to love Tim Jacobs for better or worse."*

"What if Tim doesn't feel the same way?" Ryan had asked. He hadn't been checking his chances. Rather, he had been amazed at the possibility. He had wanted to know how far she'd carry her commitment, how long she'd wait if her husband no longer loved her and refused to change.

Sorrow had filled Kari's eyes as she answered him, and he was immediately pierced with regret for asking. "I won't give him a divorce, Ryan. I can't."

I can't.

Those two words grieved him most now as he turned left onto the highway and headed home. Their time on the beach together the other night had shown Ryan how she still felt about him. It wasn't that Kari didn't want the life she might have shared with him had they stayed together.

She simply couldn't. Her word, her honor, her relationship to God, her decision to love — all that meant too much to her to risk throwing away. That was just the kind of person she was.

Suddenly Ryan realized where he needed to be that cold Monday night. He turned his truck around and headed for church. Bible studies met there during the week. The sanctuary would be open for at least another three hours.

Five minutes later he slipped into a back pew and let his eyes adjust to the partial light. In the distance he could hear the muffled sounds of people talking and occasionally laughing. He leaned his forearms on the back of the bench in front of him, hung his head, and tried to understand how he'd made such a mess of things with Kari back when he was playing football.

What's wrong with me, God? I loved her. Why didn't it work out?

In response, Kari's words filled his heart once more. *"Love is a decision . . . a decision . . . a decision."*

If that was true, he should have decided to call Kari every day after his accident, even if he was distracted and worried about his injury. He should have decided to pursue her until his intentions were clear. He should have decided to give his love for her as much priority as he gave his football career.

He thought about the way Kari demonstrated her love to Tim, the way she was willing to stand by him even when a part of her hated the man for what he'd done to her.

Ryan fidgeted, lifted his head, looked around. Maybe God was trying to teach him something about love. Something Kari had already figured out, but Ryan never quite had.

He thought of his life, the coaching, and time he spent with his family and friends. He was pretty sure those things were spurred by love. But only love as he knew it.

Kari's love — the kind of love that could

go back to a man like Tim Jacobs and pray that God heal their marriage — that love was something altogether different.

He reached for a Bible from the back of the pew in front of him. If love truly was a decision, then right here, right now Ryan wanted to get a better understanding of how that could work. Most people Ryan knew were better versed in Scripture than he was, but even he knew where to find the love chapter. He flipped pages to the thirteenth chapter of 1 Corinthians and began to read.

The first three verses could mean only one thing. Whatever else a person did, whatever other sacrifices or acts of kindness or talents that person demonstrated, the entire sum of them meant nothing if he or she wasn't motivated by love.

That made sense. Ryan kept reading.

Verse four was where it started getting good, giving specific definitions of what love was and what it wasn't. The checklist — love is patient, kind, does not envy, does not boast — shed little new insight at first. But then his eyes ran past something that seemed newly written there that afternoon, as if it were intended for his eyes alone.

Love is not self-seeking.

He leaned back hard against the pew, thrust back to those days when he and

Kari were not exactly together, the early days of his football career. She had spent that time waiting for him with a selfless patience. Much as she was now waiting for Tim to come to his senses.

"Wait for me, Kari. When I'm not so busy, I want to be with you. Really."

Ryan felt a leaden anchor settle in his stomach. Had he actually said that to her? The memory of his words tasted bitter, as if they'd never fully digested. He looked at the verse and read once more the part that said love is not self-seeking. That was it, wasn't it? His love toward Kari had been genuine by worldly standards, but it had been completely self-seeking by God's.

When I'm *not busy, I'll call you, and* I'll *decide when the time is right?* That's really what he had been saying. But why hadn't he realized it before?

Ryan read a few more verses. In his mind, he started ticking off all the things, according to the Scripture, that love did. It always protected . . . hoped . . . trusted . . . persevered. *Persevered.* That last word hit him square in the face. If he had persevered in his love for Kari, he would have asked her why she backed off, why she seemed uninterested in him after his accident.

Perseverance?

Ryan stifled a sad chuckle. He hadn't come anywhere close. Sure, Kari could have asked him about the woman in his hospital room. But she had persevered for years before the accident and finally walked away only when it appeared Ryan had given his heart to someone else.

His spirit heavy within him, Ryan read the rest of the chapter and slowed down around verse eleven. A growing sense of hope began to fill his heart as the words soothed away his sorrow and frustration: *When I was a child, I talked like a child, I thought like a child, I reasoned like a child. When I became a man, I put childish ways behind me.*

That's the difference, he thought. He had been nothing but a child back in his football days — at least in thought and understanding. Now, though, he had a chance to do something he'd never done before.

To love Kari the way God wanted him to love her. To honor her without any thought for himself.

Tears stung at his eyes as the realization took root, because to love her now after losing all hope of being with her would be more painful than anything Ryan had ever done before. But it would be love. Real love. Grown-up love. After all the years of desiring

Kari, of wanting her and believing she'd be his wife one day, Ryan knew there was no time like the present to truly love her.

The way he should have loved her back then.

He didn't have to ask God what loving Kari would mean now that she had gone back to Tim. The Lord had already whispered the answer to him as clearly as if he were sitting beside Ryan in the cool, empty church.

Without hesitation Ryan eased himself onto his knees, wincing slightly as his left kneecap absorbed his weight. *Football,* he thought wryly. It had taken the best years of his life, ruined his chances with Kari Baxter, and in return left him with a permanently damaged body.

The Scripture verses on love came back, and he corrected himself. Football hadn't taken those things; his own self-seeking actions had. He exhaled slowly and pictured Kari climbing out of his truck, walking away for the last time.

I still want her, God . . . that's something you'll have to help me with. But right now, please . . . please, just give me the strength to love her the way you want me to.

Love her as I have loved you, my son.

Ryan nodded silently, closed his eyes,

and did the one thing that proved he had a new understanding of love — a God-given understanding. With a full and sincere heart he begged the Lord to show Kari and Tim a way to make their marriage work.

Quiet tears slipped down his face as he continued to pray. So this was how painful love could be. Painful enough for Kari to stay in a faithless marriage. Painful enough for him to give up all claim to the woman he loved.

Painful enough for Christ to give his life to save people from their sins.

Ryan slowly shook his head, moved to the core by a new depth of understanding. So this was love. The kind of love God had for his people, the kind of love Kari had for Tim.

Ryan stayed there for nearly an hour, ignoring the ache in his heart and his knees as he prayed for Kari's marriage. When he left the church that night, he realized that something deep and profound had happened back in the sanctuary, something that would forever change the way he felt about Kari, but also about his own ability to love.

He thought about the professional coaching offer that had come to him the day before, one that would take him a thousand miles from Bloomington and Kari and the marriage she was trying to save. The offer was a fluke, almost unheard-of for a high school coach, even one who had spent years in the pros. Then again, perhaps it was a divine reprieve, a gift of grace.

The job would require him to relocate in February, well after the football season was over. But at first Ryan had balked. His cabin was here, his ranch, his familiar community. He had deliberately chosen to come back here when he left the Cowboys. It would always be home.

But now . . . in light of his commitment to release Kari fully, his leaving Indiana might be the best thing for both of them. A way of illustrating a love that was no longer self-seeking.

And as he drove off into the night, the pain within him both deep and rewarding, he knew he was no longer a child when it came to the ways of love.

He was a man.

Chapter Twenty-Four

Kari slipped her hands into the pockets of a brand-new pair of navy twill pants, angled her body expertly, and smiled over her shoulder as a series of camera clicks went off.

Eight days had passed since she and Tim had gotten home from the intensive marriage seminar, the one Pastor Mark had told her about. Tim had been eager to go, more than willing to rearrange his class schedule for the chance to begin what would be a lifetime of healing between the two of them.

The two days had been amazing. She and Tim had talked intently with the counselors until it was clear what motivated each of them and how they affected each other — their dance, the counselors called it. The things they'd learned about themselves and their relationship in those scant forty-eight hours had been more revealing than all their combined communication with each other to that point.

Forgiveness happens once, the counselors had told them. Healing takes a lifetime.

Kari angled her head and smiled for the camera again.

Already she knew with every fiber of her being that she had made the right choice — a painful choice, but the right one all the same. Pastor Mark had connected them with a counselor whose specialty is with marriages in crisis, and they had seen the man three times before the seminar.

The photographer lowered his camera. "Perfect, Kari, beautiful. Now from the other side."

The genius behind the camera was Henry T. Canistelli, renowned catalog photographer, a man Kari affectionately called Hank. Nearly all of Kari's memorable catalog work had come from his hands.

Kari shifted and produced another smile.

"Kari, baby, the camera loves that face. Give it to me over the shoulder."

It felt good to get back to work. The staff at the modeling agency was grateful that whatever issues had caused her to need a break were apparently resolved.

"We'll work you full body until you're showing; then we'll do maternity spreads and face work," her agent told her. "I can keep you busy until you go into labor."

The current job was a six-hour shoot at a

desirable studio in Indianapolis. Despite the hot lights and the demand to look flawless, it was mindless work. Studio work always was. Outdoor shoots were something else entirely — keeping bugs from being attracted to her hair spray, working with natural lighting and weather conditions, freezing in the winter and sweltering in the summer — and trying to look good through all of it.

With all she had on her mind these days, she was grateful her agent had lined up six consecutive studio jobs. She'd get through those, then take another break for the holidays.

"That's the way, Kari." Hank grinned at her over the top of his camera. He was thirty years her senior, with a New York accent thicker than fog. "Perfect. Let's try the other shoulder. The friendly-young-mother look you're so good at."

She turned her back to him and glanced over the shoulder as if she were looking back at a trail of children or smiling at a best friend's joke. After Hank finished clicking, Kari relaxed. "It's all you, Hank. I just show up. You make the magic."

Hank adjusted a French beret on his head and chuckled. "You got that wrong, pretty girl. I've worked the business for years, and talent like yours doesn't come along often. Wife, lover, friend, girl-next-door, you name it. Any look you want and ageless beauty to boot — that's what you've got."

Kari laughed, enjoying the easy banter she and Hank always shared. "Well, then, I guess I better thank the good —"

Hank held up his hand and interrupted her. "I know, I know —" he raised his tone in friendly imitation — " 'I better thank the good Lord because he made me look like this and I wouldn't be nothin' without him.' " Hank nodded his head patiently, as if he'd heard the explanation a hundred times. "Well, you never know, kid. Maybe there's something to that faith of yours." He wiggled his fingers in her direction as if he were casting a spell. "Maybe that explains the unearthly sparkle in your eyes." He shrugged. "Whatever it is, if you could bottle it, you'd make millions."

In response Kari merely smiled and pointed heavenward. Hank's view of God was jaded at best, but Kari figured she was in his life for a reason — even if only a few times a month at photo shoots. Besides, she couldn't help but like him.

Five more outfits needed to be photographed. Kari gathered up the next one and headed toward the dressing room.

While she was changing, she thought about the second day at the marriage seminar, the day the breakthrough had happened.

"It comes down to your fears," one of the counselors had explained. "When a relationship isn't working, fears are usually the base of the trouble."

He asked them to think about their greatest fears regarding each other, and after five minutes of silence, tears had filled Tim's eyes. He looked at the counselor and swallowed hard. "She loved Ryan Taylor before she loved me. How was I supposed to measure up to that?"

"So what's your fear?" the counselor asked Tim, his voice tender, quiet. Even before Tim could answer, Kari felt a new sense of understanding wash over her.

"I guess —" he shifted his gaze to Kari — "I guess I always thought I wasn't good enough for you. I thought you deserved someone better."

The woman counselor interjected. "And what about you, Kari? What is your deepest fear where Tim is concerned?"

Kari remembered the way Tim's friends had responded to her at the faculty party. The answer was simple. "I was afraid I wasn't smart enough."

They talked about coping behaviors and how people always responded to their fears one way or another. In this case, Tim had coped by spending time with a woman who appreciated his intelligence. Kari, though, had handled her fear by withdrawing from Tim and busying herself with activities that made her feel competent.

"So you see the dance," the male counselor said to Tim. "The busier Kari became, the deeper your sense of rejection grew, and the more attracted you were to the other woman. It was a dance in which the steps took you farther apart every day."

Tim and Kari had stared at each other, amazed at the aptness of the counselor's description.

"At this point in your marriage," the counselor went on, "there are three anchors available to you, anchors that — if you choose to use them — will keep your marriage from destruction. If you choose to ignore these anchors, you probably can't expect your marriage to survive."

Tim took her hand while the man spoke. Though she still had feelings of doubt and anger and moments when her heart wanted to think about Ryan, the feel of her hand in Tim's was more comforting than she had expected.

The counselor turned his attention to Tim. "First, because of your tendency to binge drink, you should give up any form of alcohol completely."

"I . . . I tried that."

"Now that we're making it part of your counseling, if you can't stop on your own, you need to check out one of the Christian treatment programs. We'll give you a list."

He barely paused, but shifted his gaze to include Kari. "Second, you should be completely faithful to each other, both emotionally and physically."

"And most important of all," the woman counselor interjected, "you should both commit to understanding your individual fears and changing the way you cope. And that means the *d*-word — divorce — should not be included in your vocabulary."

The male counselor nodded. "Remember, each of these anchors is up to you. By making these choices, you will be able to change the steps to your dance and work toward healing."

When the counseling session was over, before they went home, Kari and Tim had walked hand in hand through a wooded park together, talking. They promised to dance more closely together from that point on.

A quick knock at the dressing-room door told Kari she needed to put the memory aside. "Okay, beautiful, time's up," Hank said. "Let's work these sets and get home."

"All right . . . coming."

Kari adjusted the next outfit and put the finishing touches on her appearance. She, too, was eager to finish the job and get back home.

She and Tim were getting follow-up counseling with a Christian psychologist in Bloomington. Their next appointment was this evening, and Kari had at least an hour's drive back home before that. She smiled to herself. The counseling sessions were sometimes difficult and painful, but thinking of them made her feel a sense of hope. A tender, tentative sense of a hope that could mean only one thing: Her broken heart was beginning to mend.

Fifty-five miles south, at the Silverlake Apartments, Angela Manning sat at her kitchen table, sipping coffee and contemplating Tim's disappearance. She simply couldn't comprehend what had happened. Their relationship had been going beautifully. There were a few tensions, but that was normal, wasn't it? Angela had been sure that things would calm down once

Tim's divorce was really in the works.

Then one evening while she was at the library, he had simply packed up and disappeared, leaving only a short note to explain his change of heart.

Her heart ached as she picked the note off the coffee table and read it for the hundredth time since he'd gone back to his wife.

Angela,

I'm sorry. I've made a terrible mistake, and it's destroying me.
I need to be with my wife, and you need to move on. Forgive me.

Tim

At first Angela had wondered if the note was some kind of bad joke, Tim's attempt to scare her. But when he didn't show up that night or the next, she began to panic. Never had she intended to get involved with a married man. But once she had, the only thing that kept her going was a strong belief that his marriage was over and his future was here with her, at this apartment just off campus.

To think that Tim might never have been serious about her, that he had perhaps allowed the affair to continue with no intention of being with her on a long-term basis, was more than she could bear. It made her feel cheap and sordid and used.

Just like the woman her father had left home for.

She felt the sting of tears in her eyes and took a sip of coffee, remembering the shock of those first few days after Tim left.

When she realized he'd gone home to his wife, she told herself he'd be back. He had left only because of his guilty conscience. When he realized what he'd left behind, he'd start divorce proceedings — the way he should have months ago — and then come knocking on her door.

But after a week had passed, Angela began to have doubts. Had Tim's wife come back to him so willingly? Tim had said she was staying with her parents before. But now, were they already living together? in their house?

Angela couldn't stand the thought, so for the past two days she'd left hourly calls on Tim's office voice mail, desperate to talk to him. She'd even considered going to his office and waiting for him. She drummed her fingernails against the coffee mug. If he didn't call her back today, that's exactly what she would do. She had no choice.

Because now that she'd fallen in love

with Tim, it didn't matter whether or not he was married. All that mattered was being with him. All she could think about was —

The phone rang.

Angela jumped and sloshed coffee on her jeans as she rushed to pick up the receiver. It was Tim; it had to be. Of course he'd call her back. He loved her as much as she loved him. This going-home thing was only part of the separation process, something he had to get out of his system. Yes, that was it.

A ray of hope shone across her heart, and she clicked the button. "Hello?"

There was silence for a moment, and then Angela heard someone breathing on the other line. Apparently Tim was upset and having trouble speaking. She was about to say his name when a man began talking. "Hi, Angela. It's me."

Angela felt the sting of disappointment. "Who is this?"

The caller uttered a single chuckle, and something about it sent a chill down Angela's spine. "Don't you know, baby? It's Dirk."

Frustration filtered through Angela's veins. Dirk Bennett? Hadn't she gotten through to him yet? The kid was obsessed. The fact that they'd slept together didn't mean she wanted to marry him. Besides, he was so young. After being with a man like Tim Jacobs, there was no way Angela could go back to a boy.

She released a sigh that conveyed her irritation. "What do you want?"

He was silent for a while, no doubt weighing her reaction. "Well . . . I know you're not seeing the professor anymore, and I wondered if you'd go out with me tonight."

She rolled her eyes. "No, Dirk. I won't go out with you tonight or tomorrow or any other night. Our dating days are over. Are you reading me?"

Dirk's breaths grew louder and closer together. "Don't you understand, Angela?"

There was something odd about his voice, and Angela felt the chill again. "Understand what?"

"Ever since we fell in love, I've been making plans." His voice was louder, angrier than before.

Angela glanced at her watch and considered hanging up on him. Tim was probably trying to call, and here she was carrying on a conversation with a deranged guy she hadn't dated in a year. She massaged the bridge of her nose and tried to be patient. "What plans?"

Dirk hesitated, his voice softer again.

"Plans to marry you, Angela. I have everything worked out."

Angela couldn't have felt more disgusted if a dozen spiders had been released down the back of her sweater. "Are you crazy? I have no intention of marrying you." She shuddered at the thought. "I've got to go."

"Wait!" She was about to hang up when Dirk's voice sounded again. This time his words were couched in nothing less than hatred. "The professor doesn't want you, Angela. He's back with his wife. I saw them together the other day. Holding hands."

Angela's breath caught in her throat, and a searing pain ripped across her heart. No! It wasn't possible. Tim was only taking some time to collect his thoughts; he wasn't really back with his wife. It had only been a few weeks.

"Did you hear me, Angela?"

Dirk's tone frightened her, and this time she did hang up. When the phone rang fifteen seconds later, she took it off the hook and hid it beneath a pillow. Then, for the first time since Tim moved out, Angela buried her face in her hands and cried.

An hour later, when her sobbing had eased, she stretched out on the sofa and considered her options. She didn't like any of them until —

She had an idea. It was deceitful, even downright dirty. But the more Angela thought about it, the more she believed it could work.

At the very least, it would get Tim back to her apartment one more time. After that it would be simple to convince him to stay. She'd gotten him to fall in love with her once; certainly she could do it again.

The idea grew and took shape until Angela was convinced it was the right thing. If she had to lie and manipulate a little, well, too bad. It was the only way she could think of to save what she and Tim shared.

Otherwise how would she survive?

Angela considered the coming holiday season and her busy class schedule. Her idea was brilliant, but she wouldn't act on it until after Christmas break. That way she'd give Tim time to change his mind without her having to lie to him.

She smiled, feeling better than she had since Tim walked out. One way or another, she would win him back.

It was merely a matter of time.

"Angela! Talk to me!" Dirk shouted into the phone for nearly a minute before giving up and slamming the receiver back down. He tightened his fists, noticing the way his biceps bulged beneath his T-shirt.

If only she could see him, see the way he'd worked his body into a piece of art. She'd never give the professor another thought.

Some kind of annoying boy-band music was playing in the dorm room next to his, and he pounded his fist against the wall. "Turn it down!" Almost instantly the music grew quiet. But Dirk barely noticed. He couldn't stop thinking about his conversation with Angela.

How dare she mock his offer? ridicule him without giving him a chance? Dirk ran a hand through his hair and knew it was thinning because of the pills. His trainer had warned him that on the higher doses, hair loss was possible. He paced across the room once more and stared at the picture of Angela tacked near his bed.

This was all the professor's fault. In fact, maybe the man had tricked Dirk. Maybe he was still making stops at Angela's apartment. Ever since Dirk spotted a second car parked in the professor's driveway, he'd been sure that the man had reunited with his wife. But what if he was still seeing Angela on the side?

The thought blinded him with rage. He

grabbed a glass on his nightstand, threw it on the floor, and smashed it with the heel of his boot. His heart pounded as he thought about his precious Angela, blinded by the lies of a two-timing loser like Professor Jacobs.

Dirk dug his fists into his thighs and gritted his teeth. There was only one way to know for sure. He'd have to start watching her apartment again. Not every night like some kind of deranged stalker. But often enough to catch the professor if he really was stopping by. Often enough to know if that was why Angela was giving him such a hard time.

His calendar hung on his bulletin board nearby, and he yanked it off, pulling the tack out in the process. Thanksgiving vacation was in two days, but after that he'd start watching Angela's apartment at least three nights a week. He'd switch the days around until he could catch Professor Jacobs in the act.

Then he would scare the professor away once and for all.

Even if he had to break the law to do it.

Chapter Twenty-Five

Thanksgiving day was unseasonably warm that year. John Baxter found he needed only a light sweater when he slipped out on the front porch after dinner.

It was a typical Baxter holiday — warm and bustling and loud. Kari and Tim were in the kitchen wrapping leftovers. Erin and Brooke had taken the children out back for a game of tag while their husbands, Sam and Peter, tossed a football with Luke. And Elizabeth was in a heated discussion with Ashley about the importance of spending more time with Cole. John loved the presence of his family, but he needed to clear his thoughts. He closed the door behind him and found Pastor Mark Atteberry sitting on the steps outside, alone.

He laid a hand on his friend's shoulder. "I'm glad you and Marilyn could join us."

"It's been great." Mark turned, his eyes veiled in peace and contentment. "We need more of this. One-on-one with the Baxters."

John leaned back and fixed his gaze on the bare trees that lined the driveway. "Can you believe it? Tim and Kari in there together, as if their marriage wasn't all but over a few weeks ago?"

"It's amazing." Mark kept his eyes on the horizon. "Goes to show you how good God is." He paused, and his eyes narrowed. "I was praying for them during dinner. They're trying so hard, being so careful with each other." He hesitated. "I take it Ashley and Brooke don't approve of his presence today?"

John sighed and took a seat next to the pastor. "It'll take some time, but they'll come around. They want Kari to be happy."

Mark stared across the front yard. "She and Tim have been attending Sunday morning services. I keep hoping they don't run into Ryan Taylor."

A breeze stirred the nearby trees, and John thought of Kari's fishing trip with Ryan. "She'll always have feelings for him."

"Yes."

"But she loves Tim more."

"I think so. She tells me love's a decision." Mark stroked his chin. "I like that. She's *decided* to be married to Tim for better or worse, and something beautiful is growing out of that decision. It's really something."

They were silent for a long while, and the smell of fresh-baked pumpkin pies wafted out the window behind them, mingling with the distant scent of burning leaves. It was John's favorite time of year, the season when memories of his family, his children's younger days, were close enough to see and hear and touch.

Mark inhaled long and slow and tapped his knee. "How's Ashley these days? I haven't heard much about her since all the troubles with Kari started."

John felt his eyes water. "Life has never been easy with Ash. Not when she was a young girl, and not now."

"She was a cheerleader in high school, wasn't she?"

"Briefly. Until she decided she wasn't the type."

Mark nodded. "That's right, I remember. And wasn't there one boy who always pursued her?"

"Landon Blake. Ran for the cross-country team, graduated same year as Ashley. His family used to go to Clear Creek Community Church, but they moved into town, and now they go to one of the big churches near the university."

"Whatever happened between Ashley and Landon?"

That's what John liked about Mark Atteberry. He pastored by heart. His concern for his congregation went far beyond their participation in church activities. He cared for them as people, cared about their lives, whether they were once-a-year Easter attendees or families like the Baxters, who were anchored in the history of the fellowship. Because of that, he was one of the best, most loving and effective pastors John Baxter had ever known or heard of.

John considered his question about Ashley and Landon. "It's a long story."

"I figured." Mark smiled. "Tell me about it. I've got time."

Dessert was still an hour away, and the two men were not in a hurry. "We always thought Ashley would go to college. Like her sisters. Maybe teach art or manage a music studio nearby." He paused. "We knew she was different, but we never thought she'd dive off the deep end." John gazed across the brown grass, and suddenly he could see Ashley pulling into the driveway the summer before her senior year, marching defiantly into the house, and demanding more time with her friends.

"She'd met some people at a coffeehouse down by the university. Most were three or four years older than she was, caught up in some kind of seventies retro movement."

That was the year, John explained, when she began dressing differently, wearing tie-dyed skirts, and walking out of the house without brushing her hair. Several times that summer, John and Elizabeth had shared their misgivings with her.

"We suspected she was drinking, maybe even dabbling in drugs because of all the changes we'd seen. But she was careful not to get caught, and we couldn't be sure." John shrugged. "We didn't want to force the issue."

In the end, nothing had come of their talks other than added tension. When she got caught drinking at a high school party that spring, no one was surprised. Least of all Landon Blake.

"He came by the house after that and told me he loved Ashley. It was something in his blood, he said. No matter what decisions she might make, he'd love her until the day she died."

"Big words from a high school boy."

John considered that and nodded.

"Landon's always been old for his age. More mature."

From an early age Landon Blake had been serious and high-achieving, with movie-star looks and a wiry athleticism. He was active in track and field and was easily one of the most popular boys in their class. Girls were always after him, but he was interested only in Ashley. And each time Ashley turned him down, he grew more infatuated with her.

"I heard from some of Ashley's friends that Landon was teased for his devotion to her. He didn't care. He told me once he'd keep asking her out until she said yes."

John remembered Ashley's reasons for not saying yes as clearly as if he'd heard them yesterday. "He's too good for me, Daddy, too all-American. He's bought into the system — the faith thing, the work thing, the save-money-for-a-house thing. He thinks life is work and marriage and kids and retirement. But why? What's it all for?"

Like all the Baxter children, Ashley was entitled to reduced tuition at Indiana University because of John's position. But she had no interest in even applying.

"She went to Bloomington Community, didn't she?" Mark knitted his brows curiously, and again John was impressed at his memory.

"Yes, got her associate's degree in graphic design, and we actually thought she might grow up." A troubled sigh escaped from deep within, and John shook his head. "We still felt that way when she left for Paris."

"Paris. That's where she got pregnant?"

"Yes." Those two years were the most difficult John and Elizabeth had ever faced as parents. Ashley had rarely called, and each time she did, it was as if a piece of her had disappeared forever. Later John and Elizabeth learned that Ashley had met a well-known French artist who ran a studio in downtown Paris. Their romance had been little more than a whirlwind. Beyond that, details were sketchy, though everyone assumed the artist was the father of Ashley's child. "Whatever happened there, it scarred her. She came home jaded and cynical, pregnant and more determined than ever to stand against everything we'd taught her to believe. The only reason she landed here is because she had nowhere else to go."

"That's when she had her accident." Mark didn't have to ask. Everyone at church knew about Ashley Baxter's accident. People had prayed around the clock that her unborn child might survive the impact, and miraculously he had.

"Sometimes I think the lawsuit was just another one of a long list of things that hurt her. Of course, she'd never agree."

"If I remember right, it was a lot of money for a young girl."

John nodded slowly. "Especially a young girl whose life was completely out of whack."

According to Ashley, the lawsuit had been the best thing that ever happened to her. She'd been six months pregnant when she was rear-ended by a national freight-delivery truck. The impact had totaled Ashley's car and put her in intensive care with a concussion and broken ribs. Contractions had started immediately, and doctors had feared the baby might have been brain-damaged in the accident.

The story received considerable local attention because the freight company had a history of similar accidents — many in which a faulty brake system was to blame. Given the fact that the company had disclosed that information *before* the collision, any lawyer with a day-old law degree would know there was money in the case.

Four months later, when a healthy Cole

was five weeks old, Ashley's attorney settled out of court with the freight company for two hundred thousand dollars.

Overnight, Ashley had become the owner of a three-bedroom house in an upscale neighborhood close to the university and had begun a life of what John liked to call drifting — taking a few art classes at the university, hanging out with her friends, doing some painting. "Cole's the one I feel sorry for. He doesn't have a daddy, and his mother really hasn't grown up yet."

Mark stroked his chin again. "Sounds like she hasn't changed much since coming back from Paris."

"No."

"I guess I didn't realize. . . ."

"Poor Cole." John crossed his arms and met his friend's eyes. "I try to take the place of a father for him. You know, get down on the floor and play with the little guy. But Ashley's always dropping him off so she can find a quiet place to paint or hang out with her friends at the coffeehouse. It's almost like she's still in high school." He searched for the words. "Still trying to convince the world that no one can tell Ashley Baxter how to live."

The breeze was picking up, and storm

clouds gathered in the north. The temperatures had dropped considerably just in the time they had been outside, and snow flurries were actually forecast for the late evening. John stood and stretched, gently squeezing Mark's shoulder. "All that to say — pray for her, would you? As Cole gets older, he'll soon realize that we're his real parents and his mother's nothing more than a mixed-up kid."

Mark rose to his feet as well and patted John on the back. "I'll pray. And anytime you need to talk, I'm available."

John felt grounded again. He remembered his favorite Bible story, the one about Peter getting out of the boat and walking on water. The big fisherman was walking along quite nicely until he looked at the waves and began to sink.

As much as possible, John tried to live his life without looking at the waves. But when he did, when the lives of his grown children caused his faith to waver even a little, God always sent someone to illustrate the words of Christ: "You of little faith . . . why did you doubt?"

John felt certain that in this, his most trying season yet, the Lord had sent Pastor Mark to fill that role. It was a certainty that kept his eyes where they belonged —

off the waves and straight ahead to the outstretched arms of Jesus.

Inside the house Ashley heard the men stop talking and move toward the front door. She wiped the angry tears from her eyes and hurried into the empty dining room so they wouldn't know she had been listening.

So that was how her parents saw her — as an irresponsible single parent who cared little or nothing for her son?

Ashley's shoulders tensed, and she grabbed a dishrag and wiped the crumbs from the dinner table. Fine. If that's the way her parents wanted to be, she could make a life without them. She didn't have to bring Cole to their house. She had a dozen friends who would gladly watch him. Why burden her parents? Especially if they felt like she was passing off her duty on them.

Out of the corner of her eye she saw Kari and Tim, side by side at the kitchen counter stretching plastic wrap over a bowl of mashed potatoes. They were talking quietly together about something Ashley couldn't make out. The sight was practically nauseating. Was Kari so willing to pick up where she left off with Tim, even after his blatant affair? That he could even show his face at the Baxter house was nothing less than astonishing.

She remembered her father's blessing over the meal and how in the quiet space afterward Tim had spoken to the entire family.

"Obviously, you all know about the troubles Kari and I are having." Tim had the attention of everyone at the table, his voice somber, humbled. "I've made some very bad choices, and I'm sorry. Not just about hurting Kari —" his eyes glistened, and Ashley wanted to spit at him — "but about hurting all of you too." He reached for Kari's hand. "We're trying hard to work through our issues, and in the meantime your support means everything to me." He looked at Kari and then at the others. "To both of us."

He cleared his throat. "I won't ask for your forgiveness, though. I want to earn it."

Ashley rolled her eyes as the memory fizzled. The entire speech was Tim's pathetic attempt at making things easier for himself, so that he could show his face around Kari's family without feeling guilty.

She glanced at her sister, working there beside her husband. There was a glow of faith in her eyes — not just faith in God, but in Tim as well. It was a faith Ashley could not fathom. If Tim had cheated on Kari once, certainly he'd do it again. And even if he didn't, Kari would have to live her entire life with the knowledge of Tim's betrayal.

Kari was crazy, standing by Tim when a real man was clearly still in love with her. Ashley considered Ryan Taylor for a minute and knew that if it weren't for Kari she would have asked him out herself. Yes, he was like her parents in some ways. But there was something daring and different about Ryan, something that made him more appealing than Landon Blake had ever been.

She ran the dishrag over the table once more. If marriage required the type of devotion Kari had for Tim, Ashley was glad she was single.

In the next room, the patio door slid open and Luke came in, breathless, an old football in his hand. Brooke's husband, Peter, was close behind, and both men passed her without saying a word. Hadn't there been a hundred times when Ashley and Luke played catch with that same ball after dinners like this one? *You were my best friend, Luke. What happened to us?*

The question was one that filtered through her mind constantly when she was at her parents' home, but Ashley never voiced it. *I should have stayed in Paris for all anyone cares about me.*

She tuned in to the sounds around her: the gentle clanking of dishes and the whoosh of water running in the dishwasher; a football game on the television in the next room and the mingled sounds of conversation and laughter. Everything about the moment felt like something from a Hallmark commercial.

Forget the fact that Kari was nearly four months pregnant by a husband who until a few weeks ago had been living with another woman. Right now there wasn't a person in their family who wasn't feeling sorry for Kari.

Poor Kari this, poor Kari that.

Ashley snorted and moved the dishrag to the opposite side of the table.

Then there was Brooke. Never mind that she and Peter had gone as far from their parents' faith and values as Ashley had. Brooke and Peter were always welcome around the Baxter home, always talked about in a favorable light. Mom and Dad never nagged them or complained about them. The reason was obvious, and it irked

Ashley endlessly. Brooke and Peter were doctors, just like Dad. They might not go to church, but at least they'd done well for themselves, followed after Dad into a respectable profession.

But not Ashley — no, sir. According to her father, she hadn't had the sense to grow up yet.

She looked across the room at Brooke and Peter. Like everyone else, they seemed happy this Thanksgiving Day. Why wouldn't they be? In the card game of life they'd been dealt nothing but aces, hand after hand after hand.

People constantly praised Erin. No one seemed to notice that she was practically phobic about the prospect of her husband's getting a job out of state. Erin was a kindergarten teacher, a sweet girl, a Christian. What reason did she have for feeling lost or left out that afternoon?

And Luke? He'd gone from being the carefree ray of sunlight in a childhood marked with absolute certainty to . . . to a self-serving ignorant conservative who did little but judge those around him. Especially Ashley.

Ashley gathered a handful of crumbs, marched into the kitchen, and shook them into the sink, wedging her way between

Kari and Tim with a curt "Excuse me."

She wasn't halfway back to the dining room when she heard Tim whisper to Kari, "What's eating her?"

Ashley blocked out Kari's response. What did it matter? They were the ones with the problems, weren't they? Tears flooded her eyes as she grabbed a sweater. Rather than risk questions from her parents about what was wrong, she headed out onto the empty back porch.

Alone outside, she watched a pair of birds chasing each other in the darkening sky, diving one way then the other, taking turns in the lead. Then she looked back toward the house. Through the windows to the family room she could see the others talking and laughing.

Your lives are a mess, and you don't even know it. She exhaled sharply. They looked happier than any television family ever had. And maybe they were.

All except Ashley.

Chapter Twenty-Six

Kari was bound to run into Ryan Taylor again, and on Christmas Eve it happened.

After six weeks of counseling and working to put the pieces of her marriage back together, Kari was hopeful that complete healing was just around the corner. She and Tim were making progress with each session. They were more honest with each other, but also more tender, more careful not to wound.

Early in their counseling Kari had come clean about her emotional affair with Ryan. The admission had been hard for both of them. But then they had talked the whole thing out with the counselor. To their relief, the knowledge that *both* had strayed became a source of mutual understanding as well as pain.

Since then Kari had been particularly pleased with her progress in one area of her healing — her thoughts of Ryan were less frequent now.

But all that was threatened on the December Sunday morning when he appeared in her Sunday school classroom.

The church service had been over for ten minutes, and she was alone, putting away supplies, when she heard his voice behind her.

"Hi."

Her heart lurched at the sight of him standing in the doorway. "Hi," she answered. She dusted her hands on the back of her skirt.

He seemed careful not to let his eyes fall to her abdomen, which was firm and rounded, leaving no doubt about her condition. She felt her face grow hot. *He must know by now; that's why he isn't surprised.* She silently chided herself. Why hadn't she told him about the baby? It would have been better coming from her.

He held an envelope in his hands, and he looked nervous, as if they were meeting for the first time again. "I . . . I wanted to wish you a Merry Christmas." He held out the card. "This is for you."

No, Ryan . . . don't.

She made her way across the schoolroom and took the envelope, keeping her distance, her eyes never leaving his. "I'm . . . Tim and I are back together." Her hand came around her abdomen self-consciously. "We're having a baby."

Ryan slipped his hands into his pockets, and Kari struggled to read his eyes. "Pastor Mark told me."

Suddenly Kari was overcome with the nearness of him, trapped again in the memories of their night at the lake and the truths she'd learned there. Tears flooded her eyes. "Ryan, I . . . I can't be your friend." She was too choked up to speak, and she shook her head, a series of sobs jammed in her throat.

He folded his arms tightly in front of him and breathed in hard through his nose. "I know."

Her knees trembled beneath her skirt, and she desperately wanted him to leave. A meeting like this could only set back everything she was trying to do with Tim and the counselor. Tears gathered in her eyes, and she looked down at her feet.

"Being with you that day . . ." She struggled to swallow. "It was wrong, Ryan. I never should have allowed myself to —"

"Kari." His tone stopped her and she met his gaze once more. "I didn't come here to ask you to be my friend or to make you feel bad." He gave her a sad smile. "I just wanted to give you a Christmas card and tell you something."

She could smell his cologne, and she

tried not to think about how good it was to see him again. Instead, she waited for him to continue.

Ryan leaned against the doorframe. "Every day for the past six weeks I've prayed for you, Kari."

"Prayed?"

Ryan nodded, his eyes never leaving hers. "Yes . . . that you and Tim would work things out." He bit his lower lip and hesitated. "Obviously my prayers are being answered."

They made small talk for a few more minutes, and then Ryan glanced at his watch. "I need to go." He refrained from hugging her but lifted a hand as he walked away. "Merry Christmas, Kari."

After he was gone, she opened his card and felt her breath catch in her throat. Inside he'd written this simple message: "Thanks for teaching me what love really is."

Their conversation played again in her mind. His eyes had said he still had feelings for her. And the pounding of her heart had answered that her own feelings hadn't changed. In fact, only one thing had changed since their last meeting.

Their determination to let each other go.

Ashley often used Sunday mornings to run errands that hadn't been finished during the week. If she happened to be out when church ended, she would sometimes swing by and pick up Cole. That Christmas Eve was such an occasion. She'd even considered attending services with her family, but in the end she'd been too busy. She'd go some other time. New Year's Eve, maybe, or Easter.

She parked her red Honda in the church lot, ran her fingers through her short-cropped hair, and was heading toward Cole's class when she saw Ryan Taylor standing in the doorway of one of the Sunday school rooms.

For a moment she considered approaching him and giving him an update on Kari, but before she could make a decision he turned and walked the other direction. Who had he been talking to? Her curiosity got the better of her, and she walked slowly toward the place where Ryan had been. She leaned in, but the room was empty.

"Ashley?"

She spun around and saw Kari stepping out of a closet. Her face was tearstained, and she held a handful of glue bottles and child-sized scissors.

"Hi." Ashley felt strangely guilty. "I was just getting Cole."

"Cole's class is at the other end of the building." Kari straightened and pulled her hair back from her face. She looked weary, as if she were carrying an invisible burden too heavy to bear.

"I . . ." Ashley shrugged and decided to be honest. "I saw Ryan and thought I could catch him before he left."

Kari rolled her eyes and began stacking workbooks. She spoke with her back to Ashley. "What were you going to tell him?"

"Look, Kari, I'm not trying to make life difficult for you." Ashley sighed. "But if you ask me, Ryan's a much better —"

"I'm not asking you!" Kari's voice was harsh, and it sent Ashley back a step. "Besides . . ." She smoothed her hands on her skirt and hesitated. "Besides, Ryan feels the same way I do. That what we shared is better left in the past."

"Ryan said that?" Ashley had worried about her sister's judgment before. But if Kari thought Ryan Taylor was no longer head over heels in love with her, she was definitely in need of help. "Ryan will love you until the day he dies. Why do you think he was here?"

Kari leveled her gaze at Ashley. "To tell me he was praying for me."

"See!" Ashley tossed up her hands.

"That's the same thing. He's waiting just in case things don't work with Tim. Of course he's praying."

"Not like that." Kari's eyes were wet, and now Ashley felt bad for pushing the issue. "He's praying for Tim and me to be happy together."

There was obviously more to it, but Ashley didn't have time to analyze the issue now. She had to get Cole. Besides, there was no point to the discussion. Kari was determined to stay with Tim no matter how unhappy it made her.

"Look, I'm sorry for bringing it up." Ashley paused, and though the conversation might naturally have led to a hug, she simply said, "See ya," and waved as she headed for her son's classroom. By the time she got there, her parents had already promised Cole lunch at his favorite restaurant.

Ashley thought of the shopping she still needed to do for tomorrow, and she shrugged. Lately she hadn't wanted to burden her parents, but if they were offering . . .

"That's fine. Take him out to lunch. I'll pick him up later today."

Her mother reached for her hand and squeezed it. "Come with us."

Ashley remembered the Thanksgiving

conversation her father had with the pastor. "That's okay. You go. I have things to do." She stooped down and rubbed noses with Cole. "Be good for Grammy and Papa."

Cole's eyes twinkled. "I will, Mommy." He held up a piece of paper folded into a brightly colored box with a lid. "Here . . . I made this for you." He grinned. "Teacher says it's the best Christmas present of all."

She opened it, and inside was a colored picture of the baby Jesus with these words: "Jesus loves me, this I know."

Ashley let her eyes settle on the message, and doubts flashed across her mind. Jesus might love Cole — who wouldn't? — but he obviously didn't care much for her. She smiled at her son and tousled his hair. "Thanks, honey. You did a great job."

Five minutes later Ashley pulled into a gas station a mile from church. A sign told her she needed to prepay inside and she moaned, quickly sifting through her purse for a twenty-dollar bill as she headed toward the building. The stores wouldn't be open late, and she was in a hurry to be finished. Three people were ahead of her in the cash-register line, and she stood impatiently, gazing around, still thinking of this morning's conversation with her sister.

Kari had to be crazy letting a guy like Ryan Taylor go.

The line inched forward, and something caught Ashley's attention. She looked out and saw a silver Chevy truck pull into the parking lot. The driver looked familiar, and as the truck pulled up to the pump she had no doubts.

It was Ryan; there was no mistaking his profile.

Ashley watched him get out, read the sign, and head inside. She silently admired him. She didn't care for sports, but who couldn't appreciate a build like that? If only he weren't in love with Kari . . .

He spotted her immediately. "Hey, Ash, how are you?" He hugged her loosely, a smile lighting up his eyes.

"Good." She grinned and glanced at him. "You're looking gorgeous as always."

"Why, thank you, ma'am." One eyebrow lifted appreciatively. "Same to you."

This was what made Ryan different from Landon, she thought. Ryan wasn't in love with her. He could laugh with her, tease her, talk to her without ever making her fear that a wedding proposal was in the making.

She crossed her arms and lowered her chin. "Saw you talking to Kari at church today."

His eyes widened subtly. "Ashley Baxter, at church?"

Barely a foot separated them as they waited in line, and Ashley elbowed him in the ribs. "Come on . . . it's not like I have an aversion to the place." She shook her hair and tucked a strand behind her ear. "I went to get Cole, but my parents already had plans for him." She angled her face, making eye contact. "You left before I had a chance to say hi."

Ryan's eyes lost some of their sparkle. "I had a Christmas card for your sister."

"Ah." Ashley nodded big. "My faithful sister."

It was Ashley's turn at the counter. She paid for her gas, went outside and filled her car, and met Ryan by his truck. Ryan leaned against the driver's door and studied Ashley. "Kari's doing the right thing."

Ashley sighed and gazed at the distant cloudy sky. "He'll do it again."

"They have a child to think about now." Ryan shrugged. "I have a hunch he's finished wandering."

She clicked her tongue and shook her head, exasperated. "Kari should be with you."

Ryan smiled and raised his chin, his expression suddenly guarded. "It's a moot point, Ashley."

A car pulled up behind him, the driver anxious for an empty pump. Ryan opened his truck door and slid inside. "Did you eat yet?"

Ashley loved the way his casual grin challenged her and made her feel desirable. "No." She fingered her keys. "I'm starved."

He motioned toward her car. "Follow me."

"Okay." Ashley's answer was out of her mouth before she had time to think about it. She jogged back to her car as a mix of emotions fluttered within her. Lunch with Ryan Taylor? What would Kari think? For that matter, what was Ryan thinking?

She followed him and chided herself for letting her imagination run away with her. Ryan had known her since she was nine years old. He was lonely and wanted nothing more than an hour's conversation with an old acquaintance.

He led her to a salad bar restaurant that they both agreed was one of their favorites. An hour after lunch was over, they were still chatting about their lives and laughing about days gone by.

Ryan leaned back in the booth and anchored his forearms on the table. "I'm stuffed."

Ashley pushed at her fork and napkin. "Me too."

She had always convinced herself she didn't need a man in her life, but her time with this particular man was tempting her to revise her theory. She wanted their lunch date to go on forever. *He could never be attracted to me,* she reminded herself. *I'll always be Kari's little sister.*

But almost as soon as the thoughts were formed, Ryan looked at her, his expression more serious. "How come we never did this before?"

"Well —" Ashley's heart skipped a beat — "I was always Kari's kid sister." She was teasing him, and he smiled in response. "Never mind that I had a crush on you until my twelfth birthday."

Ryan's eyes danced. "Twelfth birthday?" His jaw dropped, and he pretended to be crushed by her revelation. "You gave up on me when you were only twelve years old?"

"Let's see —" Ashley stared at a ceiling tile and then back at Ryan — "I believe you were busy dating someone else back then." She lifted her chin, feigning hurt feelings. "I was a serious twelve-year-old, you know. You just didn't appreciate the woman I was behind those braces."

They both laughed, and Ryan leaned forward, searching her eyes. "Do you know how good it has felt being here with you?"

Ashley's world seemed to tilt. She warned herself that nothing could ever come of an attraction to Ryan Taylor. The whole family knew he was Kari's old boyfriend. It would be impossible.

Wouldn't it?

What was this feeling of shyness engulfing her? She rolled her finger through a few bread crumbs on the table. "For me too."

"We should've done it sooner." He cast her a crooked smile. "Sometime after your twelfth birthday."

"Yeah." She giggled and tried to fathom what he was thinking. "Hey, are you busy? Today, I mean?"

His eyes danced. "What are you cooking up now?"

"I have an idea."

"Shoot." Ryan tossed his hands in the air. "It's got to be better than anything I've got going today."

"Let's go Christmas shopping." She sat up straighter. "I need to get to the mall. And since Cole's with my parents . . ."

"And I have absolutely nothing for Aunt

Edith, the woman who has everything." He slapped his hand on the table. "You're on."

They spent the rest of the afternoon together, shopping at toy stores and boutiques and laughing at the other frantic shoppers.

In one upscale department store they spotted a mannequin head sitting atop a mound of discounted sweaters. "Wonderful!" Ryan picked up his pace, grabbed the head, and kept walking. "Aunt Edith has always wanted a second head. She loses hers all the time. Where do I pay?"

They laughed so hard they had to stop to catch their breath, and when Ryan returned the Styrofoam head, he casually slipped his arm around Ashley's shoulders. "Okay, little sister, tell me why a pretty girl like you is still single."

"Simple." She pushed back the thoughts of Paris and grinned. "I haven't been in love since I was twelve."

"Hey." They kept walking, and he tapped his shoe playfully against hers. "I'm serious."

She sighed, still recovering from their laughter. "There are guys. I'm just not all that interested."

He nodded slowly. "Fair enough."

The afternoon had darkened into twilight when they finally finished shopping. Her parents would be having their usual Christmas Eve gift-wrapping session, and she knew she should pick up Cole. But she and Ryan were hungry, and Cole could wait. He had more fun with her parents, anyway.

They picked up a pizza on the way home and took it to Ashley's house. Ryan set his coat down on a chair just inside the front door and let out a low whistle. "Very nice."

Ashley carried the pizza to the table and returned to the living room. Ever since they'd walked through the door, there had been a change between them. As she watched Ryan make his way around the room, admiring her paintings, she knew what it was.

The casual air between them was gone. And in its place was something they hadn't had time to consider.

He turned from her work, his eyes full of admiration. "Are these yours?"

"Yes." She could feel the smile playing on her lips. "All of them."

"Ashley — they're amazing." Ryan shifted his attention to one of her pieces. Her heart soared. It was her favorite — a landscape at sunset with tall grass blowing in the wind and a faded barn in the background. Ryan cast her a glance over his shoulder. "These should be in a museum."

She had always been private about her artwork. Her parents had never really approved of her pursuing a career as an artist. Usually it seemed simpler to keep her work to herself. When her parents came to visit, they generally breezed through the room with little more than a casual comment. Something like, "Nice, Ashley" or "I see you've been busy."

Cole was the only one who actually admired her paintings.

Until now.

Ryan nodded toward the sunset painting. "What's the story behind it?"

It was the first time anyone had ever asked her to explain a piece, and she was flattered almost beyond words. "It reminds me of home." Her voice was soft. "The way I saw it as a child."

She spent the next twenty minutes giving him details about her canvases. *He thinks I talk about this to everyone,* she thought. But the stories behind her paintings were glimpses of her soul, places that had never been exposed before.

Not here in Bloomington, anyway.

Ryan and Ashley worked their way to the kitchen for pizza, and after dinner he stretched. "I better get going."

She grinned. "Aunt Edith?" The night had flown by, and Ashley wished there was a way to buy a few more hours.

"Yep. Plane comes in at nine."

Ashley tried to keep a straight face. "She'll like the candy. But the mannequin head — now that would have been an amazing gift."

They both laughed as they walked toward the front door, and Ryan looped his arm around her neck, drawing her close for a familiar embrace. But when the hug ended, his arm stayed. He drew back just enough to see her face. "I had fun today, Ash."

She felt shy again, something that had happened only a handful of times in her entire life — but twice today. "Me too."

The moment changed and suddenly the air was charged with an attraction so strong it took Ashley's breath away. Ryan's smile faded as he kept his hold on her. His eyes burned with intensity and unspoken questions, and before they could say another word the space between them vanished. Slowly, tenderly, Ryan brought his face to hers and kissed her.

It was not the passionate kiss of a man desiring to take advantage of her. Instead, it was a kiss that knocked on the door of possibility. He kissed her a second time, and then Ashley felt his body tense.

He pulled back, breathless, and took hold of her shoulders. "Ashley —" he shook his head — "I shouldn't have done that."

She felt as if she were being dragged underwater. Ryan's words made no sense. Hadn't he suggested having lunch together? Hadn't he spent the day elbowing her and tickling her and putting his arm around her?

A chill ran down her spine, and she took a step back. No matter what Ryan might say, he couldn't deny his attraction to her, not after the time they'd spent together today. "It's not a crime to kiss me, Ryan." She did not waver in her gaze, challenging him to admit his feelings. "I'm not twelve anymore."

Ryan groaned and stared at the tiled floor. When he looked up, she saw a world of pain in his eyes. "You're wonderful, Ashley. You make me laugh, and whenever I'm around you, I feel better about life." He dropped his head again and rubbed the back of his neck.

She took a step closer. If he needed to be convinced, she was up to the task. "We've known each other forever." She rested her hand on his shoulder. "Whatever happened today, we're both feeling it." Her voice dropped to a whisper. "Am I right?"

Ryan looked up, and his expression was coated in anguish. "If you mean, am I attracted to you . . . ? Yes. I am." He took her hand from his shoulder and held it. "But it wasn't fair for me to kiss you, to make you think I could go out with you that way."

The sting of his rejection was more painful than anything she'd felt since coming home from Paris. Tears nipped at her eyes, and she removed her hand from his grip. Her tone was quietly angry when she finally found her voice. "It's Kari, isn't it? You're afraid of falling for me because of her, right?"

"No. I'm not afraid." He leaned back against the doorframe. "Kari loves her husband, and that's how it should be. My time with her is over."

Ashley worked a hand through her hair. "I don't get it, Ryan. What?"

He said nothing, and suddenly Ashley understood. Though he might never see Kari again, Ryan's heart was still not free.

She took two steps back and crossed her arms firmly in front of her. It was the only way she knew to ward off the cold that had crept into the room. "It's too soon, isn't it?" She bit her lip to keep it from quivering, and a sad, slow sigh made its way through her teeth. "How long will you love her?"

She couldn't breathe as she waited for his answer. Ryan reached for his keys, his eyes watery. Then he stepped back toward the door and said just one word.

"Forever."

As he drove away from Ashley's house, Ryan gritted his teeth and tightened his grip on the steering wheel. What had he been thinking? He shook his head, reached to turn the radio off, and knew the answer. He hadn't been thinking at all, not from the moment he asked Ashley to lunch. What had happened at the gas station to make him act so crazy?

He knew that answer too. There she was, laughing, teasing him, flattering him, and looking so much like Kari that his heart hurt. How could he resist? Why not spend a day with a beautiful single woman he'd known most of his life? Certainly Kari wouldn't have a problem if the two of them hung out for the afternoon.

As the hours passed, Ryan had enjoyed

himself more than he'd imagined. At times the whole experience at the mall reminded him of another shopping trip. The one he and Kari had taken after his father died. The day he had first admitted his feelings for her.

But not until he kissed Ashley in the doorway of her home had he fully understood his motives.

As awful as it was, being with Ashley today had been a way to trick his heart, a way to lessen the pain of losing Kari again. Ashley and Kari looked so much alike that he could almost convince himself she *was* Kari.

But while Ashley was practically a mirror image of her older sister, that's where the resemblance made an abrupt stop.

Kari was kind and compassionate, devoted almost to a fault. Ashley was a free spirit — artistic, stubbornly independent, and wary of anything conventional. And also, he had discovered, surprisingly vulnerable and hungry for attention. It had been unfair of him to kiss her, wrong to make her think he had serious intentions when he honestly didn't. He was attracted to Ashley, and yes, he'd had a good time with her. But she would never be the right woman for him. Not when every time he looked at her he couldn't help but think of Kari.

His guilty thoughts ate at him all the way home. He pulled in the driveway, parked, locked the truck, and walked into his kitchen and sat at the table. There in front of him, where he'd left it for the past few days, was the contract. The one that offered him the coaching chance of a lifetime.

He had hesitated about the commitment for only one reason. Although he and Kari would never be together, Ryan still loved living here: the sweet smell of wild grass around his cabin in Clear Creek; the way the Bloomington community pulsed with both family values and academic excitement; his familiarity with every intersection and business establishment; the memories of his father.

Ryan stared at the contract and released a pent-up sigh.

But now, in light of his evening with Ashley — and the kiss that had done nothing but confuse her — there seemed no point in staying. Every time he passed the university, he'd wonder if Tim was being faithful to Kari. Every time he went to church, he'd wonder if he would see the two of them. And after the baby was born, he'd have to live with the reality that if things had turned out differently, the child might have been his.

And when he ran into Ashley, things would never be the same around her either.

He ran his eyes over the front page of the coaching offer, and suddenly he knew it was the right thing to do. Hadn't it always been his dream to coach a pro team once his playing days were over? Wasn't this contract the exact thing he'd been hoping for when he ran into Kari again that first Sunday?

He grabbed a pen and slid the document closer. In the time it took him to sign his name, he committed himself to a future that would change his life and send him to the East Coast for what could be years.

He had always told himself that if the opportunity to coach professionally came up, he'd hang on to his house and his property. But now, in light of his situation and the decision he had just made, the place didn't seem so important. Ryan decided he'd call the real estate agent after the holiday. Then he'd meet with his coaching staff at Clear Creek High School and tell them the news.

In a few short weeks, he'd pack his bags and start life over again in New York City.

As far away from Kari Baxter Jacobs as he could get.

Chapter Twenty-Seven

Friends had always told Kari the fifth and sixth months of pregnancy were the best, and by the time February rolled around, Kari had to agree. Her parents were having a dinner party for Brooke's birthday tonight, and Kari was glad to be rid of the morning sickness and the padding that seemed to appear on her hips that first trimester.

Now the extra weight she carried was nothing but baby, and her sisters were unanimous in their predictions that she would have a boy.

"You look just like I did," Ashley said nearly every time she looked at Kari. "A thin-hipped balloon-belly girl."

Kari knew she would get bigger in the weeks that followed, but she had no idea how that was possible. Her skin seemed stretched to the limits already, and her ability to eat a big meal had ceased a month ago. She thought of the child she'd miscarried and thanked God that this baby lived.

The counseling sessions with Tim were

going better than she dreamed possible. Though he'd been tempted, he hadn't had a drink since before Christmas. And they were going out one night a week, sometimes just to talk about how far they'd come and how much they had to look forward to.

Her bedside table was stacked with books about what to expect during pregnancy, and in the evenings she and Tim pored over them, studying the line drawings of unborn babies and trying to imagine what their baby might look like — whether the infant's eyes had developed and whether he or she already had hair.

"You'd think we'd have this thing memorized by now." Tim slipped his arm around her as they sat together in their den one evening. Their physical relationship had taken time to rebuild, but every week her affection came more easily.

"I can't get enough of it. It seems like my due date will never get here."

"It's probably like that every time. Whether you have one child or five."

Kari believed it.

The baby continued to turn and move within her, and despite her sisters' predictions, she was certain the child was a girl. She and Tim talked about names and decided on Jessie Renée, after her great-grandmother, a faithful woman Kari had heard about but never known. For a boy they decided on Timothy Joseph — T.J. for short. But in Kari's mind the boy's name was little more than a technicality.

She and Tim decided to wait until the baby was born to find out if she was right, and at the ultrasound she had to remind her doctor not to give away the secret.

Tim had stood beside her while the doctor slid the tool over her abdomen at one of her visits, his eyes trained on a small monitor. "Well, Kari, it's a healthy baby —"

"Don't tell me!" She raised a hand, and Tim and the doctor smiled.

"Just kidding. You couldn't get the truth out of me now if you paid me."

"We *are* paying you," Kari teased. "But don't tell me, okay?"

Each passing week, each stage of development, made Kari more keenly aware of all she and Tim were sharing because of their hard work and God's gift of healing in their marriage. The feelings of joy and gratitude would sometimes catch her unaware, swelling her heart with joy and stinging her eyes with tears. And though at times she still thought about Ryan, she no longer ached at the thought of what they had missed.

He'd moved on, too, which was a good thing — taken a job coaching for the New York Giants. He had called her parents and told them good-bye before he left, asking them to pass on the news to her. She was glad for him, sure this position was another example of God's goodness in their lives. It was the kind of job he had always wanted.

Kari took a stack of china plates and laid them out around her parents' table. The entire Baxter family would be coming tonight — the first time since the holidays that they'd all been together for a meal. Kari was looking forward to it.

Tonight was also the first time they'd get to meet Luke's new girlfriend, who was going to stop by for dessert.

Kari and Erin had discussed the situation at length and jokingly decided that — as always — the girl didn't have a chance with Luke's sisters gathered around.

"At least he knows we care," Erin laughed when they talked about it earlier that day.

"Yeah." Kari grinned. "The girl has no idea."

She finished setting the table while Erin and Ashley helped their mother in the kitchen. Already the delicious smells of her mother's cooking were filling the house: savory roast chicken, fresh steamed vegetables with basil and rosemary, and her mother's famous whole-grain bread. This was the kind of meal they'd grown up with — designed by their mother to be both healthy and delicious.

"Foods affect the way we feel, the way we look, the way we act. Even the way we love," Mom always said, and no one doubted her. She had a master's degree in nutrition and had worked part-time as the hospital's meal planner for a decade before she got sick. "It's part of my job to make sure you all know how to eat right."

Kari's stomach growled, and she patted her swollen belly. *Guess you like Grammy's food too, huh, little Jessie?*

Her father got home from work and took a seat next to Tim, who was watching a basketball game on TV. Minutes later Brooke and her family arrived, and the conversations around Kari grew louder. These were the sounds Kari had missed since leaving home, the sounds Erin would miss if her husband took the out-of-state job he was considering.

Luke walked into the kitchen and tossed his backpack on the floor near the table. "I told you about Reagan, right? She's coming by for dessert?"

Kari watched her mom stop stirring a pot of beans and stare at the backpack. "Take it to your room, please."

Luke grabbed the bag. "I told you, right?"

"Yes, Luke. We'll be on our best behavior."

Kari saw Ashley roll her eyes as she drained the steamed vegetables. "Don't worry, Luke. We'll make sure our masks are in place."

"Don't start with me, Ashley. Maybe you can be gone when she gets here."

Elizabeth sighed. "Really, you two. You might try to be nice to each other. It's Brooke's birthday, after all."

"Fine." Ashley kept her back to Luke.

Kari watched and wondered if their changed relationship hurt Ashley as much as it hurt Luke. *She's too angry, God. Show me how I can help her.*

Luke shrugged and flashed a smile at Kari. "At least my *other* sisters will be nice to Reagan." He left the kitchen with his backpack and jogged up the stairs.

"Hey, Brooke, check out this play." It was Peter calling from the next room as Brooke strode into the kitchen, out of breath and frowning.

Brooke glanced at the television screen in the next room and nodded absently.

"Mom, where's Cole's ibuprofen?" She grimaced. "Maddie has a fever again. We almost didn't come."

"When did she get sick? I heard from Thelma across the street that three children were hospitalized with strep throat just last . . ."

The conversations continued until dinner was ready. Then all ten of them — everyone but Maddie — gathered around the table.

"Let's pray." Their father bowed his head and waited until the room was quiet. "Lord, we thank you for this family, for letting us gather together, and for Brooke's birthday. Thank you for creating her to be among us, and let this coming year be one of blessings and discovery for her and her family. Bless this food that it might nourish our bodies. In Jesus' name, amen."

The talking began almost immediately.

"Pass the chicken."

"Mom, you did it again! Everything smells delicious."

"No one can make bread like you."

"Dad have you heard anything more about the grant the hospital's trying to get for a new wing? Supposed to be another forty rooms."

"Ashley, your old tennis coach is going

to our church now. He said to tell you hi."

The discussions took place simultaneously, yet everyone seemed to understand and be able to participate in all of them. There was talk among Elizabeth, John, and Ashley about an art course she was taking. Erin's husband, Sam, wanted to know how many weeks were left until Kari's baby was due, and Erin shared a story about one of her kindergartners who brought a frozen fish into class on pet day. When the laughter died down, Luke filled in by giving them a blow-by-blow report of his debate team's recent victory.

It was a meal Kari knew she'd remember fondly in months to come, when she was busy taking care of a newborn and learning how to be a family with Tim and the baby. Before long, dinner was over, and dishes were being cleared when the doorbell rang.

"Must be Reagan." Ashley tossed a contrived smile at Kari and the others. "Everyone put on your mask."

Erin and Brooke giggled, and Luke nodded at them. "Thanks." He narrowed his eyes at Ashley before pushing back from the table. "She can sit by Kari."

Kari looked at Ashley and cocked her head. "Come on, Ash, be nice. How often does he bring a girl home?"

Ashley leaned over the table and whispered, "I am being nice. I'm just saying let's be on our best behavior." She leaned back and raised her eyebrows. "After all, not many girls can live up to Luke's perfect standard."

When Luke and his new girlfriend entered the room, the discussion stopped and the table fell silent. "It's a blizzard out there," Luke said as he tossed Reagan's coat on a chair and brushed the snow off her head.

All eyes were on Reagan. She was tall and athletic looking, bigger boned than most of the girls Luke had dated. From the easy way they looked at each other, Kari could tell they had been friends for a while. She wondered if this was the girl her brother would marry.

Luke made introductions; then he and Reagan sat down next to each other as far away from Ashley as possible. When everyone was seated, they sang "Happy Birthday" to Brooke.

"Thirty-five, is it?" Luke teased her. She'd already opened her presents, and Luke's had included a bottle of vitamins for seniors.

"Thirty, thank you very much." Brooke lifted her chin and smiled.

Peter leaned over and kissed her on the cheek. "Though you don't look a day over twenty-one, my dear."

"Oh, please . . . I hope that's her birthday gift." Ashley shook her head and winked at Brooke. "No one deserves a compliment like that, even on her birthday."

Reagan said little, just watched and listened, responding to Luke's whispered comments with a sweet smile.

John was the first to draw her into the conversation. "Tell us, Reagan — how'd you get mixed up with this crazy guy?" He elbowed Luke, who was sitting beside him.

Reagan laughed, and Kari decided she liked her. She seemed at ease with the Baxters, and something in her eyes looked genuine, solid. Mom and Erin began serving pie.

"Well," Reagan looked at Luke, and Kari saw it. However long the two had been dating, their relationship was more serious than any of them had known. The look in the girl's eyes was unmistakable.

She was in love with Luke.

Reagan continued, "Luke was playing a pickup game at the school gym, and I walked in with my basketball. They were short one person, but —" she cast Luke a teasing look — "someone in the group didn't think I could play with them."

"So anyway, Mom —" Luke raised his eyebrows and dug his fork into the pie in front of him — "have I told you what a good cook you are?"

"Go on, Reagan." John chuckled. "It was just getting good."

Reagan nodded, and her eyes danced as she made contact with several of them around the table. She certainly wasn't shy, but she wasn't bold or obnoxious either. Kari looked at her sisters and saw that they were caught up in the story as well. Even Ashley. This girl was good. She'd won them all over in a matter of minutes.

The tale continued about how Luke had refused to let Reagan play on their team. So a few possessions later, when a spot opened on the other team, Reagan had taken it.

Luke started to stand. "Anyone need anything from the garage? I'll be in there hiding until —"

Reagan tugged on his sleeve, and he sat back down. She lowered her chin and turned teasing eyes toward him. "You can wait. Your dad asked, after all."

Luke groaned, and Reagan laughed lightly. "Our team beat his, but I don't think that's what won him over." She cast him a look of mock curiosity. "That wasn't it, was it?"

Both Luke's elbows came up on the table, and he covered his eyes. "Here we go."

Reagan leaned forward. "I think it was the three-pointer I buried in his face to win the game." She nodded, as if looking for some kind of confirmation from him. "Yeah, that was it."

John laughed so hard his face turned red. "Well, it's about time someone showed him how to do it."

Chuckles rang out across the table, and again everyone began talking at once. They found out that Reagan had grown up in North Carolina and was attending Indiana University on a volleyball scholarship. She attended a church that met on campus, and by all appearances she seemed to have a quiet and genuine faith.

When Reagan and Luke left for a movie half an hour later, Kari and the others waited in silence until the front door closed. Then they all looked at each other and giggled the way they'd done when Luke was thirteen and a neighbor girl would come calling for him.

"I think I hear wedding bells," Erin

squealed and nodded conspiratorially toward their mother. "Don't you guys?"

Kari grinned. "I like her."

"Definitely. Give it a year." Brooke stretched and looked at her watch.

"I'll second that." Ashley stood and cleared several dessert plates on her way into the kitchen. Kari was thankful her sister had been polite while Reagan was there, and now she seemed genuine in her response.

Elizabeth just smiled quietly and shrugged. "You never know. God has a plan for everyone's life. Reagan just might be part of the plan for Luke."

The conversation continued, but after hearing their mother's comment, Kari was no longer listening. Was it true? Scripture backed it up, of course, but still — a specific plan? For everyone?

Kari bit her lip as the voices around her faded. Had she really listened to God when she and Ryan were dating? Or had she somehow missed God's plan?

She looked at Tim, deep in conversation with Erin's husband. Even now, the sight of him filled her with equal parts of love and pain.

She thought about the slow course of their healing, how painful it really was, how much Tim's affair had cost them. Physical intimacy, for instance, was still a problem. No matter how badly she wanted to work things out, she froze every time Tim touched her. The counselor said it might be months before that changed.

Lost in thought, she stood up from the table and began to stack the remaining dessert dishes. The counselor had handled the issue carefully.

"We'll take it one month at a time," he had told them in a joint session the first week they met with him after the intensive marriage seminar. "A physical relationship has to be rebuilt over time as trust is regained. For now I'd avoid anything too intimate." He had laid down a set of guidelines to oversee their physical contact for now. Back rubs were good, he told them, and kissing was fine if they were both willing; but beyond that, any physical intimacy was off-limits, at least until the counselor deemed them ready to move on.

The counselor's mandate came as a relief to Kari. Obviously, one day their lovemaking would be good again. But for now she couldn't imagine being intimate with Tim. What if he compared her to his former student? What if he had a disease?

That issue had been covered too. It was

simple, the counselor told them. Tim would have to be tested. Twice. The first test came a week after meeting with the counselor and was negative. The second test was coming up in a few weeks.

Kari sighed and carried the dishes into the kitchen. A shudder worked its way through her body. She couldn't imagine how things might have turned out if Tim hadn't chosen to come back home. They'd probably be going through divorce proceedings about the same time the baby was born.

Her mother was right. God had a plan for everyone.

There was no point looking back, wondering whether she'd gone left on life's path when God would have had her go right. Whatever wrong turns she might have made, today God's plan was for her and Tim to rebuild their marriage — no matter how painful the process. Her job was to believe that God could take the broken pieces of their lives and turn them into something beautiful.

The counselor had said something the other day that she hadn't considered before.

"Recovering from an affair can take up to a year, and during that time you'll go through seasons." He looked from Kari to

Tim. "You've both struggled with feelings for other people, but you, Tim, are the responsible party here. The seasons are bound to affect Kari more than you, at least on the surface."

The seasons were these: fall, a time for anger; winter, a time for mourning; spring, a time for healing; and summer, a time for new growth.

Which meant that Kari's anger was normal — a good thing because she still had moments when she was furious. She rinsed a dish at the sink, barely listening to the conversation about Reagan and Luke still going on in the dining room.

She thought about how hard it had been to stay by Tim's side, even after he returned to her. There were days when she still wanted to hate him, nights when she was disgusted even to sleep in the same room.

But those days were growing fewer and further apart, and she could see the Lord's handprint all over the growing relationship she shared with her husband. With time and counseling, her emotions seemed to be coming full circle. She once again felt Tim's love and was convinced they were learning new steps to their relational dance.

New steps. That's what it amounted to. The two of them were learning the steps that would bring them together, a dance that would take them into forever. A dance that could be nothing less than God's plan for their lives. She dried her hands on a towel. Her mother was right. God had a plan for each of them, and this . . . this rebuilding time with Tim was part of hers.

The snow was coming down harder than before, and weather reports predicted it could dump two feet before it was done. On the way home, Tim and Kari stopped at the market and picked up enough groceries for the week, just in case.

By the time they got home, snow had turned the driveway white, and the drifts covered the first three steps leading to their front door.

Kari sat motionless in the passenger seat and stared at the walkway. "Think it's safe?"

Tim followed her gaze. "What?"

"The steps." She turned to him, her hand over her round belly. "It rained earlier. What if there's ice under the snow?"

"Nah." He looked at his watch. "It's still early. There won't be ice until later."

She felt the baby kick beneath her fingers. "You really think it's okay?"

"Honey, there's no ice." He smiled widely and opened the car door. "I'll go first and show you."

He trudged through the snowdrifts and was glancing back at her, giving her the okay sign, when he connected with the first step and slipped. Like something from a slapstick comedy, his arms flailed out to his sides, and he landed flat on his back, disappearing into the snow.

"Oh!" Kari climbed out and marched as fast as she could toward Tim. "Honey, are you okay?"

"I think so." The words were muffled, and as Kari reached him, she saw why. The snow had fallen on him, leaving him with a white beard. His eyes were the only part of his face visible. He looked like he was made of snow.

They stared at each other for a moment, wide-eyed; then Tim spit the snow from his mouth. "Like I said, no ice."

The giggles had been building in Kari since she caught Tim's surprised expression as he fell. Suddenly she couldn't hold them in any longer. Laughter poured from her as it hadn't in months, and she collapsed beside him in the snow, brushing the wet stuff off his face as he, too, laughed out loud.

By the time Tim made his way up the steps and helped her do the same, they were laughing so hard they could barely breathe. As they collapsed on the sofa in the front room, Kari had tears in her eyes. "The look on your face . . ."

"Right, go ahead and laugh at a poor injured man."

"Well, a poor injured snowman . . ."

The laughter continued until finally they were both exhausted. Only then did Kari realize something she hadn't before. This was the first time they'd laughed together, really laughed, since long before Tim moved out.

After months of anger and betrayal and grief beyond words, a seed of love and laughter deep inside them had survived. If they could laugh together now, after the long seasons of fall and winter their counselor had described, it could mean only one thing.

Spring was on the way.

Chapter Twenty-Eight

Prayer was as much a part of Dr. John Baxter's life as breathing. But it had been weeks since he'd felt the urge to pray as strongly as he did the next afternoon, less than twenty-four hours after the dinner party for Brooke.

Generally when the desire to pray was this urgent, it was attached to the face of someone he dearly loved — one of his children or possibly Elizabeth. But the prompting that kept calling him to prayer this day was not connected to any of them.

John waited until he'd seen his last patient and then locked himself behind his office door. Almost immediately he slid to his knees and closed his eyes.

What is it, Lord? Is someone in trouble?

For a long while there was silence, but then very strongly the image of Kari came to mind. That was it! He was supposed to pray for his second-oldest daughter. Of course. The baby wasn't due for three months yet, but she'd had a doctor appointment that morning. Maybe something was wrong, some kind of complication. His mind raced with the medical possibilities.

There were too many to consider.

Instead, he prayed feverishly for Kari and her unborn child, for protection and mercy and kindness and grace. Most of all, he prayed that God himself would speed the healing between Kari and Tim so they could be the kind of family Kari wanted . . . the kind their baby needed.

Normally as John prayed, the burden would lift. But this time, the longer he stayed on his knees the more desperate the sense of need became. After nearly thirty minutes of beseeching God on his daughter's behalf, he finally fell silent.

What else, Lord?

In response a face came to his attention, but not one John would have expected. Knowing it was what God wanted him to do, he closed his eyes again and considered the man whose image filled his mind. Kari's husband, Tim.

John prayed for Tim as he hadn't in a very long time, asking the Lord to be close to the man, wherever he was that day, and to offer him hope and cleansing and salvation beyond anything he'd ever dreamed possible.

This time when he finished praying, he felt a peace and assurance in his soul. But he felt something else too. Something unsettling. He moved more quickly than usual as he gathered his things and prepared to go home.

Halfway there, he realized it wasn't just an unsettling thought that filled his heart.

It was a sense of impending doom, a sense that no matter how much he prayed or how fast he drove, something terrible was about to happen.

Five minutes before Tim Jacobs left his office that day, he got an idea. Instead of heading straight home, he would stop at a florist's shop and buy Kari the biggest bunch of red roses the shop had.

After all, they had cause to celebrate.

For one thing, it was exactly three months until the baby's due date. But the day marked an even more important milestone for them. They'd started laughing again. The night before had been the best Tim could remember having in months. Years, even. For the first time, Tim had the sense that Kari had really forgiven him — not just *wanted* to forgive him — and that they were going to make it after all. And that called for at least a dozen roses.

There was one more thing worth celebrating, something he tried not to dwell on too much: Angela had done nothing to pursue him.

Initially he'd been sure she'd call or come by his office, confused by his sudden departure or sure she could get him to change his mind. But apparently his note had been clear. Other than a long series of voice-mail messages she left on one particular day, she hadn't been in touch.

Though he occasionally felt the desire to call her and apologize, he knew the counselor's advice was wise. He had to stay away at all costs. Once an affair was over, there could be no going back.

He gathered a stack of papers and had one foot out of his office when the phone rang. It was unusual for him to get calls this late in the day, and he almost left it for the voice mail, but then he reconsidered. What if it was Kari? Maybe there was a problem with the baby or she needed him to bring home something from the store.

Tim propped open the door with his briefcase, tucked the folder of papers under his arm, and grabbed the receiver. "Hello?"

There was a strange sound, and after a few seconds Tim realized someone was crying on the other end. His stomach tightened. "Kari?"

The caller didn't answer, and the soft crying sounds stopped. "It's me."

Angela's voice hit him like a physical blow. Tim sat down on the edge of his desk and swallowed. It was the call he'd been dreading. "Hi."

She sniffed. "I . . . I know you're back with your wife. But I had to call you. Something's come up." Another few sobs sounded. "Tim, I'm . . . I'm pregnant."

As the words filtered through his brain and into his soul, Tim slid slowly down the side of his desk and landed on the floor, the folder under his arm falling next to him. He rested his head on his knees and tried to calm his racing heart.

A hundred fears ignited in his gut, and nausea came over him sure and fast. If Angela was really pregnant, then everything he'd clung to, every hope that someday Kari and he would share a marriage that would outshine even their early days as a couple — all of it had been destroyed in an instant.

He closed his eyes and imagined having two children by two different women, children who would know their father's sins as clearly as they knew their names. Even if

Kari was willing to stand by him while his illegitimate child was born to Angela Manning, they could never have the wholesome family life he so desperately desired.

And all of it — every dying dream — was entirely his fault.

"Tim, are you there?" He heard fresh tears in Angela's voice and a frustration she'd never revealed before.

He inhaled. The floor no longer felt stable. "I'm here."

"Well . . . what am I supposed to do?"

His mind worked to find a focus point, to accept the truth of what had happened. "Uh . . . right." He would have to tell Kari first, break the news to her tonight. The last thing he wanted was to see Angela Manning without his wife's knowing about it. "Are you sure? You took a test?"

"Of course I'm sure," she huffed. "What happened to us, Tim? You told me you loved me, remember? And yes, after two people live together for weeks on end, a pregnancy is a real possibility."

He knew he should feel compassion, and he did. He was sorry for her, even sorrier for her unborn child. But something in her tone caused him to know without a doubt that he didn't love this woman. He never had. She had been merely a diversion, a mistake. And somehow that made the situation worse.

"I'm sorry, Angela." Tears welled in his eyes. That was an understatement. "I don't know what to say."

There was a pause, and she sniffed again. "We need to talk."

Tim massaged his temples and felt the beginning of a migraine. "Okay. Tomorrow, noon, in my office."

As he hung up the phone and gathered his things, he felt an ache in his chest and knew it was his heart breaking. From that moment on, nothing about his future would ever be the same again.

And now he had to go home and tell Kari.

Dirk Bennett's body was colder than it had been in his entire life. His fingers were numb, and his teeth chattered. But deep within was a fire, a passion that made the night seem almost warm.

He gazed out the window of his pickup and stared at Angela's apartment.

Soon, my baby . . . soon.

A small, hinged box sat on the front seat beside him, and he reached for it, feeling his arms ripple with the motion. They were muscled enough that it was almost difficult to bend them. Gently, tenderly, he lifted the box lid and stared at the diamond ring inside, the one he had purchased more than a year earlier.

The ring he would place on Angela's finger the moment she said yes.

And Dirk knew without a doubt that moment was coming. He'd watched Angela's apartment off and on for the past three months, varying his schedule and convincing himself more every day that he'd been wrong about the professor. The man wasn't still seeing Angela on the side.

At the same time, Dirk had tripled the number of pills he was taking. He smiled. The pills were the best thing to happen to him since meeting Angela. His body was drawing looks from half the girls at the campus weight room.

There was no way she'd turn him down now.

He closed the lid on the ring box, set it back on the seat, and opened the glove compartment. Life would have been much simpler if Professor Jacobs had stayed away from his girl to begin with.

Dirk blinked and rubbed his fists over his jean-covered thighs. An image came, and then another and another. Angela with the professor at lunch. Angela and the professor walking hand in hand near her apartment. The two of them going into her apartment and turning off the lights.

It didn't matter that the man wasn't seeing Angela anymore. Dirk gripped his steering wheel so hard his knuckles turned white. If the professor were there in front of him, he'd still . . .

Everything was suddenly hazy red and blurred around the edges. Dirk tightened his grip on the wheel and held his breath. He hated Professor Jacobs for what he'd done. If it wasn't for him, Angela would never have left him. If the professor hadn't gone after his girl, life would be —

Dirk fired his fist into the dashboard and left a hole several inches deep.

He studied his fingers and wiped at three spots that were bleeding. Fear joined the dance of emotions on the floor of his heart. *What's wrong with me?* The action had relieved some of the rage, but not all of it. He opened the glove box and fingered the revolver inside. As he did, a truth dawned on him.

If he was wrong, if for any reason Professor Jacobs was still seeing his girl, there would be no point in scaring him off as Dirk had originally planned.

It was time to make wedding plans, not

wait in the wings while Angela Manning disgraced herself in a sordid affair. No, the situation was far too serious to mess around with just scaring the professor away.

Dirk wiped his bloody knuckles on his pants leg. At this point, he would have to handle the situation differently — very differently. Even if it cost him his life.

He started his engine, clicked open the gun's chamber, and peered inside.

Good. Plenty of bullets.

That meant he didn't have to go to the store. Instead, he had time for dinner and some homework. Then he'd come back, walk up the inside stairs to Angela's front door, and give her the ring.

The rage he'd felt moments ago was already fading. In fact, he felt pretty good. As long as no one got in his way — by ten o'clock that night he and Angela Manning would be engaged.

Chapter Twenty-Nine

Kari was in the baby's bedroom trying to decide what shade of pink wallpaper would look best with the pastel bedding she and her mother bought earlier that day.

It didn't matter that everyone — even Tim — thought she was having a boy. She still had a deep sense that the precious child growing within her was a girl.

She felt the baby turn and placed her hand on her abdomen. An active girl.

Kari could hardly wait for the chance to meet her daughter face-to-face, cradle her close, and watch Tim experience his first moments of fatherhood. Brooke had told her that having a child humbled a man, and Kari didn't doubt it. She could imagine Tim staring at his own flesh, face-to-face. Realizing the depth of his vulnerability, knowing that every decision from that point on would affect and shape his child.

It was a transformation that was bound to strengthen the new bond between them.

Kari wandered across the room and

stared at the baby's only toy, a stuffed white baby eagle that perched precariously on the dresser. It was from Tim, his first gift to their child.

"White because God gave us a clean new start with this baby," he had told her a week ago when he brought it home. He'd waited until they were seated near the fire that night before presenting her with the gift. She'd held it in her hand, admiring the detail on the wings, the feel of the plush body.

Tim ran a finger over the toy and let his hand settle on hers. "And an eagle, because eagle families are forever. And one day when we're past all this, we'll have forever too."

Kari blinked, but the memory remained. She reached for the stuffed bird and nuzzled it against her face. The white synthetic fur was whisper soft, and she could picture their daughter, a few years from now, carrying the eagle around by the wing. It would be her favorite, probably a dull gray by then, and most of the fur would be loved off. But Tim's words about the small, sweet toy and the meaning behind it would be as fresh and new as ever.

Kari heard a noise and spun around to find her husband looking at her from the doorway. Since they'd been back together, he'd made a point of being home earlier than he had in the days before his affair. It was one of the ways she knew he was trying.

"Hi." She smiled at him and guided the eagle on a miniature flight not far from her face. "Our girl's going to love this." She set the bird back down. "I didn't hear you come in."

The corners of Tim's mouth made an attempt to lift, but his eyes were sad. He crossed the room and massaged his fingers into her shoulder as a shadow fell across his eyes. "How was your day?"

Concern rattled her heart. "Good." She angled her head. "You okay?"

"Yeah." He searched her face, his hand still gripping her shoulder. "Fine. Just a long day."

She wanted to believe him, but his stooped shoulders and worried expression gave him away. "You sure?"

"Yep." He drew a slow breath. "I have some papers to check. I'll be upstairs."

It was an hour after dinner when he found her in the living room writing in the baby book. A Celtic instrumental arrangement played in the background, and the smell of roast chicken still lingered in the house.

Kari tilted her head back and met his searching eyes. Whatever was eating Tim had not dissipated, and again she felt her stomach tighten. "Finished with your papers?"

"No." He drew a deep breath and shoved his hands in his pockets. "I have to go back. I forgot a stack on my desk."

"Oh." Immediately Kari wondered if Tim was lying to her, if he had plans to go somewhere else instead of back to work. She dismissed the thought. Tim was beyond lying to her; it was one reason their reconciliation was going so well.

She stood and stretched, forcing her voice to be casual. "Want me to come?"

"That's okay." For an instant he seemed frozen in place. Then he came to her and took her hands in his. "May I tell you something?" His voice was quietly intense.

"Sure." She held her breath, desperate to know what was going on in his head.

His grip on her hands tightened. "What happened to us was my fault, Kari. Completely my fault."

She felt herself relax. Was that all this was? A bout of delayed guilt? "That isn't true, and you know it." Her thumbs gently massaged the tops of his hands. "We both made poor choices."

Tim shook his head. "Your being busy didn't make it okay for me to have an affair. No matter how lonely I felt."

An expectant silence lay between them, as if Tim still had something important to say. She lowered her brow. "That's why you're so distant tonight?"

"No." He searched her face, her eyes. His mouth was open, but he didn't seem to know what to say.

"What?"

He let his gaze fall to the place where he held her hands. When he looked up, his eyes were wet. "Nothing. It's just —" She waited, trying to read him. "I'm so sorry, Kari. I'm sorrier than you'll ever understand."

She gently pulled her hands from his and wrapped them around his waist. She had to stretch out her arms to do it. "I know."

He held her as close as her protruding belly would allow. Their faces were inches apart, and Kari wondered if this would be the moment when their lips might finally meet. They hadn't done more than hug or hold hands since they'd been back together. But with his emotions so raw, a kiss seemed possible.

Instead, Tim smoothed a finger over her eyebrow and traced it gently down the side of her face. "I want you to remember something."

Kari waited, her heart beating hard.

"No matter what else happens, I never want to hurt you again."

Their eyes held, and gradually the distance between their faces dissolved until their lips came together. Tears stung at Kari's eyes and spilled down her cheeks. The salty taste mingled with their kiss, and the feelings between them grew.

It wasn't the type of passion they'd once shared, though Kari imagined one day it would be. Instead, it was a kiss of infinite sadness for all they'd loved and all they'd lost and all they'd never have again. But it was something more as well. It was a kiss that hinted at a hope that was from God alone.

Kari pulled away first. She reached for the car keys on the coffee table. "Go get your papers. I'll be waiting."

"You're so beautiful." He studied her face as if he were trying to memorize her. "You're the best thing that ever happened to me, Kari." He kissed her once more. "Do you believe me?"

"I do." She wiped at her tears and handed him his keys. "I believe you with all my heart."

As Tim bid her good-bye and drove away, Kari realized it was true; she really did believe him. And with everything inside her she prayed that his days of lying were over. Because after all she'd been through since summer she was sure of one thing.

If Tim Jacobs ever betrayed her trust again, it would kill her. Even if it took decades for her heart to stop beating.

Tears streamed down Tim's face as he drove toward his office. He clutched the steering wheel, furious with himself. He'd had the perfect opportunity to tell Kari, but he couldn't. It had been physically impossible — not with her spirit opening to his and sweet trust written boldly across her face.

He exhaled through clenched teeth. Now he'd have to wait until he got back home.

He'd rather drive off a cliff than look into Kari's beautiful eyes — eyes that believed in him again despite his affair — and tell her that Angela Manning was pregnant with his child. It was the worst possible situation he could imagine, and he had no idea how any of them were going to survive it.

He was racking his brain for possible solutions long after he reached his office and gathered up the stack of papers. He was about to leave when an idea struck him.

Maybe Angela was wrong about the pregnancy. Maybe she only suspected it and wanted his support just in case. Either way, suddenly he knew he didn't want Angela Manning in his office tomorrow at noon. He needed to get this over with tonight.

He set the stack of papers down on his desk.

What if he wrote her a note telling her how committed he was to Kari? Then he could drop it by her apartment tonight, hand it to her, and tell her he had to go. He wouldn't even step inside. Just hand her the note, tell her Kari was expecting him, and leave. When he got home, he'd tell Kari the truth, and somehow they'd find a way to handle the situation.

The plan continued to take shape as he sat down, pulled out a sheet of paper, and scribbled a letter to Angela. Enough to tell her he was sorry and yes, if she was pregnant, he was responsible. But no matter what else she might need from him, he could never again give her his heart.

Because whether or not she was pregnant, his heart belonged to his wife, where it should have been all along.

He tucked the note in his pants pocket, grabbed the stack of papers once more, and headed for his car. As he started the engine, he had the strongest impression that he should scrap the plan and go home instead. That somehow God himself wanted him to avoid seeing Angela Manning that night at all costs.

Well, that feeling was probably because of the counselor's insistence that he stay away from Angela no matter what. Tim knew that was sound advice. But the reason for the rule was the danger of repeat affairs, and there wasn't even a remote danger of that tonight.

Seeing Angela now was merely his way of avoiding a public meeting with her and perhaps a scene.

Surely God wouldn't have a problem with that.

He turned onto her street, parked his car, and closed his eyes. *Please, God, let Angela be wrong. But either way, please be with me.*

Slowly, moving like a man twice his age, Tim climbed out of the car and took the first steps toward his future. A future he desperately prayed did not involve Angela Manning and an illegitimate child.

Dirk Bennett pulled up in front of Angela's apartment and turned off the engine. He saw no point in sitting outside. He clutched the ring box in his left hand, more determined than he'd ever been.

He opened the car door and made a motion to get out, but then he remembered the gun. The professor hadn't been around for weeks, months even. But what if he was here tonight? What if after all of Dirk's plotting and planning and waiting for the perfect moment, Professor Jacobs was with Angela tonight?

Rabid anger flooded his being at the very possibility, and in a flurry of motion he grabbed his revolver from the passenger seat. Dirk's hands trembled at the thought of seeing the man and putting an end to the affair once and for all.

Then he shook his head, exhaled slowly, and willed the tension in his shoulders to ease. It wasn't going to happen. Nothing could ruin his plans now. He eased the gun back toward the seat beside him.

Nothing, unless . . .

Unless Angela didn't catch the vision of what he'd planned for the two of them. Unless somehow the professor had convinced her that everything she'd shared with Dirk was simple and shallow and worthless. Unless she took one look at the ring and laughed at him, refused to see him, ordered him away from her apartment.

The thought had never occurred to him before.

Sure, she'd said no in the past, but that was back when she was seeing the professor. Back before his weight-training program, before he'd built his body into a piece of art. Minute by painful minute, workout after tiring workout, pill after pill after pill — and all of it for Angela Manning.

If she turned him down now, everything about life as he knew it would be over.

A strange buzzing filled his head, and it was difficult to think. If she didn't say yes, he knew ways to convince her. He clutched the revolver more tightly and hid it in his pocket. Wouldn't want to scare her. Then with the ring in one hand and the gun in the other, he climbed out of the truck and slammed the door shut.

He hadn't taken four steps when he spotted the professor.

What was this? Was he seeing things? Dirk blinked, rage filling every vein and capillary, strangling his chest and heart and mind. But the vision didn't change.

Instead, he watched Professor Jacobs walk toward the front door of Angela's apartment building.

Anger grabbed at his throat, suffocating him. Dirk was unable even to draw a breath without doing something to stop the man. He pulled the gun from his pocket and ran to catch up with the professor.

"Hey!" Dirk raised the gun, his temples pounding with fury. The professor's face was frozen in a mask of surprise as Dirk positioned his finger on the trigger.

"This one's for Angela."

At the sound of her name on his lips, Dirk pulled the trigger. Once. Twice. Three times, until the professor dropped to the sidewalk with blood spilling from his chest.

Only then did the anger clear enough for Dirk to realize what he'd done.

He stared at the professor lying on the sidewalk. Stared at the red pool forming around the man and ran for his car, his heart screaming within him.

As he pulled away, it occurred to him that he'd ruined everything. Every dream of marrying Angela or making a life for the two of them, every thought of finally living a life like his brothers' was laid out on that sidewalk, dying.

Right there beside Professor Tim Jacobs.

The moment Tim hit the ground, he instantly made two observations.

First, the pain was only minimal, despite the fact that he'd taken all three bullets straight on. He felt a hot, throbbing sensation at the center of his chest, but other than that he might have been lying on the sidewalk by choice.

It was the other observation that worried him more: He couldn't move, not even a little. And it was that reality that sent him beyond pain and fear straight to terror. Because as badly as he wanted to convince himself he was all right, clearly something was very wrong.

He heard footsteps, cries. Though he couldn't open his eyes, he knew Angela was at his side.

"Tim!" She knelt beside him, her voice frantic. There were other voices, bystanders gathering around, and she shouted at them, "Somebody call 911!"

Her fingers took hold of his and squeezed. "Hang on, Tim." She screamed the words and began to weep. "Dear God, no!"

He could feel pavement beneath him. Pavement and warm, flowing blood. Desperation seized Tim, and he tried as hard as he could to speak. He had something to say. Even if it took all his remaining strength he had to say it before it was too late.

Help me, Father. . . . I'm in trouble.

Voices gathered around Tim, shouting orders, murmuring concerns, asking each other whether he was breathing. Tim could feel no pain now, only a deep urgency.

"Someone stop the bleeding." It was Angela's voice.

"Is he breathing? Check if he's breathing and —"

"Has anyone called the ambulance?"

Tim didn't care about any of it.

The only thing that mattered was that he was about to die in front of Angela Manning's house. When Kari found out, she'd think he'd been lying about everything. Then six months down the road she would learn about Angela's baby, and that would be even worse.

He struggled again to formulate the words he needed to say. "Angela . . ."

"Tim!" Her grip on his hand tightened. "Hold on, baby. Someone will be here any minute."

He struggled for nearly a minute and finally opened his eyes. What he saw confirmed how serious the situation was. Angela's face was a mask of pure fear. "Oh, Tim," she said. "Who did this to you?"

Tim remembered the face of the angry young man. *This one's for Angela.*

"He . . . he knew you."

A realization dawned in Angela's features. "Was he young?"

Tim didn't try to answer. It didn't matter who the shooter was; all that mattered was saying what he had to say. He thought about the letter in his pocket and wished he could reach for it. Instead, he drew a rasping breath. *Please, God . . . I must talk. . . .*

He swallowed, and finally the words came. "I'm . . . sorry." Every syllable was an increasing effort, and at the core of his being he knew he was dying. "About . . . the baby." He sucked in a breath and heard the wet rattling in his lungs.

Blood. It won't be long. . . .

"No, Tim." Angela's weeping grew louder, and he felt her breath on his face. When she spoke it was in a whisper, intended for his ears only. "Tim, I'm not pregnant. I . . . I made that up so you'd come back to me."

What? The whole thing was a lie? Cool relief flooded Tim's body faster than the blood ebbing from his veins. He drew another breath. He couldn't feel any part of his body except a stinging wetness in his eyes.

"Could . . . you . . ." The fluid in his throat made it almost impossible to speak. "Could you . . . tell Kari . . . I'm sorry. Tell her . . . I love her."

He could see pain in Angela's eyes, but compassion as well. "Don't talk like that, Tim. You can tell her. You're going to be fine."

He heard sirens wailing nearby, and then a shuffling of feet. Four paramedics came into view, and one of them shouted, "Step aside, please."

Tim was glad for the help, but he was certain it was too late. Angela let go of his hand, and her face receded into the darkness. He heard concern in the terse voices of the paramedics.

"Respiration's shallow."

"We're losing his pulse, and we need a . . ."

The words faded. His eyes closed again. Suddenly Tim's thinking was clearer than ever before, his sorrow clearer still. The truth was, it was all over. He would never see his Kari again, never hold her in his arms and beg her forgiveness for dying this way, never feel the weight of his newborn child against his shoulder.

The consequences from his year away from God had, in the end, cost him everything.

He pictured Kari and their baby and knew somehow that she was right. The child was a girl. A sweet girl who would go through life without her daddy. But oddly enough, along with the sadness, words kept drifting through his mind like gentle winds. Words he had memorized as a child, words he had found written in the front of his Bible that first day he came back home to Kari.

" 'Fear not,' " Pastor Mark had quoted, " 'for I have redeemed you . . . I have summoned you by name . . . you are mine.' "

Redemption. That was the word that kept coming up, time and time and time again. For so long he hadn't wanted to believe it, hadn't thought it possible. But now he knew with absolute certainty the truth of what Kari had showed him, what the Lord now whispered in his soul.

Fear not.

The Lord was a God of redemption for anyone who repented and turned to him. And Tim had repented to the depths of his fading soul.

I have summoned you by name.
Yes, Lord.

As his heartbeat slowed, as he drew his last breaths, Tim was overwhelmed with a sense of deep sorrow, deep regret for all he had allowed himself to be, for all the times he'd chosen to go his own way instead of following the Lord. And yet even at the heart of his sorrow, he could feel a pinpoint of light begin to open. A spreading knowledge of a love and peace that were deeper and more infinite than anything he'd ever known.

You are mine. Fear not.
I'm sorry, Lord.
. . . for I have redeemed you.
Yes, Lord.
You are mine.

As he moved away from all he'd known in this life, his sorrow combined with the deeper peace and love — love that would guide him into his Father's arms.

His last thoughts were both simple and profound. He was grateful beyond words that he wasn't going to spend eternity in hell.

Because the year he'd already spent there was long enough.

Chapter Thirty

Kari was already sick to her stomach with worry by the time her father called. Tim had been gone nearly three hours to do what should have taken forty minutes at the most. The possibilities screaming through their silent house were so loud she could barely concentrate.

She answered the phone on the first ring. "Tim?"

"Kari, honey, it's me. Dad." Her father's voice was tired, tinged with sorrow and grief and a fear that Kari had never heard before. Not even years ago when her mother was sick.

"Tim's late." Kari's heart pounded in her throat, and her words sounded forced, robotic. "He should be home by now."

"Tim's in the hospital, sweetheart. There was an accident."

"What?" She squeezed her eyes shut, her knees shaking from the rush of terror within her. *Please, God, no!*

"Is . . . is he okay?"

"We have to get to the hospital." His

tone was still fearful. "I'll pick you up, honey."

"What about Mom?"

"She's at church. Sometimes her Bible study goes late. I'll leave her a note to meet us at the hospital." He hesitated. "I'm on my way."

When she hung up the phone, Kari was sure her father knew more than he was saying, but she was too afraid to ask questions. Instead, they rattled about in her head. *What has happened to Tim? Was the accident near the university? Did someone run a red light, or was his the only car?*

She was waiting outside the house, bundled in a jacket that didn't quite cover her belly and shivering madly, when her father pulled up. On the drive to the hospital she wrapped her arms tightly around her middle and struggled to find her voice. Her teeth clattered as she spoke. "How come . . . they called you?"

Her father kept his eyes on the icy road. "The paramedics knew he was my son-in-law. They thought it'd be better if I called you."

They were silent the rest of the way. When they walked into the hospital, one of her father's friends, an emergency-room doctor, quickly ushered them into a private room. He stood opposite them and directed them to take seats.

Kari wanted to shout at the man. *Tell me what happened. Don't make me sit down. I want to see my husband.* Instead, she meekly followed his directions, as if her body were listening to what her mind refused to acknowledge.

Her father spoke first. "I told Kari there was an accident. That's all she knows."

"Right." The graying doctor across from them had a kind face, but his expression was gravely serious. When he spoke, there was no urgency whatsoever. "I'm afraid I don't have very good news."

That's when Kari knew something was terribly wrong. Something much worse than she'd originally thought.

"Where is he?" she demanded. "I don't care about the details. I just need to —"

"Kari." The doctor took her hands and fixed his eyes on hers, willing her to listen. "Your husband was shot."

The room began to spin. Breathing and speaking were out of the question. Her father slipped an arm around her shoulders and whispered, "Kari, hang on now. . . ."

The rushing sound echoing through Kari's head made it almost impossible to concentrate. She tried desperately to understand what the doctor was saying, but she caught only bits and pieces. Something about three bullets. Considerable bleeding. Paramedics doing everything they could.

But no matter how hard she tried to hear, the man's words blended together — all except his final words, which stood out in sudden, horrific clarity.

"He didn't make it, Kari. I'm sorry."

"No!" She pulled her hands from the doctor's and laid them across her swollen abdomen, refusing to understand. It wasn't possible. "No! Tim's at the office. He had some papers. . . . You have the wrong man."

Her father tightened his grip on her while he questioned the doctor. "The shooting was on campus?"

Even in her desperate condition she could see the doctor's expression change. "He was shot outside an apartment complex . . . just off campus."

At that moment a contraction tore across Kari's middle, and she doubled over in pain. *No . . . please, God, no!*

Her words dissolved into a series of anguished moans that rolled over her again and again until she no longer recognized her voice. Her father threw strong arms around her and held her tightly — she didn't know exactly how long — until she was calm again. And then came the questions, the agonizing questions she didn't want to think of but still needed answers for.

She lifted her head and stared at the doctor through streaming tears. "Did they arrest her?"

The doctor furrowed his eyebrows. He looked first at her father and back to her. "I'm told the shooter was a young man, nineteen years old. He fled the scene, but police have him in custody. He confessed everything."

A small ray of hope pierced the darkness in Kari's soul. "So he wasn't at Angela Manning's apartment?"

The doctor hesitated. "I believe he was."

And the hope died.

"Ms. Manning spoke with police. She'll be a key witness when the case goes to trial." He leaned forward and studied her carefully. "Are you okay?"

Kari nodded. "I think so." The contraction had eased, but any relief she felt was quickly replaced with the questions. But only one that mattered.

Why?

Why after all the progress they'd made would Tim lie to her and go to Angela

Manning's apartment?

Why would somebody shoot him?

And why would God let him die?

She ached from her knees to her elbows. Her body shook more violently with each passing minute, as if the cold that had settled over her, in her, would never go away.

Her father brought his face close to her ear and spoke softly. "I'm so sorry, Kari."

Her abdomen tightened again, but not as hard as before. She closed her eyes. No . . . no, it couldn't be true. The whole story was just a bad dream.

"Tell me it's not true, Daddy, please," she wailed, desperate for some sign that it was all a lie. When none came, she sobbed louder. "Why? Why, God? Why Tim? Why now? Why?"

She heard no answers, not from her father or the doctor or even from God — not at that moment. So she did the only thing she could do. She cried for Tim and for herself and for their unborn child. For all the changes Tim's death would mean.

And in that instant she felt a part of her die too.

Because far worse than the pain of losing Tim was the indescribable loss of knowing he had lied again, that she still hadn't been enough for him, even after all they'd been through. Of all the terrifying emotions strangling her heart, the gut-wrenching feeling of betrayal was worst of all.

"Kari." The simple act of looking up at the doctor took all her remaining energy. He handed her a folded piece of paper. "This was in his pocket." The man's eyes were moist. "I thought you should have it."

She opened the note as her father's friend left the room. She tried to focus on the words, but her hands were trembling too much to make sense of it. Her father gently took it from her and in a quiet voice, seeped in strength and sorrow, he began to read.

" 'Dear Angela . . .' " He paused, and Kari figured he was scanning it, wondering if these final words from her husband would send her over the edge.

Kari's heartbeat doubled, and she swallowed back a lump in her throat. His last words had been for Angela, not her. The fact felt like a knife in her heart. She squeezed her eyes shut for a moment. "Go ahead, Dad. I want to hear it."

He shifted the letter to his right hand and clutched her knee with the other. " 'Dear Angela, I'm sorry about what happened between us, but you need to know something. I don't want you coming by my office tomorrow — not tomorrow, and not ever. And I don't want you calling me. What we had together was wrong; it was a lie, and for that I'm truly sorry. But I don't love you. I never did. I'm in love with my wife, and that's where my focus is and must be for the rest of time.' "

Fresh tears, warm and soothing, flooded Kari's eyes, and she buried her head against her father's shoulder. A blanket of unearthly peace settled over her, and she felt herself relax. Tim had been faithful to her. No matter how bad it looked, he had never intended anything more than to set Angela Manning straight, once and for all.

Her husband's last message eased the pain of betrayal but intensified the loss a hundredfold.

"Is that all?"

Her father's features clouded, and he shook his head. "There's more."

Again fear aimed a blow at her stomach, and another gentle contraction came. What now? Something worse? She held her breath. "Read it, Dad . . . I need to know."

He nodded and focused on the note once more. " 'One more thing. If you are pregnant, I'll have to take responsibility.' "

"What?" Kari whispered the word, and nausea consumed her. She fought the urge to run to the bathroom; instead she stood frozen in place while she considered the horrible possibilities. If Angela was pregnant, their children would be just months apart. Possibly in the same class at school.

She remembered Tim's anguish from earlier that night, the way he'd seemed strangely burdened. Now it all made sense — though the reality of it all left her chilled.

The pain in her abdomen came again, and she hunched over. Her father motioned into the hallway and in seconds the emergency-room doctor returned. "She's having contractions," her father explained.

The doctor frowned. "We need to get you on a monitor, Kari."

He moved to help her, but Kari held out her hand. "I'm fine." The pain was easing and she straightened up again. "I have to see Tim."

Her father's friend looked concerned, but he nodded. "We're still cleaning him up. You can see him after that."

Words wouldn't come, so her father answered for her. "Thanks, Mike. We'll be okay. Get a monitor ready just in case."

The doctor nodded and left the room. For a long while there was no sound in the room but Kari's weary sobs and her father's occasional gentle words. "Hang on, Kari. . . . We'll get through this. God will pull us through."

Deep in her soul she believed that, trusted that somehow she would survive, that her child would be fine, and that somewhere down the road she might even be happy.

What she didn't understand was how she would get from here to there.

At the moment, she wasn't sure she could remember how to breathe, let alone care for herself and her child without Tim. In a matter of hours she'd lost her husband, her marriage, her dreams for the future. All of it was gone. And even though God would help her survive, one question still strangled her heart.

Where are you, God? Where are you in all of this? Kari felt another contraction, but it was milder this time. "I'm okay. They're fading."

"Are you sure?" Her father placed his hand gently on her belly. "Preterm labor is nothing to mess with."

"I'm sure." She sighed and was about to ask her father to help her find Tim's body when they heard a knock at the door. A nurse poked her head in. "Ms. Jacobs, there's a woman here to see you. She says it's urgent."

Kari glanced at her father. "Probably Mom." The idea of repeating the details of Tim's death was overwhelming, but she longed to see her mother. She nodded to the nurse. "Send her in." The woman disappeared, leaving the door open.

A minute passed, and a beautiful young woman with tearstained cheeks and swollen, electric blue eyes appeared at the door. Immediately her eyes fell to Kari's middle. As they did, something changed in the woman's expression. Kari knew instinctively that it was her. The other woman. And she felt her heart sink to her knees.

The woman folded her arms tightly in front of her. "I'm Angela Manning."

Kari felt her father's arm around her shoulders, but she kept her eyes fixed on the woman in front of her. So this was Angela? The one Tim had left home for, the one who had nearly destroyed her marriage.

The one who might even now be carrying Tim's child.

Kari was utterly drained, her head still spinning with the reality that Tim lay dead in a nearby room. But somehow now she had to find the strength to face Angela Manning. *Father, I can't do this.*

And then, surprisingly, came the quiet

answer in the depths of her soul. A surprising but comfortingly familiar answer. The one that hadn't made sense months earlier.

My grace is sufficient for you, daughter.

And like that, Kari could breathe again. Her world was still upended, but she could breathe.

Angela stared at the floor for a moment, then looked back at Kari. The regret in Angela's eyes was raw and deep, and suddenly Kari felt something she'd never expected to feel in the presence of Tim's lover.

Compassion.

"I'm sorry, Mrs. Jacobs." Tears pooled in Angela's eyes. "It was my fault he was killed."

Kari had no idea what the woman meant, but a ripple of anxiety coursed through her while she waited.

Angela swallowed hard. She glanced at Kari's father and then back at Kari. "I . . . I told Tim I was pregnant, but —" a sob slipped from her throat — "I lied to him. I wanted him to come back to me." She hung her head again. "He came over to tell me he wanted to stay married to you."

The sorrow consuming Kari doubled. It

was the same message he'd expressed in his letter, but hearing it on this woman's lips . . .

She felt her knees buckle and sway under the heavy irony. The reality that her husband had been killed not because of his cheating or his lies but because he wanted to do the right thing.

Suddenly Kari had to know what happened. "Who shot him?"

Angela folded her hands nervously in front of her. "His name is Dirk Bennett. I dated him for a while last year, and he . . . he became obsessive. He thought the reason he and I weren't together was because I was seeing Tim. But that wasn't true. . . ."

Kari stood there staring at Angela Manning, too shocked by this news to feel anything but terrified and dazed. Tim had been killed by someone stalking Angela Manning? The whole thing was so absurd. He should have been home with her, helping her choose wallpaper and curtains for the nursery, tiptoeing with her past the hurts of yesterday into the new life they were building together.

That's what he should have been doing. Instead of going to see his ex-lover and getting himself shot.

Angela looked up again. "I was there when they were working on him." Her voice caught, and she pinched the bridge of her nose. "He wanted me to tell you something."

Kari swallowed back the sobs lodged in her throat and leaned hard into her father's arm. She wanted to hate this woman for what she'd done to Tim and their marriage. For how she'd lied to him and cost him his life.

But clearly Angela Manning was hurting too, not only from the grief and guilt but also from the certainty that she could have prevented Tim's death. Besides, this woman was the only person who could share with her Tim's dying words. Kari found that she could summon no hatred, just a new wave of tears that filled her eyes and spilled onto her cheeks. Speaking was out of the question.

Her father had been silent throughout the interchange, but his quiet strength beside her was all that kept her upright. He seemed to understand her need to know. He cleared his throat and looked from Kari to Angela. "What did he say?"

Angela met his gaze, and Kari saw resignation — that, and a deep understanding that no matter how sidetracked Tim had become, the only one he had ever loved was Kari.

"He told me to tell you he was —"

Angela's face was red. She scrunched up her striking features as a series of small sobs racked her body. When she was able to talk, she took a tissue from a box in the center of the table and blew her nose. "I'm sorry."

Kari was trying to be patient, but she wanted to know every one of Tim's final words, especially since they had been directed to her. "He was what?"

Angela sniffed. "He said to tell you he was sorry . . . and that he loves you. And that he'll always love you."

At that moment the nurse returned and looked at Kari. "I need to speak to you for a minute, please."

Her father took gentle hold of her elbow, and Kari looked back at Angela once more. There was an awkward silence as Angela slipped her purse onto her shoulder, her tears gradually resolving into an icy dignity. "I thought you should know the truth."

Kari could only nod. "Thanks."

They left the waiting room, one after the other — Angela to the dark night of uncertainty and regret, Kari to a fully lit hospital room that was even darker, a room where her husband lay cold and still and dead.

Her heart raced as she and her father followed the nurse down a long hallway to a closed door. "Your husband is in here, Mrs. Jacobs." The woman's voice was gentle. "Take as long as you want."

Kari blinked, and as she opened the door, she realized the initial shock of losing Tim had worn off.

The paralyzing pain that engulfed her now could never be mistaken for anything but real.

Chapter Thirty-One

It was two days past her due date, and the pains were coming every six minutes. Kari found her parents in the kitchen eating breakfast. "It's time." She felt the corners of her lips rise slightly, about as far as they ever did since Tim's death.

Her father was on his feet. "Are you sure?"

She nodded. "I'm ready."

John, Elizabeth, and Kari rode together and didn't make small talk. What could they say? What could any of them say? Tim should have been driving her to the hospital, and no one could escape the fact that he was missing from the moment.

Kari sighed and stared out the window. She was learning to accept the loss of Tim, but none of it had been easy. A contraction came, and Kari doubled over, groaning out loud and causing her father to pick up speed. She blew short hard breaths through pursed lips the way Brooke had showed her. She hadn't had the heart to go to childbirth classes without Tim, even though Brooke and her mother had offered to go with her. So Brooke had given her a quick set of instructions. She had said that learning to breathe through the contractions was the most important part. But the pain was long and merciless.

Like everything else about her life these days.

Gradually the contraction eased, and Kari leaned back against the seat, remembering all she'd survived these past months. The news articles detailing how Tim had been shot in front of his lover's apartment, and the article a week later explaining that Dirk Bennett, the shooter, was being tried for first-degree murder. The funeral service where Pastor Mark talked about the beauty of redemption and how Tim and Kari had found peace before his death.

Everyone had been supportive. No one, not even Ashley, had mentioned that perhaps his death was for the best, that maybe Kari would be better off without a husband like Tim Jacobs.

Kari wasn't stupid. She knew people had to be saying some of those things behind her back. There had been a time when she might have been tempted to say them herself. But not now. Not after the way they'd come together before his death.

They were within the city limits, and her dad was driving as fast as he safely could. Another wave of pain swept over her, and she clenched her jaw to keep from screaming. "Dad . . ." The contraction took her breath away, and she rocked forward, trying to survive.

"Two minutes, baby, two minutes. Hang on. We're almost there."

Kari closed her eyes when the pain eased, praying for strength. She knew God would see her through the physical act of labor. It was everything that came afterward that worried her.

Being a single mother . . . explaining to her child what had happened to Tim. Kari had no idea how she'd do any of that.

Oh, Father . . . it's so hard. Tears welled in her eyes, and she began to cry, deep inner sobs that came from a place that was still raw, still grieving the fact that Tim had died, still hurting over the memory of his last words to her and the sad irony that she had lost him just when they were finding each other again.

Her father hit the brakes. "We're here."

Kari opened her eyes and saw a nurse with a wheelchair waiting outside the emergency-room door. "You phoned ahead?"

John Baxter was already out of the car opening Kari's door. "Absolutely." He smiled warmly at her as he reached down and helped her from the car to the wheelchair, wiping her tears with a brush of his thumb. "I don't want my grandchild born in a hospital waiting room."

The next fifteen minutes were a blur of preparations and contractions as the nurses set Kari up in a labor room and monitored the baby's progress. After a few minutes the doctor appeared and did an exam. "I'd say it'll be sometime in the next hour." He patted Kari's hand, and she could feel his sympathy like a warm blanket — both soothing and smothering. It seemed like everyone in Bloomington knew what had happened to Tim — how his poor, grieving widow had been six months pregnant and waiting stoically for her husband's return when he was shot and killed in front of his girlfriend's apartment. She appreciated the doctor's concern as well as that of everyone else. But she hated how it made her the object of pity wherever she went. Especially here, giving birth to her first child only months after burying her husband.

Another contraction hit, and Kari thought she might pass out from the pain.

The doctor gripped her hand as she rode it out. Then he angled his head, studying her tear-streaked face. "You okay?"

Kari nodded. "I'm ready to meet my baby."

He grinned. "That's a girl. Listen, you have some family out in the hall. Shall I let them in?"

"Sure." She tried to smile.

When the door opened, Ashley and Cole filed in with her parents. They were followed by Brooke and Peter, both wearing their white coats and ear-to-ear grins. Behind them was Erin with word that Sam would be by later, and at the end of the line was Luke with an entire bouquet of white roses. They gathered around her bed, laying their hands on her knees and shoulders and smoothing stray pieces of hair off her sweaty face.

The pains were coming faster, harder, and under normal circumstances Kari knew she would not have wanted company. But these were the people she loved, her family — the ones who had stood by her all her life, whether they agreed with her or not. As long as they were willing to be there, she would not consider asking them to leave. Besides, they wouldn't stay long. They had planned that only her mother would stay with her through the delivery.

The group was quiet, all eyes on Kari, when her dad cleared his throat and took her hand. "We didn't want you to be alone in here."

Kari swallowed and waited until she could speak. "Thanks."

"They came as soon as I called." John glanced at the faces. His chin quivered as he looked back at Kari. "No matter how long it takes, we'll be outside the door if you need anything."

She nodded, unable to do anything but groan as another wave of pain crashed over her. When it passed she met the eyes of each of her family members, her breathing labored, sweat beading on her forehead. "I love you guys."

There were smiles and whispers of "We love you too" all around her, and again her father took control. "We need to go. Let's pray for Kari and the baby."

Everyone nodded and no one, not even Ashley or Brooke or Peter, showed any signs of hesitation. One by one they joined hands until the only broken link was between Luke and Ashley, who happened to be standing next to each other. Finally Luke smiled at his middle sister and reached out his hand. And with that the circle was complete. Tears shone in every eye, and Kari felt her heart lift at the love she felt amidst her family.

Her father looked at each of them, one at a time, then bowed his head. "Lord, you are gracious and merciful in all things, even this, the pain of new life. Father, we ask you to let the baby come quickly and without stress or trouble of any kind, and we pray that you keep both Kari and her child safe in the process." His voice cracked, and Kari felt the familiar wetness fall upon her face. She knew her father must have been deeply touched by the way they'd all come together here. Especially Luke and Ashley. "I've prayed it a million times before, Lord, but let me say it again. Thank you for my family. Other than you, Father, they're the most important part of my life."

Almost as soon as the prayer ended, Kari jerked into another contraction, and this time her dad motioned for the nurse to join them. The woman entered the already crowded room and checked the readouts from the monitor. "Okay, Kari, I think it's time."

The others filed out of the room — all except her mother, who held her hand and walked beside her as she was moved into the delivery room. Kari was grateful they had planned it this way.

The final phase of labor seemed much shorter than the first, and within thirty minutes the doctor was urging her to push one last time. As she did, Kari felt a great sense of relief. Seconds later the room was filled with the bleating sound of a beautiful, newborn cry.

"Congratulations, Kari." The doctor held up the squirming baby, and Kari could hardly believe it was really happening. "It's a girl."

A cry escaped from Kari's throat. She fell back exhausted, overwhelmed, elated. Her mother was at her side, squeezing her hand and kissing her forehead. "Oh, sweetheart, she's beautiful."

"I knew she was a girl. God told me months ago." Kari smiled and noticed that she was no longer crying. Instead, an unspeakable joy coursed through her heart and soul, a joy of relief and awe and amazement at the miracle of life.

"There's something very special about a daughter." Her mother brought her face up against Kari's. "I remember exactly what you're feeling now." She paused, and her happy tears felt damp against Kari's cheek. "Now you know why I love you so much."

"Her name's Jessie Renée."

"That's beautiful, Kari. Your great-grandmother would have loved her."

A delivery-room nurse appeared at her bedside with the infant clean and wrapped in a blanket. "Thought you might like to meet your daughter."

Gently, as if the baby might be made of glass, Kari took her and held her close. "Oh, Mom . . . there's nothing like it. I can't believe how she feels in my arms."

Kari stared at her tiny daughter, awed by her. She had been wrong the night of Tim's death. The best part of life wasn't over. Hope lived on — her baby girl was living proof.

God's plans for her were not dead; they had merely been revised, made new.

As new as the precious life in her arms.

Strange sounds filled the morning air, but Kari couldn't force her eyes open. What was it? Almost like someone was singing . . . no, humming . . . right here in her hospital room.

The tune was familiar, and though she was still half asleep, she finally recognized it.

Great is Thy faithfulness, O God my Father,
There is no shadow of turning with Thee;

Thou changest not, Thy compassions
they fail not;
As Thou hast been Thou forever wilt be.

The humming became clearer still, and Kari figured her father must be in the room. It was his favorite hymn, the one he always sang when God's hand was so clearly at work among them. The humming continued into the chorus, and since Kari was almost fully awake, she joined in.

Great is Thy faithfulness!
Great is Thy faithfulness!
Morning by morning new mercies I see;
All I have needed Thy hand hath provided —
Great is Thy faithfulness, Lord, unto me!

She opened her eyes then, and her heart stopped. How did he . . . ? Who'd told him about . . . ? It wasn't possible.

The man sitting in the chair beside her, rocking little Jessie as carefully as if she were his own, was not John Baxter.

It was Ryan Taylor.

Kari's heartbeat returned, and she stared at him, unable to speak.

"She's beautiful, Kari." He smiled at the baby through wet eyes. "She looks just like you."

Kari blinked so she could see through her own tears. "Ryan . . . I don't . . . how'd you know?"

"My mom told me about Tim." He gazed down at the infant and kissed her downy forehead. "I made her promise to tell me when the baby came, and I guess she talked to your dad. He called yesterday around noon, after Jessie was born." He looked up and met her eyes. "I caught a flight a few hours later."

She studied him, not sure she understood. "Why?"

He ran a big finger delicately along the baby's brow and looked from Kari to little Jessie and back. "A long time ago you told me something I'll never forget."

"I did?" Kari's heart was beating almost out of her chest, and she couldn't keep up with the emotions that assaulted her.

Ryan nodded. "You told me love is a decision." He paused and glanced at her tiny daughter. "I thought I loved you, Kari." His eyes found hers again. "But it was a selfish love. Not the kind of love that honored you. Definitely not the kind of love you had for Tim."

She watched his eyes fill up again, and hers did the same. Finally he swallowed and found his voice. "After you went back to Tim, I had a little chat with God and realized you were right. Love — real love — *is* a decision." He nodded once. "So I decided then and there I was going to love you the way you wanted to be loved. And that meant letting you go."

The baby stirred. Ryan adjusted his position and spoke in little more than a whisper. "It was a decision to —" His voice broke, and he hung his head for a minute as a single tear fell onto Jessie's cheek. Ryan sucked in a quick breath and wiped the wet spot with his thumb. Then he looked up at Kari. "A decision to love you in a way that nearly killed me."

There it was.

His real feelings were out in the open, and she could think of nothing to say. The loss of Tim was still too raw, too recent, for Kari to even begin reading her heart on all she felt now in Ryan's presence.

Ryan's face grew more serious, and he blinked back another tear. "I'm sorry about Tim. That's not how . . ." He inhaled sharply and stared at the ceiling for a moment before returning his attention to Kari. "I'm sorry."

The tears flowed freely down Kari's cheeks now, and she nodded. "Me too. We were . . . we were moving in the right direction."

They were quiet awhile. Eventually Ryan looked down at the baby and allowed himself a crooked smile. "She's perfect. A complete miracle."

Kari waited a minute, her eyes fixed on her little girl's dainty features. "So . . . you're in New York?"

"Yes." He cocked his head, studying her. "Coaching the Giants."

She nodded. "That's what I heard." Her mind searched for something neutral to say. "How's it going?"

"It's good." He smiled sadly. "I miss home, but you know I've always wanted to coach at that level."

She sank back against her pillow and soaked in the sight of him — strong and handsome and familiar, cradling her newborn with awkward tenderness. Her heart refused to do any more than that; the possibilities on either side of her private path of pain were more than she could consider. It was too soon or maybe too late ever to go back. Either way, this was neither the time nor place to consider what might lie ahead.

Besides, Ryan's life was in New York now, and hers was here with her family.

Where it would always be.

She forced her emotions into check.

"When do you go back?"

"I took a week off. If it's okay, I thought I might help you get settled or something." He grinned. "You know, leap tall buildings, change diapers, that sort of thing."

She smiled, sad and thoughtful, and glanced at the plush toy eagle, the one Tim had bought before he was killed, nestled at the foot of Jessie's hospital crib. He should have been here, should have been sitting across from her holding their daughter, cooing at her.

Kari closed her eyes for a moment. Somehow, someway, Tim *was* there, smiling down at them from his place in heaven, his place of redemption.

The thought filled her with equal parts of peace and pain. "Tim was so excited about the baby. We were learning. . . ."

Ryan had no answer, just listened. Watched her face. Waited for her to say more.

All she could manage was small talk. "I'm keeping the house." She gazed briefly at little Jessie. "I'll stay at my parents' for a few weeks, but when I'm back on my feet, the baby and I will go home."

Ryan leaned forward in the padded hospital chair, carefully balancing the sleeping child. "It'll take time. Getting on with life again."

She sniffed. "Yes."

His eyes grew dim, glazed with things he wasn't saying, feelings he knew better than to express. He blinked and the moment passed.

"Well, Kari girl —" he gave her a half-smile — "the way I see it, you could use a friend. Someone to listen and take walks with. Maybe hold the bottle when you're feeling tired." He shrugged. "At least until I leave."

A dozen questions came to her mind at the possibility, but the lump in her throat was too thick to voice them all. Instead, she smiled through her tears and asked the only one that mattered. "Then what?"

Ryan reached out and gently massaged the tips of her fingers. "I'll always be a phone call away. Whenever you need me, Kari. No matter how many miles are between us, I'll be here for you."

Kari waited a moment, studying him, feeling safe and protected as she always did with him. "I'd like that."

She pictured the coming days — she and her daughter going home to the temporary nursery set up at her parents' house, having Ryan stop in to visit and watching him hold Jessie, sharing these tender next few days with him.

Saying good-bye at the end of the week.

She locked eyes with him, remembering the passages of time they'd walked through together. All her life she'd been saying good-bye to Ryan Taylor. This would be just one more.

She sighed.

As with so many times before, there was no way to predict what tomorrow held for either of them. In some ways they'd come full circle. And though they might not see each other again for a month or even a year, Ryan was right. He would be there for her.

And somehow . . . somehow for today that would be enough.

A Word from Gary Smalley

For several years I've been dreaming about creating fiction, putting together a series of novels that would illustrate what I believe God teaches about relationships. During the past thirty years, I've written many books about how to restore broken relationships. But nothing touches the heart, nothing fleshes out the truth quite like a good story.

A Dream Come True

A few years ago I came across a novel by Karen Kingsbury and read it on a long flight. Halfway through the flight, my son Greg elbowed me in the ribs. "Dad . . ." He looked nervously around to see if anyone was looking. "You're crying pretty loudly there. Everything okay?"

I had no words. I simply pointed to the book and kept weeping.

Karen's books were the first ones that ever really made me cry. Since then I have read everything she has written. It is clear to me that God has given her a special gift, an ability to create stories that not only touch hearts but also change lives.

In no time at all Karen became my favorite fiction author. She also gave me an idea. As I came to know her, suddenly I could see my dream of collaborating with a fiction writer taking shape. My themes and lessons about relationships . . . her storytelling. We had a meeting that summer, and God gave us the ideas for our Redemption series.

The series will follow the lives of John and Elizabeth Baxter and their five adult children, each of whom is trying to find his or her way in life — sometimes with God, sometimes without. The series will follow the paths of pain and pleasure, tragedy and tears that take place in the lives of Brooke, Kari, Ashley, Erin, and Luke.

The Baxters, their spouses, and friends experience the same struggles each of us faces — the longing for lasting love, the hurt of broken relationships, the fear of the unknown, questions about the future, the sorrow of loss, and the joy of restored relationships. Over time you'll come to know the Baxter family as if they were your neighbors or members of your own family. My guess is you'll even see yourself in one or more of them.

At the end of each book Karen and I will

provide questions that can be used for book clubs, small groups, or as a guide for your own personal reflection.

The bottom line is this: The Redemption series is my dream come true, fiction that will teach and touch our longing hearts. I am convinced these books will make you laugh and cry. I know they will leave you with a deeper understanding of how you can build rich relationships with the people in your life.

I hope you enjoy the ride.

REFLECTIONS ON RELATIONSHIPS

Most of us are like the Baxters: We want intimate relationships, but we often go through life dazed — hurting and being hurt by those we love. In the process we end up with broken, fractured, distant relationships.

In Kari's case, her relationship with her husband — the man with whom she wanted the deepest, most intimate relationship — was battered and broken. She had a decision to make: Would she stay with him and love him no matter what, or would she do what most people thought she should do — give him the divorce he demanded?

Kari made a tough choice. She decided to love Tim unconditionally.

Love is a decision. Not always an easy one.

You may be facing a similar situation in your life. Maybe your marriage is distant or even broken, and you need to decide what to do. Maybe you are like several of the Baxter children and feel disconnected from family members. Maybe you've been hurt by a friend and have to decide whether or not you will stay in the relationship.

Whatever your situation, there is hope. God can redeem our broken relationships and restore them to wholeness. God can give us the strength and grace to love in the midst of difficult circumstances.

If you are struggling with a difficult marriage, I am concerned for you. I pray that God will redeem and restore that relationship. As you recall, one of the tools God used to restore Kari and Tim's marriage was something called a marriage intensive, an intensive counseling experience that helped Tim and Kari understand how they were hurting each other and how they could rebuild their marriage. That same help is available to you. If you would like to attend a marriage intensive or if you need other relational help, I urge you to contact us at:

The Smalley Relationship Center
1482 Lakeshore Drive
Branson, MO 65616

Phone: (800) 84-TODAY (848-6329)
FAX: (417) 336-3515
E-mail: family@smalleyonline.com
Web site: www.smalleyonline.com

A Word from Karen Kingsbury

When Gary Smalley contacted me about writing fiction with him, I was thrilled.

When he said, "Think series," I went blank.

For weeks I prayed about the series idea, asking God to show me a group of plots that would best exemplify relational truths taught by Gary Smalley and the staff at the Smalley Relationship Center.

Ideas would come, but they seemed too small for something as big and life-changing as the dream Gary and I had come to share.

Then one day I was on a flight home from Colorado Springs when God literally gave me the Redemption series — titles, plots, characters, themes, story lines, and all. All of it poured out into my notebook while goose bumps flashed up and down my spine.

Generally I don't find myself crying when I write a synopsis for a novel. I can imagine the tears it might bring. I know where the story will most affect my heart. But I don't actually weep.

On that flight, though, the tears came steadily. I could literally see the Baxter family, each person, and in those hours I came to know them — their fears and desires, their strengths and weaknesses, the things that would devastate them and the things that would give them hope. I cried for all this series would put the Baxter family through. But I also cried for the ways they would emerge victorious because of their understanding of love — and because of God's merciful redemption.

In some ways, the books in the Redemption series will read like many of my other novels. The characters will be flawed, their problems the same ones you and I face despite our faith. The difference is this: Though each book will stand alone as a novel to be read and enjoyed, the whole story will not be finished until the end.

Until the final book, *Reunion.*

Normally I do not leave my readers wondering what happened to the characters. But in the case of the Redemption series some questions will always be left unanswered, some issues unresolved until the very end. In some ways I wish I could tell you now what will become of John and Elizabeth, Brooke, Kari, Ashley, Erin, and Luke.

But I can't.

The books that lie ahead are written on the pages of Gary's heart and mine, but they have yet to be typed across the pages of my computer screen. As they emerge, we will bring them to you.

Bookstore shelves are filled with all sorts of novels, but my favorite ones always contain a love story. Not the lighthearted boy-meets-girl tale, but the story of heart-rending, unforgettable love. Real love. I believe that's what God gave me that day on the plane — a series of real love stories that have the power to change the way we feel and think and love.

My prayer and Gary's is that as you enjoy the Redemption series, you will gain a deeper understanding of how God can redeem broken relationships, how love shines its brightest in the shadow of his presence. Perhaps in riding out the next few years with the Baxters, you'll find yourself expressing your new understanding in your own relationships.

And maybe, just maybe, the Redemption series will help change the way you live together. The way you love.

I leave you with the message of *Redemption* — that no matter who you are or where you've been, no matter the roads you've traveled, God loves you and wants to be in a deep relationship with you. The Bible tells us that God "is passionate about his relationship with you" (Exodus 34:14, NLT). He cares so much about restoring your relationship with him that he sent his own Son to the cross to redeem you. The Bible says that accepting God's gift of redemption is the first step toward a restored relationship with him.

If you need to know more about the redemption God has for you, I urge you to contact your local Bible-believing church and talk to a pastor — someone like Pastor Mark at Clear Creek Community Church. Then make a decision to accept that redemption while God's salvation can still deeply affect your life.

But don't wait. The truth is, we often don't have much time to make things right. If we ignore God's redemption here and now, tomorrow might be too late. The best time to say yes to God, yes to a restored relationship with him and others in your life, is always now.

Thank you for traveling the pages of *Redemption* with us. I hope you'll pass this book on to someone else, then keep your eyes open for *Remember*, book two in the Redemption series. The answers to some of your questions are being written even now.

In the meantime, may this find you walking close to God, enjoying the journey of life, and celebrating his gift of redemption.

As always, I'd love to hear from you. Please write me at my E-mail address: rtnbykk@aol.com. Or contact me at my Web site: www.karenkingsbury.com.

Blessings to you and yours, humbly,
Karen Kingsbury

Discussion Questions

Use these questions for individual reflection or for discussion with a book club or other small group.

1. Which character did you most closely relate to in the book? Why?
2. What character would you most want to be like? Why?
3. Where did you see the redemption theme playing out in the book? Which characters in this book dealt with issues of redemption, and how were those issues different for different characters? Describe how redemption was played out in the lives of key characters.
4. Where have you seen redemption in your life? Reflect on a time when you were in need of God's redemption and found it. How did that happen?
5. What characters best exemplified the type of love you would like to have in your relationships? How did those people express their love?

6. *Redemption* dealt with a variety of relational struggles. Which one did you most relate to? How is your struggle similar? How is it different? What do you feel causes you to stay stuck in your struggle? What will it take for you to move beyond your struggle?

7. What did you think of Kari's resolve to stay married? How did she demonstrate that resolve? Was it something that came easily for her? What threatened her resolve?

8. List some of the attributes that might describe the love Kari had for her husband. How can those same attributes be helpful — or even possible — in your life?

9. What finally turned Tim around? What kept Tim from loving Kari as he had promised to love her? Which of those hindrances do you see in your life? What can you do about it?

10. How did you feel about Ryan Taylor? Describe the kind of love he had for Kari during the first half of the book. How did that love change? In what relationships do you love people the way Ryan initially loved Kari? What can you do to change?

11. Many people gave Kari advice about

her situation. If Kari had asked you for advice, what would you have told her? Why?

12. If Tim had come to you for advice, what would you have told him? Why?

13. If Ryan had come to you for advice, what would you have told him? Why?

14. Kari's siblings are important to her. Describe the relationship she has with each one. Describe the relationship you have with your siblings.

15. Describe the relationship between John and Elizabeth Baxter. What were some of the subtle signs and practical ways they showed their love for each other? What are the practical ways you do or could show your love to the people in your relationships?

16. How did John and Elizabeth's marriage affect Kari and Tim's marriage? What impact does your marriage (or your other close relationships) have on the people around you?

17. Clear Creek Community Church played a significant role in the lives of several of the Baxter family members. What positive influence did the church people have on various family members? Was the church's involvement with the family effective, or

would you have wanted Christians to handle things differently? Explain. What role do your church friends or leaders play in your relationships?

18. The counselors at the marriage intensive told Kari and Tim about their personal dance. This involved recognizing their deepest fears, analyzing their coping behaviors, and recognizing how this pattern was causing distance between them. See if you can identify your own dance and the way it plays out in your closest relationships. Are the steps of your dance bringing you closer to the people you love or putting distance between you?

19. What relationships in the Baxter family still need restoration and redemption? What relationships in your life need redemption? Where and how will you find that redemption?

20. Throughout *Redemption* God found creative ways to speak to the people in the story. How does God speak to you? At the same time consider the ways of the enemy and his distracting voice. In what ways is the enemy trying to distract you?

Additional copyright information:

Most Scripture used in this book, whether quoted or paraphrased by the characters, is taken from the *Holy Bible*, New International Version.® NIV.® Copyright © 1973, 1978, 1984 by International Bible Society. Used by permission of Zondervan Publishing House. All rights reserved.

Some Scripture quotations are taken from the *Holy Bible*, New Living Translation, copyright © 1996. Used by permission of Tyndale House Publishers, Inc., Wheaton, Illinois 60189. All rights reserved.

The Scripture quotation in chapter 23 is taken from the New King James Version. Copyright © 1979, 1980, 1982 by Thomas Nelson, Inc. Used by permission. All rights reserved.

Lyrics on pages 536–537 are taken from the hymn "Great Is Thy Faithfulness" by Thomas O. Chisholm. Copyright © 1923, Ren. 1951 by Hope Publishing Company, Carol Stream, IL 60188. All rights reserved. International copyright secured. Used by permission.

The employees of Thorndike Press hope you have enjoyed this Large Print book. All our Thorndike and Wheeler Large Print titles are designed for easy reading, and all our books are made to last. Other Thorndike Press Large Print books are available at your library, through selected bookstores, or directly from us.

For information about titles, please call:

(800) 223-1244

or visit our Web site at:

www.gale.com/thorndike
www.gale.com/wheeler

To share your comments, please write:

Publisher
Thorndike Press
295 Kennedy Memorial Drive
Waterville, ME   04901

LT FIC SMALLEY
Smalley, Gary..
Redemption

JUL 1 2 2005